THE PRIDE OF LEO

BOOK 5 OF THE ZODIAC SERIES

PAUL SATING

PAUL SATING

Editor: Cindy Niespodzianski

Cover Design: Jake at jcalebdesign.com

ISBN-13: 978-1-7322617-8-5

THREE FREE FANTASY NOVELLAS

THE ZODIAC SERIES

To Cindy Neispodzianski. Thank you for making my word chains sound reasonably entertaining.

1

OLYMPIA

Months After Cancer

"HEY, FREAK."

My stride hitched, assuming someone was talking to me. Throughout my six-thousand-year life, nicknames stuck to me like statically charged lint sticks to socks, so why would this one not be included in my litany of titles?

But I wasn't the target of the felonious name. The taunt had come from a tall human, on the desirable side of six feet tall. His long appendages dangled, his fingers nearly reaching to his knees. Gangly, but not awkward.

Sunglasses obscured the gangly man's identity, along with a hoodie, pulled up to cover his head. I doubted I knew him; I didn't know many people in Olympia, having only lived here after moving from Seattle just over a month ago. That larger city was too expensive, so Cancer and I tried our luck in the state's Capital. I knew less than a dozen mortals, and they all came into my life at the soup kitchen where I volunteered.

I had just stepped off the bus and was walking toward the

soup kitchen in downtown, passing the Red Lion that was once the Governor Hotel. The new ownership's banner hung at an angle as if hastily erected during an overnight hospitality siege.

I had planned on crossing over to Legion Way through Sylvester Park, but the park's grass glistened with the sheen of sprinkler systems and sun, and I didn't feel like getting my new sneakers wet. Half a week's salary went into obtaining them, and without a vehicle, my feet were my primary mode of transportation. I had a long day ahead and wet socks made for cold feet, and as a demon, Abandoned though I may have been, the Overworld was already could enough. This realm did not need my help. The sidewalk suited my purpose, even if it added thirty seconds to my walk commute. This route also gave me an excellent observation point to watch this aggressive guy.

The gangly man who drew my attention to the park wasn't alone. Five others stood behind him in a v–formation. After my time in the mortal army, I couldn't help notice how slack their formation was.

I scanned the park to a bench on the other side of a large gazebo clinging to a few spots of white paint. A slim man looked up toward the group from his seat on the bench. Squinting, he took in the gangly, hooded man. As I continued along the sidewalk, I pulled my bag closer. I didn't know much about the city yet, but I didn't need to be a native, nor a genius, to recognize this first sign of trouble.

The slim man on the park bench had the same sense. His hand slid to the side of his leg, where it wrapped around the sling of his backpack. Slowing my gait, I paused behind a big-leaf maple tree, whose branches spread a shadow. At this time of day, my presence could not be hidden from the group, but at least I would be obscured.

The four–lane street to my left streamed with cars and busses, normal for work week midday. Traffic crowding

Capitol Way was a constant of this small Pacific Northwest city. Vehicles filled the lanes, and pedestrians filled its sidewalks. My presence wouldn't stand out to this group, so I hung by the tree, interested in seeing how this played out. No one else seemed to notice.

"Yeah, I'm talking to you," the gangly man said, strutting forward. He and his entourage approached the gazebo, less than fifty yards away.

"I thought I told you I didn't want to see you around here anymore. You stupid or something?" gangly barked at the man on the bench.

The slim man rose slowly, slipping his backpack on in a fluid motion that neither hinted nor displayed aggression.

"Shit," I whispered.

I did not like this. The slim man moved with the caution of cornered prey, buying time while figuring a way out. I didn't know him from anyone in the group, but I knew six-on-one spelled peril. This had the potential to be a serious crime, and every indication around Sylvester Park signaled I was the only one aware of it.

"Leave me alone," the slim man said. His voice was soft, but direct, higher-pitched than I expected. It reminded me of Taurus's voice, one of the last incubi I wanted to be reminded of at this point. I was questioning a lot about myself and my recent history of decisions that led to my Abandonment, and the memory of Taurus right before I killed him in self-defense was still too vivid. A raw reminder of my troubles.

The slim man moved laterally along the bench.

The trees lining Capitol Way provided enough cover for the group. A hill ran the length of the park on Seventh Avenue, rising fifteen feet to meet the street and topped with a row of bushes and trees that made great cover for nefarious activities.

When the gang saw the slim man sliding along the bench, they moved to cut him off.

"Shit. Shit. Shit."

I stepped off the sidewalk and down the slight slope to the nearest tree. Turning sideways, I peeked around it and watched as the group shepherded their victim toward Seventh. His escape route cut off, he was probably unaware of the danger he was putting himself in. I glanced up and down the road, not seeing a police vehicle or anyone who passed as an authority figure. On sidewalks crowded with government administrators, elderly shoppers, artists, and hipsters, not a single uniform made an appearance. In the Underworld, Lucifer's Council has armed demons everywhere. Not so much in the Overworld, as if those who ruled it trusted the populace. What a concept.

"Where are the Lucifer-blessed police when you need one?" I grumbled.

"Come here!" a rough voice yelled.

The slim man tried to pull away. A burly brute, desperately in need of a shave, dove for his target's backpack and snagged a pocket. Slim attempted to bolt, but the other man's size prevented him from moving further than the backpack strap's reach. The brute gave it a yank as the slim victim slid his arms out of the strap and sprinted away.

"Grab him!" the gangly leader snarled, giving chase along with his cadre.

While keeping my eyes on the situation, I dropped to a knee behind the tree, hurriedly unzipping my backpack. The zipper caught halfway—snagged.

"Shit!" I repeated. Look, after spending the better part of two years around the American Army personnel, I can hardly be blamed for the complete disintegration of my vocabulary.

Slim sprinted across the green. He was fast, putting distance between himself and most of the group within a few strides. Unfortunately for him, one younger man, his hair split by a shaved zigzag pattern, measured him step-for-step.

Lunging, Zigzag sprawled out, swinging his arm in a

sharp scissoring movement that took the slim man's feet out. He went down with a scream, landing and rolling through the wet grass.

Wet sneakers were in my immediate future.

The rest of the gang caught up. One, his hair a mass of loose curls like an overused shower poof coming out of a month-long heroin binge, lifted one of the forest-green garbage cans and slammed it down on the slim man before he could raise a protective arm. A metallic clank rang out as trash met human.

Glancing away from the unfolding scene, I searched inside my backpack for my halberd.

Creed, being a magical halberd of mysterious origins, was as stubborn as my father's perspective on unquestioning obedience to Lucifer and His Council. A long time ago, I learned the halberd had a mind of its own any time we were physically separated. According to Aries, the ancient Founder who gifted it to me, I was the only one who could wield it. Somehow, it knew if someone other than me touched it. Proof came in a few unfortunate—not for me—incidents. I did not have to fear anyone stealing it, but I sure as heaven needed to worry about mortals seeing it. Thus, the backpack.

The park was empty except for this group, their intended victim, and a few stragglers who navigated the bordering sidewalks. Even if the pedestrians noticed, which I suspected a few did from their quick sideways glances, none intervened. I had to help this human, and I needed Creed.

Beyond the gazebo, underneath a tall tree, the group surrounded the fallen victim, who shielded his face with his hands.

I glanced down the street again, gripping Creed and hoping for a lucky law-enforcement break. The foot-long, four-inch circumference truncheon appeared to be nothing more than a solid piece of dark, petrified cherry to the uninitiated. With a flick of my wrist, I could transform it into a six-foot halberd.

Creed was power. More importantly for this situation, I was dangerous.

The slim man stood and raised his fists, a scowl coloring his face. He didn't look like a victim or someone who would accept what this group aimed to dish out.

They circled slowly, their steps, careful.

"I told you what would happen if I saw you out around the city, didn't I?" the gangly, hooded bully snarled.

"I don't care what you want," the slim man said. "I have as much of a right to be here as anyone."

Gangly flicked his hand. "No, you don't. You're a freak. Told you last time, I better never see your freaky face again, or I was going to fix that ugly mug."

A sly smirk undercut the slim man's high cheekbones. He wiggled his fingers. "Come and try then."

The others *oooh'ed* and *ahhh'ed*.

"Shut up!" the group's leader ordered. Most refused, still snickering behind balled fists. He turned on the slim man. "I'm going to break you, freak."

"I'm still waiting for you to try," came the response. Their target inched backward.

I pressed Creed against my thigh, inching from behind my cover. I wanted to give the target the opportunity to hold his own. Plus, if this resolved before I needed to get involved, I wouldn't have to use Creed. During the day. In public.

Gangly snarled and lunged.

So much for that plan.

I stepped into the park, still trying to keep a low profile.

Gangly swung and the slim man ducked, sending his sunglasses–wearing enemy swirling away. He spun to counter his aggressor's momentum. The move only drew more laughter from the gang, enraging the man behind the sunglasses.

"You fucking freak. You're gonna pay for that!"

He lunged again and the slim man dodged once more, swinging a fist into the hooded figure's back as he passed. The smack was sharp, a solid connection.

Raising both fists, the attacker half-cocked his head at the gang. "What are you waiting for, idiots? Jump her ass."

Her?

Then the context of this confrontation hit me. If I despise anything more than Lucifer's Third Council, it's bullies. After six thousand years of being ostracized because I was the Segregate, the only demon ever born without magic, I understood what it felt like to be treated differently. And I despised demons—and people—who did that to others.

The group cinched their loop around the slim man. Zigzag moved to the left, Worn Out Shower Poof to the right. The burly man and the other spread out, circling as the instigator moved in.

"This ain't ending good for you," he spat. "If you're not smart enough to stay holed up in your freak house or stay out of town, we'll make sure you can't walk back into it."

The slim man didn't wait for the group to corral him. He sprang, his fist connecting so hard with the bully's face I could hear the splintering of the plastic sunglasses from three dozen yards away. The bully's head rocketed, and he stumbled backward.

Burly Boy moved in for the attack. The target spun and thrust a kick into his thigh, kicking his leg out from underneath him. He screamed in a voice too high-pitched for someone his size.

"I'm done!" Burly Boy whined, holding his leg and limping at an impressive speed toward the intersection in the opposite corner of the park, where a handful of window shoppers gawked at goods through glass.

Though it gave him a temporary advantage, the move threw the slim man off-balance as the others neared.

The slim man might be able to hold his own for a while, but he would have to be seriously bad ass to last more than a half dozen minutes against a half dozen pieces of trash.

I lifted Creed. "You ready?"

The halberd-in-truncheon-form warmed in my hand.

I sprinted forward, giving Creed a shake. The truncheon extended. A six-foot weapon of destruction, its double-ax head sprang to life, the asymmetrical and half-moon axes promising violence from the top, while a wavy dagger jutted from the bottom.

"Please don't make me regret this," I whispered to the halberd, knowing full–well it would do whatever it wanted.

I never cast magic with Creed because I couldn't control its spells. The weapon had once shown me its full promise in an apartment in Kaiserslautern, Germany, when an assassin attempted to, well, assassinate me and an angel named Cassie. Since that time, Creed's magic had only shown itself on a few sessions where I practiced in privacy, and always of its own accord. I wasn't even sure how to engage its magic, stubborn as that halberd was. Magic happened when Creed wanted it to, and not a moment before. The only gifts I partially controlled were my heightened inherent senses.

The haft vibrated. Was Creed laughing at me?

One man with a fluffy beard partially covering a long scar on his cheek, turned as I approached. His eyes widened almost comically when he saw me sprinting at him with the three-bladed weapon.

I lowered Creed and swung before Scar Boy figured out his next move. The haft of Creed connected with the man's ankles as he attempted to leap over my strike. Wood cracked on bone, the halberd using the man's momentum and lack of grounding to send him flying. He landed in a heap behind me as I continued toward the next bully.

This one had close cropped hair, the sides shaved in a military style. He tried to jump out of my way, but I thrust

Creed to my side, looking like a marching band baton twirler. Creed clothes lined Military Man. The air sucked from his lungs at contact, and I left him behind, gasping and clutching his throat.

I didn't want to use too much force, but like I said, Creed has a mind of its own. Taking care of Military Man was something he decided, not me. I was just the halberd's executor.

I stopped, raced back to check on the human to make sure Creed had not done too much harm, and received a nasty surprise for my consideration. Scar Boy had grabbed the discarded garbage can during my distraction and sent it crashing down against the back of my head, knocking me flat on the ground. The world exploded in brilliant white light, and my mouth filled with the musky combination of dew and city water sprinkling systems. I tried to roll over but he was on my back, sending punches into my kidneys, shoulders, and skull. I kicked and scrambled, hoping to knock him off-balance and get to my feet before he knocked me out. I couldn't get myself free. After a few rounds of punches, he made the mistake of mistakes. His hand slid along my arm to where I held Creed in a weakening fist.

"Don't." The word came out as a croak.

Either he couldn't hear me or he was too stupid to heed my warning. His hand continued past my own to the haft of Creed. As soon as his skin contacted the weapon, energy bound in the fires of Hell surged through Creed. First forming a blue light at the point of skin and petrified cherry, the flame of the Hellfire spread rapidly in a ball around the man's hand, heating to a brilliant white. There was nothing I could do. He was on his own as Creed extolled the punishment.

At the zenith of its brilliance, Creed's energy sent the man flying backwards into the large white gazebo fifty yards away that hadn't had a paint job since the Ford Pinto was popular. The man crashed through its shingled roof and to the floor in a cloud of dust.

I steadied myself and surveyed the scene, trying to ignore the splitting headache and sore ribs.

These were much better odds.

The intended victim had Gangly in a headlock. The bully was bleeding from a spot between his eyes, presumably where his sunglasses had snapped. With their leader corralled, the others were all mine.

Shower Poof and Zigzag glanced at each other as I neared. I read their silent exchange. Neither looked confident about the outcome, and that's exactly where I wanted them.

"You two have a choice. I'll let you walk away, but you go now. You don't help the idiot back there, and you never bother this man again. Sound like a deal?"

Zigzag glanced once more at Shower Poof before nodding and turning to a full-out sprint toward the popular coffee shop across the park. Shower Poof hitched his pants and growled, his nose wrinkling as his lip curled. He was about to make a terrible decision.

"And let that bitch prance around the city? Getting away with everything at the job? Carl ain't going to put up with that anymore. No way. That chick needs to know her place." The confidence in his voice shook me. No one could be this stupid.

"Wrong answer," I said.

I shifted Creed from hand-to-hand, despite its length. It was a tall weapon, taller than me by almost half a foot, but sometimes it felt as light as a demonic notebook, only with far more balance. The haft slapped against my palms each time I caught it. Shower Poof's eyes traversed the gap along with the halberd. Mesmerized like most people who witnessed the weapon's charm, he was too intimidated to realize how stupid of a decision he just made.

"You were saying?" I asked with a wicked grin.

Instead of doing the right thing, the smart thing, Shower Poof made his move. I ducked under his fist and smacked him across the back with Creed. He arched, his arms flinging out to the sides. The strike had hurt, Creed hardly in a forgiving mood.

He turned.

I raised an eyebrow. "You sure?"

Doubt skittered across the man's face. But he still came at me. As I raced forward I saw a flicker of regret. Planting the wavy dagger into the ground five inches deep, I grabbed the haft with both hands and jumped. Rotating laterally, I spun, my feet crunching into the man's back. He fell into the wet grass, and this time I did not give him an opportunity to decide on how this fight went.

I grimaced. "This is going to hurt you more than it will hurt me." With a quick shake of my hand, I collapsed Creed into the truncheon form and brought it crashing against the back of the man's head, knocking him unconscious. I stood and wiped off my pants. "Dumbass."

The fight was almost over. The last thing I had to do was pull the slim man off Carl the Bully.

The intended victim was allowing his pain and anger to get the better of his judgment. He now had Carl pinned underneath him, his knees pressing down on the other man's arms. The slim man slammed his fist into the bully's face, over and over. Even at this distance I could hear the pinned man grunt with each strike. He was defeated.

I wanted to stop the slim man from doing something he would regret for the rest of his life. I knew what it was like to be a killer, after all.

I moved alongside the pair, out of arm's reach. I did not want him seeing me as an enemy. Tucking Creed against my leg so it was out of view, I raised my other hand in the universal sign of friendship.

The slim man did a double take, recognition flickering in his eyes.

"I'm a friend," I breathed, nodding my head to the side

toward the fifteen-foot statue at the back edge of the park. Scattered around it, limp bodies of the group lay. He looked at what remained of the gang, holding his fist in the air, but not bringing it down.

He said, "You did that?"

I nodded. "How about ending this? I think he got," I said with a dip of my head toward the bully, "what he deserved. If he's an idiot, he'll come back. But I don't think that's going to happen." I straightened and looked around the park. Whereas no one got involved before, dozens of people had stopped along the sidewalk to watch. Some had their mouths covered. Many were on their phones.

"Shit."

"What?" the slim man asked.

"I think we're going to have a visit by Olympia's finest pretty soon," I said. "I'd get up if I was you."

There are few things in life I'm ever correct about, but predicting the arrival of police at this scene was one of them —of course. Bad luck and all that. Olympia's entire police force showed up—I'm being hyperbolic, I know, but there were a *lot* of them. When all was said and done, they were kind enough to only cite us for the incident, though it took an hour-long interview to get to that point. One of the conveniently interested witnesses mentioned my use of a weapon, but when the cop saw Creed—in its truncheon form—he was satisfied.

I was grateful they didn't attempt to take it, even for hasty examination. The snub might have been a shot to Creed's ego, but the halberd's cockiness needed to be checked.

"You promise no more trouble?" the cop asked.

I nodded at the beat up old model Mustang idling at curb-side and the beautiful soul of a demon behind the steering wheel, her halo of brown hair glistening in the sun. "Nope. I was going to head into work, but I missed the start of my shift because of this. They wouldn't be happy about me walking in looking like this." Cupping my hand, I made an up-and-down motion at the blood and mud that stained my pants and shirt.

The cop jutted his chin at the gang. "Those guys are idiots, but they're not going to stay locked up forever. Keep yourself and your friend away from them."

I nodded. "Will do. Thanks."

Once the slim man finished his interview, we took a second to commiserate.

"I'm sorry about this," he said.

Rarely do I see eye to eye with someone, literally, not metaphorically. The slim man was my height with short, sandy hair and some light stubble along his rounded jaw. For the life of me all I saw was a human being. Nothing more. Certainly nothing to hate.

I waved away the apology. "Don't worry about it. It's no trouble."

He shrugged. "I heard that you missed your shift. I hope this doesn't get you in trouble with your boss."

"Nah, they're pretty cool. Plus," I said coolly flipping my hand, "it's not like they pay me much. If they've got a big problem with it, I can always find someone else to pay me too little for too much work. Anyway, the cop said he would stop by and let them know what happened. So that should help." I looked at him. "What about you? Are you okay? This won't get you in trouble with anyone?"

"Not anyone new," he replied.

"These guys been giving you trouble for a long time?"

He snapped his eyes shut, holding them like that for a few, long seconds. There was a long story hidden in there.

"Sorry. My name is Zeke. Ezekial really, but I prefer Zeke. Well, that's what my friends are allowed to call me. I figure, you and I connected over a brawl with bullies, so you're more than welcome to call me Zeke." I tried to laugh and lighten the moment a little, feeling wholly inadequate for the crap this man had to deal with. "And... I'm sorry this even happened."

The man smiled, but it held sadness. "It's not yours to apologize for, but I appreciate it. I'm Steve, by the way."

"Nice to meet you."

He shook my hand. "Likewise. Thanks again. Hope to see you around sometime."

Cancer smirked when I approached her car. The window rolled down, she cat-called me before I reached for the door handle.

Bending, I smiled. "You sexist. I'm not a piece of meat to drool over."

One eye widened, a playful look dancing across her smooth, brown skin. "Don't worry; I like more meat on my ... meat. Get in."

As we made our way back to the apartment, Cancer tapped on the steering wheel. "So, what was that all about?"

"You would think with a world war kicking off, humans would have better things to do than hate one another. Apparently, I'm just a dreamer," I said bitterly before explaining how the day unfolded.

At a few points, Cancer scowled. "I've heard and seen some dumb crap ever since we were Abandoned. I'm not surprised."

I sat forward. "What do you mean? Things that happened to you? Stuff like this?"

"Of course, Zeke. I'm a black woman to these mortals. That makes me prime real estate for ignorance and stupid comments. It's nice, what you did for that man. But it's hardly isolated; don't fool yourself."

"It's bullshit."

"I know."

I slapped my leg. "I mean, no one bothered to help or get involved, not until we had the upper-hand. Then, all of a sudden, everyone cares. I got cited by the cops. Me! All I was doing was helping someone, and I got cited. Where is the fairness in that? It's just like everything else."

She cast me a sideways glance. "Are you comparing your situation to what that mortal goes through?"

It was a dangerous question. In terms of intelligence, I might be a butter knife in a drawer full of steak knives, but I was smart enough to know to be deliberate in answering. Our Abandonment had changed a lot, but one thing it had not altered was Cancer's outlook on life. She was still thoughtful of others, always considerate and giving. She helped the people of Baghdad, nursing untold scores through a war that ravaged their city. She faced down a familial enemy, the most powerful succubus in Hell, to ensure justice would not fail me. Ultimately, it did, but Cancer did not. When she spoke, it was best to shut up and listen, because her words always came from the right place.

"Absolutely not," I said in a rush. "What he went through … what he *is and will* go through is bullshit. Everything is. It's just unfair."

She shook her head.

"What's that about?"

"What?"

"You. Shaking your head. You've got something to say. Just say it."

Her shoulders rose and fell. "One of these days you're going to have to let go of what happened. You're not the only one who got screwed by the Council. I did too."

"I know. I didn't say you hadn't been."

One finger uncurled from the steering wheel, pointing at the sky as she made her point. "Yet, you don't hear me complaining about them as often as you do. Why is that?"

We passed a few city blocks before I could comment. "Doesn't it bother you that Chax got away with … everything? That Seraph hid him so he could avoid accountability for what he did to you and your family?"

I met Cancer in Baghdad, where she was serving as a nurse in a neighborhood in the Khadra district. She had asked for help with a terrible curse she believed had been placed on her family that affected all of her relatives across generations, breaking them down, killing them long before their natural course. I helped—at least I tried—to get it removed by someone from the rival family by attempting to get them to recite a counter spell. Chax Vicu was in that rival family and served in a different brigade of the Army. With Bilba and Ralrek's help, we almost got to him, but the incubus escaped back to the Underworld. Making matters worse, his threat of being connected to a powerful family was true. Seraph, the most powerful succubus in Hell, was his aunt. She cast the deciding vote for my Abandonment.

"Of course it does. How could it not?" Her voice was level, but her hands gripped and rotated around the steering wheel. When she spoke again, the edge was gone. "But Zeke, I can't let that drive my actions. Talk about exhausting... and I'm already exhausted enough from... our Abandonment. Chax isn't worth it."

I wanted to confront her on that. Chax and what he got away with *did* matter. I wanted to remind her that she was in the Overworld amongst mortals, and growing weaker through her newfound mortality caused by being dispatched to this unnatural—for us—realm, while he was living it up large somewhere in the Underworld. Fat, dumb, and happy all because he had a powerful aunt.

Her furrowed brow told me to keep my big mouth shut. This was stressful enough. The war overseas was growing larger, and she was not there to help. She did not need me reminding her of the unfairness of how her life was panning out, especially now that the toll Abandonment was already wearing her down. I had never seen Cancer look so exhausted. Not even back in Baghdad, when she was the only care-provider for an entire suburb of Iraqis. Not even when she was saving a young boy's leg that had been shredded by a bomb. Not even when all Heaven was breaking loose around her. She was stressed enough about this situation, even if she was too stubbornly positive to admit it.

So instead of putting it on her, I focused it on myself. "I hate it Cancer. I swear, if I ever get the chance to make the Council pay, I will."

A nasally sigh later, she replied softly, "I know, Zeke. I know."

No matter how much I adored and respected her, I was not convinced Cancer truly knew how much I meant it.

2

OLYMPIA

Blop.

The old man with grimy hair and a kaleidoscope of liver spots tipping his nose looked at the goulash I slopped on his plate before finding my eyes. "What's that?" he asked in a voice so rough I swore he cleaned his throat with a steel wool brush.

I stared back at Sprinkles. "It's Tuesday. That's goulash. That's how this works. You know that."

Sprinkles always complained about the free soup kitchen food, no matter what we served. Three days ago he shouted at me from across the small dining room because the spaghetti noodles were too hard. A week before that, the bread rolls were too brittle. Before that, the soup was too cold. Even the free ice cream was supposedly too warm. Sprinkles —I haven't been brave enough to ask how he got that nickname—was never happy. Not miserable by any stretch of the imagination, but complaining fulfilled him in some fascinating and disconcerting way. Honestly, Sprinkles just enjoyed griping. Probably because it helped him feel part of the world that ignored people at the very bottom of the socioeconomic ladder.

In the months since my Abandonment, I had volunteered at the soup kitchen as often as possible. Aries the First had taught me of the mortal struggle of homelessness. In part, serving at the kitchen helped me honor the ancient Founder's memory. Working here also helped to understand the struggles of these humans more intimately than I ever imagined I would. Not only their struggles, but them, as people. Their wishes and desires, their hopes and dreams. The things they loved. The things they hated. I saw they were not that different from me and my demonic brethren. In a surprisingly short time, I considered a few of them as friends. Someone like Sprinkles would never truly replace my best friend Bilba, but I enjoyed the nights when he came to the kitchen. Nasty comments about our food aside, Sprinkles seemed to enjoy teaching me about the city of Olympia, making it feel like I had lived here for years already.

"How should I know that?" Sprinkles replied, cocking his head to the side, a tick anytime something agitated him that I'd noticed from our first conversation. A lot agitated Sprinkles, though I was not about to judge him. I had a roof over my head and food in my belly. Even if I didn't have my true home, my friends, or demons except for Cancer I trusted around me, I had far more than those who depended on the soup kitchen for what was likely the only meal they had each day.

"You should know because we served it last week," I answered, rotating the ladle. "And the week before that. And the week before *that*. We serve it every Tuesday, Sprinkles."

His head cocked to the side again. "Was probably garbage then too."

"You complained about it then," I agreed with a nod, "but I saw your bowl and you finished everything. Looked licked clean."

"Because I was starving, most likely," he said, his eyes giving me the once over. "Looks like you could do with a few bowls of this slop yourself. What do you weigh? A buck-fifty?"

No one ever said I was the biggest demon on the block, but my Abandonment had done wonders for my figure. Call it stress or a lousy diet, but I had dropped a few more pounds than I could afford. Now, I was a leaner and meaner fighting machine, just without much of the 'fighting machine' aspect. Without the comforts of Hell, I was more active than ever. I was in the best shape of my six-thousand-year life, which was saying something since I never was terribly out of shape—short period of personal darkness after becoming Hell's only murderer aside.

"Leave him be," Mary, a woman in her fifties, said after lightly slapping Sprinkles's arm. "He's a good boy. Does good work. Not his fault he's not a blubbering slob like yourself."

"Mary," I said, giving her a wink at my defense, "one of these days I'm going to have to take you out to dinner to thank you for all your kindness."

Sprinkles grunted. I think it was a laugh.

Mary waved a filthy glove that was more thread than glove at me, her face painted in humor. "You couldn't handle me, boy. I'm expensive."

"Frisky is more like it," Sprinkles interjected. "That's what word around the camp says."

"Oh, you," she responded with a laugh polluted with a dry cough.

I ladled goulash into Mary's bowl, giving her an extra half-spoon and another wink. "Get moving, you two. You're holding up the line."

The dinner rush was always the busiest time for the kitchen which was one reason I volunteered for this shift instead of breakfast. The flow was steady at this time, mostly during the hot evenings. As the calendar creaked toward the middle of August, the days were warmer and staying that way later. The heat drove Olympia's homeless into the shelter en masse. The soup kitchen didn't have air-conditioning, thankfully for my demonic nature that was still having a hard time adjusting to Overworld temperatures, but that didn't seem to matter to our clientele. We operated out of a building owned by the mission, on the east side of the city. The mature trees surrounding the property shaded it from direct sunlight, keeping it cool for these mortals who were constantly exposed to the elements. Someone mentioned this place was a defunct automotive repair business, but it looked more like a tiny aircraft hangar than anything ever used to repair cars. The building was as old as my ex-boss at The Book Abyss, a bookstore in the Fifth Circle of Hell. The kitchen had a distinct advantage over my beloved Fifth Circle bookstore; it wasn't nearly as chaotic as Dialphio's place.

Thinking of The Book Abyss and the wonderful succubus who owned it was difficult, no matter how good of a mood helping Olympia's homeless made me feel. I missed the store dearly, but only half as much as I missed its owner.

I broke eye contact with the next man in line as the longing pressed down on my chest.

Sometimes, especially when Cancer was working long shifts, the longing became the worst part of my Abandonment. The longing to be home. The longing to be around the familiar. The longing to be a demon, even one with no powers. The feeling would pass, it always did, but when I was feeling it, feeling homesick, it sucked.

I hadn't spent any significant time at home since I was forced into the American Army to fight a war in Iraq, a service record which was expunged by Lucifer's Third Council, making it as if I never existed to the Army.

So, yes, not only did I need to be home, partly for me, partly for the chance to get my hands around Chax's throat and force him to remove the curse from Cancer and her family.

But now, I never would, thanks to Seraph's scheming. She

concocted a lie about me blaspheming Lucifer and used that to convince the Third Council to Abandon me, along with her familial enemy in Cancer.

Abandonment has serious consequences for demons, consequences that went beyond the emotional and mental. Consequences that were still settling in.

Cancer is a nurse and had relied on her magic to save lives. Abandonment stripped her of her magic. The psychological impact was severe. Without her Water Abilities, Cancer struggled to be the positive light I knew in Iraq. She had been through difficulties and gave so much of herself and always remained positive. Now she spent most days, evenings, and some nights working, like she was trying to make up for the help she was unable to give with her magic.

Having been the only demon in the history of Hell without magic, I never knew a life with that type of power until my first mission to the Overworld when Aries the First handed Creed to me. The halberd made it possible for me to use magic, something I didn't learn for quite a long time, and not until I was staring down death and sticking my tongue out at it. Until that time, I knew how it felt to be different, and I tried to use that experience to empathize with Cancer. Was I helping? I was trying, and that was all I could do.

The worst thing about Abandonment is probably the reason why demons deny it even exists. It is perhaps why Lilith Sunstone, my supportive and loving-yet-stubbornly naïve mother, refused to allow my father to bring up the topic. Denial has a way of allowing her to pretend Lucifer would never allow this to exist. The factual truth of Abandonment goes beyond being forced to live a life without magic amongst the mortals in the Overworld. Abandonment, at its core, is the process whereby a demon becomes mortal. A slow death sentence. Dress it up all you like. The Council sentenced me and Cancer to die.

And we were powerless to change it.

I could have spiraled into a dark pit, but the healthier I was, the better I might be able to confront the Founders. And help Cancer. Volunteering at the soup kitchen kept me in a relatively good head-space because I felt I was fulfilling Aries's legacy.

Aries, that wonderful sparkling cloud of positivity, served the homeless mortals in his time in the Overworld, and he opened my eyes to not only their predicament, but to that of the homeless in Hell as well. I promised myself to spend my last few years as a mortal doing everything I could to continue the spirit of Aries's work. The soup kitchen was just the start. As I learned more about the Overworld, I would find better ways to serve them. Today, the soup kitchen. Tomorrow, the entire Overworld.

"What are you smiling at, dummy," a gruff voice pulled me out of my reflection. "I'm hungry."

I blinked stupidly, looking up into the browned face of a man who may have been in his forties or who could have been going on seventy. Deep lines etched his face and his sunken eyes hinted of a difficult life, yet his hair had few gray strands. He lifted his tray and shoved it in my direction.

"Oh, sorry," I stumbled, filling the ladle and giving the man a bonus mound of goulash out of guilt. My eyes slid to Sprinkles, who sat at a table with Mary. He watched my every movement, and his lips rippled at my kind gesture to the other man.

As the sun traversed the sky outside, we wrapped up the meal. The dining area emptied long before we finished cleaning.

"Is it okay to head out or do you need anything?" I asked Stacy, the kitchen manager.

A plump woman in her early thirties, Stacy was full of joy. I don't think I met anyone, immortal or mortal, as happy as this woman. Too young for gray hair, strands of it still interrupted her brown bundle captured underneath her hair net.

She was busy scrubbing pots at the sink, three of which leaned haphazardly. With a small bit of bad fortune, it wasn't beyond realistic to imagine someone finding her underneath an avalanche of stainless steel in the morning.

She waved a purple–gloved hand at me. Soap bubbles covered her arm down to her elbow. "We're fine, Zeke. Thank you for all of your help again tonight. Pretty crazy crowd."

"Spawn of Satan, I swear" I said with a smile, having recently picked up on the colloquialism and finding joy in the irony of using it.

Stacy giggled as she scrubbed away the evening's work. "Just wait until winter. Those cold rains move in off the Puget Sound and these folks lose their minds. They'll be pounding at the door, demanding to come inside before we show up for shift." She stopped her scrubbing to face me, her eyes locked on mine. "You ready for that?"

I shrugged. "Of course. Though, if I'm being honest, I'm not sure I'm ready for the cold." I grimaced. Summer was cold. I had been through Overworld cold months on previous missions. Those times, I could never find warmth. This was my life. Winter was my future. I really wasn't ready.

Stacy stared at me a moment longer. "Are you sure you want to continue doing this? I'm not joking. When the weather turns, they get demanding. It's rewarding work, or else I wouldn't be here, but not all volunteers can handle it."

I squinted. "Do you lose a lot during the winter?"

Stacy bit her lip. "People want to help the homeless, but there's a limit. And that limit usually starts at the point where they are inconvenienced."

"You're not going to scare me away."

"I hope not," she said. "I enjoy having you around. You've got a great attitude about this. One of the best I've seen in someone your age. Young people never seem to truly care that much about others. You're different."

Oh, if you only knew, I thought with a smirk. A human in

her thirties referring to a six-thousand-year-old demon as young was hilarious. Abandonment was so surreal at times.

Snagging my backpack from the chair in the back office, I stepped back out into the kitchen. "Well, I plan on being here for quite a while." Stopping in the open dining area, I smelled the musty walls seeped in Pacific Northwest dampness. Walls that had seen a thousand stories of hopelessness and despair. "This is important work. They need help, and I have the spare time. I have no plans of abandoning this kitchen or these people because of the cold. Actually, I wish I could help more often."

Stacy's cheeks wrinkled in a smile. She stopped scrubbing. "I'm glad to hear that." As I turned to leave, she added, "And if you're serious about it, I can always add you to the schedule a few more nights every month."

"Deal."

"Thank you," she said, resuming her work. "No more lingering. I'm going to finish these last few pots and then head out myself. Someone your age needs to get home so you can enjoy the exhilarating nightlife Olympia has to offer. Hanging out in the kitchen is not going to get you a girl-friend. When are you on the schedule again?"

Slinging my backpack over my shoulder, I wrinkled my face in thought. "Thursday, I think. I'll double check when I get home. Either way, you're going to see me again, long before you're ready for more Zeke."

She giggled. "I doubt there are any ladies who get enough Zeke. Now," she said, her cheeks turning a rosy red, "get out of here so I can focus on getting these pots cleaned so I can get home. My husband thinks it's my role is to serve him because he's too tired to cook his own meals, so my night is just beginning."

"Have a good one, Stacy," I said with a wave, nudging the door open with my hip. "Thanks for letting me do this. I'll see you."

My steps hitting the sidewalk that would lead me back to my apartment were light. For as many lousy humans as there were in the world, there were a hundred like Stacy. Sometimes, that's all I needed to remind myself of in order to get through another day.

3

OLYMPIA

WHO DIDN'T ENJOY a good Christmas movie, even in the summer?

Cancer was at work. That meant I could lounge around the apartment, wearing only a pair of shorts, even putting my feet on the coffee table without getting in trouble. A king in his castle. Watching a Christmas movie. In the summer.

There's just something about human art that speaks to a demon's rudimentary nature. With the overabundance of free time, whenever I wasn't working or volunteering at the soup kitchen, I practiced my forms while movies played in the background. One fateful day I tripped across *A Christmas Carol* and discovered I was a huge fan of the black and white film, which was ironic considering its topic and my status as one of Lucifer's spawn.

After the past week's scuffle in the park, I dedicated at least an hour every day to practicing my forms with Creed. The bullies terrorizing the man in Sylvester Park were more than a nuisance. They were a warning about becoming lazy with my forms. I don't want to say I got lucky in the fight, but things might have turned out differently had the gang been more professional … or immortal.

I started with *Rising Dawn*, my basic warm-up exercise, before moving on. *High Sun* helped me warm up my shoulders. *Silencer* was a more aggressive form that helped my low guard while strengthening my quadriceps and lower back. *Frigid Bite* came next, requiring slashing movements which tested my balance and upper body strength. That was followed by *Endless Dreams*, my last. In a perfect Overworld, I would have the room to practice my final form, but *Shadows Fall* required leaping and full-circle swings. Not exactly an apartment-friendly form. It was during *Endless Dreams* that I focused my thoughts on Lucifer's Council, but I'd reserve *Shadows Fall* for the rulers of Hell, should I ever have the chance to deploy it.

The jovial spirit of the Christmas movie playing in the background severed the severity of my exercises, but a part of me believed that was a deliberate subconscious effort. I didn't want to be this angry; I just didn't know how to not be. *A Christmas Carol* helped this practice be about disciplined maneuvers and not hot vengeance.

So did my ability to heal. During my first mission to the Overworld, after chasing Aries around a museum in Seattle and subsequently being hit by a car, I discovered I could recover abnormally quickly from injury. I was back on my feet later the same day, phenomenal, even for a demon. The fight in the park was more of an exercise than an opportunity to be pounded on, but from what I could tell, my ability to heal wasn't effected by Abandonment.

It was a curse of Lucifer to have recovery skills like mine. After the accident in Seattle, Beelzebub was the first to suspect something was different about me and he clued me in to a part of my nature I'd never noticed before. Now, I accepted and appreciated it. It was something unique about me, not gifted by possessing Creed. Something about me I could be proud of. One of my few such attributes.

Shaking Creed, the halberd collapsed to its truncheon

form. I set it on the coffee table. With a grunt, I laid on the couch and took in the struggle that was Ebenezer Scrooge being visited by yet another Ghost of Christmas. This version —seriously, why do you mortals re-make movies so often?— was a later one, from 1970. Every time I watched it, I giggled at the way Scrooge tells the woman in the red dress and floppy hat with her hands in a furry muff that she doesn't look like a ghost, to which she replies a curious "Thank you."

Humans may think movies from this age are cheesy, but all things are relative. When you're immortal, a movie this old could be considered a new release. Decades for humans are nothing more than moments for us. The movie made me appreciate how quickly mortal Technology Abilities developed, along with making me ponder if that very same magic would supersede demonkind's within the next few centuries. Whereas demons have still not devised a way to get through the issue of bedrock blocking satellite signals, mortals have global positioning systems, synchronization that allows all phones around the world to sync time, satellites in deep space, and the Internet. Demons could learn a lot from the mortal Technology magic, but something tells me Lucifer's Council has specific reasons to not hurry in pursuit.

The most wonderful manifestations of mortal magic are movies, and they're also one of the enjoyable elements of Abandonment. So many to watch and so little time to do so, though I will guiltily and readily admit that I had watched different versions of *A Christmas Carol* at least twenty times just over the summer. A wonderful story with more than a few moral anecdotes some members—all of them—of the Third Council could learn from.

My attention was pulled away from the snowy scene where Ebenezer sees himself as a small boy by the seal on my demonic notebook burning with azure blue of the Hellfire. The seal of Lucifer, an upside-down triangle sitting atop a lower-case 'v'. Two lines from each of the top corners of the triangle lanced the lower third, extending toward the small 'v'. Short, looping lines projected from the tip through the upper reaches of the letter, looking like a handlebar mustache. Someone from the Underworld was writing.

I sat up and scooted forward on the couch, pulling the notebook closer and flipping it open. Black letters were already appearing on the paper, tight loops scratched out by an invisible hand. A few demons knew I possessed demonic notebooks, wonderful devices that allowed demons to communicate over great distances and between worlds by linking to each other through our signatures in the other's notebooks. My ex-boss Dialphio, my best friend Bilba, my mother, and my enemy–turned–friend Ralrek were the only demons I knew who had them. Every one of them had note-books because of the owner of The Book Abyss. She made sure we were armed to stay in contact when I was kicked out of Hell.

"I might need a magnifying glass," I mumbled to no one in particular.

RALREK: *You there, Zeke? What are you up to?*

I grinned, feeling like being a smartass. I hadn't heard from the tall demon in a few weeks, and I was missing him. So I replied like a smartass.

ZEKE: *It's Ezekial. Doing fine.*

RALREK: *Don't be a smart ass.*

Nothing like getting called out immediately on your smar-tassery.

ZEKE: *I know no other way of being. Everything okay?*

RALREK: *Can't an incubus just write a friend?*

I took a second before scribbling my next note. Since my Abandonment I tried my hardest to not put my guilt, fear, and anxiety on those from the Underworld who I wanted to maintain a relationship with. None of them were at fault for my predicament. That guilt lay squarely on the shoulders of the five demons who sat on Lucifer's Council.

Three. Three demons, I remind myself after a flash of guilt. Michael and Azazel had voted against my Abandonment, so it wasn't fair to fault them. They had done what they could under the circumstances. But the other three? All the fault in the Underworld lay at their feet.

Ralrek did not deserve to suffer my emotional tumult.

ZEKE: *Hadn't heard from you in so long I figured you'd fallen into the pit. That, or one of your boyfriends, or all of them, finally got smart and broke up with you.*

After a long pause, my eyes drifted back to the movie. Figuring Ralrek got busy, I had just sat back to enjoy the film when I noticed letters appearing on the page again. I pulled the notebook onto my lap at his new message. This wasn't going to be a quick check in.

RALREK: *Ha, ha. Broke up with the last one.*

I waited. And waited. Nothing else was forthcoming.

ZEKE: *Sorry to hear. When?*

RALREK: *About two weeks ago. Best for both of us. We're different demons, wanting different things out of life.*

ZEKE: *If you're both happy, then I'm happy. Sorry if it sucks. You're probably lonely. I am too. You know you can write whenever you want?*

RALREK: *Not lonely. Do you know how many incubi hit me up to have drinks now? I never get a moment's peace. Can't fault them. If I wasn't me, I'd want to go out with me too.*

There it was. The true Ralrek. Until the Third Council hired us to find an operative named Gemini, Ralrek and I despised each other. We couldn't be around each other for more than a few minutes before barbs and insults flew. His self-assuredness always rubbed me the wrong way, and that probably had something to do with my lack of confidence. He had enough for a small village of incubi. But it was during that mission to Kaiserslautern to find Gemini, where I caught Ralrek doing the unthinkable. While searching in a nightclub —it was official business, I swear—I caught him with a human man. A rule-follower from the first day, Ralrek was breaking one of the big ones. At the bar, in an intimate embrace. Same–sex relationships are no big deal, but for a demon to become intimate with a mortal is the taboo of taboos. It's almost as bad as blasphemy. Seriously. I think Lucifer would blow his non-existent horns if he knew one of his kind coupled with anything other than a fellow demon. I'll never forget Ralrek's expression when he saw me seeing them. After we got over our initial shock, we talked it out and moved forward—it was just a very rough ride on a very bumpy road. That proved to be a major bonding experience in our relationship. Once Ralrek was convinced I would never betray nor reject him for who he was attracted to, he showed vulnerabilities. In a very short time, we had overcome thousands of years of animosity. To me, this new Ralrek was nothing more than a lovable, cocky incubus, and I had no problem reminding him of that.

ZEKE: *Careful, you're likely to catch something.*

RALREK: *Funny. What about you? Have you and Cancer done the deed yet?*

ZEKE: *Done the deed? Seriously? What are you, eight hundred years old? Wow. And no. It's not like that.*

RALREK: *Though you'd like it to be.*

ZEKE: *Why do you say that?*

RALREK: *Because you would with every succubi ever.*

ZEKE: *Now who's the funny one?*

RALREK: *You don't know how much I envy you, being in the Overworld around all those mortals. I'd love to meet those hipster men you say are all over Olympia. Have you met any?*

ZEKE: *I've come across a few of them.*

RALREK: *It's got to be exciting. Have you stopped by Joint Base Lewis McChord? You're close, right? So many men-in-uniform. Lucky hellhound! Well, except for the Abandonment thing.*

ZEKE: *I can't get on base. Remember, our military service was wiped clean. No more ID card. No more access.*

RALREK: *Such a shame.*

I could almost see him shaking his head of thick, oil-black hair. And smiled. I filled him in on my work at the soup kitchen before telling him about the scuffle in the park, giving him plenty of details on what the gang of thugs looked like to help satiate his belief that all mortals were attractive.

RALREK: *You're just trying to fool me. Remember, Zeke, I've been to the Overworld three times. I know how many hotties live up there.*

ZEKE: *Doesn't feel like it. Trust me, as much as being near the Third Council sucked, I still miss Hell. It's home. But I am getting used to it here. Don't know if that's a good or bad thing.*

RALREK: *You're not missing much.*

I waited for more to appear in Ralrek's response, but nothing came. Quill to paper time.

ZEKE: *You there?*

A few seconds passed before the response began scribbling out.

RALREK: *Just thinking.*

ZEKE: *About?*

RALREK: *Just life.*

Ralrek was being short for a reason. Learned behaviors are hard to overcome, sometimes impossible, even for immortals who have essentially an eternity to correct their course. A proud demon for thousands of years, he struggled to admit his shortcomings and failings, almost as much as he struggled to ask for help or guidance. A deeper issue was at play here, but it wouldn't come to light unless I pulled it out.

ZEKE: *Everything good with you and Bilba? Has he pulled his head out of his ass yet and apologized for the way he treated you?*

I don't believe in living life with regrets. There is nothing you can do about the past. But one thing I still wished for was being allowed to stay long enough to help Ralrek and my best friend through their issue over the former's attraction to mortals. Unfortunately, Bilba still had to get over some personal brain blockage about Lucifer's prohibition of demon-mortal relations.

RALREK: *About what?*

I sighed, pressing the quill to the paper a little harder than necessary.

ZEKE: *You know blessed well what I'm talking about. Has he apologized?*

RALREK: *Oh, that crap about mortals? Yeah. We're good.*

ZEKE: *If you're good, then what's going on? You sound different.*

Another pause. More slow scribbling.

RALREK: *Nothing. Just miss you. So, why don't you do an incubus a favor and figure out a way to send some of those new mortal movies. You know how terrible ours are. That's probably why you got yourself Abandoned, so you can get access to all the good stuff. Find one of those black marketers to sneak them in. Do that for me, will you? If you do, I might continue to keep an eye on your family.*

ZEKE: *That's illegal.*

RALREK: *And?*

I laughed.

ZEKE: *How are my parents? I heard from my mother a few weeks ago, but ...*

I lifted the quill. I didn't want to think about Kanthor Sunstone, my father. My thoughts drifting in his direction was never an enjoyable experience. Even in his absence, he annoyed me. That's what happens when you are never good enough for someone who should unconditionally love you.

Ralrek finished answering my own question.

RALREK: *They're good, from what I can tell. No worries there. The Council leaves them alone.*

ZEKE: *Glad to hear that.*

RALREK: *Listen, Zeke. I'm going to take off. Check in with us. We're worried about you.*

ZEKE: *Thanks, bud. You can write more often, and not just*

when you want me to break the law for you. Tell Bilba to write. It's been a whole twelve hours.

A smiley-face stick figure scratched itself out on the paper, which I pulled away to decipher—it was truly that poor of a drawing, even for a stick figure.

And Ralrek was gone. Once again, I was alone. Just me, Ebenezer Scrooge, and the ghosts of Christmas past, present, and future.

I WISH I COULD SAY MY DAY ENDED GLORIOUSLY AFTER THE conversation with Ralrek, that I sat around watching movies, eating lousy food, having a few drinks, and scratching my nuts until they were raw. But that's not what happened at all.

By the grace of Lucifer, Yahweh, Mother Nature or whatever forces moves the world, I had picked up my demonic notebook and took it to the bedroom. I fully planned on cleaning up the place. My job at the downtown bookstore gave me enough hours to feed myself and slow the withering of human currency from a mysterious friend in my last moment in Hell. What it failed to provide was a way to keep me sane when Cancer was working—which was all the time. Not that I'm faulting her for having a couple jobs. She was actually making enough money to be solvent. But it took her away from the apartment most days—all days—leaving me alone too often.

So I found myself bored out of my mind. So bored I was cleaning. Had I decided to do anything else, I might have left my demonic notebook out on the coffee table. Which would have raised questions for the visitor who suddenly appeared unannounced and most definitely unwelcome.

The sizzle of air, like a dozen fat slices of bacon cooking in a pan of oil, preceded the rift opening. A rift is a type of doorway between the Underworld and Overworld, used by the powerful and elite. Hell's rulers—and probably Lucifer Himself—are the only ones I knew who were allowed to use them.

Squads of Major demons managed gateway operations in the Underworld which allowed common demons to travel between Circles, a rarity. But rifts were a different story altogether. They were the way immortals popped into the world of mortals, so they needed to be carefully managed. One of the few wise decisions made by the Council. Shit could go real wrong, real fast, if just anyone had the power to open one. The few who do that without permission from the Council have a tendency to end up on the wrong side of dead. Whoever was coming through was a powerful demon. It didn't take a mathematician to realize the odds were not in my favor of this being friend over foe. I was suddenly important to someone important.

As the rift peeled the air apart. I snagged Creed, almost dropping it. I shook it to activate the halberd, and held it at middle guard. Held laterally, high up my chest, I trained with the position that was good at warding off a threat while also providing an opportunity to give them a face-full of steel if they persisted in threatening. The three blades gleamed in steely glory.

"Let's try not to almost take a toe off next time?" I asked of the magical item.

The petrified cherry did not respond.

My eyes didn't move from the rift as my skin prickled. This was my first post-Abandonment visitor from the Underworld. I didn't want any visitors unless it was Lucifer Himself crawling on His knees, begging for forgiveness and offering a golden carriage on the other side, ready to whisk me away to a palace in whichever Circle I deemed lucky enough to have my residency. But if there's one thing I know about the Underworld, Lucifer and His Council, it was that none of them would ask forgiveness. Remorse and regret were not emotions those types felt.

The blue flame crackled louder, its energy feeding from the Hellfire in the depths of the planet. Fully formed, it filled a quarter of the room. A shimmering scene unfolded in the center of the ring of flame.

A slender leg in tight black slacks broke the barrier between the worlds. A dead giveaway. Three of the Council members had slim legs. Two were incubi. One, Azazel, was an ancient demon and had legs thin as bones. The other was Apopis, the shape and size of a broom. This leg had form and curves in all the right places, ensuring ocular stimulation. A form that made anyone with a healthy sexual appetite feel alive. And there was only one succubus in the Underworld influential and powerful enough to use rifts.

The black-clad leg stepped through, followed by its twin and the rest of the body belonging to the blond with icy aqua eyes. Her face betrayed no emotion—well, unless you consider sternness an emotion. I swear, she didn't even blink. At least she had the decency to not fake congeniality.

"Mr. Sunstone," Seraph said, shifting her shoulders to the right in a quarter turn, and waving her hand languidly. The rift collapsed in on itself with a sucking sound, leaving me with one of the five rulers of Hell.

I didn't lower Creed. "What are you doing here? I don't remember sending out house warming invitations. And how in the heaven did you find me?"

She sniffed. I think it was supposed to be a sound of humor. It failed. A line had been drawn between me and Seraph, one etched in something more permanent than the brimstone Hell had been carved from. I was beyond false platitudes.

She raised an eyebrow, too arched for my tastes. "Do you honestly think we don't know your whereabouts, that we haven't been tracking you from the moment you stepped foot back here?"

The false levity in her voice annoyed me almost as much as her presence. "I didn't step anywhere. I was Abandoned. Remember? You were the one to cast the deciding vote. Who knew I would have to remind you of that? You seemed really satisfied when you cast us out."

Seraph's gaze traveled around the room as if she found our rental furniture more interesting than me confronting her. "You're doing well for yourself. I'm not surprised."

"What do you want, Seraph?"

Without squaring her face on me, Seraph's eyes snapped in my direction, sliding down to Creed before finding my face again. "If you would do me the favor of putting that ... *thing* away, I want to have a conversation with you."

My hand tightened on Creed's haft, which warmed in my palm. I lifted the halberd a few inches to shoulder height. Careful not to shake it, I jutted it in her direction. "What? This little thing? Why in the world would I disarm myself? Especially here in the Overworld, where you could make my day a lot worse with the flick of your wrist?"

For a second, Seraph went rigid. But if the Founder was anything, she was a calculating and deliberate succubus. Dangerous beyond measure. So dangerous she could quickly squelch any and all fear. If I had not been so attentive, if my senses were not so acute to the sights and sounds around me, I might have missed it. Unfortunately for her, I hadn't.

She slowly raised a hand. Her hand jerked, less fluid than I remembered. A murkiness fell over me. A listening ward.

I covered my smirk at detecting her spell. The special ability was so satisfying.

"Please?" she asked.

To trust the Council member or not; that was the question. My gaze never wavered. Her cheekbones, too pronounced, too jagged, flushed. Almost blotched. Her hands, bonier than I remember.

Moments stretched. Seraph clasped her hands at her waist, her thin fingers pressing into the backs of the alternate hands.

I lowered Creed, giving it a quick shake. The haft cooled. The double-ax head and wavy blade bottom collapsed inward. No matter how many times I saw Creed birth itself into and withdraw from the world it was an amazing feat. The weapon held so many secrets, secrets I had yet to understand, but its epic magic was undeniable. Back in its foot–long truncheon form, I gripped it at my side. Respect was a two-way street, and this Founder had none for me so I would not return an unpaid favor. If she changed her mind about keeping this civil, I would have the weapon exploring her insides before she could finish her incantation.

"Why do I have this dishonor of your presence?" I said, moving to sit. I wanted no obstacles, not even my coffee table, between us. That way, I could get to her in a flash if her intention proved malevolent. "I've been in the Overworld for months and none of you have bothered to check in, not that I expected or wanted it. I thought our mutual interest was severed the moment you sentenced me to death."

Seraph moved to the other chair, her stride short and choppy. She sat without turning her back. Her hands gripped the arms, and I noticed how knobby her knuckles were. "Your Abandonment did not mitigate our interest in you, Mr. Sunstone."

"I don't imagine anything will. My interest in you and the Council's business ended the day you voted to Abandon me and Cancer."

"My, my, my," she said, her head bobbing slowly. "These past few months have made you slightly more belligerent."

I gave her a cocky smirk. "I'd like to think it has made me more confident, less likely to listen to bullshit, of which you are full, Seraph. You're not welcome. I think you understand why. If you don't," I said, raising the truncheon, "I can remind you."

The chances that the Council didn't have one of their spies constantly following us were slim. If I were a gambler, I'd bet my meager savings on the fact Seraph knew Cancer lived with me, and that put Cancer in danger if she were to pop home early from work. Their family feud was ferocious enough for curses, so I doubted we would find a peaceful resolution if my roommate's shift ended unexpectedly.

"How is Cancer?" she asked as if she read my thoughts, her voice flat.

Seraph was trying to antagonize me. Two could play that game. "Better than Chax, I imagine. How is your nephew? Still cursing people? Tell him I miss him, would you? Tell him... I'm dying to see him again."

My response hung like a dagger hovering near her throat. Her piercing eyes widened, sparkling with heat. "My... nephew is none of your concern."

"Concern." I mocked, shaking my head. "Nothing you have to say is any of my concern. But yet, here you are, in my home. The last time I checked, I didn't invite you in, so you're infringing on my right to exist, which ticks me off. The longer you delay, the more dancing we do, the more irritated and less likely to listen I will be."

Her fingers rolled, tapping out a cadence on the chair arm as she watched me. "Family is a funny thing, wouldn't you say, Mr. Sunstone?"

"How so?"

Her hand flopped over. "Well, look at how they act, and how they differ. For example, how many times were you in trouble with the Council, and how many of those times did your wretched parents have to witness your downfall? Your mother loved you through all of it, yet your father? When was the last time you heard from him?"

"Lucifer, how much energy do you waste snooping into my life? And why does it matter to you?"

She tapped the end of the chair. Tap. Tap. Tap. "Family is important. Even family you don't particularly enjoy being around. Blood is blood. You do what you can for them. You do everything in your power to better their lives. At least that's how I see family. I find it interesting that you see it so very differently. I don't know why, and I don't particularly care. My priority is on taking care of mine."

My patience was running out. "Is that why you helped Chax? Why you allowed him to torture Cancer and then sneak out of Iraq before he could be held accountable? Is that the price of family allegiance? Even for a Founder, that nepotism is abusive, wouldn't you say?"

The tapping stopped. "Chax is none of your business, Mr. Sunstone. How many times do I need to tell you that?"

She was trying to sound dangerous, putting an edge to her tone that would have bullied me a few years ago. Now it was nothing more than an annoyance. "He is, as long as your family's curse effects Cancer and hers. Since you took it upon yourself to waste my time, how about we get down to why you're really here? Let's chat about some real business for a change. Like the business of removing the blessed curse? Not just from Cancer, but from everyone in her family."

"Like I said, Mr. Sunstone, I'm not here for that," Seraph said, one eyebrow raising slightly.

"Lucifer H. Christmas, Seraph, I'm done entertaining you." I was gripping the arm of my chair, making the upholstery creak in protest.

"Your involvement with Chax was more than an annoyance. I don't expect you to understand, and I frankly don't think you would care to, considering your... circumstances. I had hoped you would fulfill your promise, that you would not become what Beelzebub was sure you would. He had you pegged from the beginning, do you know that?"

This was an interesting event. Underneath the listening ward, everyone in the Underworld, the Council members included, were ignorant to this conversation. Seraph could say whatever she wanted and no one but her and I would know. That was how she framed me after her visit to Baghdad, reporting false details of our confrontation over Chax and Cancer, allowing her to twist the details of the situation into a lie that I had blasphemed Lucifer.

After that, what else could the Council do? Either way, this was the end of me. A quick death if I pissed them off enough, or slow rotting away of my immortality? Which was worse?

I might as well have some fun with this conversation if she was going to throw other members of the Council under the chimera carriage. "Did he now? Exactly how did our illustrious Prince of Demons have me pegged?"

She smirked. It was an ugly, gawkish expression. "He knew you were trouble. We were hesitant about your rebellious nature. That was never a secret, not even to you. You always knew you were different, didn't you? One reason Beelzebub took your assignment to Seattle was because he wanted to validate his suspicions."

"And here I thought he wanted to do it because he had a personal vendetta against Aries and wanted to see if the Council would allow him to get away with committing murder."

Seraph didn't even flinch at the accusation, validating my opinion. "He suspected you were always going to be trouble, that there had to be certain... properties due to your status as the Segregate. It's not easy, anticipating the actions of a demon like you, someone so unlike anyone who ever existed. As the Segregate, you were more than a case study. Yes, we were fascinated with you. But it went beyond that."

The memory of our pre-mission brief for Aries flashed through my mind. Beelzebub asserted that the ancient demon's spells could not affect me were he to attack. Aries never did, so I never discovered the truth. Since that mission, I had participated in enough sparring sessions and fights to know that magic *could* injure me. Why wouldn't a First of his name, probably the oldest demon alive at the time, do likewise?

In a flash, the realization hit me. "Beelzebub lied. Aries could have killed me if he wanted to."

Seraph shrugged. "We can't be sure about that. Not completely. You are unique, in all respects. Which is why we had such high hopes for you, why we tested you so often."

"Taurus? Gemini? Every mission? For what? To put me in harm's way? That's a lousy thing to do, even for the Council."

"There were other reasons, Mr. Sunstone," Seraph replied, her eyes dashing down to my hand so fast I would have missed it had I not been paying attention. "You present many challenges. Your involvement with this issue between my family and the Nijals was just one more. More than a simple irritant. I'm trying to accomplish certain things, and I can't have you ruining my plans out of some ridiculous sense of chivalry."

"I prefer to call it empathy," I countered. "It wouldn't hurt you or anyone on the Council to develop a sense of it, though I don't expect any of you being capable of that. But why don't we put it to the test?"

"How so?"

I pointed at her, holding my finger steady. "You. I want you to recite the cure for the curse."

Her blue eyes went from my finger stabbed in her direction to my eyes. She chuckled, a sound she forced through her throat. "Recite the cure? Don't be ridiculous."

I jabbed my thumb back over my shoulder toward my bedroom. "I still have the counter spell. I grab it, you read it."

"Why would I do that?"

I raised my hands in a half–shrug. "Empathy. Being able to

understand what Cancer and her family are going through because of an old, meaningless rivalry that involved demons long-since Abolished. The same who started this mess but aren't around to suffer the consequences of its continuation. Because it's the right thing to do."

Seraph shook her head. "Such a shame."

"What is? You're testing my patience. Has anyone thrown you through a rift before? I'd gladly volunteer to be the first."

Her mouth evened, eyes hardening. It was an intimidating look, one that six months ago would have set me on edge. Now, it had no effect but to stoke the fire burning within me. "You can't create a rift to throw me through. Additionally, it's not wise to threaten a Council member."

I never felt as good as I did when I shrugged at her comment. "Well, without a rift, you've got no quick access to the Underworld. That means you're in the Overworld, alone with me. And if I remember my early lessons, the Overworld is the only place where demons are vulnerable to death. Well, except for me." I brought Creed up and carefully wiggled the tip so that it didn't spring to life and skewer my leg. "I can kill demons wherever I want. Probably the Upperworld too. So, without an escape, bad things could happen. You could have an unfortunate accident, say, tripping over my coffee table." I moved Creed in front of my face, even with hers across the room, staring at it as if I was inspecting the dark wood. "Who knows? You could fall onto a blade I carelessly left lying around. That would truly be unfortunate. Would you be the first Founder to die in the Overworld? Well, besides Aries. You know, the First of his name you had a small part in murdering?" I hated the sound of my voice in my ears. It shook with adrenaline and I feared Seraph might misinterpret it. "So let's not even bother exploring that possibility." I inched forward. "I'll grab the counter spell and you'll recite it. Then, everything will be settled and you can be on your merry way back to torturing some other unfortunate demon. Shall I retrieve it, or should we go our separate ways and hope you don't have an accident? Who do you think would replace you on the Council, anyway?"

In the years since Aries gave Creed to me, I never imagined brashness like this. Back then, I was the Segregate, the only demon in the history of Hell without magic. An outcast. A loner. Only Bilba braved befriending me in all those magicless millennia. I'd only ever had one girlfriend, and she hung out with me only because she wanted to share details with her friends about what it was like to date a loser. I didn't even get to the second level with her. Creed changed all that. I was confident in the face of bullies, obnoxious succubi, and even Council members, of which Seraph checked all boxes. By the time Gemini went on trial, I could stand in front of the Council knowing I didn't have to quake every time they said "boo." That confidence had only grown.

Seraph's lips moved wordlessly. Never had I thought I could watch a Founder unravel. Her face twitched, lips wrestled and nostrils flared. She closed her eyes—she actually closed her eyes!—as she drew a calming breath. When she opened them again, the steeliness returned. Her voice was level when she spoke. "If you want to retrieve the counter spell, you may, but," she said, holding up a finger, "let me warn you. A counter spell is useless. It won't help Cancer, but it may help you feel better about yourself."

I had been about to stand. Seraph's comment caught me halfway out of my chair. I hovered over the cushion in an awkward pose. "What do you mean it won't help her?"

An assured confidence flowed over Seraph's face. Her bony cheekbones rose. "I could recite a counter spell a thousand times, Mr. Sunstone, and it won't do a thing for Cancer or the curse. The only way the curse can be removed is by the person who placed it. No one else can take away what was done."

Her cocky message was devastating, delivered like a

kidney punch. If what Seraph was saying was true... I let the thought go. It couldn't be true.

As if reading my mind, Seraph raised an eyebrow. "So you understand? Me, Chax, none of my relatives can remove the curse. It was set generations ago and the succubus who cast it is Abolished."

The meaning hung in the air. I didn't want to recognize it, because acknowledging its existence would mean Cancer would never get better.

Seraph spoke softly, a hint of caring in her tone, which irritated me more. "I'm sorry to be the one to tell you this. But it is the Lucifer–honest truth. The curse is permanent. It cannot be removed. I'm sorry, Mr. Sunstone."

Somehow, her apology only made my fire intensify.

"Where is Chax?"

Seraph's eyes flickered. "Chax? I told you, Mr. Sunstone, he doesn't factor into any of this. He's not your concern."

I held up a finger. "Oh, I disagree. He's definitely my concern."

"Why?" The single word hinted at danger.

"Because, *if* you're correct about this, and the curse is permanent, then someone needs to pay. I don't imagine you would volunteer yourself. Fortunately for you, I'm currently accepting applications from anyone in your family. I figure Chax, the despicable little cherub that he is, would be a great replacement."

Her top lip pulled back in a snarl. "I don't appreciate you threatening my family."

"And I don't appreciate you violating my personal space and time. Nor do I appreciate you bothering me. And for some reason, I'm pretty ticked off that you are so cavalier about what is happening to Cancer and her family. Did you want to taunt me, is that it? Just to let me know the Council is still stalking me, so I spend the rest of my very short life looking over my shoulder at every sound? Or was it the double whammy? You wanted me to know that Cancer and everyone in her family is screwed in perpetuity? Is that what you have become, Seraph?" My pulse thumped in my ears. I knew I looked like a babbling impling, but I no longer cared. "You know, I used to think Beelzebub and Apopis were having a run-off for Most Despicable Council Member, but you stole the title from right under their noses."

At that, she stood, her hands slapping to her thighs. I stood too. Her hand rocketed in the air. Mine went to Creed. Her movement opened a rift through which she could run back to the Underworld. I extended my senses into it to see how far into Hell I could peer No further than inches. Penetrating the rift felt like sticking my face into a vat of thick honey. Malleable, I could push in, but I could not see or sense anything.

I pulled my hand away from Creed.

She watched every movement. When it was obvious I wasn't going to Abolish her, her shoulders relaxed. She was even careful to cover that reaction as best as she could. "I pose no threat to you, Mr. Sunstone. I'm leaving." She lurched toward the rift, pausing after she placed one foot through, as if it gave her confidence that she could escape before I could make her insides become her outsides. "But know this. You are being watched at all times. You pose too much of a threat. To both us and the angels. Tread carefully. One wrong move and…"

Now it was my turn to blink in confusion as her statement trailed off. "Why? Why are you telling me this? It seems like that would give me an advantage, knowing that you have adorable spies following me everywhere. I don't need any favors, least of all from you."

She shrugged. "Then don't consider it a favor. In actuality, it's not. The less we have to worry about you, the more time we have to focus on other… more relevant things, the types that have an impact on the Underworld, unlike you."

Ouch.

"I would encourage you to focus on your life here," Seraph continued, one arm and shoulder through the rift. I was losing my chance, but I hadn't thought through the ramifications of doing harm to a Founder. What consequences would I face if I acted now? What would those I cared for face?

"In an ideal world, you would," she continued. "Embrace your newfound mortality and enjoy its novelty. Otherwise, you'll exhaust yourself. Because your time here will be long enough. Continuing to be a problem to immortals will do you no favors. Think on that."

"Wait." I stopped her before she vanished. "What do you mean, about my time here? I thought Abandonment meant I lost my immortality? Are you telling me I'm not mortal?"

Her smirk was smug. "You are, most definitely. But your mortality isn't like any others we've Abandoned. So unlike Cancer's. Her demise will be quick, by the grace of Lucifer. Yours won't be. Yours will be long, and excruciating, especially if you don't change your ways."

"What are you saying?"

Seraph gave an ugly, scoffing laugh. "I'm saying, Mr. Sunstone, because you do not have natural Abilities, we cannot know how fast your mortality will decay. We can only hazard a guess how long before you are Abolished... die, as mortals say," she nearly purred. My teeth ground. "Long after Cancer is gone, you will still be here, slowly rotting. Make the best use of the decades ahead. That is a more fulfilling way to live out your mortal life."

With the last jab, Seraph disappeared, and the rift blinked out. She was back to the safety of the Underworld and beyond my reach.

In a moment of frustration, I snagged Creed from my pocket by its knob and flung it against the wall. Six inches of the truncheon sank into the drywall and I immediately regretted the repairs I was going to have to make. Frustrated, I dropped into the chair and threw my head back, closing my eyes and wishing that the demon known as Zeke did not exist.

I never saw Creed pull itself free and zip across the living room. But I felt the smack against the side of my head when it took its revenge.

Outdone, even by a stupid piece of petrified wood. That summed up my life.

4

OLYMPIA

DIALPHIO: *Ezekial?*

Are you there?

Aren't you supposed to have your notebook by you at all times? Didn't we discuss that?

Why aren't you answering?

Now I'm worried.

That's it. I'm writing to Cancer. If I find out you're okay but avoiding your notebook, you and I are going to have words. Don't think I won't twist your ears.

If ever there was a tonic to the toxics injected into me by the aqua-eyed Founder who dropped bad news into my living room, it was my ex–boss Dialphio. The owner of The Book Abyss, the best blessed bookstore in the Fifth Circle, Dialphio had become somewhat of a mother figure to me over the years. My own mother didn't need to be replaced, she was an incredible succubus in her own right, but there was something to be said for one who was unrelated but could care as if for their own child. Dialphio was that.

And I had screwed up.

After my sentencing of Abandonment had been announced by the Council, I was made to promise everyone I cared for that I would carry a demonic notebook so they could reach me at anytime. Dialphio was the most vehement in her message, making me swear at least a dozen times that I would always have one nearby. I fulfilled the promise for a few weeks, but as I fell into a routine and—if I'm going to be honest with you—sulked at my Abandonment, I slacked on my end of the bargain. For what it's worth, I meant to adhere to my promise, but sometimes I got distracted, busy, or simply didn't think I was important enough for demons to want to check on me. At least today I didn't have that excuse. The notebook had been on my bedroom nightstand since before Seraph's visit, and since the Founder blessed me with her unannounced gut punch, I was too distracted. Now I had Dialphio to answer to.

ZEKE: *I'm here. Sorry, got caught up in things.*

Within seconds, a new message appeared.

DIALPHIO: *I told you, always have the notebook by you.*

ZEKE: *I would have, but things got crazy.*

I explained the events of the afternoon.

DIALPHIO: *Oh, I'm so sorry to hear that. I will reach out to Cancer.*

ZEKE: *No! Don't! I haven't told her. She deserves to know, but I'm not sure if I should tell her yet. She's going through a lot. Dealing with her Abandonment hasn't been easy. This would be a lot to put on her.*

DIALPHIO: *I don't disagree, but there may be other ways. Right now she accepts her situation. Nothing has changed since you both came back from Baghdad. Let's allow her that peace while I research.*

ZEKE: *You would do that?*

It was a stupid question. Of course Dialphio would. She was a walking encyclopedia. And if she didn't know where to look, she knew where to look to find where to look.

DIALPHIO: *I am grabbing you by your ear the next time I see you.*

I didn't have the heart to tell her she'd be waiting a long time. Thankfully, she still had her immortality, so she would be able to live long enough to see me not fulfill my promise.

ZEKE: *I appreciate any help. I'm sure you can imagine, but it's not easy to do research on curses in the Overworld. They don't have reliable information here.*

DIALPHIO: *I don't imagine they do. Give me time, and I'll let you know what I find. Until then, how are things?*

I filled her in on the most recent events in my life, including the fight in the park.

DIALPHIO: *It's not like you've been busy causing trouble. Glad to see you haven't changed much.*

I imagined Dialphio's pale cheeks turning pink at her own humor. She was the embodiment of caring. She cared about everyone and everything. A hugger to her core, I wish there was a way the demonic notebook could convey that behavior. A Dialphio hug would be a wonderful cure right now.

ZEKE: *You know me.*

DIALPHIO: *Oh, I do. Stubborn to a fault. Speaking of your stubbornness, how have your studies of the* Histories *come?*

Ah, *The Histories of the Balance*, the informative book that contained information so dangerous the Council destroyed it during one of my missions only for Dialphio to surprise me with a copy to bring on my Abandonment.

ZEKE: *Honestly?*

DIALPHIO: *Since when have I ever wanted to hear stories? If I wanted those, I would just read one of these fiction books you made me start stocking. Have you been negligent?*

ZEKE: *Nah, I've been reading it, but honestly, Dialphio it's not easy. In all the time I had this copy and the original, I made it through a tenth of the blessed thing. Some of that stuff is pretty dry, and everything else is over my head.*

DIALPHIO: *Admittedly, it's not for everyone. But it still is vital that you read it. I had hoped that would be a daily habit.*

ZEKE: *It was. At the beginning. I sort of fell off over the past few weeks.*

DIALPHIO: *Don't give up hope. Read the book. You are the only one who will truly understand what it says.*

ZEKE: *What? You're way smarter. My chances of understanding it will fall far short.*

DIALPHIO: *I don't hold Creed. You are the one to interpret the* Histories.

ZEKE: *Me?*

Yes, sometimes I can be eloquent.

DIALPHIO: *Of course you, who else? That book is the key to unlocking Creed. You read the passages. You know its history.*

ZEKE: *But its history doesn't make sense.*

DIALPHIO: *How so?*

ZEKE: *All this stuff about the Balance and liberation. And One. I don't get any of it.*

DIALPHIO: *Unfortunately for both of us, I don't know much more. I can't see into the future, but we do know about the past. Well, those of us who read do. The rest of you are hopeless. I can help you in terms of what it means for Creed to maintain the Balance and liberate, for which it's very clear the* Histories *mentions the holder of the halberd is the liberator. That's you, by the way. I can tell you anything I know about One.*

This was an interesting proposition and encouraging twist in my day after the previous disturbing visit. When I had been the target of an assassination attempt along with an angel named Cassie, she had mentioned that name, One, before slipping into a rift back to the Upperworld. Dialphio had mentioned One back in The Book Abyss. The *Histories* mentioned One. But beyond that, I knew as much about One as mortals seem to know about the good nature of Lucifer. Nothing in books outside of the *Histories*, no authority figures talked about One, and my parents definitely never brought it up.

ZEKE: *So fill me in. What is One?*

DIALPHIO: *One is everything.*

ZEKE: *See? That right there makes absolutely no sense. Let's role-play, Dialphio. Pretend I'm the dumbest demon in the history of demons.*

DIALPHIO: *Well, that's not difficult to imagine.*

ZEKE: *So funny. What would you tell me if that were true, which I'm not saying it is?*

As I waited, I imagined somewhere in the Fifth Circle, my ex–boss was giggling like a chirping bird. She continued.

DIALPHIO: *One is the creator of everything. The All. I've told you this before.*

ZEKE: *Not in great detail.*

DIALPHIO: *We didn't have time.*

ZEKE: *True.*

DIALPHIO: *Seriously, I know we didn't have much time, but context could be helpful. The theory goes; All created One. One is the material consciousness of the All.*

ZEKE: *Wait. Wait. This is 'helpful'? You're getting ahead again. What is the All?*

DIALPHIO: *The All is the All, dummy. It is everything material and immaterial. Seen and unseen. It is this mortal coil, the solar system, the galaxy, the universe, and the universes beyond the universe. The clumps of universes. The clumps of those clumps, and more. It is everything, even the nothingness in between the everything. It is All.*

ZEKE: *Space is… that big?*

I had an overwhelming and unnerving sensation of the blue dome above the Overworld, the sky I had always feared floating off into during my first visits. To think about what was beyond it made my throat form into a solid block.

DIALPHIO: *No one knows for sure. That's the wonder and mystery of existing. We get to pontificate and entertain thoughts so immense that we can't possibly grasp or comprehend their nature.*

ZEKE: *I see nothing entertaining. So, the All is everything, and it created... or... whatevered One. So what did One do and why is he important?*

DIALPHIO: They. *One is not he. Not she. They are they. And they, are the consciousness of the All, eternal. Powerful. I guess you could say One is responsible for our physical reality. Everything that supports the planet, the trees and birds, the animals, mortals and immortals.*

It was becoming clearer now, all the information wrapping into a finer point.

ZEKE: *Lucifer and Yahweh too, right?*

DIALPHIO: *Yes, even them. All subservient to One.*

ZEKE: *And here I thought Lucifer and Yahweh were equal, subservient to no one. That's what I've been taught.*

DIALPHIO: *That's what we all were taught. And there's a reason for that.*

ZEKE: *Reason being?*

DIALPHIO: *What better way to control a populace than to make them think they have an authority figure to answer to? An authority figure who is not out of reach, but who can directly impact them? One is too vast of a concept for demon and angelkind to wrap their heads around. Not very effective, even if One were so inclined, which no evidence supports, and I cannot imagine they would be. They've got universes, the eternal plane, to worry about. How could they possibly have time to meddle in our affairs? But Lucifer and Yahweh are a very real part of the world. Now that's a different story altogether. Power and control.*

ZEKE: *In that reasoning, wouldn't One be the ultimate authority figure which everyone must answer to, anyway? I don't see how it's any different. Lucifer? Yahweh? One? If we always have to answer to someone, then there is always someone who has the power.*

DIALPHIO: *The main difference is One does not have a vested interest in our politics and our Balance, whereas Lucifer and Yahweh do. They are motivated to meet their goals, One is only motivated by protecting the All. What we do here is meaningless in that perspective. I guess you could say I agree with you, but where we differ is that we answer ultimately to the All, and it doesn't care one way or another. It just is.*

In my mind's eye, I could picture Dialphio sitting at her desk in the rear of The Book Abyss, ignoring customers while she scribbled furiously. I hoped she had good help in the store.

ZEKE: *Wow, that's depressing.*

DIALPHIO: *Is it? Once we see we are the masters of our own fate, isn't that liberating?*

I thought about it, the wheels in my head breaking free of the rust of months of doing nothing more than existing. She was right. It was liberating, in those fractions of seconds I could wrap my head around it. Which I was admittedly struggling to do.

ZEKE: *It is, I guess. It's just a little strange.*

DIALPHIO: *I understand. Take some time with it, but don't get lazy. You need to grasp this so you can understand yourself.*

ZEKE: *Good luck with that.*

After confronting one of the Founders so aggressively, I wasn't sure I even understood myself.

DIALPHIO: *This is serious.*

I read the response in Dialphio's motherly tone.

ZEKE: *I understand, but it's a lot to take on. Looking at Lucifer as nothing more than a figurehead? Now I'm trying to understand that out there, somewhere, is something even more powerful? Too much.*

DIALPHIO: *Lucifer is more than a figure, a lot more, wouldn't you say? Look at your life. Look at where you are. That was done by his Council, not Lucifer. Imagine what He could do. Don't take this lightly. Simply because they aren't the ultimate authority doesn't mean that they aren't an authority.*

ZEKE: *Makes sense.*

DIALPHIO: *Does it? Do you understand what that means? If Creed comes from something above the power and reach of*

Lucifer, what does that make you in the eyes of Lucifer and His Council?

This time I didn't need to think because the answer was too frightening.

ZEKE: *A threat.*

DIALPHIO: *Exactly. So study your* Histories *and think. What you told me about Seraph visiting, that's concerning. I fully expected them to be watching you after Abandonment because you are one-of-a-kind. You and I both know that. You were before you had Creed, but now they have something tangible they can see to fear. I think that is only the tip of the demon's tail of their fear. You're a bigger threat to them than I think you realize. You need to tread carefully. I'm keeping my ear to the ground here and I can tell you, things are moving.*

ZEKE: *How so?*

DIALPHIO: *Your first mission, the Aries mission. That story you tell about your return. Do you remember it?*

ZEKE: *Of course, how could I forget? They had me strapped to a donkey and paraded through the Fifth Circle to serve a prison sentence because I refused to murder Aries.*

DIALPHIO: *After that, small pockets of demons willing to speak against the Council began taking form during your imprisonment. Word spread at the same time you applied at the bookstore. It's been spreading and growing, gathering momentum.*

ZEKE: *Those pockets never seemed to grow, though. Up until they booted me out of Hell, I never felt supported by more than a handful of demons, and they were either family or friends.*

DIALPHIO: *Can you fault them? They're afraid. They need something concrete to believe in before they fully commit. A reasonable course of action, I would say. Give them that and they may surprise you. Before you do, you need to study the* Histories.

Since Abandonment, I had been too distracted to think about asking Dialphio the question I wanted an answer to. After Seraph's news ramped up my need to engage in life again, I figured now was a better time than any.

ZEKE: *Dialphio, how is there a second copy of the* Histories? *The original was burned by the Council. It was in my possession at the time. You had no idea until I admitted what happened. So how did you make a copy?*

After another long pause, so long I figured a customer had pulled her attention away, her new words scratched out from a quill from another realm.

DIALPHIO: *I've made copies of that book. It's too precious to only have a single one. The book was always a threat, would always be a threat. I knew that the minute I first read it. That is not a risk I was willing to take when certain… rumors sprang up.*

Rumors? How early did she have knowledge about the book being the focus of someone's fire spell?

ZEKE: *What knowledge, Dialphio? Did someone tell you what was going to happen?*

Another long pause. My eyes widened when I read her response.

DIALPHIO: *Let's just say I have friends in high places.*

5

OLYMPIA

APPARENTLY TODAY WAS National Demonic Letter Writing Day. Kicked off by Ralrek's missive, followed with the troubling correspondence with Dialphio, it ended with a dinner at the small pinewood table situated between the kitchen and living room. Complete with two wobbly chairs. Only mine was occupied. I'm sure at some point in my near future, I will have had one too many drinks, sit in the blessed thing and bring it down in a humiliating heap. But for now, it held, allowing me to try to enjoy my plate of lukewarm spaghetti.

Then Lucifer's seal on my demonic notebook burned blue with an incoming message. Third of the day. I flipped it open. My mother.

LILITH: *Hello Ezekial, it's your mother. I haven't heard from you in a few days, so I wanted to check in. How are things?*

I stared at the black letters on the white parchment. How were things? What could I tell her? What did I want to tell her? Sometimes I think my mother forgets how old I am, a demon grown, ready and capable to face the Under and Over-worlds on my own. If I told her about the brawl in the park, she would become overbearingly protective. If I told her that Dialphio was helping me sneak around behind the backs of the Council, she would become disquieted. What would she do if I told her earlier today I threatened the life of an ancient demon, a Founder? She might just sprout angel wings. Best to proceed carefully then—and when I say that, I mean, I needed to lie.

ZEKE: *Things are great, mother. The job is easy, and I'm spending my free time in the soup kitchen.*

LILITH: *The homeless thing? Are they paying you well? Two jobs. Oh, I worry about you, Ezekial.*

Every time we wrote, I mentioned the soup kitchen. Then every time I mentioned it, she seemed to struggle with what it was. None of the Circles I'm aware of have institutions to serve the homeless like Stacy's kitchen. Going out of the way to help the homeless is a novel concept to demons, but not so novel that it would be so confusing or hard to grasp. My mother was only in her mid-thirty-thousands, far too young to be suffering from senility. Yet, here we were, going back to the basics about the kitchen.

ZEKE: *Did I stress you out again?*

I asked instead of mentioning that she might be shooting toward old age on a one-way trip.

LILITH: *No, son. Why would you say that?*

ZEKE: *No reason. I haven't heard from you in a few days either. Have you been busy?*

LILITH: *Oh, you know how things are around here. With the house and my business, I'm always busy. I like it that way.*

My parents weren't busy. Not really. As empty-hivers for years now, they had no real obligations beyond daily life. My father had his job working on a crew for the Hellfire, ensuring the installed safety mechanisms prevented it from raging into the Circles of Hell and destroying all demonic life. My mother had her side hustle, which was nothing more than a pyramid scheme. Neither me nor my father were allowed to call it a multi-level marketing scam. She got upset whenever that was mentioned. I stayed far away from references to pyramids.

The last time I checked, she was selling fingernail extensions. Supposedly, the newest demonic fad was to embrace the stereotype mortals have of us—them—and wear long, black and pointed fingernails. Difficult to grow, some genius developed extensions and now, mother said, everyone was wearing them. Bilba had been painting his fingernails black for a few centuries already, and his were real and trimmed to be functional. I could only imagine what he thought of the fad.

ZEKE: *Staying busy, huh?*

LILITH: *I'm trying to. The business is booming. I brought on twelve more recruits in the last few weeks. I'm even expanding my products. Who knows how long this nail craze will last, and I don't want to be stuck holding cases of them when everyone goes back to normal nails. You should see these things, Ezekial. They're putrid. Oh my, young demons. But they sell.*

ZEKE: *That sounds interesting.*

It didn't.

ZEKE: *Congratulations. And father? How is he? I haven't heard from him since that first letter after my Abandonment. For all I know, he could've fallen into the Acheron Ocean.*

I didn't expect an immediate response, and none was forthcoming. Every time we wrote, I asked her about the incubus who spawned me, the silent partner in their marriage. My father was a staunch supporter of Lucifer's Third Council. An obedient slave, if I'm being honest. If the Council told him to jump into the Hellfire instead of tend it, he would not take a second's pause to ask which of his feet they wanted to strike first. As focused on compliance as he was, we rarely saw eye to eye. That aspect of our relationship only worsened over the last few years, deteriorating after I started working for the Council. Once I gained insight into how they operated, I couldn't keep my knowledge to myself. Sharing it with my father was probably the wrong idea, in hindsight. He saw me as unnecessarily rebellious. I saw him as a non-thinking minion. We moved further and further apart, and now that I was going to spend my remaining days in the Overworld, repairing our father-son relationship was a flight of fancy.

In all honesty, it didn't bother me he didn't check in. Me owning notebooks made him nervous, Mother said. Even if he was okay with that, we had little to discuss that wouldn't lead to both of us writing in all capital letters—shouting just isn't the same in the written form. It was better this way.

LILITH: *Oh, you know him.*

Boy, did I.

LILITH: *He's busy as can be with a job. They're working him longer hours every year, it seems. Comes home later and more exhausted than I ever remember. Poor soul. He told me to make sure I said hello.*

Did he? I wondered. I didn't ask.

ZEKE: *Glad to hear about his job. On a positive note, that has to help with the bills? Yours, too. It's nice to know I don't have to worry about you keeping the house.*

LILITH: *Yes, it definitely helps. We could even finally repair the kitchen. How great is that?*

Lilith had partially destroyed the kitchen in a cooking accident years ago. Kanthor has Construction Abilities, but they are weak. I can't remember the last time I saw him use them, even for minor home repairs. To hear he finally repaired that space after years of us looking at the blackened scars left behind from my mother's botched meal, was somewhat of a surprise.

ZEKE: *What made him do that?*

LILITH: *Don't be silly. You know your father didn't lift a hammer. He hired someone.*

ZEKE: *He hired someone? Like* paid *coin to someone else?*

I tried to write that line in italics to communicate my surprise, but it just came off sloppy and was a waste of paper, so I gave up after the first few letters.

LILITH: *Yes! It's so nice to have it looking like it does now. No more apologies when the ladies come over for tea or meetings.*

ZEKE: *I don't know; I think I'm going to miss the blackened wood. It added a unique aesthetic to the house.*

Her response was delayed, and I imagined the implied message of me being back in the Underworld hit her hard. It was unintentional, but that didn't lessen the impact of the reminder of my permanent absence. As much as I had stopped enjoying visits to their house because of the ever–reliable arguments Kanthor and I got into, their home was still home to me, and it always would be.

Thankfully, I was saved by a lifeline from a dear friend. Just underneath the unanswered comment to my mother about her damaged kitchen, a note from a different demon was scrawled out on the page.

BILBA: *Hey, Zeke.*

I don't want to sound like an ungrateful son, but catching up with my best friend was a much more enticing event than a torturous conversation with my mother. Both of us were pretending to not recognize the fact we would never see each other again, and that we were okay with it. Mother is much worse at faking than I am. Our conversations usually dried up after a few minutes as we ran out of things to say, and this one was no different. We had the rest of my mortal life to struggle to think of conversation starters. We needed to save up.

ZEKE: *Mother, Bilba is writing. I need to see what he needs. He's working on something. I'll write soon.*

Her response was almost immediate, validating my suspicion that I had unintentionally upset her.

LILITH: *Promise?*

ZEKE: *I do. As soon as I can.*

LILITH: *Take care, Ezekial. I love you.*

ZEKE: *I love you too.*

BILBA: *Zeke?*

ZEKE: *Hey Bilba. Sorry about that. I was talking to my mother.*
BILBA: *Oh, I can let you go.*

I could not scribble out my message fast enough.

ZEKE: *No, that's fine. I want to catch up. What's going on?*
BILBA: *Tons of stuff. It's been ridiculously busy. How are you?*
ZEKE: *A little bruised and beaten, but still as gorgeous as ever.*
BILBA: *You mean, still as single as ever?*
ZEKE: *If I was into mortals, I wouldn't have time to sleep.*

BILBA: *Big talk for a tiny demon. What are you up to now? A hundred and fifty pounds?*

ZEKE: *Stature jokes? Wow, you're really running out of material, bud. For your information, I'm one-sixty-five, thank you very much. Speaking of demons and mortals, I heard you and Ralrek worked through your issue?*

BILBA: *Yes. We had a long heart-to-heart. A few of them.*

ZEKE: *What made you change your mind?*

BILBA: *I don't know. I saw the way he interacted with them during our deployment. Heavens, I spent forever around them myself. They're not bad. A lot like us, actually. I can see why he developed feelings. So, I guess I needed time to process my own biases and realize we're taught to think that way, but those teachings aren't etched in brimstone. They can change. I did.*

I smiled, relieved at Bilba's validation of Ralrek's earlier message.

ZEKE: *Glad to hear that. I really am. That needed to happen a long time ago.*

BILBA: *I know. But at least it did. He forgave me and we've move forward.*

ZEKE: *That's great to hear. So now you can focus on finally setting up that nonprofit for Deception users?*

BILBA: *That's the great news, Zeke. I gave up on that. Well, I didn't give up, but it's not something I'm going to put my energy into right now.*

My quill hovered over the paper. I didn't want to open a can of maggots with the next question, but this was Bilba, and he could get easily distracted with issues of the heart, especially when looking for affection from his mother. For our second mission from the Council, we were sent to the Eighth Circle to retrieve an ancient and powerful magical Horn from a demon named Taurus. During our trip, Bilba found his long-absent mother. After the mission, Bilba was allowed to stay, but their reborn relationship lasted only as long as his coin kept her flower shop business open. Predictably, when that happened, she no longer had motivation to repair thousands of years of damage to her son's emotional well-being. If there was a demon in the Underworld I despised nearly as much as the Council, it was Fellia Ravenous.

Putting quill tip to paper, I scratched out my question.

ZEKE: *Your mother?*

BILBA: *No. Not her.*

ZEKE: *Are you two in communication again?*

BILBA: *Sorry, I didn't write to talk about my mother. I wanted to check in on you and see how things were. I also wanted to let you know what I've got going on. Sorry if it sounds harsh.*

I wanted to tell him that was music to my ears, but I refrained.

ZEKE: *No worries. So what is this excitement I'm picking up on? It sounds like there's potential for good news?*

BILBA: *YES! Great news, actually. I was selected for the Passage. Can you believe that?*

ZEKE: *The Passage? Like, the real Passage?*

The Passage is the high–level test given to powerful magic users who had proven their skills and shown potential. The Council approved very few applicants. It was a major accomplishment just to be selected, but if he was successful, completing it would make Bilba a Major demon.

BILBA: *The one and only. I'm stoked.*

ZEKE: *You should be! That's awesome. The Passage, man. But isn't it a little early? You're barely six thousand. I thought you had to be older to qualify to apply?*

BILBA: *So did I. But I got the selection letter last week and it's authentic. I'm going to take the Passage!*

The skeptic in me was screaming, raging, doing a dance with flailing arms, anything it could to get my attention. Bilba was young to be approved for the Passage by a few thousand years.

This could change his life. Bilba, a Major demon. I shook my head.

ZEKE: *I can't believe it. I'm so happy for you.*

BILBA: *Thank you, Zeke. I couldn't wait to tell you. I just had to make sure the letter was real. I thought someone was screwing with me.*

ZEKE: *Nah, you deserve this. You're an amazing caster.*

I squashed the stupid skeptical voice in my head still doing the awkward jig, demanding I give it attention. Right now, I needed to be happy for my friend.

ZEKE: *When do you start training?*

BILBA: *Not sure yet. I just found my mentor, Melchiot Zeistane. My father actually got the recommendation from someone he works with. She's pretty expensive. Had to take out a loan. But I can pay it off over the next century, which isn't too bad. Hopefully, once I'm a Major demon, I can do that quickly. I'm done being in debt, so becoming a Major demon is really going to help me and my dad. First, I have to take care of him. He had to refinance the house so I could get the training. But after that, I'm attacking the loan.*

ZEKE: *A century? Ouch, that's painful.*

BILBA: *But worth it. If I pass.*

ZEKE: *You will.*

BILBA: *And here's the thing, Zeke. It's the real reason I wanted to write you... well, besides bragging a little. I feel bad about that.*

ZEKE: *Wait. Hold your good news. Why would you feel bad about bragging?*

BILBA: *Well, because you're...*

ZEKE: *Abandoned? You can say it. It's not a dirty word. Seri-*

ously, it's okay, Bilba. I'm glad you told me. Please don't feel guilty about sharing good news. I need some.

I filled him in on the two major events of the week.

ZEKE: *So as you can see, good news from home will do me an Underworld of good at the moment. Please don't feel you can't share, okay?*

BILBA: *Deal. My other news might brighten your day even more then. My mentor, Melchiot, is a Hex caster.*

ZEKE: *No way!*

Hex Abilities were nearly unheard of. In fact, I thought it was nothing more than an urban legend when I first heard about it during deployment. It was Bilba who told me it existed. When it came to matters of magic, Bilba already knew more than I ever could in my lifetime, even if I was still immortal. He soaked up everything and anything to do with magic, its history, applications, and cutting-edge trends.

BILBA: *Yes, way. You know what this means?*

I did. Bilba had told me before. Hex magic was used to cast curses. But that wasn't what had me excited. The Ability could also destroy them, real or imagined.

ZEKE: *Yes.*

I wrote in a shaky hand.

BILBA: *Don't tell Cancer yet, okay? I don't know Melchiot at all. We haven't even had our first session. But as soon as I'm more comfortable, I'll start asking questions and see what I can uncover.*

ZEKE: *This is awesome, thank you so much!*

BILBA: *Of course, Zeke. It's the least I can do. If I can't help you with this Abandonment crap, not yet anyway, I can at least do something good.*

ZEKE: *Just don't take too long.*

I wrote with a wink, as if my best friend could see it.

ZEKE: *She's not herself, and I can't tell if it's the curse or just the reality of being stuck here. Either way, she could use good news. We both could.*

BILBA: *I won't screw around, I promise. As soon as I know something, you will.*

ZEKE: *You're the best, buddy.*

And I meant it.

We finished catching up, but he had to prepare for his preliminary tests. His studies were going to take up most of his time now, but he promised to check in as often as he could. He apologized for being so silent lately, and I told him it was ridiculous. Of anyone in Hell, Bilba was the last one who needed to apologize. Dialphio would challenge that assertion that she wasn't at least neck-and-neck in the running, but I'm sure she had already hired somebody to replace me in The Book Abyss. I planned on holding that over her head every time I could—we had that kind of playful relationship.

It was hard to close the cover of my demonic notebook. When I did, I felt the world close off between me and my best friend. Yet, but for a day that included an unnerving confrontation with a Founder, I couldn't have asked for a better switch in momentum.

Now, I just needed to keep my big mouth shut about this glorious turn of events when Cancer came home.

"YOU LOOK LIKE YOU JUST GOT AWAY WITH SOMETHING." THE door clicked closed behind Cancer.

I hit the pause button on the remote—yes, I was re-watching *A Christmas Carol*, please don't judge—and struggled to contain my grin. In the hours since Bilba's message, I reminded myself over and over to not let Cancer know about the most recent development. For all Bilba knew, Melchiot could be the most miserable succubus in the Underworld, and knowing my father, that was saying something. Even if she was kind, she might not have the ability to lift the curse.

There were too many variables, too many unknowns, to risk telling Cancer right now. No false hopes.

"No, just enjoying the movie," I said, turning off the TV.

Cancer bent to unlace her white sneakers. Kicking them off, they landed one, across the other, on top of my sneakers. Great, smelly nurse shoe funk. Cancer collapsed in the chair, her head flopping back. Her loose curls fell over the back of the chair as she gazed at the ceiling.

"Tough day?" I asked.

Her hand circled in the air lazily. "No one appreciates nurses. Especially doctors. Definitely doctors."

One of the major reasons we could move out of Seattle to Olympia was Cancer's job at Capital Medical Center. Well, it was the nice, fat sign-on bonus she received that paid for our move. The job itself is what kept a roof over our heads. But the hospital was getting its money's worth, which was not surprising since they had her commitment for the next two years. She worked in the hospital's bariatric clinic—something I could barely pronounce and definitely not understand. But it was the first good opportunity to come along that would get us out of Seattle, so she took it. Though she said she enjoyed her work, she often looked like she'd just run a marathon.

Cancer slapped the arm of the chair, her eyes snapping wider. "What did you cook for dinner? I'm starving."

Now I had an excuse to allow my inner-grin to spread, a lie hidden behind convenient truths. "I thought we could have a special night."

Cancer pulled her jaw in toward her neck, a flash of playful skepticism on her face. "What did you have in mind, Ezekial Sunstone? I'm not the kind of lady you can wine and dine and have your way with. Well, not easily."

I wagged a finger. "No, you're not. But you wish you were. Too bad work gets in the way of your nonexistent love life. Anyway, I was thinking about taking you out to eat. My treat. It's a nice evening, and I've been stuck in here all day. I could do with fresh air. What do you say to Italian?"

Now her skepticism turned real. "What? Are you done with chicken wings? I never thought I'd see the day."

"Pfft. I'll never turn my back on that... ambrosia. If mortals ever needed proof Lucifer and Yahweh are real, it's chicken wings, I swear. But no, I know you're not a big fan of them because you're weird and all. Plus," I said, turning more sincere, "you work hard enough to have a meal of your choice. What do you say? Should we head out?"

"Zeke, I just got home. It was a long day. I've been on my feet for." She paused, lifted her arm to check her watch, and let it flop back to the arm of the chair. "Oh, heaven, if I know. Hours? I'm completely worn out."

As I moved toward my bedroom to grab my wallet, I shouted over my shoulder, "And you're completely hungry. Everything in life is a choice, Cancer. Either you go for Italian with me, or you suffer my grilled cheese again. The decision is yours."

"The gods are cruel," she shouted. From my bedroom door, I heard the chair squeak as she stood. "That's plain dirty, Ezekial Sunstone."

"I know."

Cancer walked into her room, pausing in her doorway to glance at me, a playful look on her face. "Seriously, how hard is it to not ruin grilled cheese? Yet, you do it consistently."

"It's my special skill. Don't be jealous."

"Yes, jealous. That's what I am," Cancer said, trying to sound harsh but unable to hide the twinkle in her brown eyes. "Just give me a chance to get showered and then I'll be ready."

The important thing to get through life, for immortal or mortal—though I imagine I needed to stop saying that since I was no longer part of the former—is that attention to detail can help avoid a swath of issues. If you watch what people do instead of what they say, you can learn a lot about their true motivations. Cancer might have complained and griped about going out for dinner, but she took the world's fastest shower and was back in the living room, dressed, her hair pulled into a tight bun, as I finished lacing my sneakers.

"Hungry?" I said with a chuckle.

"Starving," she said forcefully, slipping into her slides and slinging her purse over her shoulder. "Let's go, slowpoke."

"Race you," I said, sprinting past her, throwing the door open and running down the stairs. I turned to see an empty stairwell. I started forward when Cancer's smooth legs made their appearance from the landing. "You didn't even try to race."

"Because I'm not five hundred years old," she laughed. "Maybe you should try acting your age? Plus, who wants to sweat right before they go to dinner?" Joining me on the sidewalk, Cancer slid her arm into the crook of my elbow, hooking me to her. "Come on, handsome, let's stuff our faces with pasta."

We walked a few blocks to Casa Mia. This part of the city was a mix of fast-food joints, small businesses, and the Salvation Army services building crowded with homeless. We took a side street around the back of the building so I could check on a few mortals I knew from the soup kitchen.

"Hey Sprinkles, you staying out of trouble?" I asked when I saw the grouchy old man lounging underneath the building's overhang, only his upper torso shaded from the sun.

His lips opened and closed like a cow chewing its cud. "Ain't no trouble to get into. Too hot. Plus, I'm hungry. You working the kitchen tonight?"

I shook my head. "No can do. I've got a date."

Cancer snorted.

Sprinkles looked from me to her, and back again. "More like you've got a captive. Honey," he said to Cancer, "if the police can't help, let Sprinkles know. I'll save you from that young punk. Just say the word."

Sprinkles's charm offensive was in full gear. Obviously the heat couldn't sap that from him.

Cancer giggled. "Thank you very much. I think I can handle myself. But if I need reinforcements, you'll be the first one I call."

"If I had a phone, my number would already be in yours," Sprinkles teased.

"Only if I didn't block it," Cancer served back.

The half-dozen other homeless people lounging around near Sprinkles whistled and hooted, giving him a ribbing as we made our way down the street.

He called after us. "Remember what I said, honey. Just say the word. Punk, when will I see you again?"

"Thursday," I shouted over my shoulder. Tugging Cancer toward the restaurant, I said to her, "I'm super hungry. Didn't want to say anything in front of them."

Cancer's eyes fell to the sidewalk. "It's sad, isn't it? So many of them."

"Too many," I acknowledged with a nod. "Only a few months here and I think I fully understand why Aries did what he did, what pushed him to put his own life on the line for them. I thought I understood, but I really didn't. For someone his age, who accomplished everything he did, being able to help these people must have been fulfilling. A great way to spend his last few years. I hope he would have been proud of how I'm trying to help."

She tugged my elbow to her side. "He would be, Zeke. Don't doubt that. You give so much."

"I don't give enough."

"Don't do that to yourself," she said. "It's not worth it. We do as much as we can."

We neared the spot along Plum Street where it split into two halves, divided by a grass rise and a long line of maple trees in full foliage. The deep green leaves soaked in the summer sun. I looked at the small businesses on either side of the road. Except for cars, the street was nearly empty. Humans, I discovered, didn't like to walk places unless driving was inconvenient. Seattle had far more pedestrians. In this smaller city, with its copious parking, people never used their feet—which is really strange to a demon who spent six thousand years in the crowded Fifth Circle, where only the rich could afford chimera carriages and the rest of the population walked everywhere.

It was slightly surreal, this void of life among the living. This constant isolation from one another, everyone closed up in their cars, honking and yelling at each other, must be one reason the mortals were so horrible to each other. My mind drifted back to the fight at Sylvester Park.

"No matter how much any of us do, I don't think it makes a difference," I said.

Cancer pulled up short. "What do you mean?"

I turned to face her, my arm waving through the air. "Look at this, Cancer. Look. Listen. What do you hear? What do you see?"

Cancer did a slow turn, taking in the small slice of suburbia. She shrugged. "Nothing much. Just another weeknight. Nice and quiet."

I pointed. "Exactly."

"Exactly what? You're confusing me."

I cocked my elbow, offering it to her once more, and we continued toward the restaurant as I shared my troubling thoughts. "Half a world away, a war is going on. You spent years there. I spent enough months in Baghdad to know how savage war can be. Yet, look around us. Life continues as if everything is normal. Everything is normal. None of these humans appear troubled by what is happening on the other side of the planet, even though there are what, twenty-something nations fighting and killing? These humans can't be bothered. About anything.

"Last week, at the park. That bothered me, especially when I think about the context, the larger picture. You would think in a time of war, people would not only be sensitive to their own safety, but the safety of others. Yet the entire time those six assholes tormented that man in the park, no one intervened. A few glanced at the scuffle when it kicked off, but none of them cared, Cancer. None of them. If I hadn't been there, who knows what would have happened."

"But you *were*," she said in a soft, caring tone. No matter how harsh the world was, it couldn't dent Cancer's caring attitude, her armor. "And you made it better for him. So see? What we do matters."

"How can you say that after everything you've been through? After everything you saw over there? I'm sure worse happens in the hospital?"

One shoulder rose. "Not where I work, but the ER sees tragedies all the time. I wouldn't say it's worse. Just different."

"But you've told me about victims of violence."

"Yes," she said carefully.

"In war, you expect to see that kind of stuff, but not here," I said, raising my arm and waving it around us. "You would think they would be happier, that they wouldn't be so horrible to each other. You wouldn't think we just walked by a social services building with fifteen humans sitting outside who have nowhere to sleep tonight, never mind something to put in their stomachs. How many clusters of homeless do we not know about just in this city? What about all the cities around the entire world? Does anyone care? Their lives are so short; why wouldn't they do all they could to help one another?"

Cancer was quiet for another block. I hoped my comment about short lives didn't upset her. The restaurant was a parking lot away. When she spoke, there was no frustration in her voice. "They're mortals, Zeke. Overwhelmed by the demands of life, trying to do the best they can. And we can help them with the short time we have here."

"But will that even make a difference?"

"It's worth a try," she said, tugging on the strap of her purse aggressively enough for me to know my complaints were starting to irritate her. "If those who can affect small change don't try, then nothing changes at all."

"I don't know. It's like they're as broken as we—as demons," I said, correcting myself, "are. I thought when we were Abandoned that it would be different, but it's not really. At all."

"It's up to us to change it, Zeke. Did you learn nothing from me yet, going all the way back to Baghdad?"

I took a deep breath, attempting to soothe my frustration. At mortals. At their apathy for each other, at the randomness of life that sends some spiraling in the wrong direction. I was also spinning at the fact the Council Abandoned me for doing right by someone else. Months ago, standing atop a high-rise in downtown Seattle and looking over Elliott Bay with Cancer, I had hopes and dreams. Now, serving the homeless as best as I knew how, I felt like I had fooled myself all along.

Screeching tires behind us cut off any response. I spun, long before Cancer reacted. My heightened senses gave me an advantage to mortal and immortal in that respect. Since my Abandonment, they only seemed to sharpen. I swear, I heard the tires the moment the driver slammed on their brakes.

The driver, whatever they had been thinking, was too late for the human they ran into.

"No!" I shouted, breaking into a sprint.

Sprinkles was crossing the street. The car struck and his body bent at the waist, his shoulders slamming against the hood, before bouncing off and sliding twenty feet down the road.

The homeless congregating around the building scrambled to their feet and ran to the accident. The car slammed to a halt. Even at this distance, I could see the driver inside the vehicle gripping the steering wheel as if he wanted to break it, his eyes unblinking.

"Come on!" I shouted to Cancer.

I made it to where Sprinkles lay in seconds, sliding to my knees beside him. "Sprinkles? Sprinkles? Talk to me, bless it." I put my hands on the rags covering his shoulders, about to turn him over.

"No, don't move him," Cancer ordered, running up to the scene. "Call an ambulance!"

The car door creaked open, and I heard the scuff of a leather sole on the blacktop. "Is... is he okay?" The driver said in a shaky, youthful voice. No one answered him. I didn't even look up.

I yanked my phone out of my pocket and punched in 911.

"Sir? Can you talk to me? Do you hear me?" Cancer leaned over Sprinkles, speaking closely to him, neither in a shout or whisper, her voice as even as a floor. She was calmness personified.

"What can I do?" I asked.

Without looking at me, she answered. "Stay out of my way."

I was having flashbacks to our time in Baghdad, the place I met Cancer and saw her work her earthly and supernatural abilities to help others. I did as she asked, moving back toward the throng of homeless, keeping half my attention on the driver who had not slid back into his car nor completely exited the vehicle. The man was young, even for a mortal, around twenty. His complexion hinted that puberty was still holding up residence inside.

"I'm not going to move you, but I want you to talk to me if you can hear me, okay?" Cancer said.

Stepping away, my voice shook as I relayed the information to the dispatcher. Once I was away from the scene, I heard a car door click closed. Still on the phone, the meaning of the sound was clear. I spun and ran back toward the scene while still trying to give the dispatcher what she needed. I'm not sure she appreciated my heavy breaths in her ear, but I was in an all-out sprint to catch the driver before he fled. Three of the homeless crowd noticed. I was halfway back to the accident. They were closer. One of them rambled onto the hood of the vehicle and slapped it. The car's engine roared.

"Shit!"

"Sir, please try to stay calm. Help is on the way," the dispatcher said. Even the phone's metal can effect on her voice couldn't hide her professionalism under pressure.

I waved in the air as if she could see me. "I'm chasing down the guy who hit the old man with his car. He's trying to take off."

"Sir, we highly recommend you do not confront the individual. I need information on—" she was saying, but I was only half hearing.

Twenty yards away now. The car backed onto Plum Street. His tires squealed—sans smoke from the back wheels like you see in movies. I guess Hollywood lies about everything. The car peeled away, toward the interstate. I had enough time to notice his license plate. That boy's escape was temporary.

"The guy just left, so you might want to send police as well," I told the dispatcher.

"They're already on their way," she said.

Sprinkles was bleeding profusely from his head and each of his breaths came as gasps, accompanied by a gurgling that I wasn't comfortable hearing. Cancer's scrunched expression told me how serious this was. It was a look I had seen before, in Baghdad when she attempted to save the life of my noncommissioned officer. She glanced up. I kneeled across from her. We shared silent messages. Sprinkles was in trouble, and Cancer doubted she could save him.

"Internal," she whispered when I leaned closer.

"Is there anything we can do?"

Cancer shook her head in a jerky motion. "We need that blessed ambulance," she said from the corner of her mouth, then looked at the group of homeless, raising her rigid voice. "I understand your concern, but please give him space. I need to keep him as comfortable as possible until the EMTs arrive."

The gaggle moved back in an uncoordinated shuffle. I slid toward Sprinkles's feet, trying to keep his face free of any blockage of the breeze, doubting it did anything.

I laid a hand on his filthy pant leg. "Don't you dare leave me, you miserable bastard. I'm not done giving you a hard time yet."

My heart was nearly broken when Sprinkles didn't reply except to gurgle. I shivered.

Cancer scowled.

"What's that about?" I asked her.

She lowered her hand and rubbed Sprinkles's arm, her eyes never leaving him. "This. If I had my... if I had my old skills, I might be able to help him. I want to do something and I can't. I'm useless."

"Don't say that. It's not true."

"Tell him that," Cancer replied almost instantly.

I moved to her side, placing my hand on her shoulder. "I'm the resident skeptic here. You're the one who is supposed to keep me positive, remember? We're in the middle of the street, not in your hospital. You're doing more than the rest of us combined."

No sirens filled the summer evening yet.

"Still..." she started, but let the sentence drop. I knew what she meant—sort of.

Sprinkles coughed. Wet. His face contorted just before he spit up a thick wad of blood and mucus.

Cancer leaned over him, ordering, "Someone give me something to wipe his face."

As everyone looked around, seeing nothing accessible or clean, I ripped off my shirt and handed it to her.

She did a double take before taking it. "This better be clean," she said, snagging it and wiping Sprinkles's cheeks. My shirt removed most of the blood, but his lips and cheek remained stained.

A tear caught in the corner of her eye. "I can't even clean his face properly," she said, her voice quivering as she squinted, a frail attempt to hold herself together.

I had nothing to say, nothing that would fix what the Council had taken from Cancer.

I really hoped Bilba and his mentor could find something, soon. I couldn't fathom what else might help Cancer before she was too far gone.

6

OLYMPIA

SPRINKLES NEVER RECOVERED. His death created a void. It was a blow, not only to the Olympia homeless circles, but also to the staff of Stacy's soup kitchen. Even though I had only known him for a few months, Sprinkles had such a caustically friendly personality that I couldn't help but enjoy him. Something about him kept me sharp and appreciative for the levity of life. The soup kitchen felt empty without him.

I couldn't volunteer there enough after the accident. Neither could the rest of the staff. Stacy had more bodies than she knew what to do with. We constantly stumbled over each other and got in one another's way. Some nights, multiple volunteers would be sharing ladling duties. The love for Sprinkles was too much, too perfect. Stacy had to put her foot down, being stricter about the schedule. Like tonight, when she told me to go home and enjoy myself since I had already worked every night for nearly two weeks. I'm at least that smart; I did as ordered.

Heading back up Legion Way, I headed to Cancer's part-time job because I was absolutely bored out of my mind. Nothing good was on TV—believe it or not, I can't watch *A Christmas Carol* every night—and if I practiced my forms with

Creed one more time, I was going to enable the halberd's separation anxiety.

Since the accident, Cancer had taken on more work. Not just at the hospital, but she found opportunities to support local schools as a trainer during sporting events. She also worked at a gym. Not just any gym. This one specialized in mixed martial arts fighting. Cancer said she detested the brutality but needed the money. I didn't believe that. More likely, she did it to keep herself busy and focused on helping others after the accident that took Sprinkles—for the record; she did not fail him, but try telling her that.

The bright blue sky darkened as the evening matured. This far north—I was still trying to figure out latitude from longitude because they aren't used in the Underworld—at this time a year, the sky was light long into the evening. Most of the city was already inside. My free night began hours ago since the bookstore only scheduled me for a four-hour shift—not great for the pocketbook or my boredom. Without much to do and the evening still stifling by human standards, I decided it was time to visit Cancer at the gym and see what all the noise was about.

Something about the quiet unnerved me. In the Fifth Circle, us demons—those demons—are constantly abuzz, creating noise for no apparent reason. My home Circle is way too crowded to expect something like serenity. With my first few assignments to the Overworld being in its cities, I discovered this realm was not a harbor of quiet either, though it falls far short of the racket typical of demons. Olympia isn't a large city, but it's not small either. Instead, it is more a quaint collection of suburbs smashed together. And that had dulled my senses already. Dulled me to the point of comfort.

I was ten blocks away from the apartment, distracted by the slumbering neighborhoods and closed businesses, and enjoying the warm breeze on my skin. Past an eyelash place. An art studio. A tattoo shop that sat next to a barbershop for those convenient times when mortals wanted some ink to go with their new hairdo.

In the Underworld, demons can't be killed. Hurt? More than our feelings, that is? Sure. Injured? Yep. Asses kicked? Most definitely, as thousands of years of sparring against Bilba before I had Creed can attest. But dead? Absolutely not.

Fact is, I should not have been this comfortable in Olympia already. Thankfully, this jaunt to the gym reminded me of the need to be steadfast in my situational awareness. Because the only way I learn life's lessons is the hard way.

Across the street, near the corner of the garage that saw its best days when the Studebaker was a thing, a group of men and women, most in their late twenties—mortal ages were so difficult to pinpoint—lingered. I try not to judge a book by its cover, but it's problematic—after all, I've made my living in bookstores for years. This cover spelled trouble.

The garage wasn't open at this point in the evening, but the group had the look of one that was not concerned with such trivialities. Three males in black leather squatted along the wall. Two females, who appeared to be more than best friends, sat in the tall grass along the white brick side wall. Others, mostly older men, almost hovered in the dirt area along a chain-link fence. My senses allowed me to register all of that in seconds, giving me time to analyze three people who stood close together, conversing. They took turns glancing over each other's shoulders. I'm not the smartest mortal in the world, but I know what trouble looks like, and this group wasn't hanging around a rundown garage at this hour of the evening because they were socialites.

I quickened my steps while trying to remain composed. Tucking my chin to my chest, I scurried forward. Having grown up as the Segregate, too many incubi harassed me to make themselves feel better about how little they had accomplished in life. Those experiences, though not incredibly enjoyable and definitely hazardous to a pubescent incubus's ego, were helpful in learning how to deal with being different in a world that wasn't ready to accept diversity. I didn't enjoy making myself invisible, but when you already were, why fight it?

So, invisible I became.

Eye contact is a no-no if you suspect someone, or a group of someones, is trouble. I didn't mean to, but I jerked my head in their direction at a sudden flash of movement. One of the members, a tall, thin male, dashed around the corner of the garage. Had he not acted so radically, I would have never looked. The problem was, I did.

Now, the three made a human wall, shoulder to shoulder, turning their backs, and definitely stealing glances in my direction. Shielding something? Oh yeah, that's right. I don't care. Because something bad was going down across the street, and it wasn't any of my business.

I stretched my stride, which sounds more impressive than it is. Coming in on the wrong side of six feet tall, my 'stretched stride' was restrictive, even with the advantage of wearing shorts. I just don't have much to work with, and quickness is not a strength of mine unless I'm running. Right now, I probably looked as goofy as a racewalker, just without the incredible thigh muscles.

The majority of the group didn't seem bothered by my proximity, not even glancing away from playing on their phones, smoking cigarettes or vape pens, or even putting down the bottles of booze they openly consumed. But a man with a shaved head and muscular, brown forearms took note from his spot in the human wall. Ostensibly shielding me from something, he didn't completely turn around. His chin slid to his shoulder as he watched, casually but purposefully. The eye contact was brief, but direct, yet he made no move, aggressive or otherwise. He simply watched.

I don't think I breathed for three blocks.

The gym Cancer worked at part–time looked nothing like

a gym. Situated on the main street among more small businesses cooped up in aging buildings, I could have passed the
gym every day for the rest of my mortal life and never
thought of it as a place where people came to beat each other
to a pulp. White, corrugated sheet metal siding supported a
white roof twenty feet above. A red banner had been painted
along its entire length at the upper third of the wall, white
lettering announced the name. The Lion's Den. Maybe that
was why Cancer tagged the activities here as brutal? With
branding like that, you set certain expectations.

Across the blacktop, heat from the long summer day still
seeped skyward. Even from two dozen yards away, yells
rumbled from inside. Either serious aggression was flowing
behind those corrugated walls, or a bunch of people in town
had simultaneously hit a Mexican buffet line and were in a
twisted bowel movement challenge.

This was going to be interesting.

I pulled open the door and stepped into a wall of athletic
funk. The waiting room was sparsely decorated. A television
hung from the wall, set to a sports channel, of course. Three
black chairs of the plastic variety, two looked out over the
parking lot, the last awkwardly placed in a corner next to the
counter. The counter was covered in promotional leaflets and
business cards, which at first glance, had nothing to do with
mixed martial arts training, or even physical fitness. Garages,
boat excursion trips on the Puget Sound, hair salons and the
like, passively recruited the gym's patrons underneath a
shield of acrylic. A half empty water jug sat against the opposite wall. Something in the air—besides malodorous bodies—
raised my guard. I didn't have time to figure out what it was
because I was interrupted.

"Hi there. Can I help you?" The question came from a
middle-aged woman sitting behind the reception counter.
Either she was incredibly short from the waist-up, or her chair
was set at its lowest height, which explained why I looked

past her when I came in. She greeted me with a bright smile, showing a row of yellowed teeth which gave away a possible love affair with tea. Red blotches dotted her nose and forehead in an asynchronous pattern. Her eyes permanently squinted, as if she suspected everyone of being up to something.

Since being Abandoned, I made a habit of attempting to figure out how old humans were. It was a scale so small that estimating was difficult. Figuring the more I practiced, the better I would get, I did it all the time. But I was not expedient, and I took too long with my analysis because she crinkled her forehead.

"Are you here about the gym?" she asked. "Because if you are here to sell us something, we're not interested. Times are tough. We're not buying."

"No, sorry." I leaned closer, putting on a friendly smile. "I'm not even here for the gym."

She pulled back, the crinkle in her forehead deepening into an upside down V. "Then what are you here for?"

"A friend," I replied, leaning back to peer around the corner to the open bay where people stretched, did push-ups, jump roped and all sorts of other physical activities that thickened the gym's aroma by the second.

"Well, they would appreciate you waiting until their workout is done. Especially if they booked one of the classes." The woman spun in her chair, which squeaked as she reached for a stack of papers, patting and swatting the sides to make the stack even. "Unless you're a creep who likes to check out women, or men for that matter, while they work out. If that's the case, I promise, you came to the wrong gym."

I put my hands up like I was trying to push air away. "Whoa, whoa. No, I'm not... a creep." Bilba and Ralrek would disagree, but they weren't around to throw me to the lions. "She's not here to train; she's your nurse. Well, I guess, your physical trainer. Her name is..."

"You're talking about Tamika? Oh, I absolutely love her," the woman exclaimed.

Cancer had gone by the name Tamika Johnson when she worked as a nurse in Baghdad, and she reverted after Abandonment. Humans would have too many questions if she referred to herself by her real name. The last thing either Cancer or I needed after our experience in the desert with Chax, Seraph, and the Third Council was inquisitive minds.

"Yes, is she around?"

The woman jerked her head back toward the wall decorated with framed accolades for the gym from the local city council. "She's probably out there. But if she's with a customer, don't interrupt her. She's on the clock."

"Yes, ma'am."

The woman resumed fidgeting with the stack of papers as I rounded the corner to the bay. The open space was decorated with mirrors, the gym's logo, and more mirrors. Not a lot of thought went into martial art gym's aesthetics, apparently. The exposed support beams had been painted red. Large punching bags crowded one corner like stoic soldiers in formation. Most of the bags were busy being punched and kicked. To the left, a dark blue mat spread out like a calm sea. Two women in identical pink spandex pants stretched, talking with a trainer. A couple of men in headgear and boxing gloves sparred off on their own, supervised by a middle-aged man with an iron horseshoe of hair. This late into the evening and the gym was so active. As interesting as the pockets of activity were, though, it was the octagon ring in the center of the bay that demanded my attention.

Two men circled each other in the ring, fists raised, while a handful of members in tank tops and sports bras cheered them on. A few of the spectators slapped the sides of the cage, rattling the chain link, as the men danced in a circle, occasionally throwing cautious punches. Even the decidedly taller one fought without aggression or any actual confidence. That only seemed to frustrate the spectators. The longer the pair danced, throwing light jabs to test each other's resolve, the more verbose the small crowd became.

"Hit each other!" one man the size of a small mountain shouted, slapping his neighbor on the back. The neighbor gave him a confident smirk—let's be real, I'm trying to avoid stereotypes, but the reaction was cocky, not confident—along with a head nod, and slapped the cage fence.

On the other side, a tall woman with shoulders as round as coconuts gripped the cage, repeatedly shaking it. "Stop being pussies and fight!" Her comment drew a raucous round of laughter.

The crowd's eagerness for the fighters to destroy each other only distracted me for a moment. One attendee didn't seem bothered that the men weren't ripping each other to shreds. My roommate and friend. Cancer sat in a plastic chair in a small cove to the side of the ring. Piles of gym gear and, presumably, sweaty clothes were stacked along the wall next to her. I moved closer, noting the thickening fragrance of active humans. I tried to pinch my nose closed. I fought the funk, but the funk won.

"Nice place you've got here," I said, squatting and feeling something that made my heart skip. There was... a feeling, coming from intuition and probably a slight lack of self-confidence that raised my inbred sensitivity to my surroundings. Something wasn't right. I tried to keep my face straight as Cancer greeted me.

"Oh, it's glorious," she said with a tight chuckle. "Aren't you impressed? If not, careful how you answer. They," she said with a dip of her head in the direction of the fighters in and around the cage, "might get their feelings hurt, and they like taking out hurt feelings on pint-sized men with bad preferences in hair styles."

Ignoring her slight about my shaggy hair, I asked, "You're really not a fan, are you?"

Her head jerked as she scoffed. "Of fabricated violence? No, not really. I've seen enough of the real stuff in the last few years. Jaded? I guess. I don't see the need for it."

"I imagine it's just sport for them. Competition."

Her eyes never left the cage. Admirable, because these the two fighters were already boring me to tears with their avoidance-fighting. Maybe this was the peaceful protester way of engaging in mixed martial arts?

"There are plenty of other sports out there," Cancer finally answered. "The mortals seem to invent a new one every single day. If they need sport so bad, let them take one of those up, not this... debacle."

"And why do you work here again?"

Cancer rubbed her thumb and finger together, the universal sign for currency.

"Ah, I see," I said, watching a tall, bald human with a full, dark beard slam his fist on the wood stairs that led up to the cage. He seemed particularly agitated at the two fighters. "That guy doesn't look happy."

Cancer rolled her eyes. "I don't know why any of them do this. None of them seem happy. Ever. They say they're just intense, focused, but I don't buy it." Her voice lowered to a mumble. "Why do something if it doesn't make you happy?"

I struggled to not respond. Cancer was emphatic, but I couldn't say she was happy either. Something was missing in her lately, especially since our move to Olympia. I wanted to ask that very same thing, but then Cancer didn't really do anything besides work, so it wasn't a fair comparison. No one could be happy working as many hours as she did, regardless of the mental or financial relief it provided. The one thing that would change her outlook still required time for Bilba to work with his mentor before I could share that news.

While the bald man yelled at the fighters, Cancer sighed. "Don't listen to me, Zeke. It's just been a long day."

"Everything okay?"

She replied after a short pause, "It will be." Her response was the epitome of unconvincing.

"Well hey, look at it this way, you're getting paid for free entertainment." I checked that my humor registered. "Even if it's not very entertaining."

A wry smile spread on her face. "I guess it can be entertaining sometimes. You should have seen them when they practiced their entrances."

"Their what?"

She waved a finger at the fighters around the gym. "Not all of them want to fight, but most of them do, and they have these events every few months where they face other fighters from gyms around the region."

"And they fight each other? Like, for real? None of this" – my attention moved to the two men doing their best to put the entire gym under a sleep spell— "kind of stuff? They really fight?"

The prospects of hanging out at the gym were suddenly more interesting. I was not opposed to watching humans or demons fight, as long as it was consensual. If what I was watching was the lowest level of skill, maybe the good fights would make the quieter nights in town pass while satiating my need for violence, as long as someone else was the one getting pounded.

"Where have you been hiding, Zeke? Don't you know the inner workings of MMA?" She playfully put a hand on my shoulder. "Yes, they do. I hear it's quite the event. Merchandise, alcohol, tons of fights, and ring girls in bikinis."

"Sounds like the perfect way to spend an eternity," I quipped.

"Thought you'd like that," she winked. "I'll be working them, so you might as well come too."

"I might have to check that out," I said, trying to feign interest.

Cheers erupted around the cage. Both men were swinging

in wild desperation now. The taller fighter chanced a big uppercut and connected with the shorter man's jaw. A lucky strike, since the taller fighter's eyes were closed before even throwing the punch. But, lucky strike or not, it sent his opponent reeling backward into the fence, unconscious. The handful of spectators roared.

The fight over, the bald man with the full beard slapped the canvas, jumping up the three-stair steps and into the ring with the fluidity of a fairy. When his feet struck the canvas, they were nearly silent even though I noted the ring mat give under his weight.

"Who is that?" I asked Cancer.

She fidgeted in the chair. "Who?"

"You okay?"

"Yes, I'm fine. Just a little uncomfortable and… tired."

"You're tired a lot," I said quietly.

She faced me. The bags under her eyes proved both of us correct. "Yeah, well, I've been through a few trials, haven't I?"

"Sorry."

Cancer turned to the cage and the man I asked about again. "He's the owner of the gym. Seems okay, but he can be a bonehead like the rest of them."

"Not a fan? You're not going to last long if you don't like any of them."

"I don't dislike them," Cancer corrected. "As people, they're fine. It's all the macho-overload blood lust that I don't like. Think this is bad?" She wiggled a finger at the group of fighters who crowded around to listen to the bald man. "This is just the tip. Wait until they start talking about what they're going to do to the fighters from other gyms. Gross. Just gross."

What was gross was that my dumbass hadn't recognized why I was on edge almost from the moment I stepped into the gym. What I was feeling had nothing to do with my insecurities or some outdated need to protect Cancer from these jacked-up fighters. It had nothing to do with my own para-noia hangover from being watched by the far-too-large group hanging around the rundown garage. They made me uneasy, especially the brown-skinned man who stalked me with his intense gaze. The cloud that hung over me had followed me to the gym too. But with the fight over and the group two dozen feet away, I understood what I was sensing for what it really was.

I bent like I needed to tie my shoes and closed my eyes, concentrating. Creed warmed at my hip. Focus came within a few seconds, quicker each time I went into this focused state of mind. Sounds evaporated. I no longer felt Cancer at my side and even the lingering stink of sweat dissipated. I was in my zone now. And I extended my senses outward. Searching to validate my suspicions.

Completed, my eyes snapped open, and I shot up. I covered my abrupt actions by pretending to clear my throat. "Did you know any of these people before you applied for the job?" I asked, noting Cancer from the corner of my eyes while focusing on the group of fighters.

"No. Why?"

"You never told me how you got the job," I replied, trying to sound cool even though my heart thumped.

Cancer leaned forward, whipping her head in my direc-tion, making her brown curls bounce. It was cute. "How I got the job? There's nothing to it, Zeke. I heard that they were looking for a trainer to help the fighters recover, prevent injuries, and cover their asses for insurance purposes. I applied and got it after a short interview." Her eyes narrowed. "You're acting weird. Why do you want to know about all that?"

"No, I'm not."

"Yes, you are," she said, standing and collecting her bags.

I watched her. "What? You're done already?"

"That was the last sparring session. He'll close the gym

after their chat," she said, slinging a pair of bags over her shoulder with a grimace she tried to cover but couldn't sneak past me. "And I'm not interested in hanging out here all night. I've got an early shift at Capital." She gave me a quizzical look. "Why? Do you want to hang out here?"

I joined her. "Well, I did just get here. Can you give me a ride back?" I did not want to tell her that I would walk the entire state of Washington in a loop before taking the same route home that brought me past the group of troublesome adults.

"No, I'm going to make you walk back," she said as if I'd asked the dumbest question in the world.

Raucous laughter came from the group surrounding the bald and bearded gym owner.

Cancer rolled her eyes. "His charm offensive again. He turns on the personality, and the fighters flock to him."

"Why?"

"He feeds their egos, talking up the circuit. He makes them better fighters. Their reputations grow with each win. Some are champions."

"What's that earn them?"

"The prime spots on the fight cards, and a chance with bigger promotions. Those turn into more chances to catch a real promoter's eyes. It's about getting chances, sponsors, and on televised cards."

I nodded. "Bigger and bigger paydays."

"Money and glory," Cancer said, partially turning. "I sound terrible. He's not a bad guy, but I'm just not into the self-stroking types, even ones with great bodies."

I chuckled. "Those usually go hand in hand, don't they?"

"Alright, get out of my face," the bearded bald man replied with a hearty laugh, slapping a much shorter and scrawnier man on the back. The short man's tank top was two sizes too big, drooping well below his armpits. When the bearded man's palm met the naked skin of the other's shoulder, the gym resonated with the sharp smack. The shorter man stumbled forward but wore a grin that reminded me of incubi from my school days getting turned down by a succubus. Such was the status of this bearded man that the shorter one didn't say anything after regaining his dignity. The group took their dismissal from this leader as if he had just blessed them.

I extended my senses again while Cancer watched the group.

The lump in my throat must have drawn Cancer's attention. "What is it, Zeke?"

I tried to swallow the sudden apprehension. The stupid lump wouldn't budge, and I felt like my heart was going to punch its way out of my chest as I looked at the gym owner. My mouth fell open, about to share the sliver of insight my sensitive senses picked up on. The man dominating the gym was not mortal. Before I could convey my suspicions to an innocent-yet-clueless Cancer, the opportunity slipped away.

"Cancer!" The owner clapped his hands together with a smack that rivaled what he had just done to the shorter fighter. Instead of releasing them, he kept them clamped, which only made the chiseled forearms and thick biceps pronounce to the world the muscle contained within his skin. Show off. "Don't tell me you're out of here. The night is young."

As he neared, his pale shaved head pronounced a multitude of scars. His beard was too fluffy for someone who presumably enjoyed rolling around on a mat with other fighters. His eyebrows, nearly horizontal until they reached the corner of his eyes, dropped down precipitously. The last feature that jarred me—his intense, sparkling green eyes, light against his dark beard. In a fair world, they would be a dull brown, unstimulating. As I discovered in my earlier interactions with Ralrek, some immortals and mortals were lucky enough to have everything handed to them in the looks department. The gym owner belonged to that exclusive group. Ah, life and the chance of fate.

He moved in on her with a quickness that was startling for someone his size. Not that he was that much taller than me, maybe five-feet-eleven, but his physique filled the space around him. Subconscious or not, I took a step back to give him room. It wasn't envy that moved me when he hugged Cancer. It was something far more disturbing.

"Sorry, but I've got an early shift," she said as she pulled away, adjusting the bag his unsolicited hug knocked from her shoulder to the crook of her elbow.

"How long have you worked here and we still haven't got you hitting bags?" he said with a tone that tried to be charming but came off sounding like a salesperson pushing an up-sell.

"Long enough that you should know I don't want to hit bags," Cancer's response was gentle but firm, the type anyone who knew her would immediately recognize as dangerous. Back in Baghdad, she had scared half an Army squad out of a room in her unofficial hospital with just a few short words. One fighter, no matter how big, didn't stand a chance with her. Part of me wanted to warn him away, to encourage him to see the signs he wasn't picking up on. That part of me was shut down by my desire to pull Cancer away from this place until we had a chance to compare notes.

"Don't knock it until you try it," the gym owner said, holding her arms by the wrists. "You might surprise yourself."

Cancer subtly but insistently pulled her hands away, hooking her thumbs into the straps of her bags. "No thanks, Leo. I can't afford it and you don't want to have to hire a new trainer if I get injured, do you?"

E"No way," he said. "You're too valuable. But one day..."

"Sure," Cancer said.

Leo turned in my direction, extending his hand for a firm

shake that almost crushed half my bones. I nearly shook in the confirmation the moment our skin met. Leo was definitely one of us. "You her boyfriend?"

I smiled uneasily. At this proximity, I didn't need any more convincing that I was shaking hands with someone who emitted the power of fading immortality. I just needed Cancer to tell me I wasn't absolutely bat-shit crazy.

"I tried, but she rejected me," I said, faking a smile. "So now I'm just her roommate."

Cancer moved closer to my side, rubbing her neck. "I guess it would help if I make the introductions. Zeke, this is Leo Neto, the owner of The Lion's Den and, what, four-time Pacific Northwest MMA Heavyweight Champion?"

"Seven, but three of them aren't recognized because the old federation disbanded a while ago," he said with a cocky smirk, still gripping my hand and not breaking eye contact. "And who's this?"

"Leo, this is Ezekial Sunstone," Cancer started as Leo's hand released mine. "He lets his friends call him Zeke. He's—"

She never got to finish her sentence. Well, if she did, I never heard it. At the mention of my name, something dangerous flashed in Leo's eyes. Glancing at Cancer, I had just enough time to see his thick fist, led by scarred knuckles, flying toward my face.

7

OLYMPIA

"WHAT WAS THAT ALL ABOUT?" a feminine voice said some-where in the heavy shroud clogging my brain.

I groaned and rolled to my side, my eyes still pinched closed. I, too, would have liked to know the answer.

"Leave me alone," a male's voice rose to meet the question.

Other voices whispered, snickered, or chatted rapidly in disbelief. I cracked an eye open, the one that didn't feel like a pound of meat was pressed against it and waited for the blurry dimensions to clear. Forms soon became defined bodies of curious gym members. The middle-aged woman with yellow teeth from the front desk stood behind Cancer, who kneeled at my side, between Leo and me. The blue mat smelled more disgusting down here.

"Wha—what happened?" I asked as the world cleared in my good eye. The meat eye still refused to open.

"Man, Leo kicked your ass. One punch," someone laughed. My good eye found the source of the scorn, noting it was the short tank-topped man. We locked eyes, and he swallowed, turning and nudging the guy next to him with an elbow. "Totally kicked his ass."

The other man nodded.

The vision of Leo's scarred knuckles closing in on my face flashed back as I rolled flat on the mat, trying to ignore the old germs and funk I was letting seep into my shirt.

"Zeke, don't move too quickly," Cancer cautioned.

"Trust me, I don't want to," I replied, pressing a hand to my swirling forehead. "But I'd also like to get off this mat."

"Let's do this slowly then," she said, turning to the lingering crowd. As soon as they registered Cancer's oncoming request, a healthy portion of the group lost interest and moved on to other important things, which apparently did not include helping an assault victim. "Stephanie, Erica, James, help me."

Two women and a thin man shuffled forward.

"Let him get up on his own," Leo commanded from somewhere outside the periphery of my good eye. "He's not worth your time."

"Come on, Leo," the receptionist said. "Let's get you back to the office. We need to talk." By her tone, there was no choice. Stomping footsteps told me I was free from another assault for now.

Cancer's cadre helped me stand, holding me steady until everyone was sure I wasn't going to face-plant.

"Thank you," Cancer told them.

"We can walk you out to the car," Erica offered. As my vision cleared, I saw she wasn't someone I would suspect of belonging to a gym like this. Her features were flawlessly feminine. A small nose sat between two deep-set brown eyes. Her dark hair was pulled back into a ponytail that fell below her shoulders out of sight.

"Thank you. I'd appreciate that," Cancer replied as my brain was still processing the scene at a sloth's speed.

"Come on, man," James said. "Lean on me."

"Thanks, but I'm good," I said with a shake of the head that made me wobble.

"Sure you are," Stephanie, a redhead a couple inches taller than me and a literal breath of sweet, fresh air, said, jabbing her arm under my free one. "Come on, James. Let's not give him a choice."

We made it past the reception area, where the receptionist leaned an arm on the door frame of the back office, presumably facing Leo. She wasn't happy, not if her motherly tone was any hint. Into the parking lot, Cancer walked ahead to unlock her car and clear the front seat.

"Careful. Make sure he doesn't do anything stupid," she ordered the trio, making Erica walk behind me in case I decided a backward somersault was a better use of my passing out talents.

Like a sack of groceries, I was loaded into the car. Stephanie handed me an ice-pack. "Here. Keep that on your baseball of an eye." She patted me on the shoulder before slamming the door.

"Ready for me to get you home and baby you?" Cancer said as she slid into the driver's seat, starting the car and swiftly backing out of the parking spot.

On the surface streets, I broke the tense silence. "I swear, I don't know what I did, Cancer."

"I know."

I would have searched her expression for an answer, but I couldn't see from that side of my face, and turning my head made the world dip. I spoke to the dashboard instead. "What is his deal? Are you two a thing and I'm oblivious? Is he the jealous type? Looks it. Not surprised for a gym rat."

She grunted. "I have no idea what that was about. I told you, he's a cocky, arrogant ass. Most of them are. Leo's pride just blinds him more than the others, but they feed off pride and ego. I don't know if all fighting gyms are like that, but it's pervasive in this one. Those three who helped you out? They're the best in the blessed place. A few others are okay too. But that's it. The rest of them? I wasn't joking about not enjoying my time around them. I'm sorry this happened. Trust me, I didn't expect that or I would have never put you in that position. And, honestly, there have been more than a few asshole customers and Leo has never acted like that. Verbally? Yes, he can be aggressive. But getting physical and taking the chance of losing his business because he got sued for assaulting someone? Never."

"Not like you've worked there long. How much can you really know a person in a short time?" It was a loaded question, one meant to lead me to my next point about Leo's nature.

Cancer was quiet for another block, plus the time we sat idling at a red light at an empty intersection.

"You're right," she said after a long pause. "I shouldn't be surprised by anything or anyone anymore."

"That's not what I meant," I said. "You don't need to sound like a version of me; I've got enough skepticism for the both of us. I meant you can't possibly know him, or anyone in the city, that well. We haven't been here long enough."

"It's not just that, Zeke," Cancer said, pulling through the intersection now that the red light overlord gave its blessing. "We've been in the Overworld for months, and two-thirds of that has been in Olympia. We didn't know anyone in Seattle because we weren't there long enough. Heavens, we hadn't even bought all the furniture for the apartment before we were moving here."

"It was expensive," I interjected. "We were going to be on the streets if we'd stayed."

"But," she said, stretching out the word, "we also haven't been here for very long. Certainly not long enough to get to know people. Not to the level where we can say what type of people they are. Not with any confidence. Don't get me wrong. I'm not saying anyone has me fooled or that I'm quick to judge them, but I have to stop being so naïve."

"I didn't say that," I protested again, wanting to deliver the news of my suspicions, but she kept talking.

"No, you didn't," she said. "You're just trying to help, and I get that. But I'm still going to feel bad about this. I mean, your eye... it's going to lead to interesting conversations at the bookstore for your next few shifts. I hope it doesn't get you in trouble."

"It won't," I answered carefully, not wanting to delve into my ridiculously superior recuperative abilities. She would discover how well I healed soon, and I didn't want this conversation to steer away from what we needed to talk about before reaching the apartment. The Council's invasive ears waited, kept to the brimstone. Harry Nugel, a middle-aged man with less humor than hair, and my boss at The Book Worm, would never see this black eye since I didn't have another shift for two days. My eye wasn't worthy of another second. Pulling the ice-pack away and playing with the corner of it, I took a slow breath and said, "I'll be fine. Listen, about Leo."

Cancer cut me off. "You really should keep that on your eye, Zeke. It will help with the healing. And please, don't get started about Leo. We spend enough time bitching about others."

"Like who?"

A finger extended from her driving wheel hand. "Everyone on the Council." Another finger. "Your father." A third. "Chax." She had to replace her hand with the free one so she could lift her fourth. "Lucifer."

"Hey, we can take free shots at Him now, so why not? All mortals do." I quipped.

"My point," she said, "is that we don't need anymore people or demons to complain about. We've had our fill, and it's exhausting. Constant news of the war is draining. With the effects of Abandonment, I just... I don't have the energy for it now. That's all. Don't you feel the same?"

I shrugged and played with the ice-pack, trying to form an answer. Even though we had been Abandoned on the same day, my situation was still different. I was still parsing out what Seraph had conveyed. When the time came, I would share it with Cancer, but Leo was the immediate issue. Plus, I wasn't ready to drop a bucket of bad news on Cancer, even if lying wasn't on the agenda either.

"I don't know. Everything is pretty much the same as it was before. At least for me. My situation is different," I said, noting how absolutely silent she was. "I'm the Segregate."

"So?"

"So," I said, measuring my words, "I don't know how this is going to play out. Every demon before me had Abilities. Even though no one wants to acknowledge that others have been Abandoned, knowing the Council like I do, I'm sure they track those they've left behind. Track us and study the impact of long-term living in the Overworld. It's the most severe punishment because of everything it means and does to us. But I'm still different. Without Creed, I don't have Abilities. Everything I have comes through it. Maybe I'll live a hundred years. Maybe I'll die in ten minutes." I had to stop myself. The conversation was moving too close to the thoughts pinging around in my head related to the conversation with the succubus Founder. "I'm trying, Cancer. I really am. But I don't understand how Abandonment makes you feel, because for me, this is normal. Well, except that we're not in Hell, I don't have my friends around—"

"Gee, thanks."

I snorted. "I meant my boys, you know? There's no Dialphio, and Harry sure as heaven doesn't match up to her. It's colder here. Less crowded and noisy. There's no Council interfering in our lives." Boy, wasn't that a sudden lie. "Not much is different—for me, I mean. I know it's not the same for you."

"No, it's not," she said, pulling down our street. We were

almost at the apartment. Now that the Council had our exact location pegged, I couldn't be sure what threats lay in wait. They would be listening inside the apartment, I didn't doubt that. Our home was probably so loaded with listening spells they'd hear every flatulent squeak I made—which reminded me to order extra spicy chicken wings from now on.

I needed to drop the bomb, as mortals were fond of saying.

But Cancer was speaking again. "I'm exhausted. All the time, and not just from the long shifts and extra jobs. The Abandonment is wearing me down. There's grief from losing my identity, as a nurse and as a demon. I'm not helping anyone like I did in Iraq. I couldn't even save that old homeless man."

I shifted, trying to get a look at her. "Listen, Cancer. That stuff is important, and I want to talk about it. But—" I stopped myself, making sure I slowed my thoughts enough to not tell her more than I understood. Yes, I'm a disgusting male who doesn't want to upset a female—and yes, I know Cancer can handle it, but I'm chivalrous like that. If Bilba was sitting in the driver's seat, I would have acted the same. So maybe it has more to do with my caring personality and less to do with perceived sexism. I'm not that shallow. "Before we head to the apartment, I need to tell you something."

She parked and shut off the car, each step measured like she was waiting for the metaphorical explosion. "What is it?"

"Leo—"

She sighed, an exasperated release. "If you're going to rant, save it. Please. It's late. I've got to get up early, and honestly, I'm not in the mood. He's an asshole. I know. I've got it."

"No, he's not," I said, finding her eyes with my good eye. "He's a demon."

We sat, staring at each other until it felt like we were 'that' couple. You know the kind. They were the pair who liked to fight in public for the entertainment of their neighbors, feeling every unseen eye staring into the parking spot to see what juicy events were unfolding.

"He… he's one of us?" she asked, her voice betraying her shock. She pulled her head back, scrunching the fold of extra skin under her chin, making it ripple against her neck. "How… you can't possibly know that. Tonight was the first time you met him, or…" Her eyes narrowed to slits. "Have you run across him before? Is that why he punched you?"

I shook my head that was just now beginning to clear. "No, this was my first experience with him. Hopefully, the last too."

"Then how do you know he's one of us?"

I spent the next five minutes explaining my senses, how I had always had them, and how they became enhanced from the moment Aries handed Creed to me. She wanted specifics of the how and why, and I let her down. My senses were like any other natural ability. Some demons can run fast, jump high, dance like a feather. Others are twisted enough to understand complex mathematics. Too many can cook without having to be the creator—One; wow, I really needed to wrap my head around that before I talked to Dialphio again. All people and demons, and probably angels, had natural skills which improved with practice. My ability to sense who was immortal was no different.

"So you're sure he's a demon?" she asked, still unconvinced.

I nodded. "As sure as I can be. What I can do, it's not a perfect science. Take you, for example. In Baghdad, I was in that small room with you how many times before you used your Water Ability?"

"Too many," she replied, nearly on top of my question, but with enough kindness to smirk at her light jab.

I returned it. "Two or three times and I had weird feelings. Like someone is watching from within your eyesight, but you have no idea where they are. That was what it was like for me. But I was a soldier, in the middle of a war, trying to hide my immortality from thousands of mortals every second of the day. Exhausting. You keep using that word to describe how you feel now, and that's what it was like for me then. I was exhausted and losing touch with my senses because everything else overwhelmed me. It's easier now, here."

"I've been meaning to talk to you about how much free time you have," Cancer said.

The return of her personality was encouraging. "Funny. Ha, ha. My point being, now that we're here and surrounded by mortals, it's easier for me to pick out immortals. From the second I walked into the gym, I knew something was wrong. I could feel Leo. Not that I knew he was immortal, he's not. Not anymore anyway. That's what I picked up on."

Cancer shook her head, her puffs of hair wagging. "Wait. I'm confused. You said sensing immortals is something you can do, and you felt it in the gym. Now you're saying Leo isn't immortal. Which is it? Or, wait." She slapped my arm excitedly. "Are you saying someone else in the gym is immortal?"

"No," I said with a short chuckle, "what I'm saying is Leo *was* immortal. He emits the same energy as any demon, but it's faded. Fading. Like… yours. That means he's not here on Council business. He's not in the Overworld on some approved mission or trip. He's Abandoned, Cancer. Just like us."

She plopped back into the car seat, which squeaked. "Another Abandoned demon? That's crazy."

"I don't think he's the only one," I said, and told her about the group of adults at the garage. "There were too many of them clumped too closely together, but I swear, at least one of them gave off the same emissions. Stronger. But it was the same sensation. They might be connected to Leo somehow; I can't be sure. But there might be something to it."

"This is awesome, Zeke," she suddenly exclaimed, shooting forward and wrapping her arm around the steering wheel, draping it on the dashboard. "If others are in Olympia, we won't be alone. It won't be just you and me."

"Gee, thanks," I said, getting revenge for her earlier poke.

"Aw, and you wanted me all to yourself," she said, reaching over and pinching my good cheek. "Sorry, but I'm not a one-incubus... one man... wom... man. Lucifer, that sounds weird."

"I know what you mean."

"But seriously," she said, "this could be awesome. Not being the only demons in town. And if you're right, if we somehow figure out a way to ask him and get an honest answer, do you realize what this means?"

"I'm sure you're going to tell me," I said, unsure if I wanted to be within city limits of Leo again.

"If Olympia has enough immortals for you to sense two in a single evening, imagine how many of us might live here," she said, excitement filling her sentence the longer it ran. She spoke more rapidly now. "And if there are that many demons in town, how many live in Seattle? In Vancouver. Portland. There could be thousands just in the Pacific Northwest. Thousands."

Cancer was getting carried away. In all our months in the Overworld, I hadn't sensed what I did tonight on more than a handful of occasions. Tonight was a fluke. A coincidence. I hoped. Either way, I doubted there were that many. The evidence just didn't bear it out. But if Cancer was correct, the implications were infinite. How many would live on the entire coast? What about the country? The Overworld? This could be a wonderful twist in our story.

Or a setup.

"Glad to see I could brighten your night a little," I smirked. "Who knew the only thing I had to do was get my ass kicked to make you happy."

"Yes, you should stop by the gym more often." Her laugh was light, almost carefree. Proverbial music to my ears.

"Well, if you're in search of good news, I might have more for you," I admitted before she could pull the door open and carry me up the steps to our apartment.

"More good news?" Her eyes grew wide with renewed energy my news had unleashed. "Can I handle more?"

"I'm serious, Cancer," I said, grabbing her dangling hand. "I don't want to give you false hope, but I found something out that might change everything."

She tried to pull back with a slight tug. When she saw I wouldn't release my grip, and instead gave her a reassuring squeeze, she gripped my hand.

And then I told her about Bilba and Melchiot, and the possibility of his mentor's Hex Abilities finding a cure for the curse.

She swallowed me in her arms. "Oh, Lucifer, Zeke. Are you serious?"

"Yes, but please, don't get hopeful just yet," I said through the tangle of loose brown curls that threatened to choke me. "We don't know anything about Melchiot yet, but you know Bilba. If anyone could get someone to do something, it's him. I didn't want to tell you at first, but I respect you too much to keep you in the dark." No, I suppressed the stupid voice in my head screaming to remind me I hadn't shared news of Seraph's visit with Cancer yet. We would get to that. "Still, please, he needs time."

"Of course, of course," she said, swallowing hard. "Oh, Zeke, you've made my night. Five minutes ago, I didn't know how much longer I could put up with life in the Overworld. Now you've given me something to look forward to. Thank you." She squeezed again.

I wasn't sure if I wanted to tell her she was welcome or not. Best to see if this was going to blow up in our faces first.

8

OLYMPIA

SUMMER IN OLYMPIA was a warm time of year, by human standards, according to the mortals I listened to. Rarely, though, are the long days muggy. Today was an exception. Hot. Muggy. Uncomfortable for them, nearly perfect for me. Capitol Lake Park was empty at this time of evening. I was alone and loving it because I needed it.

I adjusted my ass on the park bench. Metal rungs painted forest green to match all the other green of the Pacific Northwest, wrapped under my legs into a natural, comfortable curve. Still, ass-on-metal is not a long-term formula for comfort. I imagined the designers of the park deliberately chose this material for the benches to keep people moving along. No camping out this close to the governing body of the state. With Olympia's homelessness problem, I was even more convinced it was the truth. Mortals can be cruel like that, I had learned—but so could immortals. Still, the realization did nothing for my ass.

Right now, a little comfort went a long way. After Leo's sucker punch and my subsequent admission to Cancer of his immortal history, she and I tried to return to normal, other than doing investigatory work where we could to see who else might be one of us. That was more difficult than it sounds. Finding demons, no matter how strong my senses were becoming, meant being out amongst the people of Olympia, requiring hours upon hours of walking around parks and open spaces, and a lot of pretend-shopping. Too much.

Perusing stores was the easiest way to put myself physically close to others, to extend my senses in a broad wave and test their immortality scale, if you will—Cancer came up with that name. It's growing on me. A few times per week, we would go to one of the clubs in town, but clubs had never been my thing. I couldn't dance even half as well as Ralrek. Clubs were a necessity because of the ages of the garage group I sensed emissions from. They weren't in the stay-at-home demographic. Cancer, refreshingly, was like me. She wasn't much of a dancer—she claimed she was, though I've seen her. No matter how much time we spent out in the short weeks following Leo's sucker punch, I hadn't come across anyone giving off immortal emissions. That night around the gym was definitely a fluke.

The more we looked, the less we found. Cancer's initial excitement about other demons living in Olympia waned. As it did, she suffered. Each day, she looked more distressed, growing quieter and withdrawn. I worried about her. That's why I headed to the park tonight, to find peace and figure out a way to change our fortunes, or at least hers.

Part of my actions were self-interested. I needed to find other Abandoned demons as well, because I needed to hear their stories and compare them to mine. The more I learned, the more I could pass along to Bilba and Dialphio. Any bit of information would help.

A soft breeze blew through the park, holding a slight hint of chill. I was looking forward to autumn. The way the trees were changing color—I try to avoid using the term 'decay' because of its connotations—added a diversity to everyday life. The air smelled fresh now, as if the Overworld were cleansing itself of summer's sweat.

All in all, it wasn't a total waste to sit in solitude in the park. Which was a good thing, because the way tonight was progressing, I wasn't going to trip across any wayward ex–demons. Forty minutes passed without another soul traipsing into or running by the park, except for a middle-aged woman, who slightly reminded me of Hell's nastiest succubus, doing yoga on a blanket in the corner of the grass where the silver feather grass met the stagnant waters of Capitol Lake. When I arrived and sat on the bench, she decided she was done with her routine, snatched up her blanket and belongings and departed.

I was officially alone in the park, and ready to think, while trying to avoid thoughts about the oncoming doom of Abandonment, wondering how long my decay would take. Which made me angry.

Yoga lady reminding me of Seraph also reminded me of the fact the succubus hadn't come by for another unsolicited visit. Good. My reaction to her first visit still surprised me. I'm not a violent demon but I understand it can be necessary. Every time I thought about the Founder, that value slipped. Maybe it was the fact that I had been blind to her unscrupulous nature for so long, or that she had played me for the fool too many times, but Seraph was now more than the face of the Council to me.

How easily she turned against me regarding the Vicu family laying a curse on the Nijals was an act of betrayal. She was the only one on the Council I truly trusted then. Azazel was too quiet and often came across as the doddering old incubus everyone tolerated and entertained, patting on the head before pushing him along in whatever direction they needed him to go. Michael lost my trust in him during the Gemini trial by showing his penchant for angel blood over reasonable action. Some things that tall, well-groomed incubus said in the public square in the First Circle were as unforgivable as they were unforgettable. Beelzebub and Apopis where dregs of demonhood and not worth any further reflection. Seraph had seemed like an anchor, the moral focus of the Council. But when her true colors seeped through, they were as pure as an angel's embrace.

And thinking of her made me angry. Yes, yes, I know. A lot makes me angry.

No news from Bilba had come in, about Melchiot or how supposed curses could be removed. Supposedly, his training was progressing nicely, but he was only weeks into his studies, hardly time enough to dive deep into how trustworthy his mentor was.

In respect to Cancer's curse, nothing had changed.

And that made me angry too.

The unfairness of this entire situation, everything I had to do, things other demons didn't have to worry about. I was sitting here in the Overworld virtually alone, nearly friendless, and without attractive prospects for the future, while the Council went about their lives, manipulating situations and demons to reach their next objectives. My mother and father, the couple I hadn't heard from since the day of Seraph's visit, were presumably just as happy as ever, or even more so now that they had coin to repair the Angel Oak tree home. I checked in with Dialphio, and even she sounded fine. Ralrek was no different, disturbingly so. When I was kicked out of Hell, he had promised to not give up the fight, and I believed him. But sometimes, usually during my darker days, like this one, it felt like he only threw punches whenever he could be bothered to remember to make a fist.

All of that made me angry.

Yes, spending a glorious early fall evening enjoying the sounds, smells, and sights in the city park was a good way to spend my time.

That was, until out of the corner of my eye, I saw a jogger.

It wasn't the fact that I was now sharing the park with someone else that disturbed me. What bothered me was who the jogger was.

Wearing a pair of knee-length black shorts from which a gray shirt dangled from the waistband, the shirtless man rounded the corner of the small public restroom building. His pectorals bounced with each long step. Rivulets of sweat ran down his bald head into his thick beard.

I looked away, hoping Leo hadn't spotted me, which was going to be very hard considering there were only three park benches lining the sidewalk. Hard to hide, sitting on the middle one. I angled my head forward, idly playing with my hands while waiting for him to pass. Running shoes slapped the concrete.

"Keep going, you bastard," I whispered to the ground.

Twenty feet away, he hitched his stride.

I wore a T-shirt, shorts, and a pair of sandals—thanks, climate change. I had brought sunglasses out with me, but they rested in my shaggy hair because the sun was setting and there is nothing cool about wearing sunglasses at night. Had I attempted to pull them over my eyes to disguise my identity, Leo would have surely noticed. Playing it cool should have made me inconspicuous. The hitch in his stride indicated I hadn't slipped by my new adversary.

"What are you doing here?" he said from a few feet away, pulling to a stop and sacrificing his evening run.

"It's a public park, isn't it? That usually means the public is allowed to use it," I said with enough attitude to make my stance clear.

Leo halved the distance, creeping forward. After his sucker punch at the Lion's Den, I wasn't going to willingly hand over an advantage. Rising to my feet, I put the park bench between us.

He pulled the T-shirt from his shorts and wiped his head. A huge blotch of the gray material darkened with his sweat.

"Man," he said with an exasperated laugh at his now sweaty T-shirt, "the last thing I needed tonight was to see you."

I gave him what I hoped looked like a cool shrug, even though cool was the last thing I felt. "If it's any consolation, I'm not exactly excited to see you either."

Leo snarled, still moving toward the bench. "You've got a mouth."

"Last time I checked, I did. Hope I don't lose it anytime soon. Life would be pretty inconvenient without it."

He snickered, but there was no humor in it. "You think you're funny, too. Think your jokes can get you out of trouble, help you get away with things. Someone needs to shut it."

Throughout his belligerent comments, Leo subtly circumnavigated the bench.

"Don't come any closer," I warned, holding up a finger like it was a shield. Creed was strapped underneath the seat of my bicycle, racked fifty feet away near the restrooms. Leo stood between it and me. When I first obtained Creed from Aries, I had received early lessons from the halberd. Creed has separation anxiety. At first, it couldn't be more than an arm's length away before it forced reunification. Over time, I trained with the weapon to improve our connection, and with it strengthened, I could move further and further away. With patience, and a bucket load of bruises from having Creed smash into me—usually when I wasn't looking—to reestablish a connection, I could move hundreds of yards away and still call to it. Doing so now would be easy, if required. The straps that held it to the bicycle seat were Velcro, and they would break easily if I called. With no one else in the park, that was definitely an option if Leo didn't back down.

He looked at my finger. "I'm going to break that finger and shove it down your throat."

I dropped my hand. He wasn't willing to listen. "Don't do this, Leo. I don't want to fight you."

"It's not going to be a fight."

He lunged. His quickness shocked me, even though I already knew a little about his speed. I stumbled backward to avoid him. My move was thoughtless, keeping me in his path. That was not my intention, but it was a result of not considering how to evade him.

I was on my own. And this muscular mixed martial arts fighter was feet away from compacting me into a doughnut-sized box.

Leo was on me, driving me backward. My feet tried to maintain purchase on the ground, but the speed of his charge and the power behind it soon drove me off of them. We collapsed to the grass, him on top of me. His arms wrapped around my back, and with the combined impact of his weight and the upward rushing dirt, the fists locked behind me drove into my lower back. Pain shot across my hips and up to my shoulders. His grip was unrelenting.

I tried to wiggle free, but the more I moved, the tighter he squeezed. When I tried to slip an arm between our torsos, he flexed, squeezing out any room.

Leo was incredibly strong, and I could feel his legs pushing into the ground, driving his shoulder into my gut. He rammed into me, over and over, driving the air from my lungs. I tried to push at his shoulders after the attempt to pry myself free failed. Leo's shoulders were thick and rounded with muscles in places I didn't even have. And he didn't budge.

Before long, stars shot across my vision. Within seconds, those stars became bursts of galaxies. The lack of oxygen was terrifying. I opened my mouth as if I was about to shove the Overworld's largest chicken wing into it and drew as much air as I could. The problem was, my lungs failed to expand under the pressure of Leo's assault. I'm sure if I was thinking clearly, I would have simply called to Creed and whacked this goon over the head. The problem was, when you can't breathe, you typically didn't have the oxygen to think. Definitely not clearly. You react.

Leo wasn't going to release his grip and stop his shoulder assault until I was out cold. He would probably leave me in this public park like that as well. Frustrated at being the focus of someone else's anger, frustrated from all the things I spent the evening stewing about, I drove my elbow down on the top of his head. Sharp pain shot up my arm to my fingertips, but there was a satisfying thud when my elbow connected. Leo pulled his head toward his chest to protect his face. I drove my elbow down again and then a third time. His grip weakened. For the fourth time, I elbowed him. Leo broke his hold, sliding up my body to mount me. I kicked my legs out, but Leo's balance was superb. Before I knew it, he straddled my waist and was trying to pin my arms.

"Get off me, asshole!" I shouted in rising panic.

I didn't know anything about mixed martial arts, but I knew enough about fighting to know that being mounted was one of the worst positions to find yourself.

I kicked, I swung my arms, and I scurried inches backward at every subtle shift of weight. Keep moving. That was my strategy. Simple, but effective if I could sustain it until I could figure something else out. A moving target was difficult to pin.

Giving up on holding me down, Leo seemed content straddling me. He balled his fist and raised it above his head, ready to throw it down. I waited until his fist started its descent, and then kicked with my knee, blindly aiming for the crack of his ass. I would be happy with any strike that landed on any part of him, no matter how sacred. Leo left enough space for my strike to gain momentum and drive him forward just as his balance shifted to punch. The combined momentum sent him flying. I was on my feet even as he rolled over. It was my turn to mount.

I sprinted forward and jumped like a spider monkey

through the air, landing on Leo. The problem with that tactic was, first, there was too much space between us. Second, Leo saw the attack coming. Thirdly, and maybe most importantly, Leo was a trained fighter. Me, not so much. I was just some punk fighting for survival. I was halfway down my descent to his prone form when I realized I was in trouble. Leo's arms outstretched and caught me as I fell. Using my momentum against me, he rolled on top. Mounted again. This time, the larger fighter pinned only one of my arms. The only saving grace was that my free arm was my stronger one.

"I'm going to break your face," Leo growled, bawling up his fist and sending it towards my skull. It connected with my cheek, which burst in pain. More stars filled my vision, but I was pretty sure he was making another attempt to strike again somewhere behind the growing field of white.

So I did the unthinkable. I sent my own fist, much smaller and less scarred, into his groin. Leo sucked in his breath, his eyes snapping shut and his fist unclenching as soon as mine made contact with his most tender parts. A fraction of a second later, his hands were cupping his family jewels as he fell over.

I got to my feet, panting and trying to blink to clear my vision.

"You sonofabitch," he groaned.

"I told you to leave me alone," I said, bending at the waist with my hands on my knees but watching him carefully. I wasn't going to allow him to get up. Leo was an Abandoned demon, so I had no reservations about introducing him to Creed. His Abilities would have been stripped when the Council sent him here. The advantage was mine now that my brain was working. The shift in status might be enough to get him to leave me alone permanently.

"How did you find me?" I asked, more than curious, and a whole lot more skeptical about this incident being more than coincidence.

Leo rolled to his side, facing me through one eye. "What does it matter?"

"It matters," I replied, taking a few steps away from him, a few steps closer to Creed. "Don't tell me you just happened to trip across me on this side of the city. That's too convenient."

He still cupped his genitals, gasping for air. "Sonofabitch, this hurts."

I shrugged. "Serves you right. I'll ask you one more time; how did you find me? Are you following me?"

"I was out for a run, dumbass," Leo responded through clenched teeth.

"Not buying that," I said.

"Then don't. I don't care." Leo rolled onto his back, pulling his knees up so they formed a tight angle, and raised his arms above his head. He drew deep breaths.

Now that he wasn't looking to me, I called Creed, instantly feeling the connection with the collapsed halberd. A rattling sensation in my fingertips validated the connection. Creed was trying to break free of the Velcro and I was feeling the temporary struggle—hey, I use good Velcro. Within seconds, the foot–long stick was free and flying across the park. The petrified dark cherry slapped against my open palm and the connection was complete. Creed and I were one again.

Leo had seen none of it.

I approached until I was standing above him, slapping Creed against my palm. I suppressed a wince as the wood smacked against my skin. The force wasn't my idea; I think Creed felt left out of the park fun and was paying me back for leaving it strapped to the bike.

Leo eyed the truncheon. "What are you doing?"

"I'm going to use this," I said, slamming the truncheon into my palm again, clamping my jaw against the pain in my warming skin, "on you until you give up how you found me. I'm not playing around, Leo. I'm done with your bullying.

I'm done with bullies in general. You've just been nominated to be the last one."

"You wouldn't dare," he snarled.

So I did the smart thing. I brought Creed down across the fighter's thigh. I did not use all my force, and Creed seemed to hold back more for the fallen fighter than it did for me, but Leo still screamed. That was going to leave a bruise.

"What is wrong with you?" Leo howled, holding his thigh.

I responded by slapping his other thigh, not as forcefully as I had the first one, but enough to make sure he would have matching bruises in the morning. "I told you, I'm going to get an answer out of you or your fighting career might come to a quick end."

He squeezed his eyes shut so hard the skin around them wrinkled. He held his muscular thighs, leaving his chest exposed. I could send a real message if he wasn't smart enough to capitulate.

"You're running out of time, Leo. Three seconds from now, I'm going to introduce the rest of you to my friend. Better talk." I raised Creed.

Leo raised his hands immediately. "Please. Stop. I was... I was told you were down here."

"By who?"

Leo's eyes dashed to the side. I glanced to the edge of the park to see what he was looking for, to see who he was looking for. The sidewalk was empty.

I raised Creed higher. "I'm not joking."

"A guy. A... someone from the gym, I swear," he repeated, rushed. "He told me you would be down here, and... and he told me to pay you a visit if I wanted revenge."

My arm halted. "Revenge for what? I don't even know you."

Hands still raised, Leo watched me like a rabbit eyes a fox. "Can I get up? Can we have this conversation like men?"

I stepped back. "Get up. Don't do anything stupid."

Leo rolled onto his stomach into a pose that looked like he was going to knock out a hundred and fifty push-ups. Instead, he pushed himself to his feet with a powerful thrust and raised his hands. "No trouble, I promise."

"Make sure you uphold your end of the deal," I said, taking another step back. "More important than knowing about your gym friend, I want to know why you think you need to target me for revenge. I only met you at your gym. Where, I might add, you sucker punched me for no reason."

Leo shook his head. "I've got my reasons."

"Then, you better start sharing them."

Then he surprised me. Leo's shoulders slumped, and his gaze dropped to the ground. "You won't believe me."

"Try me."

Leo lifted his chin in the direction of a welded table, painted dark green. Four seats were welded to it. His voice lost its heat and aggression. "Can we go sit?"

I accepted. We sat on opposite sides of the table. I made sure to smack Creed against the welded metal and took more than a little satisfaction when Leo flinched, a reaction he tried to cover. "Start talking."

"Man, it's going to sound crazy."

"You wouldn't believe the stuff I've heard and seen. I already know who you are. I know that you're a demon— well, you used to be." His flat eyebrows arched. "Now that the big reveal is... revealed—" I really needed to work on my action hero one-liners "—start talking."

Leo stared at the tabletop, playing with the diamond-shaped slats with thick fingers. "My... friend told me you were at the park. He's been keeping an eye out for you. When he saw you over here, he gave me a call. I didn't get a chance to finish my business with you in the gym because of Debbie. The receptionist. If she hadn't been there and pulled me into the back office to calm me down, it would have taken the entire gym to pull me off you." His eyes finally looked up to meet mine. They were steady. "And I would have enjoyed getting revenge. Every second."

My nose flared. "What the fuck is your problem? What did I ever do to you?"

"You've done so much. But you're blind to it, aren't you? Guess that's what special status does, allows you to get away with being clueless," he said.

His fingers gripped the holes in the table. After a few seconds, they relaxed and his head dropped.

"I know I should put that stuff in the past. My mother keeps telling me that, that I'm too angry all the time. It is hard, man. It's really hard."

Leo seemed troubled, genuinely so. I scrambled to place his face from somewhere in my past. Six thousand years might sound like a long time to a mortal, but to us it is the blink of an eye, only a slice of a lifetime. Flashing through my memory bank, I came up empty in the Leo department.

"If I did something to you, tell me, because for the life of me, I have no idea who you are besides the asshole who likes to fight," I said with a modicum of satisfaction.

Leo looked at me and then at the table as he shook his head. "Man, you are clueless. Everyone told me you were, but I had no idea they were so right. Do you get off shitting on other people's lives?"

I've got patience for a lot of things. Living an entire life as the only demon in Hell without magic can teach you to take what you're dealt one day at a time. To tolerate a father who doesn't fully love you because you don't allow yourself to be subjected to abuse by those in leadership positions. Stuff like that can teach you to mend fences you were not even responsible for breaking. Only having a single girlfriend in your entire life because all succubi rejected you as a freak can teach you how to survive a struggle with self-satisfaction. But my patience, like everything, had limits. Mine had been reached.

Gripping Creed by the knob, I slammed it on the table. "If you're not going to give me something specific, I'm going to wrap this around your neck until you promise to leave me alone."

"So you don't have to be held accountable?" Leo asked with a scoff. "Typical."

"What's typical?" I said, agitated to the point of starting to shake. "Accountable for what? To who?"

Leo's head snapped up. "To my uncle!"

"Are you sure your uncle isn't the bad guy in all of this? Maybe whatever happened to him isn't my fault because, whoever he is, he's the one who violated me, not the other way around? What's his name? Tell me and I might be able to tell you another side of the story."

"Aries."

I lost my breath. "Aries..." My head spun. "Aries is your uncle?"

"Yes," Leo said, his mouth twisting. "He *was* my uncle."

He wanted revenge for Aries. Leo had fallen for the Council's lie that I was the key to that ancient demon's murder, conveniently leaving out the fact that Beelzebub killed the Founder as I protested.

"Whoa, whoa," I said, sitting back and putting up my hands. "I barely knew Aries, but he left a heaven of an impression on me. He was very helpful and I have nothing but great respect for him."

"And you killed him for it," Leo spat.

"The heaven I did," I shouted back, before looking around the park to ensure we still had privacy. "I didn't do anything to Aries. In fact, I tried to help him. I was sentenced by the Council for that, by the way. Don't give me any crap about doing anything to him. If I did, why do I have this?" I snagged Creed and lifted it in the air. Leo flinched. "Aries gave this to me when I visited him in Seattle. He said—"

Leo's eyes flickered before narrowing. "What is that? Besides the tool you used to cheat to win a fight?"

"First, I'm not interested in fighting. That's your thing," I said. "I was saving my ass. Second, like I said, this was from your uncle. He entrusted it to me. Do you think he would do that with someone who threatened him?"

His two thick shoulders raised. "How do I know you didn't take that from him after you killed him?"

"I didn't kill him!"

"Then who did?"

I was only more than happy to name drop Beelzebub. "Hell's precious Prince of Demons, that's who."

Doubt flickered across Leo's face. There was something to it, something more than simple disbelief. My comment landed, if not on complete terra firma, at least on partial firma. If I was a betting incubus I would bet there was more than a seed to fertilize in Leo. He had a story, and if he was like any of the few demons in Hell I had come across who think for themselves, maybe he doubted the legitimacy of the Council enough to give me a chance to tell him the story.

So I did. I told him every detail that felt safe to share. But I didn't share everything. Leo could be another operative simply biding his time to sucker me in close enough to deliver the killing blow. Who knew? Surely, not this guy.

If he was, sharing Beelzebub's betrayal of demonkind was immensely rewarding. I didn't mention my friends because Leo didn't need to know about them. But I gave him enough to set a foundation for future trust. I didn't care about Leo trusting me. I just needed enough leverage to uncover the identity of his friend.

"So, see? I had nothing to do with Aries's death," I said, spreading my hands. "In fact, I was the only one working to save him. His mortal bodyguards took one heaven of a beating. I never found out if they even recovered. I hope so, but I don't trust Beelzebub or the Council enough to put faith in that. Yes, I was naïve. I was ignorant about the entire situation and the character of the Council. I treated the mission like a payday, not something that involved a living, breathing incubus. That's my fault, and I accept responsibility for it. The fact that Aries was such a kind demon only makes it harder for me, and if I'm being honest, I still haven't gotten over my role in what happened. I owe Aries. I'll never forget that. Your uncle means that much to me."

Leo asked, cocking his head to the side and squinting, "You're saying my uncle would have walked away, but Beelzebub tricked you into helping him open a rift to my uncle's house so he could kill him?"

"He had help, other operatives. He brought them through a rift and they ganged up on your uncle." Leo looked away and I scrambled to fill in details that would satisfy him. "For what it's worth, Aries put up a good fight. He didn't go down easily, and he took out a couple of them before the end."

It was a lie, but one that could only help. If Leo needed to hear that his uncle went out like a hero, then so be it. If the only harm my fabrication about Beelzebub and non-existent operatives did was to the egos of those on the Council, that was a price not even worth registering.

"That's how we got your name, man," Leo said, finally looking up now that I had shared the legacy of his uncle. In his eyes, I saw a chance.

"How?"

"One day, a representative on our Circle's sub–Council came by," Leo said. "The entire family had to come together. We gathered at my Nana's place. And that's when he told us, except his version was a lot different. They had no problem dropping your name. Matter of fact, they pretty much made us memorize it, man. You don't have a lot of friends on the Council, do you?"

"Do you think I'd be here if I did?"

Leo looked away, out beyond where the tall reeds blew in

a slight breeze. "Not long after, they Abandoned us." He stopped to exhale, puffing his cheeks so far some hairs in his beard stood horizontally. "This is nuts, man. I got myself in a mess and can't figure a way out. But, listen. I'm not going to screw with you anymore." He turned suddenly and jabbed a finger into the air. "Unless I find out that you are lying to me about this." The hand went back down. "But you don't seem to be. To be honest, I kind of believe what you're saying about Beelzebub and my uncle. There's been trouble between them for ages. We all knew that, the whole family did. Aries warned us about that incubus a million times if he told us once. I can't say I'm surprised. None of us will be when they find out. Still, a mess."

I nodded along. "It is."

"No, you don't understand," Leo said in a voice that was too soft for his physique. "I was so focused on getting to you that I've put off a few things. Important things."

I raised my shoulders in a half–shrug. "Well, now you'll have the time to do that since you won't have to worry about bothering me." I started to stand. "I'll let you get to whatever it is you need to be doing. Make sure you—"

Leo reached for my wrist, snagging it before I registered how close his hand was. I tried to pull back. His gripped tightened. "Before you go, can I... man, this is hard. Can I ask for your help?"

He looked absolutely defeated, with deep lines creasing his cheeks. I nodded, and he released me. "Sure. If I can."

"I promise to not bother you anymore if you can help me out," Leo said.

I grimaced. "That doesn't sound like you asking for a favor. That sounds like a condition. Blackmail almost."

"No, I swear, man. Like I said, as long as you're not lying, we're cool."

We weren't, but that wasn't the point at the moment. "So what is the favor you need?"

Leo glanced around the park, leaning closer. "Since you worked for the Council, you might know how to handle this. I've got a big problem on my hands."

An edge to his voice hinted of insecurity, which was significant for someone like him. It set me on edge. "What kind of problem?"

"I think I'm being followed," Leo said, his voice barely above a whisper.

Oh, beautiful irony.

"Can't you handle something like that on your own? Why do you need my help?"

Leo leaned close enough I could smell the drying sweat from his run and our tussle in the grass. "Because I think I'm being followed by an angel."

9

OLYMPIA

THEY SAY secrets don't make friends. Whoever came up with that didn't know what they were talking about, or had never been exposed to the immortal realm and its politics.

I made Leo repeat his revelation. He did not have much in the way of details, nothing solid he could provide. The gym owner was convinced he was being followed by an agent of Yahweh.

Throughout his description, I searched for inconsistencies or behaviors that hinted at him being dishonest, deceitful, or downright delusional. When he finished, I was convinced Leo was being honest, at least in part. The lack of specifics bothered me, but I was not so naïve as to jump into the pool of gullibility just because he promised to not throttle or sucker punch me anymore. Leo claimed the angel hung on the periphery whenever he caught sight of her. Whether at the grocery store or on his way to and from work, even outside his gym, he never got a good look. 'Just a vibe,' he said. A state of constant paranoia had him on edge, he admitted. I didn't completely believe him, but that went some way in explaining his aggression toward me.

His lack of specifics wasn't going to help me help him, but

my priority was keeping Leo only as close as needed to find out who his friend was. A recent development or not, I wasn't interested in taking chances. I blamed Seraph. Her sudden appearance in my apartment had me on edge. I still hadn't told Cancer our apartment was vulnerable to the Council's prying. As time passed, Seraph's visit became more difficult to share. The guilt of hiding such an important event from her grew heavier with time. Bilba had not delivered good news about Melchiot and the search for the cure, so I hadn't even caught a lucky break of timing or serendipity.

All in all, my mortal life would be simpler without Leo and his secret. Without it, he could have gone his way and I could have gone mine, and never the two of us should meet again—or something like that. Instead, because life seemed to enjoy crapping on me, thoughts of angels roaming Olympia went wherever I walked. True, it wasn't my fight, but if I wanted his friend's name, I had to help with his angel issue. Plus, if there were angels in town, causing heavenly trouble might not be exclusive to Leo. Who said they wouldn't come looking for me and Cancer at some point? By helping Leo, I would not only get his friend's name, but I would not be caught by surprise by Yahweh's hit squad. In fact, I was already planning my counter-attack.

Definitely chalking up this turn as a win.

Win or not, the troubling thoughts occupied me the entire next day but didn't stop me from finding the nearest drinking hole and chasing answers in the bottom of a beer stein—hey, old habits are hard to break. Half an hour after arriving, I still didn't have them, so I dedicated more time to searching in a different brew. Cancer was working at one of the high school football games and I was not in the mood to watch *A Christmas Carol* again—though that was more attributable to the fact that none of the networks were playing it. Apparently the entire 'Christmas in the summer' thing was a short-term marketing ploy meant only for the summer. What an ugly thing to do, to toy with an ex–demon's emotions about my new favorite holiday.

The bar was typical Olympia fair, the kind of place that wanted to belong in a big city like Seattle but couldn't afford the accouterments to create that level of classy ambience. Still, this hole-in-the–wall was a great place to hang and reflect without worrying about the expected behavioral standards of someone my age being in a bar. No loud darts or pool matches. No flirting with female patrons for attention, or any of the personal grooming expectations that went along with that activity. No loud boasting of accomplishments over the past weekend. Simply me and my beer and my thoughts. Just the way I needed it tonight.

And that's the way it stayed, at least for an hour. I was nearing the bottom of my second stein when the stool beside me slid across the rough, uneven floor.

"Is this seat free?" a soft voice asked.

Without looking, suppressing my internal groan at the fact there were twenty other available stools farther away this person could occupy, I answered, "All yours."

"Thanks, I appreciate it," he said. A cloud of cologne punched my nose, and I snagged my stein, bringing it to my mouth to disguise my aromatic neighbor. "Looks like a quiet night tonight."

The reason I came to this bar was for peace, not for conversation. This person was ruining my evening beer. I didn't want to be rude, but...

"Look, I've had a long day and—" My words dropped off when I saw who I was talking to. Steve, the man from the fight in the park smiled at me, warm and friendly, his broad cheekbones flushed an alcohol-influenced hue. "How have you been?"

The man pinched his lips. "Good. Been a few good weeks," he said, nodding his head. "Zeke, right?"

"Yep." I nodded. "No more trouble with that group?" I added hurriedly, "Not to bring up a bad subject."

I never claimed to be the most socially adept, usually saying whatever was on my mind. Plenty of demons had warned me how rude I sometimes sounded. But it wasn't rudeness which drove my behaviors, but the efficacy of communication to save time. Why crawl down the street when you could run? Sometimes, even someone like me understood why taking time to think through what I said, when I said it, and how it was said was be important. Thankfully, the man was more gracious than I was self–aware.

He rocked his head and laughed. It was a sound of relieved joy. "You know, I can't remember the last time I've gone this long without being harassed or bothered. Not like it was happening every day or something, but since that little scuffle... nothing. I even saw one of them the other day at the farmer's market. Do you know how much effort he went through to avoid me? He darted away, trying so hard to avoid eye contact he almost knocked over an apple stand. Barely caught it, or the thing would have toppled. Hilarious. I've got you to thank for that. Anyways," Steve said as the bartender brought him an Old-Fashioned, which he lifted to me. "Cheers to the good people in the world."

I lifted my beer stein, carefully knocking it against his short tumbler. "To good people."

Silent seconds passed before Steve said, "And to hoping it stays that way for a while. Thanks to your help, it might."

"I just did what anyone would do. I'm glad they saw the error of their ways. They didn't come across as anything more than dim light bulbs. Do you think they will? Leave you alone, that is?"

Steve pinched his lips. "I'm not holding my breath. People like that... they're slow to change. I want to believe they can, because I've seen some miraculous transitions in people's attitudes about me, but I've also seen a whole lot of ugly."

I dipped my head, finding a focus in my drink. "I'm sorry you have to go through this."

"I'm not," he said confidently, sounding every bit a man who meant what he said. "Everything we go through makes us who we are. Would I like to not be harassed? Sure, who wouldn't? Would I like people to appreciate me for who I am? Absolutely. Do I hope the world can embrace transgender people everywhere? I do, but I also don't believe in miracles. Do I expect it to happen overnight?" He paused for more than a moment's thought, giving me an opportunity.

"What's it like?"

He snorted, covering his nose and mouth with the back of his hand before facing me, a playful smile dancing on his lips. "What's it like to be transgender?" His voice wavered with a hint of a laugh he was trying to control.

I held up my hands. "No, no. Sorry. That's not what I meant. I—what I meant was—"

Now Steve nearly choked with laughter. "It's okay, Zeke. I get a lot of questions from people who are comfortable enough to ask them. Well, there are some people who are so uncouth they don't realize that we're not museum exhibits. But you don't come across like that. I've got a sense for those types. You don't ping my radar. If you have questions, ask them. I'm hard to offend as long as your curiosity comes from a good place."

"I just don't get it," I started. "Just seems like they should have better things to worry about, especially with the blessed —damn—world at war. I guess I expected more from people —" I almost said 'up here' "—around here."

Steve's eyes drooped. "Neither do I. No one in our community will tell you they get it. It's not something to 'get'. It's something we have to accept as part of our struggle."

"That's not fair to any of you," I said. "Who cares? You're human, and as long as you're not a dick, what does it matter?"

Steve's lips pinched again. "Unfortunately, you'll find small pockets of people who can't evolve past their brain training."

"Brain training," I said, running the phrase over in my mind. "I like that."

"Really captures the essence of how people can be taught what to think, doesn't it?"

"Absolutely," I said, thinking back on how easily Fivers—demons who live in the Fifth Circle—were equally easy to train while noting Steve had almost finished his drink. "Would you like another?"

"Sure, if you're staying," he replied. "So, what's your story, Zeke?"

"My story? I don't really have one."

"Everyone has a story," Steve countered promptly. "And not everyone would do what you did. No one else did, which is maybe the saddest part. Did you notice how many bystanders there were?"

I looked away, feeling demoralized by the inaction of others. "Yeah, I noticed that. I'm really sorry about that."

"Why would you be? You didn't do it. That is on everyone who stood by and watched or, worse, those who rushed away, pretending like it wasn't happening." Steve's eyes locked on his drink as his fingers twirled the tumbler in a slow circle. "I get it, believe it or not. That crap was scary. I can't be mad at someone who was scared. But the entire thing could have been stopped by someone getting involved. All someone needed to do was shout at the guys, or walk over to me and ask me to accompany them to a store or something. No one needed to get physically involved... unless they were looking for a fight," he said with a gleeful twinkle in his eyes, which were cast in my direction.

"Trust me, I am so over fighting," I said.

"Fighting rarely solves things anyway. Though, I sort of

got blinded by the blood lust for second there at the end," he said.

I chuckled. "Sort of?"

"Okay, *definitely* blinded. But it felt so good." Steve's free hand curled into a fist, his fingers depressing the skin of his palm.

I understood. There were millennia I wouldn't have minded putting Ralrek in a headlock and pounding him to mush.

Steve's cheeks flushed and he contorted his face with a shudder. "Not my proudest moment, for sure. I guess no one is perfect, except maybe God."

I wanted to ask Steve if he'd include Lucifer in that conversation but thought better of it. I was enjoying his company.

Steve said, "We all have things to work on, isn't that right? What about you? You said you're over fighting. Sounds to me like there's a story in there somewhere,"

"I prefer to stay away from it, that's all," I answered carefully, still unsure what Steve saw that day. Creed hadn't come up as a topic of conversation and I wouldn't have minded keeping it that way. "The less attention I have, the better."

Steve pulled away, playfulness still evident in his expression. "Really now? See? I told you, you have a story. I would love to hear it."

While we waited for our drinks, I gave Steve the rundown of my fabricated tale. A middle-class boy raised in Arizona who had hopes of being a happy adult, passing his days working in a multitude of bookstores because he loved to read and escape his reality. Along the way, he made and lost friends, felt and mourned love, and even went on a few adventures with friends. All of it was made up, encircling a few touchstones of truth.

"So, see? Not a very enticing story," I said, giving the slim man a warm smile. The look in his eyes flustered me. I think he realized my story was not the full one.

But he had the good graces to not call me on it. "Wow, it may seem mundane to you, but it's not. I imagine most people think that about their lives. Everyone else's life is always so much more exciting than our own, isn't that the general truth of things? But I'll tell you what, I've never met someone with such a boring life who could fight like you do. That was some impressive stuff."

Steve's charm had a way of lowering my defenses. Behind a smirk, I said, "Thanks. I was hoping you hadn't noticed. I didn't want anyone to."

Steve laughed. "It was hard not to. I had enough on my hands dealing with the loudmouth. You took care of the rest of them. How is that even possible? Are you a fighter? Boxer? Jujitsu? Kickboxer?"

Now it was my turn to laugh. I raised and lowered my hand alongside my seated body. "Does this look like the physique of a fighter? I'm not, but I can hold my own if I need to. Some of my experiences back in Arizona taught me how to handle myself. Sort of against my will." I reflexively lowered my voice at the last comment as my mind flashed back through real memories, which led me to thinking about Seraph, Chax, and Leo. I changed the subject to something that didn't involve me. Plus, I was drawn to this guy's charm, his attitude, his charisma. Steve had a dynamic attitude for someone who would have been justified shutting out strangers like me along with the rest of the world. "You have a great attitude. I envy that. I wish I could be that positive. How do you do it?"

"I don't know if I'm exceptionally positive."

"To me you come across as being very positive," I said with raised eyebrows for emphasis. "How do you do it? Can I borrow some?"

The drinks were delivered, and we thanked the bartender

who moved on to the next demand. Steve waited for him to walk away. "It's not easy, if I'm being honest. You don't know who to trust and you don't know who will accept you. And I'm not going to lie. For years, even before my transition, I spent so much energy hyper–analyzing every interaction I had. Frankly, it wore me out. For a little while… hell, a long while, I scrutinized every word people said. Even the good people, which was totally unfair."

"But understandable."

"Yeah, maybe," Steve said, cocking his head in a slight jerk. "But I'm super critical of myself and my past behaviors now when I look back."

He had me thinking. "I think everyone does that. I sure do," I said, meaning to be supportive. "It's easy to look at the things we did in the past in the context of the future, and a reality where we have more knowledge, more maturity, and the time to stop reacting emotionally. In the moment, we're not afforded those things. I'm hard on myself about the things I've said and done. I'm sure you weren't unfair to anyone. You don't seem like that type."

Steve's bottom lip pursed out. "Thank you." He drew a deep breath. "But once I learned to love myself, I saw the person I was, was not the person I wanted to be. That person wasn't broken. So, day by day, I changed. I began letting people in and trusting them first until they gave me a reason not to."

"So you were the one to take all the risk?"

Steve gave a few shakes of his head. "I don't see it like that. I was the one who joined reality."

"How do you mean?" This man's positive and healthy attitude was hard to understand. I was an outcast in Hell because of something beyond my control. I knew how much that stung. Yet, Steve seemed almost… encouraged by the challenge.

"People are people," he said patiently. "Some are ignorant

but mean well, and if I'm an asshole to them or keep them at a distance, they'll never learn. Their good intentions will never be validated. Or they might learn from the wrong person and their lack of understanding may turn into hostility, even open hostility. I think that's where people like those guys in the park went off–course. They're ignorant. And I don't mean that as an insult. What I'm saying is, they simply haven't been exposed to a few things that might have set them on a different course if they had been in their childhood. That happens and we grow up surrounding ourselves with people who make us comfortable, people who aren't different and who think just like we do."

"An echo chamber," I said, thinking about the demons in Hell who acted like Kanthor Sunstone, never risking to question anything the Council did.

"And that's why it's important to be as patient and as understanding as I can be," Steve continued.

"I think I lost my bag of patience a long time ago," I said.

"Go looking for it then, Zeke," said Steve. "We're all guilty of thinking like those guys at times. Most of us just aren't as ugly as them, but that doesn't mean we're immune. We all need to be open and acknowledge our limitations. Most people don't because it requires work, and people don't like to have to work anymore than necessary."

"Definitely not on themselves."

"Exactly," he said with a forceful laugh. "If being patient, taking on the role of educator, means more people come to understand, then so be it. The way I see it, someone on the other end is going to benefit, more than just the person I'm talking to. Another person like me. And if we all do it…"

"Then more and more people benefit," I finished for him.

"There's a large LGBTQ population here, but we're not the only marginalized community in the city," he said, now turning to face me. "How long have you been here?"

"A few months," I said naturally. Nothing like having to rely on the truth to be truthful.

Steve nodded. "So you've seen the city's issue with our homeless population as well? There's a lot of our community in that one. A lot of intersections. People don't think about that. They just see homeless and think of them as lazy people who don't want to work for a living."

I was already nodding. "Or alcoholics. Or drug abusers."

Steve nodded along with me. "You get it. Do you know how many of them are people just like me? Gay, lesbian, or not sure who they are, but all rejected by someone they depended on to accept them? Love them? And, one day, they're on the street, the only place that accepts them after society rejects them, pushes them in a corner, and then faults them for having no way out."

"Disgusting," I said harshly. Aries had opened my eyes to the issue of homelessness. In Hell, I thought about the beggar in the Eighth Circle who was happy with a few bags of chips and bottles of water I gave him. All the way to my work in Stacy's soup kitchen and how Sprinkles lived the last years of his life without a roof over his head. All so unfair.

"It is," Steve said, his eyes measuring me. "I assume you've been around them?"

"Yes," I admitted, telling him about my volunteer work at the soup kitchen.

"So you get it," Steve said. "You have a far better understanding of their predicament than the vast majority of people. With that understanding comes a heavy weight. Try not to let it wear you down, Zeke. People like me, people like them, we need good allies in order to keep fighting. We don't need you to do the fighting for us, but we need people like you to take bullets so we can deal with the seen and unseen challenges. You asked me how I can be positive, and the answer is because I need to, because it's the healthy way to handle everything I go through. Helps me get through each day. If I allowed my circumstances to weigh me down, I would wear out, and that helps no one. Make sure you don't wear out. If you do, you won't have energy to go looking for that bag of patience."

"I'd love to, but it's just not that easy."

Steve's warm hand found my shoulder. We made long eye contact, the type where someone is doing their best to send a deep message in only a few words. "It's exactly as easy or as hard as we make it, my friend."

10

OLYMPIA

To say that I didn't think about Steve for the remainder of that evening and into the next day would be an outright lie. Not only was it an excellent distraction from my Hell–related thoughts, but what he shared made sense. That, and his oozing positivity offered a welcome realization. Being in his presence, I felt better. Not because I had a better life than him, but because he made the world feel like a happier, healthier place.

We had a few more drinks after that second round and left the bar in happier but rougher shape. We promised to hang out again, but neither one of us thought to trade phone numbers. Regrettably, we would have to trip across each other to meet up again. I blamed the booze. It's always the booze's fault.

The next morning, I woke to company in the form of a hangover and a letter in my demonic notebook. The blue seal of Lucifer blazed with a new message. I opened the cover to see Dialphio had written.

DIALPHIO: *Ezekial Sunstone? Where are you? You haven't checked in like I wanted.*

Without knowing when she wrote, I was thankful for the

single–line entry. The lack of multiple entries hinted at the absence of panic and worry, so at least I didn't have that to go with my hangover. I was still riding the high of that long conversation with Steve, my new Olympia friend.

I searched for my quill, finding it under a pile of unopened mail—I still hate mail, even here in the Overworld —and began drawing out the letters through squinted eyes. The tiny black shapes seemed to shift under my hand, coming out in shaky, uneven lines. Poor Dialphio. She would need a miracle from Lucifer to decipher my handwriting.

ZEKE: *Hey Dialphio.*

I rose to make coffee while I waited. I hadn't even opened the canister when scratching came from the notebook. I brought it into the kitchen so I could pour a cup of brown gold as soon as the brew finished. I really needed coffee. And food. A lot of food. Heavy, fat food. And something for this blessed headache.

DIALPHIO: *Things are well. How are you?*

ZEKE: *Fine.*

DIALPHIO: *Are you sure? You're short.*

ZEKE: *I'm hung over.*

DIALPHIO: *I'm shocked.*

ZEKE: *Did you sell The Book Abyss and hit the road to be a standup comedian?*

DIALPHIO: *There's no way I would sell the store. It's doing too well.*

That was good news, unexpectedly good. I was happy for her and told her so.

DIALPHIO: *Why is it you're hung over? Do I need to worry about you? If you get carried away again I will find a way to the Overworld and babysit you every single minute of your life.*

The sharp smell of coffee filled the kitchen, and I smiled at Dialphio's promise to throttle me.

ZEKE: *I am fine. I promise.*

I filled her in on Steve, his story, and what he had me

thinking about. Bless it, it was so inconvenient when other people cared enough to help you grow as a demon.

DIALPHIO: *Well, that's good. I'm happy to hear you got out and are meeting people. Of course, I'm not surprised you stepped in to help someone. Let's try to keep a low profile, okay? You draw enough attention as it is.*

I had to read the line twice. Did Dialphio know about the other stuff involving Leo and his friend? How? I hadn't told her.

ZEKE: *What do you mean?*

DIALPHIO: *Oh, Bilba hasn't told you? Ralrek either? Well, you're the talk of the Fifth Circle, Ezekial Sunstone.*

ZEKE: *I am?*

DIALPHIO: *Oh yes. Lots of demons talking about you. Maybe too many. Of course, most of it is in whispers in the pubs and back room meetings. Quite the conversation piece.*

ZEKE: *Why? What did I do?*

After so long being the butt of jokes and fascinating dinner conversations, I tended to get agitated at the thought of being the focus of other's attention. One day, could I not just be Ezekial Sunstone? For. One. Stinking. Day?

I added a spruce of coffee to a cup filled with creamer and sugar, the only kind of coffee worth drinking, and carried it and the notebook out to the small balcony. Below, the dark blacktop hinted of last night's rain. Mustiness hung in the morning air. A few shops away, someone—I couldn't tell who or how old—huddled in a sleeping bag underneath a torn wool blanket. The night hadn't been cold inside the comfort of the apartment, but this person shielded themselves as if it were the dead of winter. I set my coffee down on the table, pushing it away.

DIALPHIO: *Things are changing here. I wish I could tell you they were changing for the better, but I adore you, so I'm not going to lie.*

ZEKE: *The Council?*

DIALPHIO: *You could say that. They're cracking down on a lot of freedoms. The mortal war is not helping with the constant need to draft more recruits. As you can imagine, that's causing stress for everyone; the recruits and their families. Hurts the economy to have so many pulled out of the workforce and sent to the Overworld. Of course, any threat to the economy gets demons angry.*

ZEKE: *But you said the bookstore was doing well, right?*

DIALPHIO: *Oh, yes. Some of us are. Don't worry about the store. It's fine. Your parents are as well. They're doing too well, if you ask me. I saw your mother the other day, shopping in Old Towne, and she looked good, let me tell you. Wearing a very nice dress and her purse slung over her shoulder was made of harpy feathers! Do you know how expensive a purse like that is? Anyway, we chatted for a bit. About you, of course.*

Dialphio had talked to my mother more recently than I had. I was going to have to get another letter out to her soon, especially after hearing that they were doing well. That eased my tension that I was once again a topic of discussion in at least pockets of the Underworld.

DIALPHIO: *But it goes beyond the Council overstepping its boundaries. A lot has happened in the last few years. You're at the center of most of it, and that which you're not, you're mentioned. You have the Underworld's attention. Don't be surprised when I tell you that demons are talking about you.*

ZEKE: *I don't know why they bother. I'm Abandoned, Dialphio. I can't help anyone back there except to be the subject of their jokes and ridicule. Probably a little scorn, too.*

DIALPHIO: *Stop that this instant. That's not how anyone refers to you. In fact, I hesitate to tell you this because it will probably go to your head, but a lot of these demons hold you in high regard. Whether you like it or not, you're seen as somewhat of a hero, a role model.*

ZEKE: *Me? Why?*

DIALPHIO: *Do you honestly think you're the only demon that grew sick and tired of the Council's machinations?*

ZEKE: *There certainly aren't—*

I was in the middle of writing my response when Dialphio's next message scrawled itself out onto the page.

DIALPHIO: *Plenty of us are sick of the things we've seen, the things we continue to see. Demons haven't forgotten what they did to you. To Aries. Do you think it hasn't been talked about? Because it has. And the more who share your stories, the more the facts come out. The legend of Zeke is growing. Your Abandonment might actually be helping. The Council may come to rue the day they did that.*

The legend of Zeke? That was ridiculous. I was nothing but a demon who stacked books for a living and worked in a soup kitchen when he wasn't practicing forms with his magical halberd or watching cheesy holiday movies.

ZEKE: *How so?*

DIALPHIO: *Well, for starters, your absence means you're not around to screw things up and destroy the perfect image some have of painted of you.*

ZEKE: *Ha, ha.*

DIALPHIO: *But it also serves as a firm example of what the Council is willing to do. This isn't isolated to whatever happened to you in Baghdad and the trial. It goes back to your and Ralrek's imprisonment during the Gemini debacle. It goes back to Aries. These rumors about you have legs, and each day they grow stronger.*

ZEKE: *Well, if it helps anyone, Cancer and I are not the only Abandoned demons in Olympia. A neat secret I recently discovered. I met someone else who's Abandoned, and you'll never guess who he's related to.*

I filled Dialphio in on the details of Leo, at least the story he wanted me to know. I followed up by telling her about my suspicions that at least a few of the group near the garage were ex-demons.

DIALPHIO: *Fascinating.*

ZEKE: *What is?*

DIALPHIO: *That there are at least three of you, more, if your senses are correct. Hardly surprising, but definitely fascinating. I've always heard stories, of course, but all the media frames these things like conspiracy theories, warning against buying into them. Plus, I imagine, part of me probably hasn't wanted to believe those stories either. To wonder how many of us have actually been Abandoned. This supports the movement here, that the Council has overstepped, has been overstepping. Demons are tired of it. Probably even more so than the Council is of you being untouchable.*

ZEKE: *I'm hardly untouchable.*

DIALPHIO: *You still hold Creed, do you not?*

ZEKE: *Of course. That stupid thing won't leave me alone.*

From my bedroom where I'd left Creed on my nightstand, I heard a quick succession of rattling. Wood on wood.

DIALPHIO: *Good. Until things change, you're going to need it. It keeps you on the Council's radar, trust me.*

ZEKE: *You sound confident.*

DIALPHIO: *I am. Creed is a gift from One, making you untouchable to any of our kind, the Council, or Lucifer Himself. You don't have natural–born Abilities they can strip or use against you. You're an unknowable threat and still would be, even if you were in their presence. Keep that halberd close. There's been chatter you might have enemies up there. Worrisome after hearing about this other Abandoned demon.*

I pulled the notebook closer.

ZEKE: *Shoot straight with me, Dialphio. What do you know?*

DIALPHIO: *I don't know anything for certain, otherwise I would tell you. You know that. When have I ever held back?*

That wasn't necessarily true. Throughout my time working for her, Dialphio became privy to a lot of information about my situation, experiences, and struggles. The bookstore owner was the one to educate me on Creed's nature. Without her insight, I'd still think of the halberd as nothing more than a stick with an attitude. Dialphio *had* held back on me in the past, but only until I was ready for her to share. Outside that context, I don't think bullets flew straighter than Dialphio's directness.

ZEKE: *Never. So don't start now.*

DIALPHIO: *I didn't write just to tell you demons are interested in what's going on so much so that they're not willing to wait to see if the Council will let you finally return home. There's another reason you're hearing from me. Something I need you to hear from me because I got it from a reliable source. Someone I don't question. It directly involves you and a threat on your life.*

ZEKE: *If this has anything to do with Seraph, I already—*

Again, I was cut off by a new message. My eyes widened as I read it and my throat felt like I'd swallowed my entire untouched coffee, cup and all.

DIALPHIO: *Chax is in the Overworld, and he's looking for you.*

ONE OF THE BAD THINGS ABOUT NOT HAVING ACCESSIBLE FRIENDS is that you're left to work out problems on your own. Steve was too new of an acquaintance, and far too mortal, to understand my dilemma. Cancer, love her to death, was always in scrubs at the hospital, tending to injured kids at a high school game, or over at the Lion's Den with Leo and his crew of sweaty fighters.

The fact was, I had no one but myself to help me think through Dialphio's news. I wrote to Bilba and Ralrek after the exchange with my ex-boss. My best friend replied as the morning faded to afternoon, which waned to evening and me heading out to stuff my face with chicken wings. Ralrek did write, saying he had nothing better to do. But his advice was limited, because the Overworld was beyond his reach. He admitted there was little he could do in the Underworld. Though he wasn't helpful, he promised to check in with Dialphio in the morning to see if she had anything he could help with. Before we said goodbye, he mentioned overhearing rumors of groups forming, but that they were too political for his tastes, and he hadn't checked into them. When I suggested he was likely also a topic of discussion with these groups, his interest needle barely budged.

Now, I was officially worried about him.

Any thought I had of the chicken wings curing my dilemma or settling my paranoia were dashed when I stared at the plate now containing only thin, darkened bones. Feeling no better on a full stomach, I dropped off a few extra meals at the nearby homeless camp, and made my way to hang with Cancer at the gym.

If I was paranoid before about my senses and being on guard to any threat, from Leo, his friend, or the group of adults that enjoyed hanging around garages, that emotion was throttled up another hundred percent now that I knew a true threat was in town.

I didn't fear Chax, not on the level of one–on–one confrontation. When we were deployed to Baghdad, I, along with Bilba and Ralrek, had confronted him about breaking the curse on Cancer. During that confrontation, Chax made the unfortunate and unwise decision to cast a spell against me. Little did he know then—not until Bilba blabbered—that I could sense magic as soon as a caster began their incantation. Chax's Ability was weak, and that's me being kind.

Magical abilities were not why I was anxious about him being in the Overworld. Chax was devious and connected, having access to the most powerful succubus in the Underworld. A succubus with probably limitless resources.

I was exhausted by Chax even while we were deployed. I was exhausted by all the crap the Council put me through. I was exhausted by this Abandonment. I just wanted to be left alone. Abandonment should have provided that, yet every time I turned around, one more fact reminded me I never would be. Tunneling down the channel of dark thoughts—one of Hell's amusement parks really needed to build a ride with that name,—I hoped Cancer wasn't with a customer. Being in the gym would keep me partially out of my head.

The trip could serve multiple benefits. I fully planned on having a sidebar with Leo. Our scuffle in the park showed me what Leo could do. A life in the Overworld, where I was dying more each day, was tough enough. Knowing I could physically be injured or killed and at least one powerful immortal was actively interested in my demise made having a conversation with Leo imperative.

He was a teacher, and I needed to become his student. I would help him tackle the angel while he helped me tackle advanced fighting techniques.

That is, if Leo was not the true threat when all was said and done and didn't accept my counter-offer simply as a chance to snap my neck.

Yes, I have trust issues.

The streets were quiet again. As each evening grew colder, the songs of fewer birds filled the air. Fewer children played outside—not that many mortal children ever did. Fewer runners explored the sidewalks. All of which made my journey to the Lion's Den less stimulating, especially without the females running—hey, I'm a healthy incubus, so don't judge me. Less stimulating but definitely safer because I didn't see a suspicious group of adults hanging around closed garages, nor did I sense anyone emitting immortality. Tonight's trip was a mundane excursion across the city.

At least until I reached the gym.

Crossing the street toward the backside of the white corrugated metal building, I noticed something in the back corner of the parking lot. Even on enjoyable, moderate autumn nights like tonight, where not a single puff of cloud dotted the sky, this side was noticeably devoid of vehicles. Only two large dumpsters shared the area between the gym and the neighboring deli.

Well, two dumpsters and two individuals.

I was too far away to overhear them, but watching the way they gesticulated suggested the conversation was not friendly. One of the individuals was easy to mark by his height and bald head rocking a full beard. Leo sneered at the individual. They threw their thin arms in the air. The person arguing with Leo was nearly half his size. Barely over five feet tall, they wore baggy sweatpants and a hoodie with the hood pulled up.

I slowed my pace so I could watch the interaction without interfering. It could be a lover spat or a business disagreement. But this was something precarious.

Anyone walking around the city in sweatpants and a hoodie covering their head would set any observer on edge. The fact that Leo had an angel problem ratcheted up my caution. If I approached too recklessly, I might lose the advantage of surprise.

But I would be a fool if I didn't hang back to see if Leo was completely honest in what he shared after our fight. The fact was, he had been watching me and having me watched. My relationship to Aries and what Leo and his family had been told by the Council's mouthpieces was irrelevant. He could have easily fabricated that story, a ruse to distract or keep me close so the Council or one of its operatives could strike.

No matter how often Dialphio told me I was untouchable because of Creed, living in the Overworld stripped me of presupposed leverage. They could easily take me out without touching Creed. It had happened once before, in the Eighth Circle, by a subversive succubus named Marijon. During a fight, she was able to pick up Creed by using a device connected to her staff. Dialphio might think Creed was untouchable, but I knew better. All rules had ways of being broken. If taking my time to creep on Leo and this other person would save a repeat of that, so be it. I wouldn't pay the price for Leo.

No other observers or possible angelic allies hung in or

around the bushes as I moved up the sidewalk, still out of eyesight. Leo never glanced my way. The thin line of trees on the other side of the chain-link fence behind the dumpsters appeared empty except for the squirrels that chattered angrily about the humans disturbing their peace. I shut my eyes, extending my senses. The wave rippled outward, rolling over Leo and his combative friend. Leo was emitting, of course, strongly enough to pick up from this distance. Stronger than I remembered. Or was I being paranoid? Was his fading Ability mixing with the second individual? Pushing the wave further into the tree line, I searched for any other signal. None came back. No nasty surprises lurking in the shadows at least. Leo was relatively safe from attack from anything but some pissed off squirrels.

"No, I'm not!" Leo shouted loud enough for me to hear clearly. "I'm not and I'm tired of you harassing me about this! Get out of my face. Now!"

I stretched my stride at Leo's sudden outburst. His flash point had been reached. As I experienced, Leo was capable of sudden violence. If he sucker punched someone that small, he could do real damage.

In a trot, I closed on them. The person responded to Leo's with a high-pitched screech of their own, which only made Leo react excessively. He stepped forward, towering over them to intimidate. He flipped his hand up in the air as if dispensing with the person.

The small, hooded person reached for his arm when it dropped, and he yanked it away. In a moment of slowed time, Leo shoved them. They stumbled backward, catching themselves on the dumpster.

"I'm not playing around," Leo shouted. "If you come around here again, I'm going to kill you."

I was halfway across the grass when the person said something to Leo that reached me as nothing more than a murmur underneath the sounds of the evening.

Leo sprinted at them, his fists balled.

I opened my mouth to tell him to stop, that I was here and that this situation didn't need to escalate. A splitting pain shot across the back of my head and forced my eyes closed. I winced and fell to my knees, immediately dizzy.

"No," I groaned. I knew this sensation, what it meant. Magic.

Angelic magic.

In a blur, Leo flew backwards, slamming into the corrugated metal siding of the Lion's Den.

Pushing down the urge to vomit, I blinked my eyes clear. "Stop!"

The angel's head spun my direction. They wore sunglasses, but that didn't stop me from noticing their distinctive feminine features through my blooming migraine. Leo meant to knock out a female angel, and she had reciprocated by throwing him against his own gym wall.

"Please stop," I said, this time more genially. I didn't want to present as a threat. Angel magic was strong, and even though Creed warmed at my side, I didn't want to be forced to use it. Not against an angel. Who knew what that would kick off. The angel drew enough risk by casting to attack Leo, something that might open rifts on both sides of the divide that I did not want to be near.

The angel heeded my warning, spinning away and racing around the corner of the gym. Leo swiped at her legs as she sprinted past. She tripped, going down with a cry, before leaping to her feet and casting again.

I scrambled up as the pain of her spell squeezed the base of my skull. My eyes filled with tears and I heard Leo cry out. His moans told me he was alive, somewhere behind my blurry vision. I stumbled forward until my eyes cleared enough to see. When I rounded the gym, the angel was almost at the other end of the building. I gave chase.

I raced past the Lion's Den, past the next building, and

down an alley. Her last spell dissipated with distance and time. I saw clearly and felt my normal self again. My speed returned. The distance closed.

The angel took a hard left. Another alley. I followed. This one was carved between two storage unit warehouses–a matching pair of two hundred-yard-long buildings. Our racing footsteps echoed against the kingdom of corrugated metal.

The alley between the storage units was empty. We were completely alone. That could be good or a bad, depending on the angel's disposition.

A slight pressing sensation filled the back of my skull as she began another spell. This one was much weaker. Either she was weakening, or she was casting something smaller. Let her mistake me for an innocent who only wanted to protect a friend. Her assumption worked to my advantage.

The minor spell only caused mild discomfort. My vision remained clear, and I was now within fifteen yards.

Her hand extended backward, slowing her pace. She sent a rippling wave of air at my feet. It spread out in a cone shape, rising and falling like ocean waves, one after another. The entire spell was twenty feet long and absolutely unavoidable. She had cast it at a height that prevented me from jumping over it.

Ten yards away, I made my move. Just before the white wave hit me, I leapt to the side. At the crown of my jump, I grabbed the rain gutter of the storage unit as her wave passed below. Miss. I hung for a second before pulling myself onto the roof and dashing after the angel who was making her getaway.

Within seconds, I had the distance closed to barely more than a body's length—I told you I was fast. The angel glanced backward, not noticing me above her. Once parallel, I dove, spreading my arms in a crucifix pose, aiming for her waist. I struck, and we tumbled to the blacktop in a cry of pain, anguish, frustration, and just about any other emotion you might suspect after jumping from fifteen feet off a roof when you dislike heights. My back didn't avoid the anguish of meeting pavement as I rolled, the angel wrapped in my arms. Her sunglasses flew in the opposite direction.

We slammed to a stop against the metal shed door of the opposite storage unit with me taking the brunt of the blow. The angel struggled to pull away. Eternity would not have provided her with enough chances to break from my locked hands. She smelled wonderful. Like a cool day in Eve's Sanctuary. Her hood fell off as we wrestled, and her cocoa hair with hints of blond spilled out. In the entire Under, Over, and Upperworlds, I had only ever seen one female with hair like that. One I hadn't seen in years.

In a haze of confusion, I rolled over, pinning her underneath me and staring into the most gorgeous face I'd ever seen, my breath taken away.

Cassie smiled. "Hi, Z-Zeke."

11

OLYMPIA

"MIND GETTING OFF OF ME?"

I looked down at the crystal blue, oval eyes of the angel I thought I would never see again. Mounted on her, I felt awkward and very uncomfortable. "Um, yeah. Sure. Sorry. Promise not to set me on fire?"

I got to my feet and offered her a hand. She playfully swatted it away. "You hit like a girl, do you know that? Plus, I wasn't trying to set you on fire in case you couldn't tell. I thought you knew more about magic? We can't cast fire spells, silly."

"I'd never seen one like that before," I said, trying to clear my head of the shock at seeing her again.

Cassie straightened her hoodie and sweatpants, glancing around the blacktop. "Where are my sunglasses? They were expensive."

She started to pass me. My hand shot out, snagging her wrist. "Cassie. Why are you here?"

Her eyes sparkled as her pale lips spread. "Work. Now, help me look for my sunglasses."

"How about we chat while we look? They can't be far," I countered, feeling my stupid heart skip with excitement.

Cassie, in the Overworld.

I hadn't seen her since Kaiserslautern, Germany, when she'd worked out a favor with Seraph to allow me to see her one last time to close loops from our Gemini mission. During that visit, Cassie and I were attacked by an assassin and barely escaped with our lives. It was the first time I had activated Creed's magic, killing the assassin in a beam of blue light that, to this day, I wasn't sure how I cast. Cassie hadn't provided answers then, but she had provided enough insight and nudged me in the right direction about Creed's nature, reinforcing Dialphio's research.

"That's fine, as long as you look for them more than you're looking at me," she laughed and moved away alongside the row of the shed doors.

"I—I wasn't looking at you," I said, less confidently than I wanted. She looked good walking away.

"Yes, you were," she snickered.

Shaking that vision, and the thoughts that came along with it, from my head, I flipped my hand in the air. "Well, of course I was looking at you. We're having a conversation. I haven't seen you in years, and this is unexpected. But it was purely innocent." I was talking too blessed much. "Plus, you're here. In the freaking Overworld."

"There they are!" she said, walking three doors down and bending to scoop them up.

It was a sight I both appreciated and abhorred. I looked away. This was Cassie, an angel, an agent of Heaven, an immortal enemy.

Wait, but she wasn't anymore. With my Abandonment, I lost my immortality. That meant I was no longer an enemy of angels, and they were no longer enemies of mine. Something positive was coming out of the day.

"Mission achieved," I said, eyeing her sunglasses, which she promptly braced at an angle on the top of her head. "Now, what was all that about back there?"

She waved away the comment. "Just some business."

"It looked like pretty serious business."

"I doubt I would have been sent back here if it wasn't, Z-Zeke," she stuttered, as angels are prone to do with demon's names. She was trying to sound dispassionate, but sounded humored instead. Her shoulders drooped in an exasperated sigh. "You're not going to let this go, are you?"

I shook my head.

"Fine," she said, tucking her hands inside the front pocket of her hoodie. "I've been here for a few weeks."

"In Olympia?" I interrupted in a voice too loud for the surroundings. My voice echoed down the channel created by the warehouses. I checked for prying ears. We were still alone.

"Yes," she said with a chuckle. "Why?"

"Because I've been living here for months and haven't seen you."

"It's a big city."

"Not that big," I countered, emboldened by facts.

Her thin lips twitched. "I guess so. But I don't exactly make a habit of perusing the location of my newest assignment to inform every demon of my comings and goings. That would make my life pretty dangerous."

Oh boy, this chat was going to take some time. If we weren't standing in between two warehouses on the edge of Olympia, I would have proposed stopping by a bar for a drink or two to talk things through.

I puffed my cheeks out and blew a breath of frustration, admitting, "I'm not a demon. Well, I am, technically. But things have changed. I—"

Cassie cocked her head. "What do you mean you're not a demon? Of course you are, Z-Zeke. Don't be ridiculous. It's not like I don't know that. I swear, all that stuff in the past, with Gemini, and what happened afterward? It's over. I had a mission to do, and I did it. You had a mission. You did it. We can be honest with each other... I hope we can, at least."

"No, that's the thing. I'm being completely serious," I said, and then filled her in on as many of the recent events about my mortal situation as I could.

She was quiet when I finished, turning away to pace in a small circle. "So that means you can't go back to the Underworld? They really kicked you out?"

"We call it being Abandoned," I said.

"We do too," she said, pacing. "But for us, being Abandoned means..."

I gave her a second more to continue, but her thoughts were as dark as my future. "Yeah, that's exactly what it means."

Cassie stopped, delayed briefly, and then approached with hurried steps, wrapping me in her arms. Her comfort enveloped me. The years of not seeing each other evaporated with her touch. "I'm terribly sorry. That's not right. You deserve better." She pulled away, but still held my arms. "What's the chance they'll change their mind?"

My head dropped. It was so hard to be a failure and meet her eyes. "Unless you can get your friend Seraph to change her mind, I doubt any discussions about that will ever happen."

"Seraph is hardly someone I would call a friend."

"She hooked us up so we could see each other in Kaiserslautern," I reminded Cassie.

She nodded, bobbing both of my arms in rhythm. "She did. But she only did that because she owed someone else favors. Don't let her fool you. I wish I could say I'm surprised she's wrapped up in this nasty business, but I'm not. Oh, Z-Zeke, I'm so sorry. If there's anything I can do, just ask." Those crystal eyes sucked me in as she asked, "What did you say her nephew's name was?"

"Chax." The name came off my lips like someone had brushed a bowl of oil over my tongue. "But he's a demon. There's nothing you can do."

Cassie let go of one wrist and raised a finger. "A demon in the Overworld. That makes him vulnerable." Her grin was a stark contrast to the dark implication.

I shook my head. "You can't do that. Not for me, Cassie. Though I appreciate it."

"What's the alternative? That you spend the rest of your time looking over your shoulder every single day?"

"If I hadn't been paranoid about him popping out of the weeds, I wouldn't have seen you and Leo arguing," I said with a wink. "You see? It has its benefits."

"How can you play around about something like this?" she asked. "He's a threat. You said Seraph visited you here? That means she's gathering information while trying to intimidate you. And if you're Abandoned... the time you have left draws shorter every day."

"Isn't that true for all of us, even immortals?" I grinned.

Cassie slapped her leg. "This isn't a laughing matter," she said hotly, spinning away, resuming her pacing. "Either you tell me or, when I go back to the Upperworld, I will start asking questions. Do you want that? Because I can send a missive when I get back to my apartment and have our intelligence department run reports. They might send another agent, or they may give me the assignment. Either way, fess up or I'll start researching. I'm pretty sure I'll find what I'm looking for."

Something told me Cassie always got what she wanted. Clearing my throat and my distracted brain, I decided to refocus our conversation. "What are you looking for from Leo? You still haven't told me?"

"L—Leo is... a small matter," Cassie admitted. "You'd think with the blossoming war, our Council would be distracted. Apparently, they have a lot of bored agents at the moment and everything is so tense between our Council and yours, the Underworld's, that they're hands-off when it comes to the war. Did you hear five more countries joined today? Everything is intensifying. From what I've heard, we don't want to overstep and provoke the demons, and apparently the same is true for them. Both sides ramping up recruiting troops."

"An arms race," I interjected.

She dipped her chin. "I can't speak for my Underworld counterparts, but we're spending our time influencing the Balance on matters that aren't nearly as important as a world war."

"Matters like Leo? What is he doing that is affecting the Balance?" I asked.

"He's a demon—" Cassie started, but I interrupted.

"He's a gym owner. He's in the same situation as me. Abandoned, and honestly, he's emitting quickly. He may come across as an influential demon to you, but trust me, it won't last."

Cassie stopped pacing to square on me. "Emitting? What does that mean? And how did you know he's Abandoned? How did you know he is a demon in the first place? Are you just assuming because I'm involved?"

I shook my head and explained my growing senses. The angel had a way, without words, of pulling information out of me. Cassie's mouth dropped open at a few points in the conversation.

"So you're telling me you can see Abandoned demons emitting their immortal energy?"

I nodded slowly. Emissions was not a topic I was confident talking about because I was still trying to figure it out for myself. Between them and just how in the heaven I could ever control Creed's magic instead of the halberd controlling me, I had a full plate of ignorance. But there were only so many things I could do, and only so much time in which to do them. Sensing emissions had been an accident, inherent, but so subtle I never registered it until recently. I only really started noticing it during my deployment to Baghdad, surrounded by tens of thousands of mortals, exposed to them every minute of every single day. Without that experience, I might have never noticed my growing strength. Accidental, unplanned, and unregulated. One more thing that controlled me.

Cassie whistled. "That could be helpful."

I snorted. "Sounds like you're trying to recruit me."

"Why wouldn't you join me after what happened? After what they did?"

I scratched my scruffy hair, breaking eye contact. The proposal was tempting. Not to work for the angels, but to do whatever I could to stay closer to Cassie.

But working for the Upperworld? Angels like her, I could entertain. But their upper management? No thanks. One immortal body condemning me was enough.

"Sorry, but I'm pretty much retired from the whole 'immortal struggle' game," I said, using air quotes to emphasize my point. "And I'm not really interested in getting back into it. Putting myself between demons and angels and the games they play would make me a target for both sides. As crazy as it sounds, I'm not interested in being anyone else's target. That list is long enough."

Cassie bit her lip. It was a sexy gesture, even though she wasn't trying to be. Her eyes flicked to my hip. "I see you still have your halberd."

"Creed? Yes, why?"

"Do you remember what I said about it?"

Oh, I did. How could I forget it? Before she stepped back to the Upperworld through a rift in Kaiserslautern, she had told me that the weapon came from One, that mysterious part of the All—the same force Dialphio was forcing me to understand through reading *The Histories of the Balance*.

"Yes."

"Good," she said. "Then that is where your sensing Ability comes from. The weapon is enhancing what is naturally inside you, that's all. The power of One is drawing it out. It makes absolute sense. I don't know why I didn't think of that as soon as you told me you could sense immortals. Z-Zeke, this is magnificent! This is going to help so much."

"Help with what?"

"I feel terrible saying this, but you could help me with this situation with Le—Leo," she said.

"Mmmm, that wouldn't help with the whole 'staying out of it' position I've been meaning to take. Plus, you still haven't told me what he's doing," I reminded her. "I get that he's an ex-demon and you're an angel, and the two of you aren't supposed to like each other. But if that was an absolute truth, you wouldn't like me either, and I know for a fact you do."

"Wow, who is full of himself?" she laughed.

"His previous status hardly seems worth your attention," I said, moving us on. "Especially considering he's an Abandoned demon. He's not a threat, Cassie."

She shook her head before I finished. "It's not his past immortal nature that's a concern of our Council."

"It's not?"

"No," she said. "He and his gym are shifting the Balance in Olympia."

"How so? It's just a gym where grown-ass people roll around on a mat inside a cage and occasionally punch and kick each other. Your Council is concerned with stuff like that? Even the idiots on Lucifer's Council wouldn't care about this place."

"They wouldn't because his actions favor them," Cassie said. "The Balance is all about the struggle between the Upper and Underworlds, right?"

I nodded with a smirk.

Cassie's eyes twitched. "Why are you smiling? I didn't think this was funny. Isn't that what you said?"

"It's not that. Being around these mortals, and their media and in casual conversations, it's hilarious to hear them talk about how the struggle between Hell and Heaven is one about good versus evil."

"Yeah, I've heard that too many times for my own good," Cassie agreed, sounding frustrated. "It causes a lot more work on either side. But that's too big of a problem for me. Yahweh and Lucifer need to figure that one out."

"It is so ingrained in their thinking I doubt it will ever change."

"Probably not," she said. "But don't let what is happening in this gym fool you. He has his membership focused on their internal motivations, which sort of makes sense when you think about it. I mean, have you met some of them? I did when I was a member of the gym."

My head jerked, and I chuckled. "You were a member?"

Planting her hands on her hips, she asked, "Why is that funny?"

"You don't seem like the fighting type. No offense."

"I will have you know I'm quite the fighter," she said, not sounding offended at all.

I cocked my head toward the spot where I had tackled her. "I subdued you fairly easily if I remember correctly."

"I was trying not to hurt you," Cassie countered. "I could, if you're interested?"

I held up both palms toward her. "Whoa, whoa. I'm not into that kind of play."

"I think you're just afraid, knowing what would happen to you if I didn't hold back," she laughed. It was a light, pleasant sound, like water trickling down a brook. "Anyway, L—Leo's influence is growing. They have these regional tournaments where his fighters compete against others from around Washington State, Idaho, Oregon. Some fighters from Northern California come up to take part in them. Leo's fighters do quite well for themselves. Some of them are champions in their division."

"Still not seeing the problem."

Cassie blew a long breath out, her smooth cheeks rounding. "He's charismatic. It might not look like it to people who are put off by his personality, but for the right type of person—"

"People who like busting faces while having their egos stroked?"

Cassie nodded. "L—Leo is charismatic. Don't think he's not. His gym membership is up nearly two hundred percent from just last year."

"Stalker."

Cassie gave me a playful scowl before forcefully moving the conversation back on-course. "*Most* of that increase comes from the championships his fighters are winning. And that works just like anything else. The more successful you are, the more people want to be around you."

"And the more successful everyone is, the more people who want a piece of the action? They join the gym—"

"And his influence grows," Cassie finished. "We've been watching him for over ten months. Initial reports noticed a local shift in the Balance. The Council can't afford to have a strong pocket of internally motivated humans. Both cause ripples, right? Those centered internally, and those externally, and I know I'm biased. But in a community like Olympia, which it tight-knit for its size, we can't risk more and more mortals chasing those internal needs like pride and accomplishment and individual achievement. That will throw things out of whack, and the influence will spread if not interrupted."

"And you're here to ruin his business," I said. "If his business fails, these fighters can go to other gyms, but those might not be led by such a charismatic person. The influence will fade as people fall away. Ruining an Abandoned demon's life because he's increasing human internal motivation? Sounds cruel, speaking as an ex-demon myself. Couldn't Yahweh's Council just send some of you here to increase the collective, or external, whatever, motivation of others? Go work with social groups or something. Heavens, Yahweh should know the homeless in the city need help. A lot. If the Balance requires more collective motivation to re-balance, why not put energy toward that instead of tearing down a small pocket of internally motivated people?"

Cassie's lips straightened, so pale now that they almost blended in with her light skin. "The course is set. It's all part of the Balance. I'm doing my part. If I had the type of power to change how the Balance was constructed, I would. But I'm not that angel, Z-Zeke, and I never will be."

I turned in the direction where the gym was obscured by the warehouses and the distance I had chased the angel. "That gym is all he has, Cassie. If you get too involved in this, he might lose the only thing that gets him out of bed in the morning. Be better than that."

"I doubt that is all that motivates him," she replied.

"Are you confident about that?"

She nodded. "Pretty much. I can't say for sure, but I think L—Leo is involved in other things, outside of the gym and the fighting circuit. Things that might also be accelerating the local Balance shift."

"Care to share?"

She shrugged. "Maybe. When I've got better information and won't make myself sound like a speculative fool."

Thinking about Leo being involved in something more was hardly a revelation. Without having a dog in the fight, and having discovered the identity of the angel stalking Leo, I had fulfilled my end of the deal with the gym owner. If she didn't ruin this for me, the only obstacle preventing me from receiving training from him was now removed, freeing him and me to enhance my skills.

"Do me a favor?" I said.

"Of course. Ask anything. If I can do it, I will."

"I need you to promise me you won't act against Leo without telling me first," I proposed.

"Why?" Her question came out hard, but curious. She wasn't slamming the door in my face, only shutting it slowly.

I explained my reasoning. With training, I might be dangerous enough to stay alive long enough to deal with Chax and, more importantly, Seraph. If I could do that, I could get that family off my back, possibly save Cancer's, and set a better course for my own.

"So you're asking me to step back from my work in helping reset the Balance because of internally motivated actors so you can focus on your internally motivated needs?" Cassie said.

I didn't see it like that, but understood why she would. "Sort of."

"There are other gyms where you could learn these skills," Cassie said.

"None at the top of the game like the Lion's Den," I countered. "None owned by an ex-demon who will understand my nature and use it in the training. None where I can also keep an eye on Cancer."

"You must really care about her," Cassie said, an abrupt tension to her voice.

"I do," I admitted, "and I need to watch out for her. You think I have enemies? Seraph will go out of her way to make Cancer's life miserable. She already has. And Cancer doesn't have her Abilities anymore. She doesn't have something like Creed. And... she's not doing well."

"Okay."

I blinked dumbly, trying to register Cassie's answer. "You'll do it? Before you do anything to Leo, we talk and see if there's an alternate approach?"

"I will let you know before anything is done." Cassie raised a finger. "But Z-Zeke, just know that I can't promise any alternate course of action. I have orders, just like you did when you worked for Lucifer's Council."

"I was pretty bad at following orders," I said, trying to hide the dark message behind a chuckle.

It didn't fool Cassie. "And look where it got you."

Ouch.

"Sorry," she continued, "but I'm not going to put myself in that position for him… or you. I'm going to complete my mission, but I will work with you to the best of my abilities. Is that fair?"

"What choice do I have? I need the time, and you have a job to do," I observed. "This sounds like the best solution."

"I'm glad we agree," Cassie said. "There are too many unknowable aspects, so to have something solid is comforting. Let me do my job, and I'll help you."

"Unknowable? Like what?"

Cassie looked around the alley. She tugged at the collar of her hoodie, which pulled the material tight against her chest. I think I forgot to breathe. "I can't stay much longer, but I can tell you that Yahweh's Council is very concerned about the Horn Lucifer has."

"The Horn of Taurus?" I asked, shocked to hear her mention the ancient artifact. Even I hadn't thought about it in ages, and I was almost enslaved because of a desire to possess it.

"Yeah," she said, shaking her head. "It's some powerful horn-shaped item with special properties. From the briefing we received, it gives the holder enhanced Abilities, and in the wrong hands it—"

"Oh, I know."

She blinked. "You know about the Horn?"

I whistled. "Boy, do I." I gave her a quick rundown about the mission to the Eighth Circle where we were sent to steal it from Taurus. When I finished, I asked, "What do you want with it?"

Cassie shrugged, her lips pressed together. "Do you know where it is? Where was it being held when you left?"

My mouth dropped open, about to answer, when I stopped myself. The Horn was a valuable item. Too many demons were interested in it. Someone on the Council had volunteered me to be traded to Taurus for it—and I was sure I knew which Council member was behind that move. They wanted their hands on the Horn enough to subvert their peers on Lucifer's governing body, meaning the Horn was valuable and powerful, even more so than I imagined.

I really needed to start listening to Bilba talk about all the boring books he read.

"The last time I saw it, a piece of crap demon was carrying it through a rift between Circles," I admitted carefully. I couldn't tell Cassie too much. She was still an angel, and even though I trusted her, that trust extended only so far. She might be drop-dead gorgeous and as sweet as chocolate, but Cassie was also involved in the angelic attack on the First Circle. Sure, she was there to save Gemini from being executed. That was understandable. What was not under-standable, rational, or defensible was that Cassie was part of the angel team that threw Angelfire around like a wealthy demon throws gold coins. For all the good things she was, Cassie was still a dangerous agent of Yahweh and I had too many demons still in the Underworld whom I cared about. Whether or not I wanted to get involved in the politics between Hell and Heaven, this called for practicality.

"And you have no idea where it is?" she pressed.

I pinched my lips together and shook my head, not both-ering to reply.

"That's a shame," she said with a sigh. "Rumor is, it's been lost. If you hear anything, if your friends hear anything, will you let me know?"

"Sure," I said. "But you see where I am." I raised my arms and spun in a circle, light on my toes to mimic a dancer, bringing a light to Cassie's sparkling eyes. That made me smile and forget the darker thoughts about the angel. "I'm hardly connected with the ins and outs of Hell anymore."

"Just... just tell me if you hear something?"

"You've got it," I said. "As long as you keep me in the loop."

"I will."

I scuffed the blacktop with the tip of my sneaker. "So are you going to be around town long?"

She shrugged noncommittally. "As long as it takes to complete this mission. Then I'll get my next assignment."

That was good to hear. If I could help delay her, she would be around Olympia longer. Double bonus. "Gemini here too?"

Cassie's eyes scrunched to narrow slits, cute wrinkles forming up her forehead toward her hairline. "Gemini? Why would he be here?"

"I thought you two were a team?"

"We were for the mission you busted us on," Cassie said with a light chuckle that contradicted the seriousness of how important that mission had been.

"So he's off doing his own thing?"

"I have no idea where he is," Cassie admitted, her eyes rolling in thought. "The last time I saw him was... it's easily been a year now."

"Don't you all stay in contact? Agents, I mean."

Cassie's face wiped clear of emotion, as flat an affect as if she were a wax figure. "The effective way to keep agents safe is to keep us clueless to what the others are doing. That is the way to secure operations and reduce vulnerabilities."

"Makes sense," I responded. "Can't say I will miss him."

Cassie burst out in laughter. "What? You didn't like Gemini? He played the overprotective boyfriend role really well, I thought. Maybe he played it too well?"

I gave her a sideways glance. "You could say that again. Plus, I don't think he's a big fan of me. I've got enough enemies, so one less is fine with me."

Cassie moved closer. Her cool scent tickling my nose.

"He's a professional, Z-Zeke," she said softly, her voice like a warm wind flitting across my face. "He understood your role. He also understood how you were being used and didn't fault you for any of it."

I gave her a skeptical look. "Even though I was part of why he was almost killed?"

She nodded. "You were being used by your Council. Gemini understood that and didn't fault you. *Doesn't* fault you. When he accepted that mission, he understood the risks. Honestly, there were some days he was ready for it, almost too ready. I had to slow him down more than a few times."

"He wanted to die?"

She sniffed. "No, he didn't want to die. But he was willing to, especially if it brought about reaching our objectives. That's what professionals do."

"Well, I hope no one ever asks you to make that sacrifice," I said.

Cassie made a fist and lightly bumped me on the shoulder. "Aw, that's the sweetest thing you've ever said to me." She leaned in, wrapping her arms around my neck and squeezing tight. Mine found her waist, less firmly. "But I have to get going. They're expecting a report and I'm almost late. You know how that can be. Don't want the bosses upset. So, I'll see you around?"

She let go of my neck and backed away as soon as I released my arms, which was too soon. Our embrace could have lasted a year and still would have ended too soon. "I hope so."

"Me too," Cassie shouted over her shoulder as she ran back down the alley.

I watched her go, standing there long after she was out of sight. Cassie was in the Overworld. Even though we barreled toward winter, the days would be brighter from now on.

12

OLYMPIA

HAVE you ever had that person in your life who made time disappear? Cassie was that for me. I swear we were only talking for five minutes, but every verifiable data point—at least the ones in reality and not inside the dense confines of my mind—indicated we had talked much longer.

Our conversation had started in the evening, and somehow lasted well after the Lion's Den closed, signified by the empty parking lot. No cars, no ride home. I had a long, lonely walk to the bus station ahead, which was fine. So many internal doors were opened in our chat, doors I didn't know were closed. I felt excited and elated, nervous and apprehensive, all at the same time. Seeing her made my stupid heart race. My mind went along for the ride. I had so many important things to think about already. Not only did she add to them, but she clouded my ability to think at all.

All of which, of course, gave me plenty to think about on the walk home. All of which distracted me from paying attention to my surroundings. I was a dozen blocks down Fourth Street, heading back toward the city center, when my skin prickled.

Creed warmed against my hip.

I checked my surroundings, seeing nothing out of the ordinary. Warm light drifted into the night from the homes lining the street. The café was empty, only a few lights on and a solitary body moving around, cleaning up after the day's business. Olympia had throttled down. Trouble was ramping up.

Hoping I was paranoid, I searched for what my senses were pinging. Creed grew hotter each second as the halberd warned me.

Emitting. Someone, maybe more, was emitting.

They weren't close, but the distance was closing. I sent my wave out, trying to pick up on any subtlety that might distinguish between strong immortal signatures and the dying levels I could expect from an ex-demon.

The last thing I wanted to do was overreact. For all I knew, it might be Leo. His emission signals were still strong enough to pick up now that I knew to focus on him. After witnessing his confrontation with Cassie, it made sense that he would catch up with me to find out what transpired. But I had to be smart, knowing not only was there a troublesome group of adults in the neighborhood, including at least one immortal or ex-demon, but Chax was in the Overworld. Seraph might not be too far away. No longer could I half-ass my way through life. My guard went up.

Five blocks separated me from the downtown bus terminal, which might have enough waiting passengers to discourage any threat to stop being a threat. Witnesses had that kind of effect on aggressors. Reach the terminal, assuming at least a few people waited for a late night ride; that was number one. Safety in numbers, and all that. Once there, I could use my senses with more focus and accuracy. After that, I could adjust my route and get a glimpse of who was following.

Two blocks later, my calculated plan started falling apart. Footsteps, multiple pairs, raced closer. I turned, seeing a dozen shadowy figures against the backdrop of the faint yellow street lights. Whether or not I was the target of this group, a couple things made my decision simple. One, there were a lot of them. Anyone in their right mind would feel threatened, walking down a street with a group of people running toward them. I like to think of myself as someone in the right mind. Two, it was dark. Everyone knows very few good things happen in the dark and most of those are not meant for a general audience. Last, someone in that group, at least one, was definitely emitting.

So I did the smart thing. I ran.

As I've said and feel like I have displayed, I'm fast. Very fast. The group might have had the advantage of numbers, but I had the advantage of me. That might sound a little cocky—or a lot cocky—but it is no less true. Even without giving my muscles a chance to warm, I put distance between me and the group immediately. Their racing footsteps faded.

I glanced over my shoulder in time to see them split into three groups, four people each.

I turned up Washington Street, past the theater. I blew by the small businesses, all of which were closed. Franklin Street laid to the east, Capitol Way, to the west. The park where I had witnessed a gang of bigots terrorize and assault Steve was only a few blocks further. For a second, I entertained the unrealistic fantasy that he would be chilling in the darkness and ready to return the favor, as if taking on a dozen hoodlums wasn't unrealistic.

I took a hard left and headed toward a pub that might still be open, just past the old Capitol building and its gorgeous Romanesque design.

Crossing the street, I glanced back. The group was racing my way. They were still two blocks away. Instead of stopping at the pub, I continued, taking the tight bend around Seventh Avenue.

"He's this way!" someone shouted.

The post office lay to my left and a three-story parking garage to my right. I raced around the corner of the larger structure, through the entry to the garage, and looked for an elevator or stairs. An elevator was the second of my choices. Stairs, I could climb at my pace.

Off to the right, a red EXIT sign buzzed in the night. Racing toward the sign, I bounded up. A minute later I was on the rooftop, fifteen feet higher than the street lights and forty feet higher than I felt comfortable being. Finding a dark corner of the rooftop where one of the lights cast intermittent darkness as it flickered in and out, I watched for the group.

The first small cadre arrived half a minute later, stopping in front of the Post Office, directly across the road. Three men and a woman in their early mid-twenties. I extended my senses, feeling nothing. Mortals, but mortals who still meant trouble.

I crouched behind the cement half wall, not willing to take any chances that they might spot me silhouetted against the rooftop parking lights. I chanced a peek at the street below.

A dozen seconds later another group arrived, followed by a third nearly a minute after that. One man in the last group bent and grasped his knees, wheezing.

"You're too fucking fat," a man with a hooked nose and long hair wrapped in a ponytail said.

"And you're too fucking ugly," the bent man said.

"Shut up and listen," the woman who arrived with the first group, said. She had round cheeks and a bulbous nose, and was dressed in tattered jeans and a blue jean jacket. "He can't be far."

Creed thumped against my hip.

"You're just itching for a fight, aren't you?" I asked the halberd.

It didn't respond.

Slowing my breathing, trying to calm myself, I focused my senses as the group discussed their strategy.

I pushed the wave out and grunted when it was stunted by distraction. The group argued where to search while half of them complained about the conversation being too loud. I tried to shut out their useless chatter. If they decided to search the parking garage, I would deal with that situation then. If they moved on, I wouldn't have anything to worry about. The more time I spent allowing their conversations to distract me, the less effective my sensing would be.

Concentrating, I focused on my breathing, calling back to the tactic that helped me excel at firearms training in boot camp. I risked taking a few seconds to close my eyes. Focus came. I sent out my next sense again, and it spread in all directions. When it struck the group, I nodded with a grimace. At least one was emitting.

Opening my eyes, I focused on the signatures, one person at a time. It was not the quickest work, and I wasn't sure I could do it, but this group was still arguing, giving me ample time to test my theory. Just as they broke to continue searching the surrounding blocks, I found my target. Either his emissions clouded the rest of the group's or he was the only ex-demon among them.

Hanging a couple yards behind the others was a thin man in all black. He wore a hoodie, with the hood pulled up—it's a Pacific Northwest thing, I swear. Even at this distance, I suspected he was one of the men who made the human wall outside at the closed garage the first time I visited Leo's gym. This man had been the one who watched me with a raven's eye until I was out of sight. Here he was again, and he was emitting.

The short, bulbous-nosed woman shouted orders to one group, and their leader shouted back at her. Decision made, they moved on and he followed, almost looking reluctant to join.

I let out a relieved breath as they disappeared into the night. Whoever this group was, whether working with the

Council, or just Seraph, they had aims on me. Ex-demons being involved meant this chase wasn't going to end any time soon. But for right now, I was safe. No guarantees about tomorrow.

Ex-demons. Leo was one. Leo had mysterious, unnamed friends who were interested in me.

The evening presented even more mysteries, but one thing I knew for sure was that I could no longer risk turning my back on the gym owner. Not unless I wanted him to shove a knife between my shoulders.

13

OLYMPIA

FRIENDS ARE AWESOME. Good, reliable friends are epic. Bilba was, is, and would always be the latter.

After getting home from hiding in a parking garage and freezing my ass off, I wasn't feeling rested. I tried to distract myself with a peanut butter and jelly sandwich and a good movie. Unfortunately for me, the only thing on at this time of night were B-movies, all horror, with plots revolving more around females showing more skin than directors showing monsters central to the story—of which, there was very little. The last thing I needed to see was more of the female form. Each short pair of shorts, cleavage shot, and bikini scene only made me think of Cassie. Why torture myself with thoughts of her?

I grabbed my demonic notebook, sneaking past Cancer's room. Her door was closed, and the lights were out. The succubus was going to work herself into an early grave if she didn't learn to relax. Back on the couch, because nearly one in the morning was too late to sit outside on the balcony, I cracked the notebook open. Bending my legs, my feet propped on the coffee table—Cancer would kill me if she saw,

but she was asleep and I was troubled, so this was happening
—I used my thighs as a temporary desk.

ZEKE: *Hey, are you awake?*

My eyes fell on the muted television, completely uninterested in the newest scene of a bloodied but barely dressed woman stumbling through a forest. The trees must have been magical, though. Though the scene unfolded in the middle of the night, a bright light shone through the forest, regardless of the direction she raced from the killer. Horror movies, am I right?

Thankfully, I didn't have to suffer for long. Within moments, I received a response from Bilba.

BILBA: *Hey, Zeke! What's going on? You're up late.*

ZEKE: *So are you.*

BILBA: *True, but I'm studying. You're probably drinking.*

ZEKE: *Why does everyone think all I do is drink?*

BILBA: *Funny. For the record, I don't. But you are a young, single incubus. That's kind of what we do, isn't it? Are you? Drinking?*

ZEKE: *No, I'm thinking. In trouble.*

BILBA: *What kind?*

I filled Bilba in.

BILBA: *Man, things are never dull with you.*

ZEKE: *Thanks for the insight.*

BILBA: *Seriously, are you okay?*

ZEKE: *I don't know, to be honest. A lot of things are still swirling around me, even though I'm Abandoned. I swear I haven't done a blessed thing, but it's like I'm still wrapped up in Council crap. Have you heard anything?*

A long pause.

BILBA: *I have to be careful. I've been talking with your ex–boss. Started going to meetings, too. A couple groups started popping up right after your Abandonment, but lately they've been making a little more noise, and I wanted to see what they're all about. I can't say too much at the moment, but things are moving, and maybe that's causing waves in the Overworld. It's possible.*

ZEKE: *I guess so, but I need it to stop.*

BILBA: *That's not going to happen.*

ZEKE: *Why not?*

BILBA: *Simple. Your story is important. To a lot of demons. It might be hard to understand because you're not here, and you're too blessed humble for your own good, but tons of us are pissed off. Remember what Ralrek and I told you before we walked you to the rift for your Abandonment?*

ZEKE: *I'll never forget that day.*

BILBA: *Neither will I. Neither will Ralrek. And there are plenty of others who weren't even there to send you off who won't forget. Change has been a long time coming. Before you get a big head, just know it's not all about you. Your story is an easy one for demons to latch onto, and it has inspired some to move forward. That's a good thing.*

ZEKE: *Not for me.*

BILBA: *Stop pouting. Let's plan what you can do to keep yourself safe instead, okay? No matter how you feel about it, things here are moving. Demons want change. You knew that years ago after Aries. We heard rumors all the way back then. This is progress. Let me check into some things, then I'll get with Dialphio and see what she has to say. Oh, and I've got some possibly good news.*

ZEKE: *For me?*

BILBA: *Well, for Cancer. Possibly. I stress that. Notice how I underlined the word?*

ZEKE: *What is it? We both could use some.*

BILBA: *Well, Melchiot has had me researching hexes and curses. She gave me a book from a library I'd never even heard of.*

ZEKE: *There's a book you've never heard of?*

BILBA: *Stop interrupting. Yes, I didn't know about the book or that the library even existed. I guess it's an exclusive, only for Major demons. Anyway, the book is called* The Pathway: A Guide to Hexes and Curses, *all about these ancient spells and counter spells, all of which have to do with Hex magic.*

Even if he was only beginning his research, the fact he had a resource was encouraging. The fact his mentor was helping find those resources was even more significant, since the last time we wrote he wasn't sure that she would get involved. Things were looking up, at least for Cancer.

BILBA: *Of course, I need to do a lot more studying, but I've got three pages of notes with questions for her during our next training session.*

ZEKE: *Great. Thanks, bud! By the way, how is training? Has it financially ruined you yet?*

BILBA: *It's getting close.*

ZEKE: *Sorry to hear that.*

BILBA: *Well, it is not like the Council set up a way to fund training for demons, especially underprivileged ones. It is what it is, and it's worth it. Having access to the money we made in the mortal Army would come in handy if I could figure out how to convert it to coin. And, no, before you ask, I don't want to work for them again.*

The thought never crossed my mind. Did Bilba think I was a monster?

BILBA: *And the training is going well. She has me focusing on Constructive spells. Not only new ones, but she's teaching me how to hone my reliable spells for the Passage.*

ZEKE: *Will your snakes really help you in the Passage?*

BILBA: *Funny. My boa constrictors are pretty badass.*

They were, but Bilba was my best friend, so giving each other shit was how incubi showed they cared, a fact as old as our species.

ZEKE: *They're good but easy to evade. So keep working on them, okay? I don't imagine what you'll face in the Passage will be simple, otherwise everyone would be a Major demon.*

BILBA: *True, but you should see how big I can make them now.*

I didn't want to think about what giant boa constrictors looked like, and definitely not what it would be like to fight

178 | PAUL SATING

one or two. I needed sleep, not nightmares. He knew they creeped me out after hundreds of sparring sessions during which he used them to unsettle, torture, tease, and defeat me with those slithering bastards in their smaller form.

ZEKE: *I'm glad to hear all of that, bud. Any idea when you're going to take it?*

BILBA: *No clue. Long road ahead. They don't rush. Timing is important, especially in relation to the other things we've talked about. Getting involved in too many movements against the Council is something I need to balance against receiving their approval to take the Passage.*

I tried to ignore the implication that Bilba might distance himself from groups taking up my cause because of his need to complete his test.

ZEKE: *Good. I don't want you rushed. I want you ready and safe.*

BILBA: *Aw, that's sweet. Who knew you could be a nice guy after all?*

ZEKE: *How are you doing besides that? You haven't said anything about your home life.*

BILBA: *Are you asking about my mother?*

The bluntness of his response was surprising. Had he calloused his heart, or he was completely done with her? I was rooting for the latter.

ZEKE: *Yes. But only because I care.*

BILBA: *I'm focused on other stuff. I have too many things on my mind.*

ZEKE: *Good, I'm happy for you. I can't imagine how hard it is to balance your job, what your dad needs, and training for the Passage at the same time. You're impressive. But I will deny that until the end of days, if you tell anyone. Especially Ralrek.*

BILBA: *Don't worry about me telling Ralrek. I can't remember the last time I saw him.*

ZEKE: *Really? He's gone silent on you?*

BILBA: *We check in from time to time.*

ZEKE: *But you guys are hanging out?*

BILBA: *Not really. It's not like I don't ask. He's always got an excuse, and has been acting weird ever since I got news about the Passage. Well, even before that, actually. I think he misses a few things. You. The Overworld.*

ZEKE: *Mortals?*

I wrote that with more than a little humor in mind, which is hard to translate in the written form.

BILBA: *Maybe, now that he's already single again. Not that I expect any of his relationships to last. The breakup had an effect, even if he won't admit it. I thought he would come around after a little while, but he hasn't. He's drifting, not doing much of anything.*

ZEKE: *What I would give to be home and hang out with you guys again. Maybe he just needs a little Zeke in his life?*

BILBA: *You think that's the answer for everyone. But if Little Zeke were so effective in lifting spirits, you would have had more than one girlfriend.*

ZEKE: *That is more an issue of them being picky than anything to do with Little Zeke.*

I drew a smiley face to convey my humorous intent.

BILBA: *I'm really worried about him, but with everything I have going on, it's difficult to give effort toward someone when they don't want it. Don't get me wrong; I've tried. I'm going to keep trying, but my schedule is packed. Between work, my studies, and reading up on Hex magic, I don't have much time. I wish you were around. You would pull him out of this funk.*

ZEKE: *You give me far too much credit.*

BILBA: *You would. You always knew how to for me. Him too. Ever since you two bonded on that mission for Gemini, he's been different about you. Helping him talk through things really changed him. You're good for him. Me too. So come home, you jerk.*

A few minutes passed. I imagined both of us were doing the same thing. Brains filled with alternate realities where I wasn't sitting on the other side of a rift from my friends, where we could be together to help each other through life's struggles. Entertaining realities where Bilba could take whatever training he needed for his Passage without bankrupting his father and future. Realities where I wouldn't constantly be tangled in political messes and was free to help friends in need.

Probably feeling remorse over dropping a reminder I was not home and never would be again, Bilba finally scratched a new message.

BILBA: *Hey, it's super late and I need to get some sleep. Let's check in again before next week, okay?*

ZEKE: *Sounds good, bud. Let me know if you find anything out about a counter spell. Cancer will want to know.*

BILBA: *I will, Zeke. But don't get yours or her hopes up too high. This stuff is tough, and Melchiot hasn't promised to help me more than she already has. I still need to be careful.*

ZEKE: *Understandable. Just write if you discover something. Don't make me wait.*

I stared at his last line, part of me hoping that wasn't the end. I wasn't in the mood to sleep, regardless of the late hour. In years past, Bilba and I would have sat up long into the night, playing video games, eating lousy snack food, and talking through anything we needed during the distraction of gaming. We probably held Hell's record for most nights staying up until the blue light of the Hellfire broke the world. I missed those times. I missed him.

A deep sigh rolled through my chest. At some point, I was going to have to realize and accept that those times were gone. My life was prescribed loneliness, and I felt every bit of it.

Afterward, I struggled to get to sleep. My mind was abuzz with activity, thoughts, and the forever destiny of loneliness. So I wrote to Dialphio, figuring she would know what to say. I did not expect an answer right away, since it was so late. So I allowed myself the pleasure of ignoring the terrible movie with its cheesy acting and gore, and allowed myself to fall into an unsatisfying sleep.

———

"HEY," A SOFT VOICE SAID FROM SOMEWHERE IN THE MURKINESS of my brain.

I groaned, barely registering the hand on my side, shaking me slightly. I groaned again, mumbling something even my brain couldn't decipher.

"Hey, Zeke, wake up," the voice said, accompanied by the hand, shaking more firmly. "Get up. If you're that tired, go to your bed. I've got to get ready for work. It'll be noisy out here."

Cancer. I cracked my eyes, instantly squeezing them shut against the bright orange of the Overworld sun. "What time is it?"

"Time for you to get up and either start your day or decide that you don't want to play," Cancer laughed, moving into the kitchen and banging every drawer, cup, and utensil as she made coffee.

I rolled over, hit my demonic notebook with my lethargic foot, nearly knocking it off the coffee table. The cover flopped open and the scribbled lines reminded me I had written Dialphio before going into my zombie state on the couch. She'd written back.

DIALPHIO: *Good morning, sunshine. To what do I owe this pleasant surprise?*

Pushing aside my shirt splayed across the corner of the coffee table, I searched for my quill. Not finding it, I picked up the shirt and flapped it like a towel. The quill went flying to the end of the couch by my feet. Grunting, I sat up to retrieve it.

"Good to see you've made the adult decision," Cancer said from the kitchen.

"Stuff it and make me some coffee," I replied with a grin.

"Talk to me like that again and you'll be lucky if I don't pour it over your head when it's done," Cancer replied, wearing a smirk of her own.

Quill in hand, I wrote back to Dialphio.

ZEKE: *Everything is as fine as can be expected. Can't a guy just check in on the people he cares about?*

I had enough time to pick up my shirt, head to the restroom, get dressed, and even pour a cup of very strong coffee before Dialphio responded.

DIALPHIO: *Ezekial Sunstone, if I didn't know better, I would say that you miss us. I've been talking to Ralrek and Bilba, and they both say they talk to you more often. Apparently, you're writing more? Missing home?*

That was a given. No way can someone spend six thousand years in a place and less than a handful in another and not miss the former. The Overworld was not home, and likely would not feel like my home for decades to come. If I lasted that long. Admitting I was homesick was a completely different challenge, though.

I didn't want to talk about any of the crap that had unsettled me. I wanted to connect with my nosy ex-boss and feel normal again, by force, if necessary.

ZEKE: *How are things at The Book Abyss?*

DIALPHIO: *Still ridiculously busy. I don't know what's going on, but with the uncertainty and consequences of the mortal war, with so many of our young demons being drafted, business has yet to slow. It's the craziest thing. I've had to hire another employee. Two. I now have two employees. Can you believe that? I don't even have space. They have to share a desk, your old one.*

Dialphio had hired two employees to replace me. Something about that didn't sit right. I don't know what I expected, but knowing that she had taken the official step of bringing in new demons stung. Silly, I know. Sue me.

DIALPHIO: *You're quiet. Is everything okay?*

ZEKE: *Just thinking.*

DIALPHIO: *About?*

ZEKE: *It's ridiculous.*

Embarrassing was more like it.

DIALPHIO: *How do you know it's ridiculous if you won't tell me? What's on your mind?*

I should have just told her everything was fine. Why didn't these things have erasers? Dialphio was going to draw it out one way or another. When she suspected something was amiss or that she was not fully informed, her determination went into overdrive. Getting away with anything that wasn't the absolute, and often-times uncomfortable, truth wasn't something one accomplished often when it came to this wonderful, caring succubus.

ZEKE: *I'll work it out, seriously. I'm just being ridiculous.*

DIALPHIO: *What's going on?*

On the other side of the rift, Dialphio was probably sitting at her desk, her emerald eyes burning with fierce stubbornness to get an answer out of me. I took a deep breath and acted like an adult.

ZEKE: *Everything is piling up. I know it's impish, but talking about the store, how well it's doing, and that I'm officially replaced... it just stings. Bilba is doing so much. Ralrek is in trouble and I can't help, and then you tell me this. It feels like a friend helping you get back up after getting your ass kicked and then accidentally elbowing you in the face.*

DIALPHIO: *Oh, I know this isn't easy. You know I had to hire them, right?*

ZEKE: *Of course. That's why I said it was ridiculous and didn't want to bring it up. I know it's stupid.*

DIALPHIO: *No, it's normal. Think about it. One reason Abandonment is so tough for us is not only the physical consequences of losing immortality. The emotional and mental aspects must be just as excruciating. In fact, they might be the aspects of Abandonment that lead demons to a quicker decay, at least from what I've researched on the topic. I don't imagine it's easy to watch life move on for the rest of us, and I wouldn't be surprised if it feels like you're on the outside watching life happen for everyone else while your's stagnates.*

ZEKE: *Not only stagnates, but gets worse.*

DIALPHIO: *And you feel like you're facing it alone?*

ZEKE: *Yeah, a lot. There aren't many I talk to here, and even less I can trust. Cancer works all the time. She's never around. So I'm in my head too much. Which means I'll think about your employees and pout. I get why you had to hire them. I just —*

The sentence dangled, transferred by the nature of the demonic notebook to the other side of the rift where my ex-boss was likely sitting in the back corner of the bookstore at her desk. The now-sacred place where we used to have dozens of open-hearted conversations every week. My heart ached to be sitting at my old desk parallel to hers and having this conversation face-to-face.

DIALPHIO: *You're homesick. That's natural. It's going to take time before you feel better about being there.*

ZEKE: *I don't know if I have time.*

DIALPHIO: *Take what you need. Find out how to be okay with this or it will put a strain on you that will drag you down. No one wants that. Not me, your parents, or your friends. We worry about you. We think about you all the time. You're always in our hearts, and that's something no one, not even Lucifer Himself, can take away. That place is yours forever.*

Forever.

The word used to always have much different connotations when I had forever. Forever was what I saw when I looked at the Founders, someone like Azazel, who likely witnessed every significant event in Hell's history. Forever was what I thought about when I sat alone on quiet evenings, watching the Hellfire fade, bringing serenity to troubling thoughts over my future.

Forever wasn't something I thought about regarding the

Overworld. Mortals were so temporary, flitting in and out of existence so instantaneously as to make me wonder how they lived fulfilling lives.

Now, with Bilba busy, Ralrek distracted, my father ignoring me, my mother distant, my ex-boss moving on, and me with limited time, the term held a new meaning. Forever was my future. Here, virtually alone in the Overworld, without a hope of returning home.

14

OLYMPIA

Now I think I understand what Olympia natives mean when they talk about the rainy season. As September faded, the gray took a stronger grip of each waking day. When I complained to one of my coworkers at The Book Worm, he laughed. Jerry laughed about a lot of things. He seemed to be jovial by default. But he took great pleasure in my weather cycle melancholy.

"You better pace yourself," he warned. "Complaining about the rain already is pointless. Give it another four months and then you can start. But don't worry, by then the rain will have jaded you too much to complain about it."

"Four months?" I asked, holding a stack of books I was about to stock and staring at him dumbly. "You can't be serious?"

He nodded. "Oh, I am. Completely. October is just the start. We'll have a few more days of absolutely gorgeous weather, but it won't be long before the rain rolls in. And once it does, it's going to stay until late in the spring."

"Like March?" I said, as if I could bribe Jerry into changing weather patterns.

He laughed, walking away and leaving my question

dangling like a blazebull's tail, leaving me as listless as those domesticated Underworld farm animals. From the region of an endcap dedicated entirely to the hottest epic fantasy series, he said, "Try May, maybe even early June. You're going to have fun with this, Ezekial. All gray and gloomy for months on end. Sort of like the way you act."

My mouth dropped open to make a smartass response, but Jerry was walking toward a waiting customer. Defeated, I clamped my mouth shut and let him take the small win.

"Doesn't matter, my shift is almost over anyway," I told the books in my arms.

The rest of the afternoon passed as uneventfully as most do when you work in a small bookstore in an unremarkable neighborhood on the outskirts of a small city's downtown district. All fine by me, because today was about going through the motions. Again.

Jerry was right. His comment wasn't about winning a verbal sparring match. My general disposition lately was as entertaining as watching brimstone paint dry.

I was in a funk. The problem was, like a lot of funks, I couldn't see through it to find my way out of it. Plus, I didn't have the energy even though I wanted to. The hammer blow from Dialphio's last message had set my course, and I went along for the ride.

I just didn't know how to stop. From one thing to another, Hell would not leave me alone, but neither did it allow me reentry. It was like a relationship where only one member got what they needed. Call me the unfulfilled partner.

With my elbow, I pushed aside the curtains separating the store from the employee–only area, I glimpsed something in my periphery, down the last aisle which was dedicated to military history just before I slipped into the land where no customers were allowed to roam.

The number of books we had on the topic was obnoxious, considering I rarely saw anyone venture down the aisle. In all my time working in the store, I couldn't remember selling a single copy of any of this particular stock. No one in Olympia seemed interested which was why the shadowy figure stood out. Any customer presence in this aisle was an anomaly.

I glanced around. The figure, draped in a green rain jacket, dashed sideways, disappearing behind the end cap.

Shy customer or not, my shift was over. Jerry and his sunny disposition were on duty. He could handle them.

"Are you headed out?" Harry Nugel, my boss, asked.

"Yeah," I said, lifting my rain jacket from the row hanging on the back wall. "I have a hot date tonight."

I didn't. Cancer was headed to the store so I wouldn't have to walk home in the incessant drizzle that threatened to become a maelstrom. I didn't want to keep her waiting, and I also didn't want to keep this conversation going. If there's one thing I hold dear to my heart, it is my belief no one should hang around their place of work when they're not being paid. Well, except for Dialphio's store, but that place and its owner are exceptions to all occupational laws and standards. Life is full of experiences beyond contributing free labor to the capitalist machine.

At the front of the bookstore, I noticed the customer in the green rain jacket lingering by a display. I could stop and help, and that might have been the right thing to do. But Cancer could already be idling outside, dinner needed to be made, and I had recorded a version of *A Christmas Carol* that featured puppets as actors, and I was not missing out on that experiment.

Outside, the drizzle had turned to a light spray. The air had a chill. The store's overhang shielded me from the former, for the most part. Nothing in Washington was safe from its rains.

This part of downtown was eerily still. The gray day discouraged most shoppers, except for the hearty. Occasionally, a straggler crossed the intersection into view. A couple walked into the jewelry store catercorner to the bookstore. A mother and her three children bounced to the door of a toy store just down the sidewalk. as if today was the most glorious day in history. The bookstore even received another visitor while I waited. Green rain jacket left, their hands empty. Just another browser.

Smug in my evaluation, I covertly watched. You might call it creepy, but I call it passing the time until Cancer pulled up.

Green jacket customer didn't dally until stopping at the end of the block. They whipped around, looking back toward the store. I played off being caught by pretending I was looking up and down the street. They stayed at the corner even when the crosswalk signal turned to white. They just stood there in the building rain.

A minute later, another person, this one wearing a camouflaged Gore-Tex jacket, joined them. The pair conversed at the corner. On a chilly, pissing-mist kind of day.

Unease gnawed at my stomach. Hardy Pacific Northwest people or not, no one hung outside on days like today. Huddled together and virtually squared on to each other, they were seemingly uninterested in moving. Waiting. For what? I didn't know, but I didn't like it.

I closed my eyes and concentrated, tapping into my sensing. Reaching the two cloaked figures, it washed over them without registering emissions. I cut off my senses, feeling better but still troubled.

"Stop being paranoid," I chastised myself, seeing Cancer's Mustang idling third in line at the stoplight.

I stayed underneath the overhang until she pulled in front of the store. I raced through the rain, getting a face full of Pacific Ocean spray, and jumped into the car, already dripping onto her seat.

"Bless it, it's nasty," I commented, leaning forward to drip on her floor mat instead of the seat.

"That's why I'm so late," she said, pulling onto the street. I noted that her red wool jacket had darkened thirty shades. "No one knows how to drive in this stuff. Weird, considering where we are. The other nurses at the hospital say it rains here all the time."

"So does Jerry," I commented.

"Who?"

"Book store," I said with a jerk of my head back at the building.

"Weird then, right?"

"Pretty much everything and everyone is weird here," I said, as Cancer rounded the corner. The pair of creepy people at the corner glanced our way, still being creepy. Both wore their jackets cinched tightly around their faces, preventing me from getting anything more than a cursory look. Both were white men, probably in their thirties. Nothing unique to either.

Still, I watched them, twisting to look over the headrest as we continued down the street.

"See something interesting? It's too cold and everyone is bundled up. You can't tell men from women, Zeke." Cancer laughed. "Please tell me you're not checking someone out? Please?"

I lost sight of the pair when a white van moved into the lane behind us from a side street. Facing forward again, I said, "You make it sound like that's all I do."

"It is," she laughed. "So, any big plans for the rest of your night?"

"Not really," I admitted. "I might work on my forms. Creed has been needing some attention lately. But I don't have much planned besides cooking."

"You should come down to the Lion's Den later," Cancer said. "I'm working tonight. We can hang out."

I shot her a mock look of surprise. "You must really be bored. Or you think I'm a real loser."

Cancer shook her head. Droplets of rain sprayed my

cheek. "Not at all. I just don't want you sitting in the apartment if you'd rather get out." She squinted, checking her rearview mirror and adjusting it. "What a jerk."

"Who?"

She jerked her head at the mirror. "The guy behind me. He has his high beams on. I know it's raining, but it's not that bad, and it's not dark yet."

I turned. The white van was closer now, blaring high beams, and making me squint. "He probably doesn't realize it. It is gloomy, but still light out, so maybe he can't tell. One thing I've learned about humans is they don't know how to drive. None of them. Cancer fit in. Love her to eternity and back, but my heart typically got its best workouts when I was her passenger. "Can you imagine these people driving a chimera carriage?"

"Maybe," she agreed, then waved her hand like she was encouraging a gnat to move on with its life. "Anyway, come down if you want. Seriously. I'll talk to Leo and see if he can get you into a class."

That sounded attractive, just on any other night than tonight. "I appreciate it. Let me know what he says. But I don't think I'll head back into this mess once I'm inside."

"You can have the car," Cancer said. "Just drop me off at the hospital."

"And how would you get to the Lion's Den?" I asked, giving her my best smartass look. "I'd love to see what you look like after that walk. Would your hair be so... springy after a few blocks in the rain?"

"You don't want to see what it would look like," Cancer laughed. "You could pick me up from the hospital, dummy, and drive me. Then you could come in for a lesson."

Cancer's face lightened, and not from excitement or joy of the thought of me picking her up and going to the gym together. Light danced from the rear-view mirror on to Cancer's cheeks. Headlights. I turned to see the white van close in enough to read a license plate, if it had one. It didn't.

"What is that jerk's problem?" I said more than asked. "Did you cut them off on your way to pick me up?"

Cancer's eyes alternated between the road in front of her and the mirror. "No… I don't think so."

"Are you sure? I've seen you drive. I know what you're capable of."

"Not all women are bad drivers, Zeke," Cancer replied.

"No, they're not. But you are."

An engine's roar interrupted any response. The white van revved and closed the final few feet to the back of the Mustang.

"What the—" Cancer's alarmed question was cut off in the middle as the van rammed us. She cried out.

I was jolted forward, the seatbelt locking and ensnaring my chest. "Sonofabitch!"

The car swerved, the tires clipping the sidewalk before rebounding into the middle lane.

"Turn there," I said, pointing at the approaching street. It led toward the downtown marina, away from buildings and traffic. We could pull over and check the damage before calling the police.

"Here?" Cancer asked, her voice shaking.

"Yes," I said too harshly. On edge, I checked behind us, horrified to see the van closing the distance once more. The revving engine signaled the driver's intent. "Now. Turn."

She did, and the momentum pushed me against the passenger door. I held onto the headrest, pulling myself forward, shocked to see the van slam on his brakes, fishtailing into the lane, and following us down the road toward the marina. A block later it was on us again.

"Hold on!" I warned just before the van struck, this time harder.

Cancer yelled. I yelled. The Mustang spun sideways. The

van advanced, striking near the rear tire. We spun faster; I held onto whatever I could to maintain my equilibrium. Everything blurred, but I heard a *thud* at some point during the spin, registering only seconds later that Cancer's head had connected with the driver-side window and ricocheted back in my direction. In the chaos of the out-of-control car, I couldn't make out the extent of her injury. All I could do was hold on until this ride was over.

The white van rocketed past us as we spun out into a wide gravel lot. The Mustang jerked to a halt, sending Cancer's limp head slamming into the driver's side window again before swaying back and forth. Out cold. I unbuckled my seatbelt and reached over, stopping before I touched her, remembering Cancer talking about head injuries and keeping them immobile.

"Cancer? Cancer?"

My fingers went to her carotid artery. Her pulse was strong.

I straightened my leg to allow myself enough room to pull my cell phone out of my pocket as I checked on the location of the van. After the last assault, its momentum carried it past us, toward the marina's gate. Already, the driver had circled and was racing in our direction. Any conversations with the dispatcher needed to wait.

I punched in 911 and let it ring, setting the phone on the dashboard in front of Cancer.

The van's engine roared again as it surged forward. Did the driver intend on slamming into us? This was crazy. Their intent was dark, beyond question, motivated by an aunt-nephew combo, I was sure. Hazarding a guess Cancer was not the intended target, I deduced the driver didn't care if she went out with me or not, as long as I went out.

Jumping out of the Mustang into the pouring rain, I stripped off my jacket and pulled Creed from the loop at my waist.

194 | PAUL SATING

Discretion be blessed, I was not willing to risk Cancer's safety for the attention using the halberd might bring.

As the white van bore down, its high beams spotlighting its intended target, I gave the truncheon a shake and birthed Creed to life.

The double-ax heads sprang out as Creed stretched into its full six feet. Anger surged through me, making it difficult to breathe as my pulse raced.

At the speed the van was moving, with Cancer's car sitting sideways in the gravel, any strike would kill her.

I shook with the fire of Hell and one pissed off ex–demon. Seconds lay between that van and Cancer's end unless I did something. Painful rage seared my brain. What? What could I do to stop thousands of pounds of speeding metal?

And in that moment Creed answered. The double-ax heads and foot-long dagger, previously nothing but cold steel, burst to life with flames of blue. The power of the Hellfire raged at the ends of my halberd, its intense heat not affecting me.

Fifty yards away, the van's engine pitched down. Driver, passenger, and side doors opened when the van was no more than thirty yards away. A coordinated move. Bodies tucked, rolled, and tumbled from the van as it bore down on the Mustang.

My fist clenched Creed's haft as the van closed to twenty, fifteen, ten yards. I lunged into the space between it and the car, holding Creed in front of me and slamming the dagger into the gravel. It bit deeply, throwing rocks in every direction. The blue Hellfire thundered in my ears.

I screamed as the headlights blinded me from five yards. Creed heated, the only sensation I had of the power of the Hellfire. It boomed, it fed, and it burst forward in a light that dominated the vehicle's headlights.

A blue wall rushed to meet the vehicle only an arm's length

away. Behind the flame of the Hellfire, I squinted, forcing my eyes to remain open to witness Creed's vengeance. The wall of blue rocketed into the van, collapsing the front. Glass splintered, sending thousands of shards in every direction as the van folded in on itself from the momentum pushing it forward and the power of my halberd pushing it backward. Metal crunched, rubber tires exploded. A cacophony of violence.

And then it was over. The blue of Creed's Hellfire faded as quickly as it sprang to life, now nothing more than modest flames licking at the axes and dagger. The white van was a flattened collection of metal, plastic, and shredded rubber. Glass glistened for yards in every direction.

But the fight wasn't over. Eight figures stood behind the wreckage, all on their feet and closing on me.

"I hope you didn't wear yourself out, buddy," I whispered to my halberd as the group neared.

Creed's haft vibrated.

Witnessing me flattening their van into a big Frisbee should have been enough to reconsider their next move. But the eight clones in black seemed determined to be introduced to Creed.

"Stay back!" I shouted as the group spread in a circle, three of them moving so wide they were looping around Cancer's idling car. I noticed Cancer's head slowly roll toward the other side. She was coming to. I needed to get her help. "Who are you? What you want?"

"Just you," a thick brute said from the middle of the pack. He was six feet tall and his orange hair was shaved down to stubble.

Swaying back and forth on the balls of my feet, I shifted Creed from hand-to-hand, constantly turning right and left to keep all eight in check. As they fanned out more, that became steadily more difficult. Clinking of a chain made me spin. The one woman in the group, with a bulbous nose and large, oval eyes, dangled a chain from her gloved fist. I really hoped she wasn't planning on using it.

"What do you want?" I said, trying to delay the inevitable ass-kicking. I couldn't close my eyes to sense them because of the risk. So I tried with my eyes open, which weakened my ability. As my senses extended, I picked up on someone emitting. Turning to check the distance between fighters, I noted the tall man with a trimmed goatee. His hazel skin accentuated the rippling muscle in his forearms poking out from his rolled up sleeves. This was the man from the human wall outside the garage. The same who had been part of the group pursuit through Olympia.

Here he was again, hanging a few steps behind the rest. Even though he was dressed like the others, I knew the shape this ex-demon was in. Alone, he would be a handful. With seven peers, the chances I could walk away from the fight were slim. But I saw something in the way he hung back that made me wonder. If there was a way to escape, the key might lie with him. His brown eyes held mine, but I didn't see hatred in his gaze. Intensity resided there instead.

Neither Chax nor Leo were part of the eight, but that didn't mean they weren't involved in this calculated attack. Were they the two hiding behind rain jacket hoods outside the bookstore? I really should have helped that aimless customer. If Chax was in the Overworld, if he was Leo's mysterious friend, I would have had him in my grasp. Bless it. What other reason did this group have to commit a felony if they weren't involved with Hell's twat? If I survived the next few minutes, I was going to get answers.

"Can we get this over with?" growled a gruff man with a limp, grimy ponytail.

"Got somewhere to be? Because I know your sorry ass doesn't have a woman waiting," the oval-eyed, chain-wielding woman berated, drawing laughter from the group at ponytail's expense.

"How about you leave us alone? I won't even ask why you have a problem. Just get out of here. She's injured," I said with a tilt of my head back toward the Mustang, "and I need to get her to the emergency room. The longer we stand here and talk, the more pissed I'm going to get."

The thick brute shook his orange-stubbled head and pulled a hammer from his hoodie pocket. "Ain't going to happen. We were sent for you and we plan on doing our job. Why don't you drop your stick and come along quietly? That way, you don't have to get hurt."

Holding Creed in one fist, I jammed it in the thick brute's direction. He jumped back. I smiled menacingly. "Too late. You already hurt my friend, and that pisses me off. You don't want me more pissed off, trust me. Did you see what this little stick did to your van? Imagine what it's going to do to your mushy body. I'm not sure how you plan on taking me anywhere since you're going to have to hoof it, but I imagine the police will help you with those details after I beat in your asses."

I didn't think the comment was funny, but it drew a round of raucous laughter from the gang. Theirs was the type of forced hilarity called for by social pressure and arrogance. The dangerous ex-demon did not join them.

The woman, dangling the chain in her fist, raised it. "I can't wait to wrap this around your throat." The way her jaw clenched and unclenched with tension told me she had every intention on making the promise come true.

"I don't know who you people are," I said, trying to keep my voice even as adrenaline surged through me, fed by the warmth of Creed. "What did I do that offended you so much to stalk me and nearly kill my friend?" I swiveled. Each person crept closer without providing an answer. "Well?" I shouted when I got none.

"You're not one of us," a black man with a bad underbite said.

"I'm well aware of that and glad not to be," I replied. "Though, that still doesn't explain why you've got a problem."

The only response was the scuffing of boots over the gravel. None of the group glanced at Cancer. Good. I wanted their undivided attention. If she drew their attention, one of them might get the brilliant idea to go after her, as a hostage to convince me to acquiesce.

Spinning and lowering Creed to mid-guard, I shouted, "Tell me what the fuck you want. Why are you harassing me?"

"Because you're a demon," the intense man with hazel skin said evenly. It was the first time he'd talked. His voice was fluid, smooth and rich, the type you would hear from an R & B singer, not a hoodlum bent on violence.

My mouth dropped open in surprise. I knew he was an ex-demon, but I thought I was the only one who could pick up on signatures. Cancer couldn't. Never in any of our conversations did Bilba or Ralrek say they could sense a demonic presence. Aries was the only demon I knew who ever acted like he could sense, and I couldn't be sure that wasn't driven by paranoia. Even if this ex-demon could, I expected some discretion. The demon bro code demanded we did not blabber in front of mortals.

Him knowing my nature confirmed my worst fears. Leo or Chax, or both, were involved with this group.

He flicked his hand at Creed as if he read my mind. "We saw you a few weeks back using that in a fight in Sylvester Park. You took out a whole gang."

Instinctively, I pulled Creed closer to my stomach as eight sets of eyes fell on it. The ex-demon's smooth voice didn't sound hostile or even antagonistic. He talked about Creed as if he was making a book report in the school science class.

I tried to laugh off the connection between the halberd and

me. The sound came out broken and staggered. "This doesn't make me a demon, my friend."

"Only one weapon like that," the thick brute said from behind me. I turned to face him, verifying that each member had taken a few more steps closer. I sensed again. He wasn't emitting.

"So?"

"So," the woman said, "we know that weapon belonged to a demon. We were also told to follow you because you were that demon. Pulling it out just proved us right, moron."

After minutes of threatening me with her dangling chain and verbal vitriol, I was okay punching a woman in the face for the first time in my life.

The group tightened their circle around me. They knew my background. Whether that bit of intelligence came from the ex-demon with the smooth voice, Leo or Chax, it didn't matter. Something bigger was happening, but no one informed me. Uncovering what that was, though, needed to wait until I escaped this mess. Now, to figure out how to do exactly that.

The thick brute jerked his hammer-holding arm at me. Three men sprang toward me. I adjusted my grip on Creed as they converged, noting the other gang members moving more deliberately, but still approaching. The three springers were my priority; the others needed to wait their turn.

As the staggered assault began, I dropped to one knee, holding Creed at an angle facing the closest man. He skidded to a halt, staring at the double-axes. He wasn't my intended target, just a distraction. Having halted him, I used the momentum of the other two against them. Without standing, I leveled Creed and swung in a counterclockwise spin. There wasn't that much space. The margin for error was slim. Creed's haft swept the legs out from both men at once, sending them crashing to the gravel.

Jumping to my feet, I rotated Creed over my head in

snappy rotations as I lunged toward the third man. Bringing Creed down, I struck him across his shoulders. His head lolled as he went unconscious, long before he fell to the gravel.

"Get him!" the thick brute shouted. Four, including himself, moved. The only one who delayed was the ex-demon. I had assumed the brute was the leader, but it made more sense the ex-demon was the snake whose head needed chopping to put an end to the fight.

Brute moved forward, but with smaller steps, clenching his gloved fist, rubbing the hammer's handle.

I tried to keep track of all four different approaches, but he was the biggest threat. At least, that's what I thought right up until my lower back burned. Glancing down, metal links wrapped around my waist. The chain queen had made true on her promise. I spun, trying to pull her off-balance to untether myself. But she was stocky, and I wasn't. With the weight advantage, she barely budged, grinning as she dug her feet into the loose gravel.

With a chain cinching me and her holding on for every pound she was worth, my mobility was negated. The thick brute was on me and swung his hammer. I deflected the blow with Creed, and leaned back, leading with my elbow, which I promptly smashed into the face of another attacker. His head jerked with a crunch and blood spurted from his nose as he yelled, falling to the ground with both hands to his face.

The two fighters I had knocked off their feet were back upright, more tentative now. But as they saw the other members of their group ganging up on me, they rejoined.

I still had six against me, five if you didn't count the intense ex-demon who didn't seem interested in getting involved with another of his kind, making him the smartest of the bunch.

My face was rocked when a fist caught one cheekbone. My vision blurred with tears and my cheek burned, accompanied with a tightening of the chain around my waist. A man joined the woman holding me. They yanked in unison, over and over, repeatedly throwing me off-balance. Fighting was hard enough. Fighting multiple adversaries was nigh on impossible. Doing it without being able to find my center of balance put me in a desperately defensive position.

I yanked against their pull. They resisted. I was knocked to the gravel when one man struck me across the shoulders with the stanchion from a stop sign. I don't know when or where he got it, or even how he pulled it free from the ground, but none of that mattered. The only thing that did was that he had it and used it to impressive effect. A warm sensation trailed down my back. The strike had opened skin.

My blurry vision caused by the multiple sources of pain only slightly diminished the effect of four figures hovering over me.

"Punk ass," the thick brute said one moment, and the next, his booted foot was racing to meet my face.

My bottom teeth clicked against the top when his foot connected, snapping my head back. I flopped onto my back, my mouth filling with the iron taste of blood as the gravel pressed against me. At least this group were equal opportunity leeches, making me bleed from both sides of my body.

I pried my eyes open, seeing the bottom of his boot hovering over my head. Before I had time to move, the hard rubber soul descended. In the grooves I saw a dozen smaller pebbles. My dazed mind had enough time to think about how badly those were going to cut my face before he stomped me.

The boot drove my head into the gravel. Rock bit into my face. A blackout approached.

My arm was jerked above my head.

"Don't!" I heard that rich voice say somewhere in the fog.

I tilted my head, which felt like it weighed forty pounds, in the voice's direction just as the goateed ex-demon dropped to the gravel. In a prone position, his eyes widened.

Convenient for him to now have moral objections as my vision tunneled. The jerking on my arm stopped, and it took a second to understand the ex-demon's warning. He wasn't opposed to what the group was doing; he wanted to stop what was about to happen. Because he understood the consequences.

I chuckled as one of the group reached for Creed. Allowing him access to the halberd was the easiest decision eternity ever served an ex-demon like me. Forcing him to have to jerk it free would have made him more aggressive. Best to let him follow the path to his own downfall. I opened my palm.

Hellfire burned in Creed's haft as the foreign hand wrapped around it. I couldn't see the blue ball forming, but I didn't need to. The heat in the haft radiated through my own arm.

"Tick-Tock," I said through a scratchy throat.

"What?" the thick brute said in confusion.

He got his answer.

According to Aries—who was ambiguous—and validated by Dialphio's research, the halberd was mine by right. No one else, not even Lucifer, could touch it. Even a finger on the haft would give someone an inauspicious start to their day. Under normal circumstances, I would ensure that didn't happen. This was me getting my ass beat to a pulp so I could be dragged off to some hole where Leo, Chax, and probably Seraph were waiting. Maybe even killed. Creed was about to become the great equalizer.

I grinned, tasting my own blood, as Creed defended itself.

The radiating Hellfire circle grew into and beyond my periphery. The heat had only slowly moved up my arm as Creed's repulsion initiated. Now that it was fully engaged, my entire body warmed in the glow milliseconds before Creed rejected the man's touch. The *whoomp* that followed the expansive light rocketed through the world. A sound wave of destruction simultaneously hitting the standing gang like a diesel truck—like a racing white van, driven by a madman. Their screams filled the gravel yard.

And the attacks stopped.

My chuckle turned to a cackle until I passed out.

———

"Zeke?" A soft voice interrupted my beautiful rest.

My head lolled side to side. Someone was shaking me.

"Zeke? You've got a get up. Zeke? Come on."

Cancer. Cancer was calling to me. And she was desperate.

Behind the thick blanket over my brain, I came to, realizing she was alive and semi-well at the same moment I understood where I was. Gravel bit into my back. My lips were sealed together with dried blood, the iron tang filling my mouth. Dust irritated my nose. Everything hurt.

I cracked my eyes. Worry painted Cancer's expression, her mouth turned down, as she hovered over me. Dark worry lines interrupted her usually smooth skin. Then she smiled, her round cheeks glowing. "There you are," she said, trying to sound confident and failing.

I extended my arm. "You're not getting rid of me that easily. Help me."

She grabbed my hand and tugged gently. "Slow. Sit up slow. Give yourself time to adjust."

The world spun as soon as I was in a seated position. Even pressing a hand to my head didn't lessen the sensation.

"What happened?" she asked. "I don't remember a thing after the van hit us. By the way... what in the heavens did you do?"

Instead of answering, I jerked around in panic. The world swam, the ground tilted toward the sky. I gripped the ground like my life depended on it to brace myself. As it was, Cancer saved me by the shoulders.

"What did I tell you?" she said, sounding very much like a mother. "Take it easy."

"Need to find Creed," I said in a croak.

"It's right there," she said, pointing from over my shoulder to a spot in the gravel a few feet away.

Sixty feet around the halberd, the gravel was stripped to the dirt. Creed lay, collapsed. Bodies, all dressed identically, lay prone further beyond.

I held out my hand. "Creed."

The halberd stood upright on one end, wobbled slightly, then lifted off the ground and flew to meet my open palm. Creed was cold. The spinning world slowed.

I got to my feet. "We've got to get out of here."

"I need to check on them first," Cancer said. "I don't know what you did, but they look worse for having met you."

"Good."

Cancer scurried from person to person. I did a quick count, noting the victims. The ex-demon who identified me as one of his kind and the chain-wielder weren't among the group. Surprise was not the name of the game. The ex-demon must have recognized the threat Creed was and promptly protected himself. This problem was going to have to wait. I could barely stand on my own feet.

"Are they okay?" I asked Cancer.

She moved to the fourth victim and stopped. Tucking a poof of hair behind her ear, she fell to her knees. "This one needs help," she said sharply, the type of intensity reminiscent of watching her save limbs and life in her Baghdad clinic.

I inched closer. "What's going—"

I didn't need to finish my question. The pony-tailed man was in serious trouble.

When Creed acted in self-defense, it had done what it always does with its shock wave. Previously, I had seen it direct its power on a single individual who was threatening to touch it. I'd never seen Creed send a full circle attack. Of course, I had also never seen it crumple a van, making it look almost like a flattened Origami. This time, I wasn't sure if what Creed had done was the full extent of its power, but it was devastating just the same. If this man had been the one to touch Creed, he had blessed himself. If he wasn't, then his friend royally screwed him over.

He lay in a heap of a collapsed wooden fence, rotted from years of Pacific Northwest rain. A broken fence wasn't the problem. Instead, his neat, monochromatic black outfit had one accessory he probably hadn't decided to wear when leaving the house on his murderous mission. A pole jutted from the man's lower abdomen. Shredded skin and a few clumps of meat stuck to the end, and blood streaked the two feet of metal exposed on the wrong side of his stomach. His eyes flitted like a fairy's wings.

Cancer looked up. "I have blankets and my medical bag in the trunk. Go grab them and bring them here. Then call 911."

"If we call an ambulance—"

"Do it, Zeke!"

Shambling to the car took longer than I expected. Hours would pass, maybe even a full day this time, before I felt like myself again. By the time I made it back to Cancer with the blankets and medical kit, she was performing CPR.

I kneeled on her patient's opposite side. "Anything I can do?"

Cancer shook her head, her curly hair wetted by the rain slapping against her cheeks that were a mixture of rain and tears. "I can't... I can't help him, Zeke. If I had my Ability..."

"Don't do that to yourself." I said, feeling useless as I watched her struggle to save the man's life.

She slipped a rescue mask on him and worked feverishly for another five excruciating minutes, but it was fruitless. As she focused on her patient, I slipped my fingers to his wrist to feel for a pulse. Absent. She had lost him minutes ago yet continued on, refusing to give up. She pumped his chest, squeezed air into the rescue mask, and restarted the process over and over.

"Stop, Cancer. He's gone." I placed a hand on her shoulder. "Let it go."

Her head dipped, Cancer sniffled. Her shoulders shook as she cried. "I can't... I couldn't... I'm so weak, Zeke." Her cries turned into a full sob as she placed her hands on her knees, her shoulders jerking.

"Let me get you home," I said, standing and offering my hand as I glanced at her Mustang, still idling this entire time. "Your car looks drivable. Let's see if it can at least get us back to the apartment. We'll figure out what to do then," I added sternness to my tone when she didn't budge. "We've got to get out of here. I don't want to have to explain this to authorities."

Still sniffling, Cancer's smooth hand found mine, and she allowed me to pull her to her feet. Rushing her to the car, I slid into the driver's seat while she cried toward the passenger window. I was grateful for the lack of scrutiny from her because it gave me a chance to reflect on how thin her hand was.

Troubled, we made it home in one relative piece.

THE SEAL OF LUCIFER BURNED BLUE WITH THE HELLFIRE ON MY demonic notebook as I stepped out of the shower, toweling my hair dry. I flipped open the cover to see my mother's message.

LILITH: *Hello, Ezekial.*

Standing in my bedroom, a towel wrapped around my waist and one draped over my shoulder, I place my hands against the dresser and read her note.

LILITH: *I hope everything is going well. We're fine here. I've been missing you. I know I haven't been the best mother since every-*

thing happened. I should write more, and I'm sorry that I let our busy lives get in the way. You're handling this so well. I miss you terribly. Do you have a girlfriend yet? I saw Dialphio the other day. Her store looks to be doing well. It was busy. She has a young succubus working for her. Very cute. When you come home, you will need to meet her. I think you might like her. Everything is well here. The house is being converted. Can you believe that? Your father finally found a contractor who can do it for a reasonable price, I guess. Whatever he said, it worked. They're framing now. Finally, we won't be the only house on the block still in its original form. That will be so nice. I can't wait for you to see it. I miss you, son, and I'm very proud of you, and I just wanted you to know that. I hope all is well. Please write. I love you, Mom.

I closed the notebook, my head falling. Everything was stiff and sore.

Cancer was in her shower, but her stifled crying still drifted through the closed door. Normally a letter helped me feel connected and valued. But I couldn't help my friend and didn't feel worthy of anything if I couldn't help someone like Cancer.

I was so done with today. The last thing I needed was a letter from home telling me how great everything was.

Nothing was great. Nothing may ever be again.

15

OLYMPIA

No ONE in Hell ever talked about it, and I don't remember anyone in the Overworld mentioning it either, but I had no idea that mortals had so many versions of the same movie. Underworld movies aren't nearly what mortals are able to create with their Technology Abilities, so demons like Ralrek, often value the mortal creations far more than their own. That, I appreciated. What I did not appreciate was the same story told over and over in newer versions, just with new actors and better special-effects. There was something to be said for content in its original form. Raw, real. True to the source. This newer stuff was as an insult to the beauty of original creation.

The day after the gravel yard scuffle where Creed showed me a new level of power and vengeance, I sat, senses dulled, in my living room. Alone again. Cancer was at the hospital and I was filling my day with another remake of *A Christmas Carol*. Dwelling.

The fight for my life. The death of a mortal. The fact they knew I was a demon and were sent to abduct me. Beating the pulp out of me and committing vehicular assault against Cancer was just done for bonus points. It was all too much, weighing on my mind and sucking me out of the world. Cancer had left for work without saying a word, ignoring my pleas to share her thoughts about the previous day. The way she departed didn't make me feel any more at ease.

Today was fully on course for being another shitty day.

And it got a lot shittier when I heard the sizzle of a rift opening in my kitchen. Out of instinct, I yelled, "Creed!"

From the bedroom, the connection was intense, almost as if the stick sensed my panic. The halberd flew down the hall-way. The way it whipped through the confined space sounded like a small vacuum cleaner—though I am positive the weapon would not appreciate being compared to a common household appliance. Even before the rift formed, the halberd was in my hand and activated. Cold steel awaited anyone who stepped through that tear between the Over and Underworlds. This time though, the blades weren't burning the blue of the Hellfire.

"Don't leave me hanging," I warned the weapon, wondering why it was selective in who it engaged for and who it treated to its lame metal state. Someone coming through a rift from the Underworld would have been an excellent time for an encore appearance by the Hellfire magic. The petrified cherry haft didn't respond.

I crept around the coffee table, lowering the double-axes. The shimmering image of a room somewhere in the Under-world greeted me. The details were blurred beyond the film separating the realms, obscuring the exact location. Regard-less, I was ready. Seraph wasn't going to like how this conver-sation went. I rolled my shoulders to ease the tightness from yesterday's fight. The multitude of cuts had scabbed over—scabs were already falling off—and the blemishes and bruises on my face were fading but still noticeable. Whoever was coming through would already know what happened to me, I bet. They might even be responsible for it. I inched forward to meet my visitor.

I pulled Creed back when an aged face with a long, white goatee tipped with orange emerged from the rift, the full body of my visitor still hid behind the veil to the Underworld.

"Do you mind if I come in, young Ezekial?" Azazel asked.

I raised Creed's head, holding the halberd vertically. Azazel was the oldest member of Lucifer's Third Council, I think. The others had aged better if he wasn't. Azazel looked like a walking collection of dust. His thinning hair was as white as snow, except for the tips, which still clung to hints of orange from his earlier, more vibrant life. In the time since I'd last seen him, Azazel had allowed his goatee to grow even longer, nearing his hips now. The tip was still dyed orange. So rebellious for someone of his station. Small liver spots dotted his face, and seemed to have pulled outward, like a slowly loosening circle of oil.

After being screwed by Michael and Seraph on successive missions, I could say with full confidence Azazel was the only member who I did not hold outright hostility toward. Throughout my trials with Lucifer's Council, he executed his duties with humility and grace. Even when Bilba confronted him in Baghdad about recognizing my rights, Azazel had been accommodating and patient.

Any other visitor from Lucifer's little leadership team would have received a steely rejection, metaphorically and probably literally. Azazel got the benefit of the doubt. At least, temporarily.

I turned away and walked back toward my couch. "Come in."

"Thank you," Azazel said as he stepped through.

Glancing back, I shook my head. The ancient Founder was dressed in white canvas sneakers, ripped jeans, and a button down long sleeve shirt that looked like the designer had used it to catch painted wildflowers. Whatever look the Founder was going for, he missed. His popped collar forced me to give him credit for being comfortable and confident in his style.

"Have a seat," I said, gesturing to the chair. "I would offer you something to drink, but I don't imagine your visit will be long."

Azazel raised and lowered a spotted hand, and I felt a listening ward's slime fall over the room. It was a weak version, the weakest I had ever felt, and I worried it would not prevent prying ears. "No, no. I don't want to take up too much of your time." His head swiveled to take in the living room, his hairy chin dropping open, not in wonderment but in dazed observation the elderly and infantile shared in common. "Impressive home you and Cancer have made. Quaint and comfortable. Yes, very impressive."

"What do you need, Azazel?" I asked, leaning back and raising my hands, between which I balance Creed, the ends pushed into my palms. It was a subtle hint, one I hoped he registered.

His eyes traveled to the television. "Oh, I absolutely love this movie. Wonderful selection."

"Yeah," I said dismissively, "I'm just wondering who the ghost of Christmas future will be."

His head swiveled in two brisk twitches, curiosity spotting his expression along with his liver spots. "My apologies. I don't understand."

Still balancing Creed between my open hands, but rocking it as if I were kneading dough, I stared firmly. "Seraph visited to deliver a message short on peace and kindness. Now you're here, to deliver some warning, I'm sure. So I'm curious which one of the big, bad wolfhounds will visit last to warn me away from a future I don't want to experience. Any insight?"

That flustered the Founder. Above his hairy chin, loose cheek skin quivered as he stumbled over a response. "There is no third visit. No warning."

"Then why are you here?"

Flustered, Azazel said, "Well... I... I hadn't checked in

with you since... since the unfortunate vote to Abandon you. I wanted to see how you were doing."

"Why?"

"Well... it's important to see how you're doing," he said. "For myself, you understand. I am interested in your well-being, young Ezekial."

I leaned forward, firmly grasping Creed in one hand. "Why do you care? You're part of the body that Abandoned me to this. Abandoned Cancer. Neither one of us did anything wrong, her least of all. Why should I care to spend another minute entertaining one of you?"

"Ezekial," Azazel's voice gained sturdiness, sounding so unlike the Founder I had known for years. "If you'll remember, I did not vote for this. Yes, I am part of the Third Council, and I have to support the decisions the body makes. However, that does not mean I agree with everything it decides, including your situation and that of poor Ms. Nijal. If I'm intruding on your time, I apologize. I thought a visit would be helpful. Possibly to keep yourself connected with the Underworld."

His statement felt heavier than the individual words, like there was a hidden meaning I wasn't seeing. I stayed quiet, interested in how he would fill the silence. Or if he would. A moment passed, and Azazel spoke.

"Your friend is doing well for himself. Mr. Ravenous, I mean," Azazel continued. "Quite impressive, I must say."

My eyes narrowed. "Don't tell me the Council is harassing him now that I'm not around to bully?"

"Harassing?" Azazel said, looking genuinely confused. "No such thing, I promise. Word is, his preparations for the Passage are coming along nicely. Encouraging to hear. His mentor, Melchiot Zeistane, is an impressive caster in her own right. Mr. Ravenous has done well by selecting her."

"Then why don't you give him missions so he can pay for it if you're so impressed with his efforts?" I said, holding a low growl. Bilba would never ask for a mission out of respect for me, but I could for him.

Azazel lifted his hand to stroke the end of his goatee. "Would that I could, young Ezekial. But it would serve Mr. Ravenous better to not align with the Council at the moment."

Interesting. "Why's that?"

Azazel's hand stopped momentarily before resuming the stroking. "Everything that happened over the recent past between the three of you and the Council has opened fissures that have been concealed for ages. Behind the scenes, things aren't how they appear on the outside, as you have experienced. Working with any of you would be a risky proposition, the Council has determined."

I collapsed back against the couch. Light tapping of rain droplets slapped against the balcony door. Yay, it was raining again. "So you force us into servitude, put us in unenviable positions, completely disrupt our lives, and then discard us when you have no more need of our services? Is that how it works?"

The quivering in Azazel's cheeks smoothed. In that fraction of a second, Azazel looked like how I imagined he would have thirty or forty thousand years ago. Young, virile, and confident. "Everything has its reason. Everyone has their cause. Be careful to ascribe meaning until you understand the full context. There may be very good reasons why Mr. Ravenous and Mr. Burning are not getting missions from the Council. Don't be in a rush for us to employ them again."

"Music to my ears. Why though? With this unsolicited visit, I think it's fair to give me some sort of insight."

"It is in their best interest," Azazel said, his voice rock solid.

"For whose best interest? My friends or the Council?"

"Though it may be difficult to see Ralrek struggle and Bilba move on with his life while you are here, I prefer you trust me in this respect," Azazel said. "The Council is struggling with its identity. This happens from time to time as the natural cycle runs its course. I believe we are fully in one of those moments now, a transitional time, if you will. Your friends do not need to be part of that. If you want what's best for them, be happy that they're not. Encourage them away from thinking about it if they do. Support Ralrek the best you can. Encourage Bilba in his studies. That is my recommendation."

"I see," I said, carefully. Bilba and Dialphio had delivered enough hints that things in Hell were rocky. Azazel's comments fell in line. But this was a Founder, a member of the Third Council. And the Council was a complex riddle, with many layers and many more games being played amongst them. What was real and what was not? "Is that all you needed then? To help me convince the two of them to not look for work from you? Seems you could have sent a letter or messenger to them directly. Or an assassin?"

Azazel jerked his head. "Assassin? Well... we... we don't... why would we do that?"

I studied him. The Founder did not flinch under my scrutiny. Sure, his millennia upon millennia of practicing poise for the purposes of political power might deserve credit for his lack of a reaction, or his response might just be genuine. I pressed the issue.

"Hardly a revelation, wouldn't you say? It's happened multiple times." I lifted my arm, gesturing toward the rainy day. "It's happening now, here in the Overworld. Even after everything you, the Council, have done."

"I assure you, I don't know the first thing about assassins, but if you have something to share with me, do so. It will be held in confidence."

"You're going to claim ignorance?"

"Young Ezekial, I swear to Lucifer I have no idea what you're talking about," Azazel said, his tone genial but steady.

"I came to check on you and mention your use of that halberd. You might want to be careful with the weapon. As far as assassinations, I wish I could answer you. You deserve that much."

I deserved that and more. Instead of taking the conversation down a new path, I said, "You don't know about the group that attacked us with their van? The group that almost killed Cancer? You're going to look me in the face and tell me you're clueless? Come on."

Azazel lifted both hands. "I don't know about any such group."

"Yet you know about me using Creed?"

Those aged hands spread. "You have hardly made a secret of its use, young one. There was an event yesterday. None of us can be sure exactly what happened, we can't see everything. But we can see an imbalance in the use of Abilities in the Overworld. Well... that includes angelic magic as well, but that's not the point of this discussion. Your use of magic registered yesterday. We are well aware of the fact you do not possess an Ability, leaving only your halberd as the explanation. That is a very dangerous occurrence. Which, is why I wanted to speak with you."

"I was defending myself against Hell's operatives," I said, feeling my back teeth grinding against each other. "Using it was justified."

"Justified or not, it drew attention," Azazel responded. "With everything you've been through over the recent years, is that something you want? I do not imagine so, but you are young, very young, and can be fiery. That has led you into poor decisions, I think we can both agree? I figured talking to you before someone else did was best. You need not worry about the signal, I took care of that."

"The signal?"

Azazel nodded. "The signature of magic being used in the Overworld. Imagine it like a stamp on parchment, except that it fades over time. Hours, instead of centuries. I've expunged the evidence of your use of the halberd so no one on the Council is or will be aware. A fortunate coincidence that I was the one on duty. If another had been…"

Azazel had wiped away evidence of me using magic in the Overworld? I wanted to express gratitude, but that was difficult for me to do with any member of the Council, even him. "Why… why would you do that?"

"Because it's the right thing to do," Azazel said, sounding younger than he ever had. "It was an error of judgment, one driven by necessity. I understand that. My peers, at least some of them, might not. Expunging it from the record helps us avoid the issue altogether. Be very careful when and how you use that much power again. Though it draws on the nature of the Hellfire, it is that very fact that might expose you. Even in small doses, the weapon's magic can be detected. For all I know, One purposely designed it that way to keep its holder in check. Regardless, exercise caution. I won't always be around to help."

An admission about not having the slightest clue how to control Creed's power almost fell out of my mouth. Not my fault. Azazel was rocking with my world with his candid sharing. Helpful or not, I was grateful that I hadn't stumbled into sharing something I couldn't afford to admit. No one on the Council needed to know about my incredible ineptitude. In that struggle to keep my mouth shut, I almost missed the fact that Azazel didn't warn me away from using my power or explicitly instruct me not to. He only encouraged me to be careful. Double interesting.

The ancient Founder snickered. "Of course, it cost me a favor with a long-time associate on the other side, but they have agreed to remove it from their records as well."

"The angels?" I asked.

"Of course," Azazel replied. "I have a few friends on the other side. It's difficult to work with them. One has to be patient and understanding. But those types of relationships keep a balance, so it must be done. Don't feel restricted with your halberd here, of course. In your home, you're safe to do as you see fit. This is a sanctuary."

"I suspected as soon as we moved in, just as I did in our apartment in Seattle. I imagine no matter where I go in the Overworld, I will always find myself living in a sanctuary." It was a statement with a sincere question at its core.

"You will, unfortunately," Azazel grimaced slightly. "It has advantages and disadvantages for you."

"And the Council," I reminded the Founder.

He nodded. "And the Council. Still, there are benefits. Don't discount them."

"I won't," I said carefully.

Azazel scooted forward on the seat of the chair. "I must go soon. My absence will be noted, just as my presence here will be if I'm not careful. Before I go, how are you feeling?"

I shot glances to the sides of the room, feeling like I was being watched. "Good. Why?"

"Abandonment can be hard on a demon," Azazel said, "which is why I wanted to ask after you. I'm curious how you're feeling. How you have been feeling."

I set Creed in my lap, fingering the haft as I deciphered Azazel's intent. I didn't want to pull the covers back on something before realizing it was too late. "I'm fine. With everything going on, and you giving me this information that my use of the halberd is actually being tracked and how—"

"All magic is, young Ezekial," Azazel corrected.

I nodded repeatedly. "Yeah, yeah. I get that. My point is, there are more important things unfolding that need to be discussed than how I'm feeling. The Council is aware of my recovery skills. Let's not pretend it doesn't. It's been that way since I can remember, and you have evidence from the first time you sent me to Seattle. So I'm not sure why my overall health matters now."

Azazel's hand dropped from his goatee back to the armchair. "Would you say the same about your friend, Cancer? Is she just as 'fine'?"

I narrowed my eyes to slits. I didn't like anyone from the Council talking about Cancer, especially when she wasn't here. What I liked less was the fact that Cancer was not doing okay. She hadn't been. She lost her Ability, and that depressed her. More than depressed. She was crushed by the fact she couldn't use her Ability to heal and save lives. Much of her moodiness could be attributed to that, but who would be 'fine' after being Abandoned?

Azazel had me thinking, though. There was more than Abandonment-driven depression to Cancer. A malaise. She was working ridiculous hours, that much was true. Exhaustion and lethargy, even on her rare days off, were constant companions for my roommate. A few days ago we had been sitting on the balcony, watching life in Olympia happen below, and her coffee cup slipped from her hand and smashed against the concrete four stories below. Thankfully, the sidewalk had been empty of pedestrians so only the cup took damage. Cancer had been holding it for no longer than a minute. It wasn't the first time something like that happened. A few weeks ago, she almost took off a toe when she dropped a knife while emptying the dishwasher. She walked down the stairs at a grandmother's pace. I had to move the furniture on cleaning days because even sliding the chair was too much for her. The fact was, Cancer was not Cancer, and things were only getting worse.

"She is," I finally answered. "She's working a lot, but she's doing well."

The Founder's bottom lip rolled over his top, making the long white hairs of his goatee near his lip poke out in a multitude of directions. "Is she now? That is surprising."

His last comment was leading, he was trying to guide me in a particular direction. For what purpose? Taking the bait might help me find out. "What is, Azazel? I told Seraph the same thing when she was here. I'm done playing the Council's games. If you need something, or are here to make demands, just say it and let's get it over with. This constant dancing is exhausting."

"Don't misinterpret my intentions," he responded firmly. "My concern is for you and Ms. Nijal. I don't imagine she's doing as well as you say. The operatives watching you have seen her, of course. You two spend time together, but rarely. Those reports indicate Abandonment has taken a toll on her."

So the Council was watching us closely enough to know how Cancer was doing? And Azazel was sharing this insight. Hands up for the second big revelation in a single conversation. What was the Founder's game?

"Abandonment does that to our kind, young Ezekial," Azazel continued. "It's a natural process of one losing their immortality. A tragic consequence, but one that is required."

"Required? Why in the world would it be required?"

"Even immortals don't live forever. When we lose immortality, it's only natural that we begin to decay. Because of our nature, decaying is different for us than for mortals. Their biology is consistent; they begin to die as soon as they are born. Our decay is more... aggressive once it begins. That's the only way I can say it. It's a tragedy, truly, but it is the nature of who we are."

My throat constricted as I asked, "How long... until she decays and is Abolished?"

"It's different for everyone, I'm afraid." The corners of his eyes turned down. "A better answer is deserved, but is not something I can give you. I'm sorry. For Cancer to live her remaining time as fulfilled as possible is the better way to spend her energy. You could help with that. But it is not something to fight, because she cannot win. Even with your help. With anyone's."

Accept her Abolishment—her death? Why, when the

incubus sitting in my living room could change her fortunes? The fire in my gut sparked to life. "You could allow her back into the Underworld."

Just above the line of white hair that formed his goatee, the elderly incubus's skin began to flush. The red hue slowly spread as he spoke. "Me? No, I cannot do that. The Council needs to reverse their decision."

"But you could," I pressed. "You just don't want to."

"It's not that simple."

"It's exactly that simple," I said, gripping Creed. "You could do it if you wanted to be helpful. If you want to correct this wrong."

The ruinous pattern of flowers on Azazel's shirt rose and fell as he took a slow, deep breath. "Would that I could. But the Council will not change its mind. I've had those conversations already in your time away. Dozens of them. No one is shifting, Michael and I being the only two who can see the injustice the Council caused. To be honest, between you and me," he said as he lifted his liver–spotted hand and waved a finger around before tapping his ear, "even he wavers depending on the day. Caution. Caution is what is required. But it would be a disservice to you and to young Cancer if I misled you with false hope. No, no. Best for both of you to accept this fate and enjoy the time you have. If something changes, we can address it then. But spending your days looking for something you will never find is a cruel, cruel fate." He looked around the sanctuary as if he were inspecting the corners for mold. After a moment's silence, he said, "Another benefit of living in the sanctuary is that its magical wards slow the decay. It doesn't stop it, I won't promise that. But it does slow it. There is no better place for Cancer than here, with you."

Every time I felt like I was swimming upstream, someone threw a rope around my ankles to help pull me back from the shore. This conversation with Azazel, regardless of his intentions, felt exactly like that. My mind spun around the inevitabilities of Abandonment while my heart ached to be home, around the demons and places that made me feel whole.

"So we just have to accept this?"

Azazel drew a nasally breath, long and wheezing. "I'm afraid so. Accept this and live the best life you two can. Yours will be much longer than hers, and that is important to recognize. Something in your nature that none of us understands affects your nature. The Council has asked our greatest medical practitioners about your case, and none have provided answers. They fully expect you to live an extraordinarily, abnormally for mortal standards, long life. But..."

The conclusion was clear. "But Cancer won't."

Azazel reached for his goatee before letting his hand drop into his lap. "I'm afraid not."

"That's just great."

"I'm sorry," the Founder said, sounding like he was.

I suddenly found myself not wanting to be in his presence. "I'd like you to leave, Azazel."

The Founder shifted on the chair. "I understand. I feel terrible about bringing you this troubling news, but I'm afraid I must impart one more piece before I go."

More bad news? Maybe this was a new tactic of the Council, to torture me with thoughts until I went mad. Made sense. Their assassination attempts had been crap. Why not shift strategies?

"What?" I said, clamping my teeth together.

Azazel lowered his voice, which was ridiculous considering he had set a listening ward on the sanctuary. "I have sources that keep me abreast of your situation." His eyes flickered. "All Council members do. We work independently as well as dependently. It's a complex relationship, one filled with distrust, disloyalty, and dishonor. But I have those outside the Council I trust, and they watch and listen in places where I can't always be."

"Oh, yeah? And what do they tell you about me, Azazel?"

He shook his head, the end of his long goatee swaying as if pushed by a fan. "Not about you. About another."

"Who?"

His hand slipped to his goatee again. "I never liked many of the circumstances and consequences that happened to you. The Council fears you; that's not a secret. In fact, I'm confident you have a very good idea of your effect. But that doesn't justify the positions we've put you in. Beyond that, there have been... manipulations, shall we say, to the situation. There are forces at play in the grander picture even we can't see. The possibility exists that someone may take it upon themselves to push the course in a way that favors them. That may have been already happening for some time, culminating in the way we handled the events after your deployment to Baghdad. Our attention is spread thin because of the mortal war. So is that of our operatives. Since no one used Abilities, at least not at a significant level, nothing pinged on our senses, so our attentions weren't drawn to what was becoming a problem. That's when Seraph took advantage of the situation. She has close ties to her nephew, giving her a first–hand source. That allowed her to manipulate the situation into what she needed it to be. The result was the outcome of your trial."

"My Abandonment," I said, not wanting that part left out.

To his credit, Azazel nodded. "Not only is your decay guaranteed, but you are placed somewhere where you are prone to injury and death. Convenient, wouldn't you say?"

Azazel was not here to threaten me. He was here to warn, educate, maybe even prepare me. These were not the actions of an enemy. "That's the plan, right? To put me in a position where I can be removed as a problem?"

The ancient incubus's head bobbed up and down. "I'm

afraid so. Don't misunderstand me. When I came, I wanted to check and see how you're doing. I wanted to hear about Cancer. However, the main reason I came was to make sure you had information. You need to be prepared for what lies ahead. Using your halberd carefully, responsibly, will not draw attention. I believe you understand that now. It must be in much smaller doses than what you did yesterday. Work on that because you may need that power soon. More than a few demons want your absence from the Underworld, and from any world, to remain permanent. Many of them also worry about you tipping the Balance in the angel's favor."

I was only half hearing the second part of his warning. "What's your plan?"

"Chax Vicu is in the Overworld," Azazel said soberly. "I validated that with multiple sources. Seraph has given him permission, unbeknownst to the rest of the Council. Confronting her will take time. For now, you need to be aware he is here, and his purpose is to find you. His reasons are nefarious, I assure you. I don't know the details beyond that, young Ezekial, I'm sorry."

But I did. "I think I know how to find him, Azazel," I said with a respectful head nod. "I appreciate this."

Azazel stood slowly, as if each stretch of his limbs were an individual challenge. "Put it to good use. Remember, Chax's Abilities are weak. I foresee a time when he uses them against you without pinging our detection senses. We have operatives in the region, but not many who spend time in Olympia. Even a small use of his Abilities could still result in a disastrous outcome. Be careful."

"He could send a group of thugs to run us off the road. Maybe next time they'll kill us," I said, half my mind recalling yesterday's event.

The Founder stood and opened a rift in the kitchen. "Best of luck to you and Cancer."

The Founder inched forward and stepped through without pausing. The slimy sensation of the ward lifted.

I stared at the spot in my kitchen where the rift had stood seconds before, blinking dumbly as I tried to understand what in the heaven just happened and what it meant moving forward. For me and Cancer. Was Azazel really on our side? Something told me, before this was over, I would have my answer.

16

OLYMPIA

"HONESTLY, I'M SURPRISED YOU CAME," Leo said, pulling a black jacket emblazoned with the gym's logo off his chair.

"Me too," I admitted.

We were in the back office of the Lion's Den. Though it was a Saturday, the gym was relatively quiet. Three fighters worked through individual routines in the bay. Even Debbie, the watchdog receptionist, quietly typed away without interacting.

Leo caught me eyeing her through the open door. "She's having a bad day."

"Yeah, I felt that. If it's any consolation, she's not the only one."

In the days since Azazel visited, I had spent too much time inside my apartment and in my head. Anytime I ran out to the store or stretched my legs with a run, I spent most of my energy peeking around every corner and looking over my shoulder. Wholesome couples walking dogs or their tiny humans now got my attention because I could no longer trust anyone. The delivery man's get-up might be a cover for one of Hell's operatives working for Chax. Solitary figures sitting in the grass at the park near the harbor suddenly became part of a network of spies watching my every move. Even the bartender at my favorite watering hole was suspiciously inquisitive, even though the questions were innocuous.

Paranoia aside, I was drained. Cancer picked up on that. She had asked me when I planned on working out at the gym so I could confront Leo over his ex-demon nature, and I told her I hadn't had a chance. So she did what good friends do. She set up the big boy play date herself, not asking permission. In doing so, she obligated my entire free Saturday, one of the few I got from the bookstore, to Leo, and worse, his family.

"You sure everyone is okay with me dropping in with you?" I asked.

Leo scrunched his face, throwing his jacket over his elbow. He grunted as he snagged his keys from his desk, which held exactly two pieces of paper and roughly thirty pictures of him in different fighting poses, all shirtless with rippling muscle. Similar snapshots of his conquests hung on each wall of the office, celebrating the glories of his career.

"Don't worry about it," he said. "They're cool, and it will help."

Help who? After Cancer facilitated this bro date, Leo and I had a heart-to-heart conversation to remove a few degrees of secrecy between us. I still held secrets. Not too many to be reckless. I was sure he was holding back. Opening our secret boxes, even slightly, made this arrangement more transparent, moving us closer to our individual goals. I needed his training and to find out if he was involved with Chax. The only way to do that was to get closer. A family outing, as long as I didn't act like an absolute cherub, might be the key to unlocking tons of information.

Leo was convinced the angel still followed him—I never betrayed Cassie—who was heaven–bent on causing him harm. With the annual family picnic coming up, he did not want to put his loved ones at risk. The event was the perfect opportunity, not only for me to help deal with the angel, but to ensure his family's safety.

I fingered a loose thread on the sleeve of my sweatshirt. Thankfully, today was one of the rare days in mid-October that the rain discontinued its torture. Leo said the family only got over their collective trauma of Abandonment during their first October, holding their first Overworld festive gathering. The picnic became the tradition, held at the same time each year because, well, duh, tradition.

The sun's zenith was noticeably lower, but still high enough to provide glorious days like the one we were about to enjoy. The dropping temperatures didn't stop Leo from driving through the neighborhood toward the park with his window rolled down. He said he liked the fresh air. I hated the ravenbumps—goosebumps; I have got to get better at using appropriate colloquialisms—on my arms.

"You nervous?" he asked, his eyes sliding to watch my hand rubbing my exposed arm.

I pulled it away. "No, I just feel like I'm intruding."

"Nonsense, man," he replied with the curtness usually reserved for one of his fighters. "You're going to love the family. It'll be good for them to see someone from the outside too, especially someone from back home. Trust me, they spend too much blessed time together."

"Just fair warning, I'm not much of a conversationalist," I admitted. "Actually, I can get quiet around large groups."

He sniffed a laugh. "Don't worry. My Nana will drag a conversation out of you if she has to. You won't want to deny her, not if you value your life."

We pulled into the parking lot and I helped him unload the beer and soda. Considering the inventory we held, it would have behooved us to show up earlier. The amount of alcohol we brought could serve a platoon. Today, it would ensure most of the adults would have to walk home. The loads of canned sugar we hauled meant everyone was an hour away from jumpstarting the smaller members of the family pinging off walls long into the night.

The picnic was in full swing across the park. At least three dozen ex-demons loitered, chatting and laughing, or playing board games at tables. The young ones tore up the volleyball pit as if they were searching for Lucifer's buried treasure or chased each other around the trees and tables. My mouth watered as soon as we approached when the soft breeze carried the smell of grilled meat in our direction.

"That's a big family," I said, somewhat intimidated.

"Told you we were, man," he laughed.

"You did. I just didn't expect it to be so... big."

"That's usually the definition of 'big'. Plus, they're friendly as heaven, though. Come on, let me introduce you to everyone."

I shifted the cases of beer in my arms for the fifty-yard walk. The view of the expanse of green we were crossing and the throng of ex-demons enjoying the sunny afternoon elicited a satisfied sigh.

"Leo!" A tall middle-aged incubus who reminded me of Michael moved forward, his arms wide. "About time you showed up."

"Leo is here," a squat woman with a crescent nose smiled, announcing to an older woman seated on a picnic table bench behind her.

With hair so white as to be transparent, the elderly woman smiled through squinted eyes as she searched. Wrinkles as old as time permanently attached themselves to her forehead, around her eyes, and neck, making the latter look like one of those plastic chew toys owners buy for their devildogs.

"Leo? Leo is here?" The woman's voice cracked through her rusted throat.

"Yes, mama, he's here," the crescent–nosed woman said cheerfully, before swatting a brooding young man sitting on the bench next to her, staring at his phone and ignoring everyone around him. "Help your Nana."

Leo leaned closer. "That's my brother. Harvest. Real pain in the ass. Don't be surprised if he and I get into it at least once today."

"What would a family gathering be without at least a little drama?" I said lightly, thinking of my own family and the awkward memories they provided.

"Come say hi to your Nana, Leo, and I will greet our guest," the crescent–nosed woman smiled, the corners of her lips hooking around her large nose making it appear even more angular. She opened her arms and embraced me before I had a chance to set the cases of beer down. "Welcome. I'm Alecia, Leo's mother. I presume you're Ezekial?"

She smelled like wildflowers. She didn't relinquish her grip. Locked in her greeting, the weight of the beer pulled me down. "Thank you. It was kind of you to allow me to come."

Alecia stepped back, ordering a nearby pair of boys to take the cases from my hands. They were only too excited to help, probably enjoying the feeling of such an adult responsibility even as they struggled with the precious cargo. "We're glad to have you. Leo tells me you two have a mutual friend who says you spend too much time alone. That's a shame, especially this time of year. Before long, we'll all be stuck inside for months on end and seasonal depression is like a chimera kick. Trust me, the dark, wet months don't get easier to survive as the years pass. But, enough of that. We're happy to have you. Now, I will warn you, the family might be a little overwhelming. Just smile and nod a lot and you'll get through today."

"Thanks for the advice," I said, smiling and feeling even more awkward, but allowing her to pull me along for introductions. Twenty minutes passed before I met everyone, making introductions feel more like a round of speed dating than a casual family gathering. In fairness, I was greeted with warmth and kindness at every turn, except for the brooding younger incubus, Harvest.

The tall man who reminded me of Michael was Uncle Celio. He spoke in conspiratorial tones, leaning close while eyeing Leo's brother. "Harvest is a troubled young man. Don't let him bother you."

I pinched my mouth as I nodded. "Will do. What's his story?"

Celio shrugged as if it didn't matter. After a few thousand years of dealing with Hell's Reformed Asshole, Ralrek, I understood where the line was in giving energy to brooding types. "He's just a punk. Has been for years. Not like we're all not going through the same thing, you know? Don't let him bother you. Not worth your time. If he gets smart, just tell him off. The entire family will back you up, trust me."

A trio of children trying to tag each other raced around us. Their giggles could have lifted even Harvest's mood.

"Well, I'll let you go." Celio raised his red plastic cup at me with a wink. "You need to meet mama. That's your real test. Best do it before the rest of the family wears you out."

"Everyone is scaring me about meeting her," I admitted.

"Good."

We laughed as we parted ways.

Credit to Leo, even as swarmed as he was by the family, he did not leave me hanging. "Let me introduce you to Nana. She wants to meet. Don't let Uncle Celio make you nervous. She's a real softy... once you get through the tough exterior."

He pulled me toward the white-haired matriarch. Her slits-for-eyes fixed on me the entire way. Analysis completed, judgment passed. The old woman had me so on-edge I even focused on walking correctly. My feet felt as if small bags of wet sand were tied to them, and I almost stumbled.

"Hey," I leaned toward Leo before we reached her. "Did you tell her that I'm... you know..."

"Abandoned?" Leo said too loudly before laughing. "Yes,

don't sweat it. I told them. What's the big deal, right? We all are, so it's not like we don't know what it means, man. My mother insisted you showed up once she found out. She didn't tell you?"

"No," I answered. "She said it was because I spent too much time alone. I guess Cancer is telling you all of my secrets."

"Just a cover," he said with a shrug. "Come on, this will be the easiest thing you've done since killing my uncle."

I jerked back so hard that Leo halted. He looked surprised. "What?"

"I thought we were good, that you understood what happened with Aries," I said, careful to watch my surroundings. I was standing in the middle of his large family. Surrounded on all sides. Had I just stumbled into a death trap? Was Leo leading me to the slaughter, his innocent looking Nana playing the role of Brutus? Stupid, stupid Zeke. "You said you believed me."

Leo looked as serious as I've ever seen him, his lips flat and his eyes dead. The rest of the party chatted and laughed, cooked, and played games, oblivious to this sudden tension.

Just as I readied go to fisticuffs and ruin the picnic, Leo's face broke into a smile as he leaned closer. "I'm screwing with you. Relax, man. We're here to have fun." He wrapped a meaty hand around my forearm. I was pretty sure his thumb reached his fingertip. "And I believe you. I told you, I know the politics behind what happened to him. I wanted you to relax, because I know my family can be a little overwhelming. Sorry about that."

I released a shaky breath. "You had me for a second."

"Good," he said, and then tipped his head toward the picnic table where Nana and her squad of attendees waited. "But don't let your guard down. My Nana tears up weak demons like a devildog tears up potty pads. Come on, let's go meet her."

The table was covered with platters of fruit and bread. Apples and pears in one bowl, bananas in another. A mound of muffins sprinkled with sesame seeds was recklessly piled in a basket, side-by-side with one, now half-empty, that held white rolls.

Nana sat on the far side bench, Leo's mother next to her while a middle-aged man stood behind her looking every bit the protector. Another woman, this one a carbon cut out of Alecia with blond hair, sat next to Leo's mother. She watched me as closely as Nana's protector. The close-side bench was populated by three women, one younger, roughly my age, and the other two on the wrong side of middle-age. Blue eyes on one of the older women, hazel for the other. The blue-eyed bench partner had a nose so sharply bridged it reminded me of a v-shaped folded piece of paper. The other woman had a button nose above a masculine chin.

"Nana, this is Ezekial Sunstone," Leo said, putting a hand in the middle of my shoulder blades and encouraging me forward with a hearty nudge. I didn't have a choice in which direction I was traveling. "He's the one I told you about."

I opened my mouth to greet the matriarch and her posse when Nana's protector took a jerky step closer.

Nana didn't seem to be bothered by his overbearing attitude, as if she knew the power she exuded. Wisps of white hair floated around her head in the soft breeze. Her eyes remained narrow slits against the sun as she examined me for an uncomfortably long time. "Hello Ezekial. I'm glad you could join us."

"Hello Mrs. Neto," I replied. "I appreciate the invitation. I planned on sitting around the apartment and eating lousy microwave food all day. This is much better."

Her wrinkled lips pressed against each other. "You will be expected to eat more than your fair share today. I hope you're ready. Leo is a good boy, so I hope he mentioned my expectations about you bringing an empty stomach."

Leo hadn't, but a table full of food with the grill spewing out wonderful aromas would have prevented me from betraying him even if I wanted to. "Yes, he did. I'm ready to eat."

"As am I," the woman with a button nose said, her eyes traveling up and down my body at an uncomfortably slow pace. "To eat this one."

"Might need a stiff breeze when we're done with him," the woman with the v-shaped nose agreed.

"Aunts, leave him alone," Leo said with a chuckle at my blush. "Trust me, he might be little, but he can hold his own."

"How do you know? You've taken him on the mat?" the protective man behind Nana asked.

Leo's looked at me mischievously, like he was weighing the benefits of sharing the story of our park fight. He turned back to the protector. "You could say that. He's a badass. Lots of energy. Will probably eat half the food if you let him."

"Well, he is more than welcome," Nana said, placing her hands on the table, her elbows bent at ninety-degree angles and achingly pushed herself up. The protector and Alecia raced to help, but the elderly succubus waved them away with one hand while she wobbled but remained steady.

Leo whispered, "Go to her and give her a kiss on the cheek and thank her for being invited. She's basically just given you permission to be part of the family. The others will be watching."

At first glance, Leo's statement was accurate. I felt the eyes of everyone, even those distracted with faraway conversations, the grill, and even the informal volleyball pit treasure hunt fall on me. I slid around the table. The protector made room at my arrival.

"Thank you for welcoming me," I said, my neck burning with embarrassment as I brought my face close to her cheek. She helped by turning her head to the side. I placed the light kiss on her wrinkled cheeks, the smell of faint grease wafting around me.

Not knowing if I had performed the ritual correctly, I stepped back. Seeing Alecia smiling broadly, my shoulders loosened. I would not be killed by the family; not yet, at least.

Nana waved horizontally at the other bench. "Sarah, Louisa. Make room for Ezekial so he can eat with me. Leo, find yourself a chair. I want to talk to you."

I'd never seen Leo move as fast as he did to follow her command. Even the time he sucker punched me happened only at half this speed.

"Sit, Ezekial," Nana said, her arms shaking as she slowly lowered herself.

I moved to the opposite side of the picnic table, the space now open thanks to Leo's aunts following Nana's orders. This woman ran a tight ship. I was grateful for that, especially because of the way the two aunts continued to look at me as if I was the one about to be laid out on the table and feasted upon.

"Do you have family in the area, Ezekial?" Nana asked.

I shook my head. "I don't. They're all..." Knowing that Leo had informed his family of my situation was one thing, but admitting it so openly felt strange.

Nana's expression, as stern as one of the gargoyles chiseled into many of the Old Towne buildings, wiped the nosy looks from the pair of aunts. They pretended to be interested in their meals, but I could tell they were paying close attention. When she spoke, it was with empathy. "I see. They're back home? Do you miss them?"

I snorted bitterly before I could think about proper decorum. "Tremendously."

"And you have a good relationship with your parents?" Alecia said, pulling a roll from the basket and buttering it before handing it to Nana on a small plate. Her distraction with the task seemed perfunctory, a ploy to disguise her analysis.

"My mother means the world to me," I said, grateful when Louisa passed the breadbasket so I had something to do while I answered. Why was it taking Leo so long to grab a blessed chair?

The group at the table had the courtesy to not press for details.

"I, for one, miss the Underworld," Nana said, setting a marker down as the first one to mention the unmentionables.

Ever since my first mission in the Overworld, the message had been drilled into our brains to never mention anything hinting at the Underworld. Even the most subtle references supposedly drew the attention of angels. Like a gullible impling, I believed the lie.

"Which Circle is your family from?" Sarah asked.

"The Fifth," I answered.

"Never got to travel there," the protector, still standing behind Nana, said. "We're from the First."

I nodded, not wanting to open up the can of serpents about their Circle, *the site* of Hell's greatest tragedy where three hundred demons died by Angelfire.

"That's because those tyrants who run the Underworld don't allow anyone to travel," Nana said in a biting tone. "Used to, generations ago. Imagine the wonders awaiting us if we were allowed to explore the other Circles?"

A tense silence fell over the picnic table at Nana's inflammatory comments.

"One of the benefits of being Abandoned, I guess," Alecia said with a tight laugh everyone else mimicked in their own ways.

Nana's wrinkled lips continued to grind against each other until she spoke. "It's not so bad," she said after a while. "I find I enjoy it here. I think most of the family does, except for the stubborn ones like Harvest."

"Mama, leave him alone," Alecia said only in half–hearted defense. "He was young and had a girlfriend."

"A beautiful succubus," Louisa said.

"She was," Sarah agreed, her eyes constantly flicking toward my lap.

Leo and his chair finally rejoined us.

"Welcome back," I said, relieved.

"What are we talking about?" Leo said with the exuberance of someone not sitting in the conversation centered around a touchy subject while someone's relatives got touchy with their eyes.

"Your Nana was reminiscing over the Underworld," Protector chimed in.

"She was also sharing how much she enjoys the Overworld," Alecia commented quickly.

"Don't you like it, Leo?" Nana asked. "You're doing so well for yourself."

Leo was halfway to reaching for the breadbasket already readying to dump the bowl of fruit onto his plate. He halted both actions and slowly set them on the table. "I do, Nana. It has given me opportunities I wouldn't have had back home."

Alecia studied her son and nodded.

"And you don't have a problem decaying?" Protector said skeptically, crossing his arms. "I don't believe that. Not for a second. Not for someone in your shape, with the path you had ahead."

Leo shrugged. "Can't change it."

In another circumstance, I might have called Leo out. For someone who made his living in the fighting ring, physical endurance in the form of a long, healthy life would have been a priority. Abandonment stripped him of that. No matter how successful his gym was, wasn't the octagon where he found glory? I doubted it didn't bother him, especially surrounded as we were by his loved ones. Putting him in a corner by asking him was not a smart move. Testosterone rarely reacted well with confrontation.

"What about you, Ezekial?" Nana turned the attention on me. "How have you been doing with your Abandonment? Leo tells me there is a very nice nurse who lives with you, a friend if I remember correctly, who was also Abandoned. Are the two of you settling into a routine?"

I nodded. Uncomfortable with sharing Cancer's story with strangers, I kept the focus on me. "I'm doing okay. It's not an easy adjustment, and I miss my friends and family. How long has everyone been here?"

The aunts, uncle, Leo, and even Alecia shared looks with each other before Nana formulated her response. She lifted her chin and answered. "It happened soon after the crime against Aries."

All eyes shifted to me. Did they know how intimately connected I was with Aries? I didn't want to volunteer that information if it wasn't something Leo had already shared.

"We've been here for years," Alecia said firmly, but evenly. "Right after they murdered him, they rounded us up and, within a few days, the entire family was Abandoned." Her eyes drifted to the three children in the sand of the volleyball court, disrupting the game.

I drew the conclusion, the abhorrent conclusion, for myself. "So they weren't born here?"

Alecia shook her head, biting the corner of her lip. She reached out to her side, toward the beautiful blond carbon cut out younger version of Leo's mother who had been quiet throughout the conversation. "Solia is their mother. She's been strong, but it has been hard on her and the children."

"The youngest is three years old by human standards. A little over seven hundred and forty by our kind's measure," Solia said quietly, tears welling in her eyes.

"That didn't matter to them," Sarah said caustically. "They

kicked them out right along with the rest of us. With as much feeling as if they were picking up dry cleaning."

"I'm so sorry," I said to Solia. "That's horrible."

Her eyes never left her children. "Thank you."

"Don't apologize," Nana said, her voice full of empathy and compassion. "You've done no harm to this family. Many here are too young to understand what Aries was involved in. I have been around for generations and know he understood the risks of his work. He did it for all demonkind. A true hero."

"A hero with more courage than any of those bastards on the Council. A crime." Protector snarled from his standing position.

Nana reached around and patted his arm. "Yet he is still a hero of our kind. An inspiration. Leo has told me your side of things. I hope you are comfortable around the family, because none of us fault you. We know the truth. Aries, in his wisdom, shared his thoughts with me and my brother before his death. We know who you are and we are sorry you have paid such a substantial cost. You, too, are a victim of the Council, just as we are.

"But this is the life we have to live. Our only life. We can't spend our energy being angry, because anger changes nothing. Over time, you will see that. You will learn how to take pleasure from this mortality. Maybe even more than you ever could during your immortality."

I flinched and Nana caught it.

"Hard to believe?" she asked, a glint of humor crossing her face. "I understand why. Just as we teach the young ones to enjoy theirs, so must I teach others. With immortality, you may have never felt the urgency of passing time. With mortality, we are pressed to live each moment as our last, because it may be. One of the greatest travesties of our species, the lack of understanding a terminal nature." Her head turned to the children, and the corners of her eyes trembled with oncoming tears. "They are so young; they will likely not procreate, which is a kindness. Drawing their torture out into their children's lives is a fate so cruel even angels would not subject someone to it. Fortunately, they'll never know. But you and Leo are not so young. Lucifer willing, you have long lives ahead. Enjoy your time. Enjoy this life. It can be a magnificent experience. Losing our identity as immortals is difficult and takes time. If we are honest, each of us struggled with it after arriving. Some of us are still struggling." Her ancient eyes found Harvest, who sat underneath the tree by himself, looking just as miserable as when he was sitting with the family. "He is struggling most of all. I fear. His mother has tried. His brother has tried. But he holds in his anger."

The succubus was being so honest and candid, I felt it only obligatory to reciprocate. "I understand. I don't remember a day that I didn't regret and mourn the things I've lost while also being pissed at the Council for what they've done."

Sarah drew a breath.

"Language," Leo admonished.

Alecia's eyes swelled and deflated in rapid succession.

"Oh, stop it," Nana chastised with a wry smile. "As many lifetimes as I've lived, you think I haven't heard fruity language? Do you think I offend so easily? Come now. Ezekial, give yourself time. Be kind to yourself. You have lost part of who you are. Mourning is a natural part of this experience. But look at them." Nana lifted a bony hand, her bent finger extended at the children playing without a care in the world. "Joy can be found in this life if you look for it. You never know when you will be Abolished. None of us do. For some, decay happens slowly. For others, it could be cruelly expedient. Why stress over those things we cannot know? What you have now is everything you will have in the world. You have this moment, this breath. Nothing more. So don't waste it. Come now, let's eat this firehorse food until those lazy men finally finish the burgers and ribs. I swear, they'll stand over that grill until the sun sets if we let them. Leo, go tell them I'm hungry."

Everyone at the table laughed as Leo left with a cherubic grin.

From the grill, a round man who I think I remember being named Artis, shouted, "I'm hurrying."

"Well, hurry faster," Nana said in retort, drawing more laughter.

As the sun continued its low jaunt across the sky, the food came. Hours into my first Neto family picnic, I drank to keep pace with Nana and ate what felt like twice my body weight. Spirits, of the liquid and jovial kind, were shared. Throughout the festive meal, we shared our favorite things about both worlds and what each could improve. When the conversation turned to what everyone would do to the Council if they still had their Abilities, the afternoon really got fun. It was a light conversation, nothing hostile or toxic—okay, maybe a little hostile, but this was the Council we were talking about after all. I had the sense this family was cleansed of its negativity by Nana long ago, with Harvest being her final project. What an amazing force.

For the first time since my Abandonment, I felt at home. Olympia wasn't Hell. The Netos weren't the Sunstones, yet I couldn't have been more comfortable if I was sitting surrounded by my parents, Dialphio, Bilba and Ralrek.

By the end of the picnic, my cheeks hurt from too much laughing. The goodbyes were as drawn out as the grilling had been. Nana refused to let me leave until I promised to spend more time with Leo. She also made me swear to put the upcoming mortal holidays on my calendar. It was expected, I learned, that I attend the family's Samhain—culturally appropriated as Halloween by mortals—feast. In the following months, my first Thanksgiving and Christmas were obligated to this extended family of mine. Of course, Cancer was more than welcomed to join. Only after swearing on the Satanic Bible—I did not have to *literally* do that—was I released.

Back in the apartment, fed until fat, I drifted in solitude. It struck me just how absolutely cruel the Council was to do what they did to demons like the Neto family. To the aged and to children. There was a special place in Heaven for demons like that, I swore. I'd have to ask Cassie the next time we caught up.

17

OLYMPIA

"ZEKE?" Cancer asked, doing a double take as I walked into the Lion's Den. "What are you doing here?"

I motioned toward the octagon. "I've been promising Leo I would train. I figured, I don't have anything else going on today, so why not?"

The gym still stunk, as if even the sheet metal siding held the aroma of sweaty humans. The regulars and my roommate didn't seem to notice. Cancer made her way from the stool where she had been watching the fighters and hugged me, momentarily neutralizing the funk.

Then she pulled back. "You're seriously going to train?"

"Why not?"

"They don't play around," she said. "It will be intense. Probably risky."

"Still think I should give it a shot," I replied.

Cancer's eyes flicked over my shoulder. "Give him time."

"Who?" I said, following her eyes.

Leo was coming from the reception area into the gym. His eyes were drawn down in a scowl.

"Hey Leo," I said.

He walked past me without looking up. "Hey."

I pulled my head back in surprise, looking to Cancer for insight. "What's that about?"

Cancer rotated to watch him pass, giving me a one-shoulder shrug. "I don't know. He's been like that for days. Every time I try to talk to him about something, a new routine for the fighters, stretching recommendations, stuff like that, he's been... cold. Short. Brusque. Debbie said she doesn't know what's going on. This is unlike him, according to her. I'm done trying. When he's ready, he'll talk."

I hadn't seen Leo since the family picnic. "Let me talk to him."

"Be careful, Zeke," Cancer warned. "He's been an asshole, treating everyone like dirt. Just fair warning."

"Thanks."

Leo was at the octagon, adjusting the apron and testing the metal links of the cage wall.

"You good, Leo?" I asked as I approached.

He didn't turn to face me. "Yeah."

"Well, hey, I was thinking I could take you up on some training." I looked at my sneakers and shorts and my old concert T-shirt I had picked up from a thrift store for two dollars. Hardly the look of a fighter. Creed was strapped to my bike seat, which was chained to a rack in front of the gym, making me feel especially naked and awkward. "How many times have we talked about it, and we still haven't gotten together? I can't keep pushing it off. So, are you up for it? You could give me a few lessons... returning the favor, you know?"

Help with an angel for help in the octagon. That had been the deal. A troubled mind might cloud his memory.

Leo stopped manipulating the cage chain-link and faced me. His look told me he wasn't making the connections between our deal and my comment.

"Remember how I helped you with a certain issue, and I wanted to get some pointers in return?" I said.

He took in my casual outfit. For a second, a flash of humor crossed his expression. "You want to train now? In that?"

I shrugged, taking a quick glance around the gym. "If you have time. I didn't know if you had a class going on, but it looks quiet."

"That's because the Lucifer–blessed war is costing me members. Lost another two this week. I didn't even know they got drafted until they came in to cancel their memberships."

"Sorry to hear that," I said. "Casual members?"

Leo dropped his head, giving it a few shakes. "No. Both were two of my better fighters. Losing them is going to hurt the team at the next event. One is a titleholder, so he's going to have to vacate it and lose out on a nice payday." He shrugged, a gesture full of attitude. "But what can you do? The war isn't ending anytime soon. They're drafting more and more people."

He walked past me, lifting a hand and beckoning with a finger. "Follow me. I'll have you hit the ropes to warm up your shoulders. Then we'll hit the bags while we talk. Kill two ravens with one stone."

He took the next few minutes to show me the technique he wanted to see. After warming up my legs, arms, and even my neck, we moved to a rack where I finished a long, and some-times awkward, routine of shoulder shrugs, pulls, rotations, and lifts with resistance bands. Then we moved to a heavy canvas bag, which I promptly beat the heaven out of with a series of arm and leg strikes. Well before the bag was defeated, I was sweating. My hand-me-down concert T-shirt was drenched and stretched.

Leo had me on the mat next, moving through a series of push-ups and sit-ups, even using a foam roller to work out any last kinks and hitches in my lower back and shoulders. Honestly, I could have rolled for hours; it felt that therapeutic.

My galloping pulse reminded me that no matter how good of shape I thought I was in, I had a long way to go.

Besides giving instructions and pointers, Leo was quiet, often leaving to snap at other gym members who were, as he said, acting like 'lazy wastes of skin bags'. I had no idea what an energetic skin bag acted like, but his targets were sweating as profusely as me. Lazy, they did not appear. Periodically, he returned to give me a new routine, only to yell at someone halfway through his instructions.

Back on my feet, he had me jump roping. "I was hoping to get some cage training," I said between gasps.

Leo crossed his arms, the sinewy muscle in his forearms cutting from wrist to elbow. "It's the octagon. And you think you're ready for that with the way you're panting and sweating?"

"Yeah, you think we could? Not like I'm training for a tournament, Leo. I'm trying to stop me getting my ass kicked."

"You would get destroyed," he responded, but his eyes scanned the gym as if he was searching for someone.

"Better destroyed here than in the streets." Still jumping, I managed to form the most coherent sentence I could as my heart raced and I panted in short bursts. "Possibly. I should be able to hold my own for a little while. Plus, I'll be learning the entire time. Think someone could show me the ropes?"

"You see how many people I've got here right now, man?" he said. "And they have their own routines I'm running them through. Routines they're paying me to do. Some of them are so far behind I don't know if they'll ever get caught up. They keep saying they've got other stuff getting in the way, but it's bullshit. They're just lazy. Not sure I've got anyone for you to spar with."

"What about you?"

"Me?" Leo scoffed. "Come on, man, you don't want that."

"Why not?" I said, stopping my work out and letting the jump rope dangle over an arm.

He scrunched his mouth, waving at me. "You've only been working out for a couple of minutes and look at you. If we got in the octagon, I would tear you apart. You're not in fighting shape. You're not a fighter, man. I am. And I know what I'm doing."

"True, but you could take it easy on me."

Leo shook his head. "See, that's the problem, right there. No respect for the sport. The octagon isn't the place to take it easy. If you don't fully apply yourself, you get injured. I'm not taking the chance of you doing something dumb and hurting you and me in the process. Not with the fights coming up, especially. Go see Debbie. She can get you geared up while I see what we can do since you insist on having your ass handed to you."

Debbie assisted me in finding the best gear they had lying around for my upcoming beat down.

"Are you wearing a cup?" she asked pointedly after making sure I had MMA gloves, headgear, and shin guards.

"A cup?" I asked, not in the least bit thirsty and struggling to imagine why hydration was imperative.

"For your little boys," Debbie said, dipping her head toward my most personal space.

"Oh, sorry. I'm not used to it being called that," I said with sudden realization. "Um, no."

"Well, good luck then," she said, slapping the top of the gloves in my hands. "I've got to get back to work."

Dismissed by Debbie, I walked into the bay, suddenly very focused on my family jewels. True to his word, Leo was waiting by the cage with four female fighters.

Cancer intercepted me. "Are you sure you want to do this?"

"We need to talk later, if you ever stop working," I said, my tone low. "I'm worried about a few things, and I have to handle something. If I don't get this training, I might end up getting myself in trouble with my... stick. You remember him?"

Cancer scrunched her face as she nodded, understanding my reference. "Just be careful, Zeke. They might look little, but they're no joke."

I gave her a reassured smile. "It's just training."

She rolled her eyes. "You don't know Leo's kind of training." When it was obvious I wouldn't be deterred, she asked, "Where is your mouth guard?"

I offered my glove that hid the item. "Not sure how to put this in with these gloves on."

She sighed in a motherly way. "Let me help."

By the time she'd shoved the piece of plastic in my mouth Leo was waving me over. "Come on, man."

When I joined a small group, he made introductions to the brunette, two red-heads, and a sandy blond. Leo had his bases covered. I thought I recognized two of them, but I couldn't be sure where I would have met them. "Zeke, this is Stephanie, Adina, TC, and Erica. They'll show you some moves. I'm warning you, they won't take it easy."

"Nice to meet you." I gave them a smile.

The four women, near enough to my height and build, did not return it. TC snarled behind her mouth guard. Erica smashed her fist into her palm. Adina bounced from foot to foot, her fists raised in front of her, and swiveled side to side, as if she was doing a full-body warm up. Stephanie rolled her head in a half circle as if the tension of wanting to tear me apart was making her ache.

"Get in then," Leo said, pulling the door open.

The four women raced up the stairs.

"Wait, I'm fighting all of them?" I asked.

He *harrumphed*. "You said you wanted training. What better way than to jump into an intense session? This will be good for you. Now, get in there. I don't have all day. This is a favor, right? You're not a paying customer, man. So let's go."

I clambered up the stairs into the octagon, catching my toe on the last step, stubbing it and falling to the canvas. That received a few chuckles from people outside the cage, none from inside. Leo's death squad did not look like they were in the mood to laugh about anything.

As soon as I got my foot clear of the door, it slammed closed behind me with a clang and accompanying clink as Leo locked it. I was about to ask him what he was doing when I found myself face-first against the chain-link cage.

Stephanie was behind me—bless it, she smelled amazing —shoving my face into the steel. Her forearm pressed against the back of my neck and somehow she had already snagged my left arm and yanked it behind me. I howled. The metal mesh bit into my cheek. I scrambled to ask Leo to call off his attack dog, only to notice the fighters in the gym stopping their workout routines, moving to the cage to witness my obliteration. I couldn't see Cancer behind the entertained strangers. I'd seen two of them before. A panicked second later, I had visions of vans and gravel.

The brigade of thugs who attacked us were members of the gym. I knew it!

I scrambled to fight off the star-bursts of conclusions over-whelming my brain. This could be a coincidence, but it might be more. Unfortunately for me, I didn't have time to work it out. If I didn't concentrate, I was going to be worse for wear. With two thugs on standby, they could take advantage of my diminished state once these four 'ladies' were finished with me.

Stephanie pulled me away from the cage, giving my cheek a reprieve, only to pull me to the mat. She laid underneath me with me looking up that the ceiling and wishing for the first time in six thousand years I didn't have the superior missionary position on a female. My back was to her chest, my arm sandwiched in between us, and her free arm wrapped around my throat.

Her arm was solid muscle. I grabbed it to pull it away, but it didn't budge. Somewhere outside the cage, more than a few people laughed.

I rolled side to side, trying to break free, but her grip never loosened. I slapped at her arm, I pulled, I yanked, and the entire time, Stephanie's arm dug deeper into my neck. My shoulder burned as she kept the other arm trapped.

"That's what I call leverage!" Leo shouted from somewhere as I stared at the metal ceiling and the lights hanging from them.

My mouth opened wide, trying to draw oxygen and failing.

The three other women in the cage laughed and rooted her on. Everything was quieting now. I imagine the decreased levels of oxygen going to my brain had something to do with that. Sounds dulled as my vision narrowed in on the light above the ring. I had to move fast or I would embarrass myself by being choked out within seconds of stepping into the cage for the first time.

Drawing my legs in, I pushed up on the balls of my feet then thrust my legs over my head. The move sent me circling above Stephanie. Her grip slipped as I tumbled over and behind. There was a quick wrenching on my neck in the final second when she realized what I was doing, before her hold finally broke.

Standing above her head, I scrambled to put her on the defensive. I was still seeing stars as oxygen flooded back to my brain. Stephanie rolled onto her stomach and was upright before I contemplated my next move.

I lowered my center of gravity, hands raised, preparing to throw punches and wondering how hard I was allowed to hit a woman. Before I thought for too long, another monkey jumped on my back, this time in the form of the auburn-haired Adina.

The woman was only an inch shorter than me and not heavy, but she was strong. Stronger than Stephanie. She followed her peer's move, from behind, wrapping her arm around my still–recovering neck and cramming her elbow underneath my chin. Unfortunately for her, I'd ditched using delay as a tactic.

Reaching above with both hands, I grabbed the bands of her sports bra, yanking forward as I rolled toward Stephanie. One red-head met the other as Adina flew into her co-fighter. Stephanie barely had time to raise her hands. The pair went down in a tangle of muscular legs and arms.

I now understood how the sparring session was going to go. Leo was testing me in the most unfair way he could, by having me ganged up on by multiple fighters who knew more about this ring than I could learn in the next year. Armed with that, traumatized by the fact Cancer was outside the ring with two van assailants, I didn't wait for Erica or TC to make their moves.

I spun to face the pair. They spread out in opposite directions. Cheers boomed. Beyond the two fighters, more of the gym members lined the cage, drawn by the spectacle. Faces blurred in the heat of the battle, but it was a safe bet that everyone in the gym was now watching.

"Take it easy ladies," I said as I hunkered into a fighting position. "I don't know what I'm doing."

TC snarled and Erica growled as they circled. As I rotated toward one, the other attempted to slip behind me. When I spun on that one, the other took her place. They were going to do this dance and would soon be joined by Stephanie and Adina. I needed to move now.

I closed in on TC. Her scowl turned more menacing as she took shorter steps to keep me moving, so I remained unbalanced. When I was within arm's length, she threw a combination of punches that kept me away. None landed, deflecting off my gloves. Even with the protective gear, they were solid enough that I would not want to be squarely punched by her. I closed in again as she kicked the side of my leg. The muscle knotted instantly. I did the smart thing and backed away.

"Come on, man! You wanted to fight. Now fight!" Leo shouted from outside the cage.

"I'm trying!" I shouted back, using oxygen I probably should have saved.

The mat vibrated underneath me. I spun to see Erica charging and moved just as she lowered her shoulder to hit me at waist height. She missed, and I gave her a push in the back of the head for good measure, sending her flying into the cage. She bounced off it and stumbled backward in my direction. Now it was my turn to jump on someone else's back. Wrapping my arm under her chin, I grasped my opposite bicep and snagged her head with my free hand to lock in the chokehold. I may or may not have gripped her hair tight enough to pull as she fought to break free. I squeezed harder. Within seconds, Erica's hand slapped my arm.

"She's tapping! She's tapping!" someone shouted from the cage.

"Let her go, she's done!" Leo ordered, and I broke the hold, getting to my feet and looking down at the brunette with a mixture of adrenaline and regret as she coughed to draw air.

Three fighters still occupied this enclosed space with me. Each looked ready for another go. I didn't know how much energy I had left to satisfy them.

"Let me have him," a deep voice shouted from outside the ring. I didn't turn to see who had spoken, my eyes still on TC, whose permanent scowl had slipped, revealing a woman who no longer looked like she was interested in a fight.

The crowd fell silent. Only TC shuffling and Stephanie and Adina taking recovery positions filled the void. Somewhere, Erica's coughing slowed. It was as if the fighters in the ring and those outside it were waiting for Leo to make his decision. King Leo and his pride, I guessed. Cancer had warned me about the cult–like figure he had become for many in the gym, and the way these fighters waited for his permission convinced me of that truth.

"Fine," Leo said, sounding less than happy. "See what you can teach him then."

The cage door was unlocked and yanked open by the woman with the bulbous nose. My adrenaline pumped harder at the sight of the chain-wielding maniac from the van crew. I scanned the crowd and saw three others hiding amongst them now. It wasn't until the four sparring partners walked out of the ring without even as much as a head nod of combatant respect, that I saw who wanted to finish me off.

I backed away from the door as he strode up the steps, already in fighting gear.

The ex-demon from the gravel yard jumped into the cage. He knocked his gloved hands together, and his eyes were a fury of focus. This was the one who knew enough about Creed to warn his crew to take cover right before it took out its vengeance. Now, trapped in this cage and surrounded by Leo's disciples, I didn't know if this was about mixed martial arts training or revenge.

The door slamming closed sounded like the hangman's death knell.

The shirtless ex-demon was an intimidating figure. Intensity had radiated off him the night they chased me through Olympia and again at the gravel yard. In those two instances, he had been garbed in a black outfit. Now, he only wore trunks, boots, and gloves, revealing just how fit he was.

I tried to swallow. I don't think I did.

As he jumped from foot to foot, his pectorals barely shimmied. His biceps flexed even as his arms dangled at his side. Just under the lower edge of his shorts, his quadriceps were as big as a small devildog. This ex-demon had so little body fat he would have sunk like a stone in water.

"Kill him, Virgo," Chain Queen shouted, slamming her palm against the cage.

Others in the crowd mimicked her, slapping the chain-link, making it rattle. The intensity in the gym was ratcheted up a hundred degrees as Virgo closed in.

"Be careful, man, I don't know what I'm doing," I said, swallowing while trying to not appear intimidated, even though I absolutely was and couldn't think straight as he neared.

"I know," Virgo said in that deep, rich voice.

He circled me as the crowd cheered.

I kept my guard raised, trying to figure out how in the world I was going to get out of this cage alive. Was this a setup? The possibility existed. Leo had been agreeable to training me and had weeks to think through how it could go down. To this day, he still hadn't revealed who his friend was. A handful of the van gang were members of the gym, and they just happened to be here tonight?

This did not feel right.

Planned, plotted, scripted.

Here I was, inside a locked cage with an experienced fighter, a cage surrounded by a crowd that included at least a few of his allies. The only ally I knew for sure I had was the kindhearted nurse outside the cage who had no way or means of helping. Even Creed wouldn't be much help. Strapped underneath my bike outside the gym, it would take valuable seconds to get to me. Virgo might be too fast for the halberd to do any good.

With the way this was developing, it wouldn't have shocked me if Chax walked out of one of the locker rooms. Like I said, bad.

Virgo closed in, his fists raised.

I raised mine higher, keeping as much of my face covered

as possible while still providing a narrow slit through which to view his approach. With short steps, I backed up. He closed. The crowd around shouted encouragement to him. Focusing on his fists, I never saw his kick coming. It connected with the same thigh TC had struck moments before. The powerful strike sent me staggering backward, my legs trembling. I didn't have time to worry about injury as another kick with the opposite foot landed on my other leg. Then a third, back to the right leg. Over and over, Virgo struck with kicks that pushed me back, back, back.

I moved to my left, and he easily rotated with me, much quicker and on sturdier legs than the pair quivering beneath me.

I moved to my right. He shifted.

Virgo darted forward, his fist nearing my face. I raised both gloved hands, and he hit them so hard they pushed back. My gloves bounced off my head, which ricocheted into the chain-link. Someone outside the cage laughed. I would have too, since I'm sure I looked absolutely ridiculous.

Pressed against the unforgiving metal, Virgo was on me, throwing punch after punch. I kept my head covered while bending at the waist to use my elbows to shield my gut, which was still taking a pounding. Each blow pushed more air from my lungs. Blow after blow, in rapid succession, landed on my torso and each time my guard dropped, Virgo sent punches toward my head. Sometimes I blocked them. Sometimes I did not. In those times when his punches landed, the world filled with ringing.

I was running out of energy and connection with the world. I couldn't possibly call Creed to save me either because I couldn't string together the single syllable or thought. I had asked for this. This assault was more than a show of dominance driven by testosterone and adrenaline. Virgo did not intend on killing me in front of so many witnesses, did he? The aim was abduction, wasn't it? Unless

Seraph and Chax, and any of the other multitude of names Azazel hinted at didn't care one way or another. Why would they? We were all disposable to the Council, serving with our lives if necessary, for Lucifer.

My body ached, points of pain, raging for my attention, sprang to life, begging him to cease the attack.

Virgo worked my sides, landing punches into my lats and rib cage. I couldn't take much more. My opportunity came more from desperation than strategy. As he leaned to throw another punch, I pulled my arm away from my head, risking a counterattack that might knock me out cold, and threw a punch to the side of his head.

I would like to think even for my relative pint–size, I'm strong as a chimera. That's hardly the truth, but I did hit Virgo hard enough to send him stumbling sideways. Hard enough to elicit a few exclamations of surprise from his supporters.

Virgo stumbled and started to stand upright again. I had to negate the chance for a counterattack. I dove for his legs, wrapping my arms around them. Without seeing my fresh attack, he was off-balance. Keeping his legs pinned together with my arms wrapped just behind his knees, I drove him into the mat, my shoulder digging into his stomach. He jerked in an attempt to break free. His fist found my back and shoulders, but I kept my head tucked to his side to reduce its exposure. Now that I was on top, I had no idea what to do next. I couldn't hold his legs for more than a few minutes while suffering these punches. I had a temporary position of dominance, and I could not relinquish it.

I waited for another strike to land on my back. When it did, I scrambled up his body, knowing he needed another second to follow up on the punch. Using the intervening time, I straddled him, my legs wrapped around his waist, and sat back to force his down.

"Get up, Virgo! Rip his head off!" Chain Queen shouted.

"Kill him!" someone else encouraged. I think they meant it too.

I pressed harder on his pinned arm, driving my head into the side of his and pushing. His opposite arm came up and found the back of my head. Stars exploded. We sat like that for an eternity, my legs struggling to keep his under control, while I pinned one arm and fended off blows from the other. There was no way out. I couldn't land any attacks and was constantly on the defensive. Though I had the superior position, it afforded nothing to bring this fight to an end.

I gasped for breath. Every fiber burned. Each time he kicked, he moved me a few inches. Each time he tried to free his arm, mine gave. The advantage I had enjoyed for a few minutes was drying up.

In desperation, I pulled my head up and raised my arm to strike. My arm halfway toward its zenith, I realized my mistake. I had freed his upper body completely and had to pull my legs inward to put power behind the punch. In that position, it was easy for Virgo to throw me off-balance. He sent a kick upward, connecting with the middle of my back, thrusting me forward even as my punch descended, striking the mat instead of his head.

One second I was flying over him, landing on my stomach, and the next he scrambled on top of me, yanking my arm as he put a chokehold on. My third of the fight.

I screamed as he wrenched my arm backward. The burning in my shoulder convinced me each muscle fiber was peeling from their associated tendon.

Sounds dulled for the third time but not enough to avoid the cheering at Virgo's dominant position. I squinted as I tried to snag anything of Virgo and tear it from him. Nothing was off-limits if it meant this pain would stop. Around the ring, only inches away, half a dozen faces blurred. Except for one.

Cancer's eyes were wide with worry. As oxygen stopped

feeding my brain, even her face became indistinguishable, its features wiped clear by a wall of agony.

I was vaguely aware of the ring shaking, and then the weight suffocating me was lifted.

I rolled onto my back, gasping for air and holding my shoulder.

"What is wrong with you? Get the fuck out of here!" a voice—Leo's?—shouted.

An eruption of voices protested, one indistinguishable from another. The mat shook more violently, and Cancer was at my side.

"Zeke? Zeke? Are you okay?" she said, her face so close I could tell what she ate for dinner between the hospital and the gym. More fast food. My home-cooked meals betrayed.

I pried my eyes open. Her puff of loose-curled hair was haloed by the hanging lights, hiding her face in shadow until she leaned closer. That's when I noticed the dark circles under her eyes, accented by stress lines in the corners and across her forehead.

"I think I've earned chicken wings tonight," I said through a throat dried by exertion and dehydration.

The lines around her eyes smoothed. The dark circles stayed put. "You asked for it," she laughed and slapped me on the arm.

I winced. "Wrong one," I said through gritted teeth.

"Sorry about that," she said, holding my arm. "Don't move it until I can look at it. Can you sit up?"

"Yeah, I'm fine," I said.

"But you're not much of a fighter," Leo said, hovering over me and offering me a hand. I took it.

"That's why I said I wanted training," I reminded him.

"Well, you've got some. Welcome to the Lion's Den." He barked a laugh and lowered his head to wrap my arm around his shoulder. He walked me out of the octagon and took me to his office where Cancer checked me out in relative privacy.

"Who in heaven was that guy?" I asked Leo, still holding an ice bag to my shoulder.

"Virgo?"

"Yeah, the one who was heaven-bent on separating this arm from my body." I winced when I tried to raise my arm to show him my reference. "What's his deal, and is he involved with you?"

"Involved how? He's a member," Leo answered.

From the corner of the office, seated in a black chair with thicker arms than seat padding, Cancer groused. "I don't know what happened out there. I've seen him around for weeks and he's never acted like that. I thought he was one of those quiet-but-strong types who isn't a total jackass."

I wanted to blurt out a question to see if Cancer had recognized Chain Queen or any of the other van gang but couldn't with Leo there. When she tended to them in the gravel yard, Virgo had already fled the scene. Her triage had been cursory on all but the mortally wounded member. In the traumatic situation, she might not have registered their faces enough to recall them in the gym.

If she had seen Virgo in the Lion's Den before, then maybe the gang had been tracking her movements as well as mine. I swallowed the lump. Chax was in the Overworld. Chax was near. Chax might mean to finish his family's business with the Nijal family if he didn't believe in curses as a bonus to destroying me.

Leo was seated on the edge of a chair directly in front of me, his legs spread and his hands dropped between them as he rested his elbows on his knees. His eyes never left me. "I have no idea what that was about. I have been working with Virgo for a while now. For months, man, I've been trying to bring out his aggression. Too passive, but an outstanding fighter. Undefeated. There's a sponsor in town who is interested in him. Problem is, he doesn't seem interested in them. He doesn't seem interested in much."

"Tell my shoulder that," I responded.

"Yeah, man," Leo said, sitting back. "Listen, I would have never let him get into the cage with you if I knew that shit was going to go down. You looked like you could handle the women, and I didn't want you to get too cocky. When he said he wanted you, I figured fighting Virgo would be perfect medicine to keep you grounded. I don't like fighters with big heads. They lose touch too quickly."

"I'm hardly a fighter," I said.

"And he already has a big head," Cancer said from the corner.

"Are you involved with him in something I need to know about?" I said, needing to focus on the hard questions.

Leo ran a hand through his beard. "Man, you won't get it."

Now Cancer shifted forward on her chair. "What are you saying, Leo?"

I tried to send her a warning with a look. I needed to get an hour or two alone with her so I could update her on everything before the situation became ever more dangerous.

But she wanted answers from Leo "Who is he, Leo? Is he part of that group that's been following me? I asked you to do something about them. What's going on, bless it?"

So, I wasn't the only one with secrets. "Someone has been following you?"

Cancer's eyes finally broke from Leo. "Yes."

"Why didn't you tell me?" I asked.

"First, because I couldn't be sure what was going on, and second, because I don't need you to protect me, Zeke," she answered forcefully. "It always happens when I'm here, so I told Leo. This is his gym. I figured it was just a bunch of jerks who thought they could overstep."

"We need to talk. I think I might know what's going on," I said carefully. "But let's do that when we have more privacy."

"I can leave you two alone if you'd like?" Leo offered.

"No way," Cancer and I said simultaneously.

She cleared her throat angrily. "I want an answer, Leo."

"Me too," I said. "You wanted my help, Leo. I gave it to you. I even put myself in harm's way to save you. Remember?" He didn't need to know Cassie wasn't a threat, to me at least. "You owe me an answer about Virgo. Are you and him wrapped up in something?"

Leo pushed back against his chair, rubbing his face aggressively while sighing behind his hands. "Guys, I swear, I'm not. I don't know what you think, but I'm not like that. I just..." He stopped to examine us. "I'm going to shoot straight with you. Zeke—"

"Ezekial," I corrected. "Only my friends may call me Zeke, and right now, you don't qualify."

His eyes drifted closed. "That's fair. Listen, you met my Nana. You know what she's like. She has made peace with our... situation."

His head half–cocked in Cancer's direction.

"Just talk openly, Leo," I said, flicking a thumb toward Cancer. "She knows what you are. All three of us are Abandoned demons. See? There. Out in the open. Okay? I'm running out of time and patience trying to figure out foe from friend."

"You're a—a demon?" Leo asked of Cancer.

The circles under her eyes seemed to darken as she took a deep breath. "I don't know what I am anymore, but Zeke and I were Abandoned a few months ago."

Leo's gaze dropped between his feet. "I never knew. I'm sorry."

"I don't feel safe, Leo," Cancer said. "I need you to be honest with us. What are you involved in?"

Leo slapped the arm of his chair, making Cancer jump. "Nothing, I swear. I'm not involved in anything. It's just—just that I've talked to agents of," he paused.

I wasn't feeling patient, Steve's bar lesson about its virtues forgotten for the moment. "What?" I nudged the gym owner.

Leo interlaced his fingers, squeezing and wrinkling the flesh between his knuckles. "Last year I met someone, and they told me there was a way I can make right."

"Make right?" I asked.

He waved his hand in the air as if I could see what he was referencing. "All of this, man. The entire situation. It's all bullshit, you know that. You do too," he said, turning to Cancer. "We've all been screwed over, man. I figured out a way to make right."

"With who?" I asked.

"Not with, but *for* who," Leo said. His voice was firm, hands clenched, and he fidgeted on the chair as if he was sitting on a pile of tacks.

"What are you talking about?" Cancer asked, using the same motherly voice she used for me and my squad back in Baghdad.

Leo groaned. "I was told I could earn my way back into the Underworld. Not only for me, but for my family." He spun, facing me, a pleading look in his eyes. "Man, you saw what they were like at the picnic. They're too young to decay. Kids, man. Freakin' kids. This isn't just for me," he said, pounding his chest. "This is for everyone in the family, the little ones and the adults. Nana, too. She doesn't deserve to spend her last years like this. Do you know how fast she has been decaying? I don't know what you guys have been going through, but I'm getting weaker every day. That's why you don't see me in the octagon anymore. I can't hold my weight against half the fighters in this blessed place, even the smaller ones. I have to get back. I need to get my family back. So, I looked for a way and found one."

"How?" I asked, half skeptical while also trying to contain my excitement. If Leo was even telling a half-truth, this held promise. A way to save Cancer.

Leo looked at me like answering was the last thing he wanted to do. "I can't give up my source, man. But there's a guy, here in the area. Not sure if he's in Olympia or out of Tacoma, but either way, he's got hookups in the Underworld. He said if I worked for him, he would put in a good word and get me an interview. I'm already way down the path, man. I've actually had the interview. I'm close to getting my family back home."

I squinted. "What kind of work?"

"You know, Balance stuff. That's why I started the gym. I took out a loan and opened. Don't have to worry about repaying it if I'm back home with my family. The only thing I had to do was get mortals focused on themselves. Pride, ego, individual accomplishment. You know? That kind of stuff. If I could build a large membership and get them chasing their own ambitions, I was going to get the chance to take everyone home. He said if I did my job over the next year, everyone could get home before... before they get too sick. Then I could hand the gym off to another, he said. Wasn't long after that the blessed angel started showing up."

Cassie. I would not betray her, but I needed to know what their situation was. Was she running interference or acting directly against him?

"What about the angel?"

Leo frowned, shaking his head. "When I wouldn't agree to stop pushing these mortals to focus on their goals, she got nasty. Threatened me. Harassing me and my customers, trying to drive away business. Said if I didn't stop, she'd do worse. That she'd given me enough chances. That's screwed up, man. She is interfering with my chance to get back into the Underworld! That's why I needed your help. I figured, if you could help me with her because of... you know, who you are, I would have enough time to get my family home. I didn't expect you to be cool. I really didn't. I swear, it's nothing against either of you; I'm just trying to take care of my family."

"I get that," I said after a moment's thought. "And Virgo? How does he fit into this?"

Leo's shoulders drooped. "He's just another punk with an ego problem. He came in with a group a while back and, honestly, man, I just targeted him because I could tell they all needed their egos stroked."

"And you did it, right?" Cancer asked with a biting tone.

"They were easy, Cancer," Leo said, almost apologetically. "Easy points. I was using them, I admit it. I'm sorry, really sorry, about you getting mixed up in that. I still don't understand what happened."

I rolled my shoulder under the ice pack. "Don't worry. I'll recover." I stood, looking at Cancer and nodding toward the closed door. "You ready to head out?"

"Yeah," she answered quietly and stood to collect her things.

Leo watched us. "You coming in tomorrow, Cancer?"

"Mmm, hmmm," she mumbled without turning around.

He looked at me, his green eyes losing their intensity. "What about you? I promise I'll give you pointers. I won't let crap like that happen again. I'm straight-up, man."

"I think about it," I answered honestly. "I've got a lot to think about."

I walked out of Leo's office and closed the door behind me, still unsure if turning my back on him was smart or reckless.

18

OLYMPIA

DIALPHIO: *This isn't good.*

I stared at my demonic notebook sitting in my lap, the sounds of quiet city life ebbing to and fro below as I considered Dialphio's hopeless and unhelpful response.

I had spent the last hour communicating with her about the previous day's incident at the Lion's Den. I told her everything that had happened since our last letters. The fight with the four women, Virgo and what Leo knew about him. Leo's dilemma and how his pride got in the way. I even shared the most confusing event of all, that I had unlocked a power in Creed to the point of drawing the Council's attention. Before I was done, my old boss heard my inner turmoil about Azazel's friendly visit.

After moments without a response, thin letters scratched out on my notebook paper in Dialphio's handwriting.

DIALPHIO: *I have so much to say. I wish we could do this face-to-face.*

ZEKE: *Why?*

DIALPHIO: *Some things are better communicated that way.*

ZEKE: *True.*

DIALPHIO: *Especially things of this nature. You and I don't have secrets, at least I hope that is still the case. You are special. And that halberd makes you a severe threat. I've told you that from the very beginning.*

I nodded at the paper as I scribbled out my response.

ZEKE: *You have, I just don't know what to do about that.*

DIALPHIO: *What do you mean?*

The fine point of my quill bit into the parchment. My letters refused to form. My brain would not allow them. Dialphio was correct, face-to-face would make this much easier. But if we were having this conversation in Hell, the paranoia over the Council listening would never be far away. As it was, sitting in my apartment—a sanctuary of the Council—communicating via my demonic notebook was about as safe as it got. I was probably safer than Dialphio. I thought about how I could frame my response without putting her at risk.

ZEKE: *There's obviously more to this than their distaste for Creed. I just can't figure out what it is.*

DIALPHIO: *Azazel came to you for a reason. Have you told me everything he said?*

I thought back. Putting Dialphio at risk of being discovered by the Council was the last thing I wanted, but providing her with insight would pay benefits. The game was incrementally ratcheting up. Dialphio put herself in risky positions for me, to help me deal with everything I'd faced since she came into my life. She'd done more than that, pulling back the mysteries of Creed as and when she could. If the Council only knew. That didn't mean I wanted to make things worse by adding depth to her involvement. A careful balance to strike. She was a grown succubus, though. She knew how to handle herself. if she wasn't comfortable, she wouldn't ask.

ZEKE: *Yes, everything. Azazel knew I used Creed but hid it from the rest of the Council. He's interested in Bilba and Cancer. He even hinted about political struggles. And, of course, telling me about Chax. The entire thing has me feeling crazy.*

DIALPHIO: *Why would his visit make you feel like that?*

ZEKE: *Because he's a member of the Council. I can't trust them, Dialphio. None of them. How do I know his visit wasn't a setup for something else? Every time I turn around, there is a new problem.*

DIALPHIO: *I understand. This has been a struggle you have faced for far too long. Cells of demons around the Circles are gaining momentum in their calls for change, but I fear change is slow. My gut tells me Azazel is the exception rather than the rule. He didn't visit you out of subversive malice, but because of genuine concern.*

ZEKE: *Why would he be concerned for me? He's part of Lucifer's Council, the same demons who screwed me over every chance they got. It doesn't make sense.*

DIALPHIO: *Didn't you say he talked about the politics of the Council? One incubus cannot force four demons to follow a course of action. Politics is about subtlety and patience. Careful, sometimes painfully plotted and executed moves are the key to success. Have you played the mortal game of chess yet?*

I looked away from the demonic notebook, confused. A blackbird crossed my view, from one rooftop to another. The seagull compatriots squawked criticism from the other end of the block overlooking the harbor. Chess? Games? At a time like this?

ZEKE: *No, I haven't.*

DIALPHIO: *Give it a try. It's a fascinating game. A strategic one. Both players have the same aim. To pin the other's king. Subdue it. But the king is not the force in the game. The queen has the true power, and the experienced player knows that. The important strategy isn't to protect the king, but to keep your queen safe so she can wreak havoc. The other pieces, the rooks, the bishops, the pawns are used in attack and defense. But the smart player uses them in more subversive ways, to distract from moves of the real powerful force. They keep the opponent's pieces busy while the queen destroys. That's the mark of a true genius.*

ZEKE: *So are you saying I'm the Queen?*

DIALPHIO: *Maybe not you, maybe not even Creed. Maybe it's*

a combination; you and the halberd. I'm not convinced the power of the weapon is to destroy. That may not be why the Council fears it.

ZEKE: *Oh, it can destroy, trust me.*

The van and the man broken at the end of a pole flashed in my mind.

ZEKE: *But if not to destroy, then what?*

DIALPHIO: *To preserve. The weapon is of One. We may never know its true nature. Creed may forever remain a mystery, as will One's intentions. But we can deduce a few things. The weapon being made from the creator of All imbues it with certain intrinsic characteristics. That's why even the most powerful among our kind can't put their hands on it. What other item in the entirety of the Underworld can Lucifer's Council not control if they want to?*

I gave the question consideration and couldn't come up with an answer.

ZEKE: *They can do whatever they want.*

DIALPHIO: *Exactly. Yet they can't take Creed, because it is of One. It supersedes our laws. No, Creed is not meant to destroy, it is meant to preserve.*

ZEKE: *Preserve what, though? That's my frustration. Years of being screwed with by the Council, for being punished for not doing anything wrong except maybe making a few mistakes. I'm at the point where I need answers before I totally give up on everything.*

DIALPHIO: *Don't talk like that.*

ZEKE: *It's the truth, Dialphio. It's so exhausting looking over my shoulder every single turn. There are times when I just want to lie down for Chax and let him run over me, if that's what he wants. Cancer has essentially given up, and her life is more peaceful for it.*

DIALPHIO: *Is it, though? From what you've said, that doesn't sound like the case at all. Outwardly, things may appear peaceful, but we cannot know the turmoil someone feels. Plus, you're not a quitter. If you were, they would have oppressed you years ago. No, there is definitely something more here, and you're not allowed to quit until we find out what it is.*

ZEKE: *You're not the boss of me.*

There was a slight pause in her response. I imagined Dialphio chirping like a bird in laughter back in The Book Abyss. Bless it, I missed that stinky, dusty, and overcrowded bookstore.

DIALPHIO: *Sorry, that made me laugh, and I had to tell Jade a lie about why I was back here at my desk, laughing like an imp seeing her first dingleberries. She's a wonderful replacement for you, by the way. I got lucky with her.*

ZEKE: *I'm happy for you.*

I wasn't; I was envious and jealous, and homesick, and battling rising depression—but Dialphio didn't need to know that.

DIALPHIO: *Seriously, the reason you hold Creed is not an accident. It was not the whim of the senile incubus on his deathbed. This was a carefully manipulated situation. I'm not going to say it was fated or anything tacky like that. We both know there is no such thing beyond the fate we create for ourselves.*

ZEKE: *I hope you're not saying I created this for myself, Dialphio? Trust me, this is not how I pictured my life turning out.*

DIALPHIO: *Yet it is where you are because of those greater forces. What does* The Histories *say about Creed and who will possess it? What will that person do with it?*

Of course that all–important tome would come up during our conversation. It always did. I studied the dumb book with a voracious appetite back when I thought I was doing important work for the Council. That was a long time ago, when I thought I had a chance to get something out of those sacrifices so I could make a better life for myself and my family. None of that mattered anymore. I couldn't make my own life better, nevermind the lives of my mother and father. It seemed they were better off without me anyway. I was never going to see Hell again, so my investment in studying anything related to it had dried up along the way. The only reason I cared now was because I had a chance to save Cancer.

Before I could figure out a response, letters formed on the page with a new response from Dialphio.

DIALPHIO: The Histories of the Balance, *in case you don't remember, says 'the Great Prince will bind' with Creed. Now, what that means is up for interpretation. Maybe even the interpretation of a single demon. You. Made by One, it chose you. The Histories tell us it can. I believe it did because you are that Great Prince.*

I stared at the message, easily read but incomprehensible. Great Prince?

Running a hand through my hair, I groaned. Dialphio was doing what she often did. Making me think.

ZEKE: *But I don't know what that means. What are the benefits of the job? Does it pay overtime? Maybe it's not worth taking?*

DIALPHIO: *I hope you know that I adore your personality, but sometimes your levity is unnecessary and unhelpful.*

I slapped the notebook and stared off across the rooftops of downtown Olympia. Hardly picturesque, the city reminded me of an upscale Eighth Circle. That Circle had been depressed by the financial muscle of a solitary incubus named Taurus, and Lucifer's Council allowed that to happen. Tens of thousands of demons lived in squalor while one incubus pulled the strings for the few who led healthy and wealthy lives. Someone on the Council had worked with Taurus to set me up to become his slave. They were willing to give me over, and Creed along with me, in return for the Horn artifact. The demon responsible for that event was the same who ensured I was assigned to the Gemini case. I wouldn't doubt they even suspected his true angelic nature. The same demon had sent an assassin to the sanctuary in Kaiserslautern to kill Cassie and me. The same demon who would obliterate any demon in her path if they interfered with her ambition. Friend, foe, other's families; to Seraph, none of that mattered. No innocents would, if that was what was called for. The demon who was cleverly unstoppable. A chess master.

But maybe someone could stop her. Someone like a Great Prince.

I needed to know my ex–boss's thoughts.

ZEKE: *I'm sorry, Dialphio. It's a lot to think about.*

DIALPHIO: *It's a great responsibility and needs to be taken as such.*

Unseen, I nodded.

ZEKE: *But what does it mean? What does it change for me?*

DIALPHIO: *We know Creed is too powerful for anyone in the Underworld to control, even Lucifer himself.*

My throat flushed. Dialphio's comment might have seemed innocuous to the casual observer, but after my blasphemy charge and Abandonment, I was sensitive to any mention of Lucifer, especially by someone I cared about. No stretched imagination was needed to foresee a time when someone like Dialphio would be Abandoned under the same ridiculous conditions I was.

ZEKE: *Be careful what you say, I wouldn't want you to suffer because Lucifer gets His boxers in a bunch and they Abandon you out of offense.*

DIALPHIO: *Do you honestly think Lucifer would care about these letters, even if He knew? Don't bother yourself with those thoughts. He couldn't know about these even if He had time, which I doubt He does. Plus, the moment we stop having important discussions out of fear of what might happen by those who hold power is the moment we hand them true power. The power of unquestioned compliance. The greatest sins of demonkind.*

ZEKE: *What is?*

DIALPHIO: *The moment we stopped questioning.*

I rubbed my eye with the heel of my hand. Too much. Too many implications. The Great Prince. I just wanted to be the best version of me.

ZEKE: *What do I do? I don't know how to be the Great Prince.*

DIALPHIO: *Neither do I. That's something we can figure out together.*

The autumn sun cast longer shadows as it fell from the sky. The heat it used to project onto my balcony was now a thing of weeks gone by. The Overworld was entering the season of death, a time when almost all life went dormant, a true irony to my own life.

19

OLYMPIA

THE SUN WAS STILL STRUGGLING to maintain its dominance of the dome that encircled the Overworld when I found myself back in the streets of Olympia and making my way east to a local watering hole. The air relinquished its warmth and never regained momentum. Months would pass before I would feel warm again, the way the cycle was progressing.

Up and down the street, Olympia's homeless set up shelters for the night in the doorways of closed businesses. They were careful to stay away from the open stores, out of a mixture of respect, a desire to not be a nuisance, and to stay away from trouble with authorities. One man pushed his shopping cart into a covered arch. The cart was loaded with everything he possessed, including several ragged blankets and more cardboard than the warehouses of the giant online store just up the road in Seattle. His cartful would serve as his shelter from the cold tonight.

I had my own possession that did a similar job. Mine hung from a loop on my belt. I'd read the passage about the Great Prince a dozen times in *The Histories of the Balance* and never spent much time thinking about it. For all I knew, the moniker might have originated in the ramblings of the mysterious writer of *The Histories*. The Great Prince could be a fictional character, a legend, created to provide readers with hope and a sense of power in an ancient world that modern readers transposed to their own times. Any significance the title held was meaningless except to those who recognized it, deriving power from what someone ascribed. It was dangerous to get carried away with thoughts about being a Great Prince who somehow held enough sway to unnerve Lucifer's Council. Dialphio could believe that for another millennium if she wanted, I would ponder and plod through this because it was my life, my future—if I had one.

"Hey Ezekial," Ralph, a homeless man of fifty with a scraggly beard of gray and red, smiled from his corner seat at the intersection on Capitol Way. "How are you this fine evening?"

I waved. "How have you been, Ralph? You looking for a place tonight?"

Ralph fiddled with the wool gloves he held. "Not sure. Thinking I might head over to the lake and see what I can scrounge up. Heard a bunch of stuff got dumped there earlier when some guy got rounded up. Had a breakdown at the park, I guess. Scared the crap out of a couple of old people. Cops took him and no one's seen him since. Might as well see if he left anything behind."

I grimaced, hiding it immediately. "What happened to your stuff? I thought you had a tent and a mattress?"

The corners of Ralph's mouth turned down. "Did. Trouble at the camp two nights ago and the next thing we know, there's a fire raging through it. Not that I had much, but what I did is gone. Lost everything."

"I'm sorry to hear that," I said, moving closer as I dug into my pocket to pull my wallet free. I had two twenties and handed them over. "Take these, please. It's all I got on me, but it's yours."

Ralph looked at the money as if I had conjured a harpy.

I wiggled it. "Come on, take it."

"Ezekial, I can't," he said, his eyes moving away.

Shame and pride, something I saw often from Olympia's homeless. Even in their state of desperation, it was hard for them to accept help. One of the great crimes against this community was the general apathy for their condition by the public, who preferred to attribute laziness for their condition. People like Ralph weren't lazy, but they were prideful, and sometimes that hurt far more than it helped.

I bent and slipped the twenties under the cup sitting to the side, that way he wouldn't have to take it directly from me. "I hope that helps, bud." I looked back toward the intersection, across to the pub. "If I see you out here later, I'll stop by again. I'll hit an ATM on the way and we'll see about getting you a tent if you don't find something for yourself. See you later, Ralph."

The man still wouldn't make eye contact. I had made him uneasy. The money would come in handy; accepting it was a challenge. Taking my leave was the solution.

"You're a good man, Ezekial. A good man," Ralph called out as I walked away.

The pub was dark and dreary, the kind of small business allergic to the siren's call of corporate entertainment. The dank smell of the Budd Inlet permeated the walls. No flashing lights, no expensively streamed music. No designer-influenced interior. This place lacked the plethora of large screen televisions simultaneously showing every game happening around the Overworld typical in finer drinking holes. The only lights came from the short line of beer coolers and sponsor's neon signs hanging from the black walls, always making it interesting when trying to navigate around Charlie's bar. The darkness made it the perfect place to hang out when you wanted to be alone with your thoughts.

"The same as always?" Charlie, sixty and as mean as if he was ninety, said.

"You got it," I answered, moving to the far end of the bar and taking a seat. This position gave me the advantage of having no doors behind me since the bathroom and the door to the parking lot were to my right. Both were in my view, as was the front door. I wouldn't have to spend an ounce of energy worrying about my six—my back, for those of you lucky enough to have not served in the military. This was the new reality in public spaces. Oh, joy.

Within seconds, Charlie was sliding a pint of a local porter to my end of the bar. His aim was true, as it always was, and I caught it by the handle. We'd had a lot of practice with this routine. I raised it to the bar owner. "To life, Charlie. To life."

Charlie's eyes narrowed, and he grunted, before turning away and moving to the other end of the bar to talk to a solitary man about his age. The two bent close and grumbled about 'kids' and 'these days', taxes, 'the man', and general life while I enjoyed the quaint peace inspired by beer with body and no interruptions.

It didn't last.

My beer held my attention for a while before the front door opened. The toll of living in the Overworld as the Great Prince was cut off when I saw who walked in. Charlie and his equally ancient friend stopped chattering to look at the new patron, before the owner straightened, wiping his hands on his pants.

"What can I get for you, young lady?" Charlie asked, grinning behind his fuzzy mustache and beard.

Young lady. If Charlie only knew.

I pushed my barstool back and stood, smiling uncontrollably as she smiled at me. Cassie made her way over and gave me a hug. I warmly accepted.

"What are you doing here?"

"Looking for you." She smiled, losing the expression when she glanced at the barstool next to me. She pulled a napkin from a dispenser that reluctantly gave up the precious commodity and wiped the stool. "Is this taken?" She almost sounded like she hoped it was. Charlie's was not for everyone.

I looked around in mock judgment. "Yeah, I think someone was running to the restroom. She'll be back in a second. Super cute, too. Last seat in the place. So busy, you know?"

Her eyebrows bounced up and down rapidly. "Do you have a hot date or something, Z-Zeke?"

"Don't hate me because I'm wanted," I said, speaking the first thing that came to mind that sounded cute and clever. So blessed hard to think around Cassie.

She snickered before sitting. Charlie instantly hovered, the old pervert.

"What can I get you, young thing?" he asked.

"How about an Old Fashioned? Do you make a good one?" Cassie said.

"Bet I do," Charlie said, rubbing his hands and moving away to make her drink.

I pulled back. "Wow. Impressive."

"What?" Cassie replied. "Can't a girl enjoy a classic?"

"Absolutely," I said with a nod. "I didn't think of you as going for the strong stuff."

"Why? Because… my kind are goody-two-shoes? Did you expect me to order a Shirley Temple?" Cassie snickered again.

"Well… no… I just thought, you know…"

"Your kind and your stereotypes," she said with a shake of the head and a laugh.

"Isn't *that* a stereotype?" I said, giving her a nudge with my elbow. "Like your kind doesn't."

Cassie tilted, a playful smirk spread on her thin, pale Lucifer-blessed sexy lips. "We're not nearly as judgmental as your kind thinks we are, and by your comments just now, as your kind actually is."

Charlie was back, carrying a lowball glass in his hands

and a flirtatious glint in his eyes. Every part of the exchange was awkward, so I imagined it had to be tenfold for Cassie. She handled it with grace, staring at Charlie with those crystal eyes. Eyes that made me want to reveal my darkest feelings. I was not alone. Charlie looked like he wanted to swim in her optical oceans.

Cassie leaned forward, her eyes sparkling. "Thank you so much for this. I'm sure it'll be wonderful. I can't wait to enjoy it. Me and my friend here." She tipped her head in my direction without breaking eye contact with the bar owner. "We have important things to talk about. Would it be too much trouble to ask that we're not disturbed when you get your flood of regular customers? Thanks. I appreciate it."

Charlie nodded like an impling who had been offered a lifetime supply of his kind's chocolate chip cookies. "Of course. Of course. No one will trouble you two. I promise it."

As he walked away, I stared dumbfounded. "That has to be your true magic."

"What?" Cassie laughed, flipping her hair. "I told you when we were in Germany, males can be manipulated if you know how."

"You're wicked," I laughed. "I would have thought better of your kind."

Cassie lifted her glass. "Angels can be just as devious as demons." She winked as we clinked glasses. Then she winced after sipping the Old Fashioned.

"Not any good?" I asked.

"Not the smoothest I've had." She smiled through her cough. "But it will do."

"You sure you're not a rookie? I thought your kind could only drink sacramental wine?" I teased.

"One of these days I'm going to bring you to the Upperworld so you can see what it's really like. Maybe that will break down these ugly stereotypes," Cassie laughed. It was a beautiful sound. "We can party just as hard as your kind."

I lifted my beer. "Ha, that's where I've got you fooled. I don't have a kind anymore, not unless you include mortals."

"That's not what I've heard." Cassie raised her eyebrow, giving me a sideways glance. "Word on the streets of the Upperworld is you've been causing problems. Getting yourself attention, I heard."

"Attention? In Heaven?"

"Yes. One of our agents saw quite the fight near the harbor, in a gravel yard or something. Sound familiar?"

I suddenly found my pint fascinating. Locking my thumb and middle finger around its handle, I spun it, watching the circle of condensation expand on the bar top. "Don't know what you're talking about."

"Are we going to lie to each other now, Z-Zeke?" Cassie said, her soft tone making me want to give her whatever answer she was looking for.

"No, not at all."

She turned on her barstool. It creaked underneath her, wobbling slightly. She caught herself and laughed. It was an infectious sound, and I found myself joining her.

"So how about we have the truth of it?" she said. "What happened?"

I checked on Charlie and his customer, ensuring they were still engaged and not listening. When it was safe, I gave Cassie the rundown of the incident with the thugs. Sharing was so easy with her, the immortal enemy of demonkind. Too easy. Before I knew it, I was telling her about Creed and what it had done.

Her eyes widened. "You used the halberd?"

"More like it used itself," I admitted. "This blessed thing has a mind of its own. I wish I could claim credit, but that would be a flat-out lie and you would see through it anyway, obviously."

We shared a laugh as Cassie thought, a troubled expression passing over her face.

"What is it? Something's bothering you."

Her radiance returned. "That's the strange thing for us. If it had not been for the agent and dumb luck, we wouldn't have known it was you or a demonic spell. Our sensing wards are strong, and they're pretty active in town because of the whole thing with Leo. Olympia has been receiving a lot of attention because of him... and other reasons. Using that weapon should have registered as demonic."

"But it didn't?"

She shook her head. "No, not that I've heard of. That's very... interesting."

"You're not going to rat me out, are you?" I asked. "Trust me, the last thing I need is a squad of angels harassing me too."

"I've been following you ever since that thing with Leo. I hope you don't think I've harassed you," Cassie said, then blinked and bit her lip like she said something she did not want shared.

Now it was my turn to swivel my stool, placing my elbow on the bar and my chin in my open palm. I gave her a look of playful scrutiny. "So you're following me, huh? Why is that?"

"Well I—I mean, not always. I... because I knew you were here... and Leo... and..."

It was adorable watching her stumble, something I could have watched all night long. "You can admit you missed me and wanted to hang out again. You didn't need to stalk me. Though that's kind of hot."

She swatted my arm. "You can be a real ass. It wasn't like that."

"Sure it wasn't," I teased. "I'm honored. I've never had a stalker that wasn't demonic before."

Cassie's expression turned dark. "Are you still being... bothered?"

"You could say that," I admitted, updating her on more recent events.

"That makes sense," she said, her eyes distant. "We've been hearing rumblings about your Council's activities here. Rumors are they're up to no good."

"You guys still have spies in Hell?" I asked.

Cassie nodded as if I'd asked her if she wanted to go for ice cream after drinks. "Yes, Z-Zeke. Just like demons have spies in Heaven. We've talked about this, remember?"

"I do," I conceded. "I just don't like having another reminder of the lies we've been told throughout our lives. That's one more in a long string."

Cassie's hand found mine, resting on top of it. Warmth radiated from her palm, sending tingles up my arm. I think I flushed—but I'd rather not admit that. "I'm worried about your situation. If the things I've been hearing are remotely true, you're in trouble. I don't like that. Not at all. I feel like I know you, that who you were back in Germany is the same demon I'm sitting with now."

I closed my eyes and drew a deep breath through my nose. "I'm an Abandoned demon, Cassie."

She replied softly, "You're something more."

I snorted so loud that Charlie and his friend looked our way.

"What's that about?" she asked.

"You just reminded me of something someone from home told me," I said. "She thinks I might be the Great Prince one of our books mentions. Some liberator. Just because I own Creed." I explained what I understood from *The Histories of the Balance*. Cassie listened intently.

"The Great Prince, huh?" she said, a playful smile dancing on her lips.

"What? Is that so unbelievable?" I laughed.

"Segregate. Hell's Reject. Great Prince," Cassie rolled her eyes back and forth. "By my calculations, you've got more nicknames than Yahweh has angels."

I barked a laugh, playfully swatting away her hand, which I immediately regretted.

"But that makes sense," Cassie said, resuming normal official business. "We're aware of what Creed is and what it can do. I'm not surprised you would have an authoritative book referencing the holder in high regard. Great Prince? I'm not sure about that, but you're definitely more important than you know. Why else would this be happening?"

"I don't know," I said as honestly and vulnerably as I could. "Demons keep telling me this kind of stuff, but I can't process it. I'm just Zeke. That's all. A demon... an Abandoned demon who just wants to work in a bookstore and spend time with demons, people, angels, who are important. I don't want anything more than that. I didn't want or ask for the stupid halberd." Creed burned against my side through my blue jeans. I ignored it. The burning bit but not enough to really hurt. Petulant stick. "I didn't want to have to work for Lucifer's Council. I didn't ask to be Abandoned. I didn't go looking for Cancer so I could break her curse and get involved in a family feud."

"Yet, here you are," Cassie said, not unkindly.

"Yet here I am," I said, spreading my hands. "Drinking beer in a dingy bar, albeit with great company, trying to forget everything that gives me headaches." I stopped and laughed bitterly at a new thought. "Did you know Leo wants me to take care of you?"

Cassie's forehead crinkled adorably. "Take care of me how? Is that what you call flirting? You've got a lot to work on, mister."

In the flash, I panicked, thinking I had been doing exactly that, and that Cassie had seen through my guise.

But then she swatted my hand. "I'm joking, silly. He's bothered by my involvement, I know. He's going to have to get over it."

I nodded, thinking about Leo and his struggle to get his

family back into the Underworld. Someone in that position could easily become a pawn in a bigger game. Even if his motivations were selfless, I couldn't fully trust him. "And the thing I'm still unsure about is who he's wrapped up with. There's another demon in the area who started this whole mess."

"Chax," she nodded.

Cassie remembered. I hadn't seen her in weeks and she remembered.

Before I could say anything—all of which would come out sounding ridiculously unfledged—Charlie interrupted, hovering until Cassie politely and flirtatiously had him make us another round. I don't even think Charlie realized he had been dismissed.

She nibbled on her lip. It was maddeningly sexy. "So, Seraph is deeply involved in this?"

"Unfortunately," I admitted. "I haven't seen her or Chax yet, which is a good thing, because I don't know what I would do, but I'm sure I'd be worse off afterward. She most likely won't show her face again. That's why he's in the area. But he's hiding like a coward, having someone else do the dirty work."

"What's his aim? Have you figured that out?" she asked.

I jutted my bottom lip out, feeling a wave of hopelessness. "They want me dead. Well, Seraph does. That would be a more accurate way to describe it. She's acting through him. But it doesn't change the end result... dead is dead. Unless I do something."

"And if you do something about it, something to her family, you pay?"

I nodded, taking a swig of my new beer. "Or my family or friends or both do."

Cassie sighed. "Leo doesn't seem like much of a problem in that context. I can handle him influencing the Balance here. I can also wait. I'll need to talk to my superiors, but I think I can package it in a way that they will give me time to work on Leo after I help you."

"Help me? Why would you do that? You're a…" I stopped myself, checking on Charlie and the solitary customer. "Wouldn't an angel get in trouble for helping someone like me?"

"Not necessarily. I'm not really worried about that, to be honest," Cassie said firmly. "My superiors should see the advantage of me helping." She raised a hand, stopping my oncoming objection. "Yes, I realize that sounds lousy, like you're being used, and that's not my intention. But that's how I'm going to sell it."

"Why would you want to do that? That's… I can't ask you to do that."

Cassie leaned closer, her scent made me feel like I was home in the Fifth. Only keeping my eyes open kept me from floating back. I nearly jumped when she touched my hand again, chills racing up my arm and fogging my brain. "Because of that group you fought in the gravel yard. This could be a good thing for me and you. I'm just being honest, Z-Zeke."

"The thugs?"

She loosed a tight snicker. "That's not exactly how we refer to them, but yes. The Abandoned."

"They have a name?" I rocked my head at the sound of it on my brain. "Pretty cool name, I guess. Could make a cool rock band. Maybe punk."

Her eyes danced between mine as she watched my expression for something, a sign. A look of displeasure marred her smooth complexion, and she looked away, shaking her head. "They did you no favors, the way they've treated you."

"Who? The thugs?"

"No, your Council. Your parents. Your elders," Cassie answered. "They didn't inform you about so many things. More evidence that your leaders intentionally set you up.

And that upsets me. A lot. That group you call thugs? Most of them are disillusioned mortals who have a lot in common with you."

"I feel you're trying to tell me something without saying it. What's going on?"

"Did you notice anything when you were fighting them?" she asked.

"One of them knew Creed was dangerous," I admitted. "I'm not sure how much he understood, or if the information came from someone else, but he knew what would happen if someone tried to take it from me. And that's not the only thing. I also... I can kind of tell when someone is a demon, even if they've been Abandoned. It's like when you work out and you're sweating and hot and you walk out into colder air. You see sweat evaporating off someone's body in thin, white clouds like..."

"Smoke!" Cassie said excitedly.

I nodded. "Exactly. It looks like that. Smoke. No one has ever mentioned being able to see it. I can. Demons and some of those Abandoned give off this... smoke. It's like they are emitting their immortality. At least, that's what I call it."

Cassie's eyes widened and sparkled. "So you know who the Abandoned are?"

I didn't. "They're just thugs, Cassie. I know at least one ex–demon is among them. I've sensed his emissions a couple times. They might have another one or two. Hard to tell since they always travel in packs. Beyond that, I think the rest of them are just—"

"Angels."

I was going to say they were assholes. Instead, I replied, "What?"

She leaned closer, uncomfortably close for the testosterone streaming through me. For a second I stopped thinking about demons and angels at all. "The Abandoned, Z-Zeke. I don't know why your Council doesn't educate demons, especially as one of their operatives. The Abandoned are a group of demons and angels who have been... well, Abandoned. It was only after desperate conditions drove disillusioned mortals their way that they started taking them on board too, diluting their immortal numbers. But still, there are many immortals among their ranks. Did you sense anything immortal about them?"

I shook my head as I thought about the attack. "I sensed... something. But most of them looked like normal mortals to me, except for the few who might be ex-demons."

"Hmmmm." Her shoulders drooped. "There are angels among them, too. You must not be able to sense the ex-angels because they're not your kind. But the Abandoned is a large group, much larger than the small contingent you fought. Wherever the rest of the group is, I guarantee you there are more demons among them. If this Chax character is in town, I guarantee you, he will be with them because he can hide in the signature... these emissions you're talking about."

It was hard to ignore Cassie's exuberance over this. However, I'm stubborn and forced my thoughts back to the first encounter with the group hanging around the garage. I had been distracted and not expecting to sense a demon at all. They had the advantage of my ignorance then, but not any longer.

Replaying the memory now made it as clear as the night I watched them form a human wall, as if they were trying to hide something. Something, or someone.

Cassie's voice broke my reflection. Her tone was dark, troubled. "And if I'm right, if you're being harassed by the Abandoned, your troubles just got a lot more complicated."

———⊷

TROUBLE, IT SEEMED, WASN'T CONTENT TO SHARE A DRINK WITH me. It accompanied me all the way home, and I forgot to stop by the ATM to withdraw cash for Ralph. My saving grace was his absence from the spot where I had met him earlier. That brought me a reprieve, and I would correct my forgetfulness in the morning, even if I had to go looking for him before work.

Trouble also greeted me when I got home.

I unlocked the door, hearing the low murmur of a television. Every light was off, the only glow came from the flickering screen. I paused in the doorway, listening and not wanting to disturb Cancer.

I closed the door slowly and untied my shoes, not even kicking them off in a haphazard way as I usually did. Creeping along the hallway, I peeked around the corner. She was asleep on the couch, one bent leg risked tumbling to the floor. Her head was thrown to the side, and an arm was raised above her head. Her mouth hung open. She was drooling.

As I crept past, the floorboard creaked at the foot of the couch. My roommate snorted in quick succession, the type that panicked waking brings.

"Zeke? Is that you?" Cancer's voice shook as she kicked awake, knocking the blanket to the floor.

"Sorry," I said, picking up the blanket and laying it over the arm of the couch. "I was trying to be quiet."

Cancer sat up, rubbing sleep from her eyes. In the blue light of the movie, her skin looked paler, except for the circles under her eyes, which seemed stained deeper with each passing day. "Don't worry. I need to get to bed. I can't sleep on this couch. Where have you been? I thought we could grab a bite to eat when I got home, but you were gone."

"I had a troubling chat with Dialphio today and needed to clear my head," I said.

"Is everything okay?"

"Everything's fine," I lied.

Cancer looked at me, trying to dig into my brain and pull

out the truth. Her eyelids lowered in suspicion. "You're not being honest."

"I don't want to bother you with my crap."

"I wish you would. I bother you enough with mine," she said, collecting her blanket by rolling it around her arm and holding it against her chest.

"That's because you're not any trouble. I am," I said.

"I am."

"You're not. And you don't appear happy."

Cancer pulled the blanket tighter against her chest. "I try. It's not easy."

"How can I help you be?"

"You can't, Zeke." She still wasn't looking at me. "What I would give to serve overseas. But I can't."

"Why not?"

"Someone needs to stand by your side," she answered softly. "You and me against the world."

"But... " I started, but lost where I could take any possible reply.

"It's not a problem for me. Honestly." She tugged the blanket to her neck now. "I worry about you, and if you weren't a constant target, if I didn't worry that you'd hit the bar to ignore what you face, then I could be okay leaving to serve in that nursing program for war victims. No," she said, her face snapping in my direction, "I'm not going to. I'm... I'm just thinking out loud. I'm as happy as I can be, Zeke. We're together, and that's important to me. You are important to me."

"As are you," I replied, my throat suddenly dry. "There's something I wanted to talk to you about."

"Oh yeah?"

I snagged a notepad from the table to fill in the other details. Paper could be burned, leaving no clue for nosy spies listening in on the conversation. Cancer would get it out of me one way or another, so I might as well make it as painless as possible.

I filled her in on the details of the conversation with Dialphio that were safe to share, without mentioning my ex-boss's name. I told her about the fact I was still a threat to the Council and likely always would be. I told her that my stick was going to cause a lifetime of headaches for the Great Prince. That Azazel might be the key to us staying alive. I spilled my guts about the fact that I was involved far deeper than I ever wanted to be and that I needed to prepare.

"Please don't tell me you went to drink away your troubles. It sounds like she's just trying to be helpful. That could be a good thing."

"Well, the night wasn't full of possibly good things," I said.

Cancer cocked her head. So I told her about Cassie, which took far longer than either of us had time for, but with the angel being, well, an angel, the investment was necessary. I wasn't sure if Cancer had a problem with angels. She had known they were in Baghdad too, but Cassie was a surprise.

"I wish you would have told me about her before," Cancer said.

"Yeah," I said, knowing there was a lot I should have been communicating over the past weeks.

Cancer's voice was filled with a dangerous heat only a succubus can manage. "What does she want?"

Apparently, Cancer wasn't as open-minded or free from Hell's conditioning as I thought. This was going to take some time to work through. I filled her in on the specifics of the conversation, keeping the verbalized details sanitized since we were in a sanctuary and it was almost guaranteed somebody on the other end in the Underworld was listening. Sporadically, I jotted bullet notes to fill in the rest.

Cancer tried to run a hand through her frazzled hair until it got stuck and she gave up. "My Lucifer, does it ever end?"

"My thoughts exactly. I can't talk about much now, but maybe we can go for a drink tomorrow? I owe you dinner."

"You do?" Cancer asked.

I gestured toward the kitchen. "It's not like I left you a great meal tonight."

"At least it wasn't your grilled cheese."

I huffed in a half-sad way. "Let me. It's the least I can do."

"Do you have any money for dinner?" Cancer said teasingly as she moved past me down the hall.

"I got you," I said, trying to remember if my checking account was in triple or double digits.

Cancer paused at her bedroom door, turning and placing a hand on the jamb. "Be careful with her, Zeke. Can you trust one of them?"

This wasn't a conversation to have inside a sanctuary. This was a dinner conversation. Because that's how our dinner conversations were. Public chats about demons, angels, magic, Hell and Heaven. All of which were safer to discuss at a restaurant, an affordable one, than in our apartment.

"Tomorrow," I stressed. "I'll tell you everything, Cancer."

"Tomorrow," she said with a slow head nod. "Good night, Zeke."

I stared at her closed bedroom door for a few minutes before deciding I couldn't run after her and risk sharing anything more tonight. Tomorrow. Tomorrow, I'd be honest with my roommate. About everything.

20

OLYMPIA

"I THOUGHT this was supposed to be just the two of us?" Cancer said from the other side of the table.

I smiled apologetically, glancing at the young couple nearby who appeared interested in everything said at our table. I leaned closer. "Well, it was. I wanted it to be. While you were at work today, I saw Cassie at the gym and we got talking."

"You went to the Lion's Den today?" she asked skeptically.

"Yeah, I need to stay close to Leo, and after what you saw the last time I was in the cage, more training can't hurt, right?"

"Zeke," Cancer said, "are you sure that's safe? Especially after everything she told you?"

Cancer had referred to the angel a few times during our conversation, yet rarely used her actual name. Once we left on our walk to dinner, I informed Cancer of the conversation Cassie and I had regarding the Abandoned. Cancer deserved to know, and I was done keeping things from her under this presumed need to protect her. She had more ferocity on the tip of her nose than I had in my entire body. She could keep herself safe and ward off threats as easily as I could. She needed to know about the Abandoned because it affected her.

"I can't be, not completely," I admitted reluctantly, glancing toward the nosy couple. They looked away immediately. "But I can't sit around the apartment or get distracted at the job and have them jump me unaware, Cancer. I have to learn how to fight without Creed, and I need to watch Leo. This takes care of both."

Cancer looked away. Concern etched her expression. I leaned closer.

"I'm going to be okay. I won't do anything stupid."

She browsed my face. "You've got a long life to live and a lot of enemies still to make. I want you to be careful. Promise me that."

"Stop talking like that," I said with a smile on my face, though nothing inside me was smiling. "You've got a long life to live and more friends than enemies to make who I will then need to introduce myself to. Cancer, if I do this right, I can ensure both of us stay safe as possible. Maybe even enjoy our lives. Who knows. Plus, staying close to Leo might help us find a way to do the same thing he's doing for his family."

"To get back to the Underworld?"

I nodded with a short series of chin dips. "I have to get home. You have to get back. I see how strong you're trying to be, but you can't fool me, Cancer. Your decay is taking its toll. You can try to act tough, but you're not feeling well. So before you chide me, remember I can see the same in you. You're not being completely honest either."

"I'm doing okay, Zeke, I'm just working a lot."

"That's bullshit, Cancer. Come on," I said more softly when she flinched. "Be honest with me, please."

"I have been, but I don't think you took me seriously," Cancer said, looking at anyone in the restaurant who wasn't me. "Then... I just stopped talking about it because that was easier. You're focused on other things. Important things. You have a lot going on. I'm not arguing that you don't. Taking your attention away from all this stuff isn't fair. Okay? That's all it is."

The waiter drifted to the table with drinks like he was offering an apology for interrupting me and giving Cancer the advantage in the argument. When he walked away, I leaned toward her again. "I'm sorry. I have a lot on my mind. I never meant to come across like I don't care."

Cancer was still looking at everything that wasn't named Zeke. She answered softly. "I know." Then her eyes focused on a single point over my head, past patrons and decorative plants. "She's here."

I stood when Cassie approached the table. Cancer did not. "I'm glad you could come," I said, receiving a hug from the angel. Her hair smelled lightly of fruit I couldn't place. I didn't mean to sniff as deeply as I did; it just sort of happened. I pulled back, trying to hide my embarrassment, and pulled out a chair. "Please, sit."

Cassie did, smiling at Cancer. "Hi. Nice to meet you."

"Hello," Cancer said.

I sat down carefully, my gaze shifting between the pair as if I was watching the countdown clock to an explosive device.

"I'm glad you came," I said, trying to restrict my smile to only a goofy grin at Cassie's presence, and only realizing I was repeating myself and exposing my nervousness when it was too late.

"And I'm glad we're having this conversation. It's impor-tant," Cassie replied, her eyes swaying between Cancer and me. "This will be a tricky situation if we don't communicate well, Z-Zeke."

"Ezekial," Cancer said flatly, sitting back in her chair and gripping the napkin as if it were her worst enemy. "His name is Ezekial."

I looked around for the waiter so he could take Cassie's drink order and interrupt this eruption of the figurative Hellfire. The only time Cancer had been outwardly hostile was in Baghdad, when I was serving as an American soldier. Other than that, she was the example of kindness and patience. With Cassie around, Cancer was anything but that. I didn't want to think what would happen if Cancer knew Cassie had been an angel spy involved in the attack on the First Circle that killed hundreds of demons.

"Where is that guy? Just like a cop, never around when you need them," I said louder than required, hoping to draw their attention away from one another. "What do you want to drink, Cassie?"

"Oh, I don't know. I could go for a red wine," she said, her eyes scanning the table.

"What are you looking for?" Cancer said.

"The drink menu," Cassie said, mimicking the nurse's edged tone.

Oh boy, I'm so glad I had nothing else to do with my day. Weakly trying to shift the atmosphere at the table, I teased, "What? No hard liquor?"

"With Italian?" Cassie said, as if I had just said the most repulsive thing in the world. "Do you think I'm a heathen?"

We shared a chuckle, Cancer did not join in. The waiter finally made his way around to take her order and brought a basket of warm breadsticks and house butter. The food was a nice distraction from the tension, and the three of us used it. In my rush to focus on food until the ladies eased up, I bumped Cassie's hand as she was pulling away from the bread basket. Her breadstick tumbled from her hand to the table and she gave me a playfully aggressive look.

"If you didn't want me to have starches, why didn't you just say something?" Cassie laughed.

I lifted the basket. "Here, take mine."

Cassie pushed the bread basket back. "That's okay. I can eat this one. Don't your kind have a rule about eating fallen food? Anything under ten seconds and it's still edible?"

Cancer grimaced as Cassie picked up the breadstick, broke it open over her plate, buttered one side and bit down. Her eating habits made her even hotter.

She waved the other end in the air in a swiveling motion. "Have you heard about the war? Terrible. Just terrible."

Admittedly, I had not heard a single word about the fighting in the past few days. Those pesky other troubles, like not allowing Seraph, Chax, or the Abandoned to get close to me or my suddenly not-so-friendly roommate, occupied most of my brain space.

"It is," Cancer answered. "A true tragedy."

"I must have missed something," I admitted.

Cancer pinched her breadstick between her finger and thumb at an angle, moving it back and forth across her plate as if she were drawing with it. "There was a missile attack two days ago on a small city in Israel. The Chinese. Tensions are high. England bombed northern cities in Turkey in retribution."

"They say over twenty thousand died in the two attacks," Cassie said, her eyes widening. "It's absolutely horrendous."

Cancer lifted her breadstick off the plate, the end pointing up in the air. "And here we sit, drinking and eating as if nothing is wrong."

A guilty silence fell over the table, each of us casting our eyes to our plates.

The waiter came to take our dinner orders, for which I was grateful. Not that the war wasn't important. The three of us weren't going to solve the tragic dilemma at this table over a single meal.

After the waiter walked away, I leaned forward and whispered, "It's not like we don't have important work to do here." Cassie nodded, but Cancer just gave a grunt. "What? We do, Cancer. We're talking about—" I halted and checked my surroundings, noticing that even the nosy couple had lost interest now that they were stuffing their faces. "We're talking about the Balance."

"I am well aware of the importance of what we need to discuss, Zeke. I understand this little thing between the two of you," she said, waving her breadstick at Cassie and me, "is going to nudge the Balance one way or another if you don't figure this out. That hardly compares to a war that's been raging for years, with no sign of an end. I'm sorry, but if you want to discuss the importance of the Balance, you can't look past that. It's the greatest tragedy the Overworld has seen in a very long time."

I bit back a comment. Cancer was acting like she intentionally wanted to upset me, Cassie, or our ability to communicate. During my first mission in the Overworld to find Aries, Beelzebub had warned our team to be careful about what we talked about outside of our sanctuary. But during the subsequent trips to the Overworld, I had noticed we didn't draw mortal attention during our conversations—mostly by accident, but you take your wins where and when you can. Not only could we talk about the Underworld and the nature of demons and angels, but we could use magic to a certain degree without mortals or any power players in the immortal realms noticing. I didn't know how far I could push it, but Cancer's attitude was making me want to test it, though I wouldn't.

"Nothing we do at this table or anything we do after this conversation compares to what we could be doing over there," Cancer said. "So, forgive me for being the resident skeptic. This is just ridiculous. There are things that need our attention, and then there are things like this. Let's figure this out and move on."

Cassie's eyes slid to me before finding Cancer. "What do you mean 'things like this'?"

"She's talking about Leo," I answered for Cancer.

"Dealing with him is important," Cassie said, her voice

firm, and her gaze steady on Cancer. "It may not seem like it to you in the big picture because it doesn't seem as egregious as the crimes being committed overseas. I get that. The war is a manifestation of the Balance being off. Small behaviors, small individual aims, incorrect reasoning, all innocuous on their own, become problematic when left alone for so long. They gain momentum the longer the Balance remains out of whack. We can't lose sight of the small things that shift it. If we do, we'll only be able to ignore them for so long before a small offense becomes a major issue, growing into something much worse than the war."

"What could be as bad as what is happening over there?" Cancer said, snapping off the end of the breadstick. "Thousands of people, tens of thousands of people, died this week. Just. This. Week."

"Cancer, come on," I said.

Cassie held Cancer's gaze. I was completely forgotten. "I'm well aware of the tragedies of the war, C—Cancer. I can't change it. My job is here, in Olympia, to deal with L—Leo and keep the Balance."

"To shift the Balance, you mean?" Cancer said, biting back.

I leaned forward, my forearms resting on the table. "Listen, listen. We're all friends here, trying to do the right thing. Let's try to remember that, okay?"

"You're right, Z-Zeke," Cassie said, nodding. "Cancer, I'm sorry if you feel like I'm apathetic about the war. It's a horrible situation, and I hate seeing it just as much as anyone. I do," Cassie said more forcefully when the line between Cancer's brows deepened. "My job is to do something about Le—Leo, and I always do my job. I thought we were here to figure out what we could do together to resolve this."

"I've got to be honest, Cassie. Leo isn't our biggest concern," I said, including Cancer in the conversation. "I get that he is a priority for you. But with the Abandoned targeting me, and possibly Cancer, coupled with the fact Chax is probably involved, I need to take care of that first. Just like we talked about at the storage units. Once that's done, I'm all ears. I'll help you with Leo. With a little more time, I think I can get close enough to have a real impact and maybe keep you out of the calculation altogether."

"What would that do?" Cassie asked. "If I'm not involved, that would just slow things down."

"Not necessarily," I said. Her face twitched. "Give me time and I'll work on him while we're going through this. Heavens, we can work both angles at the same time."

"Please don't swear," Cassie said, holding the breadstick like a ruler she was going to whack me with.

I lifted my hand in apology. "Promise to back off Leo so I can focus on Chax. Maybe then I can get Leo to feel safe enough to come around. We can figure out a way to meet everyone's needs. Because, I promise, he isn't going to stop unless he sees another way out."

"He needs to change his ways," Cassie said stubbornly.

"He's not going to," I said, "It's too important to him."

"See? That's the problem with this self-interested motivation," Cassie said. "Small pockets of people like him focused on themselves aren't a problem. They're annoying, but a problem? No. With L—Leo, he is too charismatic. Too many people are drawn to him. Not just in the gym. Watch what happens when the fights come around later this month. Gyms from all around the region bring fighters into town. I've seen it a few times. Each time they hold one of these big events, Le—Leo is surrounded by hundreds of other fighters. Think about how easily his reach extends in that context, drawing more and more away from where we need them to be. Fighters like him want to be like him, and the Balance shifts each time. I've got to stop him before this next fight. I've waited, but things aren't moving fast enough. If you want me to continue buying in, they need to move faster."

"What? Is the entire Balance going to shift to the Under-world's favor if Leo influences a half–dozen, heavens, an entire *dozen* fighters?" Cancer said in a scoffing tone.

Cassie's head snapped in Cancer's direction. "Don't demean the argument. Hundreds attend these fights. They return to their towns and cities, and the influence spreads. Would you enjoy solving one problem only to have another fifty spring up in its place? The growth is exponential. It happens quickly if it's not carefully calibrated. Too far to one side and you both know what happens."

I did. Beelzebub warned me during our first trip to Seattle. Armageddon. The apocalypse. The end of the world.

"At least they're not shooting and bombing each other," Cancer replied, not having the insight I was lucky enough to possess.

"This isn't helpful, ladies," I said, so distracted by the tension between them I didn't notice I was getting better at using mortal colloquialisms.

"Maybe someone like you doesn't understand it, Ca— Cancer," Cassie said, her voice rising. "But someone in my position does because we see the bigger picture. The Balance is precarious. Too much of an influence on either side throws the entire thing out of whack. It doesn't need to be a complete landslide. If angels and demons can't work together to ensure mortals maintain the balance of being motivated by the self *and* for the greater good, then everything begins to fall apart."

"Well, it's not like self–motivation is an evil thing," I said.

"I didn't say it was." Cassie said. "Pride, narcissism, self-ishness, living a life focused and driven only by self-centered actions has a ripple effect. What starts in Olympia isn't contained within the city limits."

I said, "Look, you know I don't care anymore about the immortal struggle. I don't have a devildog in the fight, but there is nothing wrong with someone being motivated by their self-interests. Without that, some of the greatest achievements of mortal science would never have been accomplished. Mortals wouldn't have done the amazing things they have. Like flight, circumnavigating the globe, voluntarily strapping into a rocket to be shot into..." I waved my hand toward the front door as if they understood I was talking about the frightening expanse of space. "They wouldn't put themselves in orbit around the planet. Adventured across the ocean by sight of the stars in the..." I gulped. "In the skies. Striding into the depths of the Amazon or out into the endless seas would have never occurred. Those things happened because of self–motivation."

"You're not listening." Cassie's bottom lip rolled into her mouth. It flopped back out with a *pcp*. "And without outward motivation, you wouldn't have the professions they have. Say, the entire medical field?"

"Have you ever met a surgeon?" Cancer's zinger cut across the conversation.

Cassie's gaze swiveled to Cancer before snapping back to me. "You wouldn't have cures for diseases. Some of the greatest leaders of all time were outwardly–motivated. Without those advances, there would have been no structure for those individuals to achieve the things you mentioned."

I held up my hands. "I'm not attacking you. I just wanted to make sure we didn't lose sight of the fact that neither side has more right or wrong than the other. Heavens, that's why it's called the Balance."

"Stop swearing," Cassie said, with a twitch of a smirk. "There's an angel in your presence, remember? So, what do we do then?"

"About?" I raised my hands to the sides in a shrug.

"Leo," Cancer said flatly. "If you weren't so distracted by her, Zeke, you'd be able to keep up."

Ouch, so much for having a good wingman.

"Sorry," I said, feeling every bit of awkward at being called out. "How about we call an official truce?"

"Over?" Cassie asked.

"Leo," I said. "I promise you I won't interfere or encourage him to influence any mortals toward self–motivation. Truce up until this tournament. Well, unless something happens and the local Balance is tipped too far? I trust you and offer my word. In fact, while I'm in the gym training as a fighter, I will use every opportunity to keep the focus where it currently is. Might even see if I can sway him to a more outward perspective to serve others. In return, you stay away. From the gym. From Leo. No interaction whatsoever, Cassie. The way I see it, that arrangement benefits you more than me, but you could repay it?" Both of their heads snapped in my direction. I found myself raising my hands as soon as my double entendre registered. "No, no. Sorry. I didn't mean it like that."

"And how did you mean it, Zeke?" Cancer said, her tone still flat, but a tight smile zipped across her face.

"She helps us with the Abandoned," I said with a shrug, trying to look nonplussed.

"What kind of help? I have to be careful what I get involved in, especially with them. My mission is with L— Leo. Like we already discussed, I received special permission from my superiors. Some. And it's temporary. Anything else you have in mind? I have to know exactly what you're looking for before I go back with another request."

"I want a clear message sent to them. They are to leave me and Cancer alone," I said forcefully.

"Is that all?" Cassie raised her eyebrow. "I expected you to demand more."

"Such as?"

Her gorgeous lips pressed together. "The Abandoned are a problem for the Upperworld, just as I imagine they are for your Council, the Underworld's, I mean. Sorry."

Cancer shrugged.

"No offense," I said. "How are they a problem for both Hell and Heaven?"

"The Abandoned actively seek out angels and demons," Cassie said. "As Abandoned, the ex–angels don't have any way of knowing for sure who is an angel, but they have spies in every major city around the world. They're constantly watching and listening for rumors of the presence of any angels. I imagine it's the same for the ex–demons."

"So their network of spies do what with demons and angels when they find them?" Cancer asked.

"Eradicate them," Cassie said simply.

"They try to kill immortals?" I said, lowering my head.

Cassie nodded again. "I can't tell you how many agents we've lost over the centuries to the Abandoned. Some great agents, as well. Remember Princess Diana? Oskar Schindler? Martin Luther King, Jr.? There were others, of course."

Cancer snorted. "Next you'll claim Gandhi was an agent."

Without missing a beat, Cassie replied. "Actually, he was one of yours. But, trust me, there are dozens more just in the past few decades. All victims of the Abandoned. I'm sure the Underworld has lost as many to them."

I sat back and whistled before a troubling thought struck me. I shot forward, drawing a surprised frown from Cancer. "But she," I said, pointing at my roommate, "and I aren't demons, so why would they care about us?"

"I don't know, Z-Zeke," Cassie answered. "But how are they to know you're not? If they've seen what you can do with your halberd, it's understandable why they would suspect your immortality. You pretty much exude it."

"And it's not like you do much to hide it either," Cancer added.

"I don't flaunt it," I said, a bit too defensively.

"So, if that's what they suspect, that explains their actions. The gravel yard incident convinced me of that. From what I know of the Abandoned, the bad news is they won't stop. I have no problem helping you with them, as long as you uphold your end and help me with Leo. Then you get out of my way when we're finished with the Abandoned. Deal?"

I nodded slowly.

Our dinner arrived. We dug in like ravenous vultures. I had chicken Alfredo and was nearly finished before Cancer peppered her dish of rigatoni. Gross. Cassie had spaghetti, which she slurped loudly, drawing Cancer's glare more than a few times. I learned in our time in Germany not to mention the angel's eating habits. Graceful and beautiful as she may be, the way she ate made an entire platoon of starving soldiers look like fine-dining connoisseurs.

In the middle of the meal, just after we had agreed on a truce, I figured the door was open enough to get the truth about Creed from an angelic perspective.

Dialphio had me thinking about my own manner of self-restriction. Cassie knew enough to provide insight during my mission in Germany, so the single question I had for her was one she might be able to answer.

"Let me ask you something," I said, my fork raking the nearly empty bowl. "You know about my halberd."

"Right?" she said, drawing the word out, a noodle dangling from the corner of her mouth, which wiggled when she slurped it. Adorable.

"Are angels immune to it?" I waited so eagerly for her response the clinking of forks on plates, thumping of water carafes being set on tables, clanging from the kitchen, was drowned out. Even the heavy smell of pasta sauce dissipated.

She blinked vacantly. "Immune how, Z-Zeke?"

"Can an angel possess it, Cassie?" I said without a hint of levity.

Her eyes slipped from mine to my side. The table blocked her view of Creed, but she knew it was there.

"Can they—you, your kind?" I said when she didn't answer.

"No, Z-Zeke, no angel could touch that weapon without suffering the consequences," she said, her words measured. "I told you before, the halberd is a creation of One. It is yours and yours alone, as long as One deems it so." Her eyes narrowed. "Why do you ask?"

"Just wondering," I said, digging back into the last of my dinner and stuffing a chunk of chicken coated in Alfredo sauce in my maw before I said too much.

Untouchable. Exactly what I needed to hear.

21

OLYMPIA

"I NEED to step out for a second, Stacy," I called over my shoulder as I bumped the push bar of the door with my hip. The brisk October day bit in greeting. As the trees turned to browns and oranges, the air had grown steadily colder each passing day, encouraging winter onward. Maybe, when it came, the Abandoned would choose to stay cooped up inside throughout the winter? Nothing like depending on Mother Nature to save your ass.

As I pulled my demonic notebook from my backpack, I pondered my general state of readiness if the Abandoned ventured out. In the weeks since the dinner chat with Cassie, where we agreed on a truce over Leo, things had progressed positively. I was hanging at the Lion's Den more nights than not. As a result, my grappling skills had improved drastically. Leo had me on a serious diet and workout regimen, even outside the ring. He was unforgiving like that. I had never felt stronger in my life.

Cassie and I hung out a few nights each week, which always made every gray day decidedly better. She said the purpose was to check in. I didn't care why we were hanging out as long as I was around her. Cancer gave me grief, but I wasn't as concerned with her unfair personal revulsion over Cassie being an angel—my thoughts, not Cancer's words—as I was about her decaying.

Whereas the weeks had been good to me and my physical conditioning, Cancer was worsening at a faster rate. So rapid it was frightening. Of course, she brushed away my concerns over her health. She said she was fine, but if she wasn't working, she was sleeping. Being honest with each other extended only as far as convenience. But who was I to judge? The few times we were home together, and she was resting, she rested hard. I could have bought and played a drum set and not disturbed her slumber. She coughed more than ever too. The dark circles under her eyes expanded to her cheekbones. She dropped plates and glasses with a regularity that had me visiting the local market for replacements at least once a week until I was smart enough to shop for plasticware.

"It's just the curse, Zeke," she would say in rare moments of vulnerability.

And maybe she was right. Maybe the curse was real. Bilba hadn't found anything so far. His mentor, Melchiot, hadn't done much, he said. But maybe Cancer's situation was more. Decay was as hard on demons as death was for mortals—well, for demons not imbued with some strange qualities like myself. Coupled with a real curse, the double-whammy was dramatic. It would explain why, after only a few months in the Overworld, Cancer looked worse than any of Leo's family, even though they were Abandoned years before us. Even though I told her about Bilba's work and my idea of working a way to get her back into Hell, she seemed worse off each day.

Cancer's health kept me on edge in addition to being Abandoned myself, the Abandoned hunting me, and Chax leading the charge.

I still hadn't found Seraph's twerp of a nephew. Though Olympia wasn't a large city by any stretch of the imagination, it also wasn't insignificant. Accidentally crossing paths with him or the Abandoned was more attributable to happenstance than luck. I used the off-hours to work out at the gym, staying away from business hours to keep the group off my tracks until I had the element of surprise. With Chax, I wasn't having any luck, and happenstance could not be bothered.

We were no nearer to finding out how Leo could get back to the Underworld. I felt terrible putting off his situation, but my priority was Cancer. Getting her home was my primary concern. Any time I asked Leo about his deal, he became guarded, wary. I didn't think it had anything to do with distrust, but more about having something good that was a limited resource. No one, immortal or mortal, shared openly if it meant they'd lose out, and that was exactly how the gym owner acted whenever I brought it up. I would help Leo and his family if I could, but I was not going to lower my guard as long as the threat from the others existed. They could unravel everything.

Two dozen yards away from the soup kitchen, it was safe enough to open my demonic notebook and see who had written.

BILBA: *Hey Zeke! Or should I call you Great Prince?*

Bilba's handwriting. Another note was being scribbled.

I slid the quill from the loop and responded.

ZEKE: *Great. So Dialphio told you?*

BILBA: *Would you prefer His Majesty or Your Greatness? She wasn't clear on which is most appropriate and we're wondering.*

ZEKE: *Full of jokes now. Shouldn't you be studying Hex spells? How is that going?*

BILBA: *Great. Melchiot is impressed with my progress. I still have a long way to go, but I'm progressing nicely, she says. I had to slow down, because I'm getting more hours at the café.*

ZEKE: *You're working at a café?*

BILBA: *I have to pay off these loans somehow, and I might as well start. If I waited until after taking the Passage I would have a century's worth of debt to pay off. This way, I can keep it somewhat manageable. I'll only be a relatively old incubus by the time I'm done repaying everything.*

ZEKE: *Hate hearing about your coin but glad to hear your training is going well. Any idea when you'll be able to apply for an actual Passage test date?*

BILBA: *Oh, that's not going to happen for a long time yet. There's so much I need to learn. But I'll let you know as soon as I give a serious look to my timeline. I promise.*

ZEKE: *And the other issue? The thing you're helping me with?*

BILBA: *I'm at home. I'll burn the page when we're done, so we're safe. The curse?*

ZEKE: *Yes, any progress?*

BILBA: *Actually, that has sort of stalled. Not that I'm not trying. I am, I swear. I found a couple other books from the library. I've been going through them. I'm just not finding anything helpful. Not that I can understand or have the skills for, at least. Not yet. Curses are a controversial topic, I guess. Some scholars say they're real; others say it's more in line with Discernment spells. All fabricated, you know? Melchiot wasn't happy when she found out I was spending so much time on the matter.*

ZEKE: *Why?*

BILBA: *She thinks it's distracting me from my studies. I flunked a couple tests. They were hard. Really hard. She said I failed because I've been spreading myself too thin. She was regretting talking to me about the curse. I don't think she wants me involved.*

ZEKE: *I thought you said she was cool?*

BILBA: *She is. I mean it, she really is, Zeke. But I'm paying her so I can pass the Passage, not to remove curses. Between us, I think she's worried about her reputation. I guess it's embarrassing, a black stain on your record, if your students can't pass. My failure would hurt her business. She has other types of classes she holds for lower-level casters, hobbyists mostly. But who wants a teacher whose high-profile students fall flat on their faces, you know? I get it. But don't worry, I've been working with her on the curse. She's not apathetic. You would like her. But she only has so much time with me and demands I'm focused when we're together.*

ZEKE: *I need you, Bilba.*

BILBA: *Please don't think I'm blowing this off.*

ZEKE: *Find something, fast. Cancer isn't doing well. I'm worried.*

BILBA: *I'm trying.*

ZEKE: *Please try harder. I don't know how much longer she has, bud.*

There was a pause. I pressed my back against the birch tree, tapping the feathered end of the quill on the page while I waited.

BILBA: *I'm doing everything I can. This is old magic, practiced by a handful of demons, at best. It's not like I can walk to The Book Abyss and ask Dialphio for a manual. Trust me, if there was someone else I could go to, I would. There just aren't any practitioners. It's like I'm learning the nature of these spells from scratch. Melchiot is my only hope. Zeke, she wants to help, don't get me wrong. But—*

Even as he was writing his response, I scribbled a quick note to interrupt him.

ZEKE: *She's busy. I know. Listen, I need to get going. Please keep me up-to-date, and congratulations on your studies.*

BILBA: *I miss you, Zeke.*

ZEKE: *Miss you too, bud.*

I drew a line under the message, a demarcation to end one message and start of another. This one was going to my other friend.

ZEKE: *Ralrek, what is your ugly ass up to?*

RALREK: *Hey Zeke, how are things?*

I blew out a breath of relief at the tall incubus's quick response. Conversations with Ralrek were a different dynamic. I could shoot straight with Bilba, but I often worried about his feelings. With Ralrek, I didn't. I wasn't sure if Ralrek was coming out of his funk, and didn't want to kick a fallen demon, but I needed to push the cart forward before I lost all momentum.

ZEKE: *Okay. Dealing with Chax–shaped issues.*

RALREK: *You've gotta be kidding me? Is that sonofabitch up there?*

ZEKE: *Seems he got special permission.*

RALREK: *Hang on.*

I waited long enough to worry someone might have seen our messages, and he was answering uncomfortable questions on the other side. I closed the book and started back toward the soup kitchen when the blue light illuminated Lucifer's seal. I cracked the cover open to see Ralrek's new message.

RALREK: *Sorry. I am having drinks and didn't want anyone peering over my shoulder at our conversation. I'm in the bathroom now, so it's safe.*

ZEKE: *You're messaging me from the bathroom?*

RALREK: *It's safe. Would you rather I announced our chat to the entire bar?*

I laughed and pushed the image of Ralrek sitting on the shitter out of my head.

ZEKE: *No, I just didn't need that picture of you.*

RALREK: *Just forgive me if my handwriting goes to heaven in a hand basket if I start pushing, okay? I'll be sure to wipe my ass with this note when we're done. That way, even someone who is curious won't want to come near it. So, Chax, huh? I imagine Seraph sent him?*

ZEKE: *That's the word.*

RALREK: *Bitch.*

ZEKE: *Yep.*

RALREK: *Wish I could help, man.*

ZEKE: *Maybe you can. Any word on the street? Have those secret cells moved forward?*

RALREK: *Got to be honest. Zeke, I haven't gone to a meeting in a long time. They're not dedicated to action. All they want to do is talk. I lost hope.*

ZEKE: *Have you gone to any other meetings? What about the other cells?*

RALREK: *I went to one a couple weeks ago. Same thing. Lots of talking. Talking. Talking. Talking. Everyone is angry, but no one does anything. They just sit around and complain, Zeke. It's pathetic.*

ZEKE: *Sounds like they need someone to kick them in the ass to get them going.*

RALREK: *You got that right.*

The bare branches of the birch had laid a carpet of browned leaves at my feet that crunched as I paced back and forth, waiting. When one didn't come, I pressed.

ZEKE: *Maybe you could be the one to spur them forward?*

RALREK: *I wish. They wouldn't listen to me.*

ZEKE: *They won't listen to an incubus who has directly worked for Lucifer's Council on multiple missions and been involved in what you've been involved in? I find that hard to believe.*

RALREK: *Not so hard to believe if you were here. I'm telling you, these demons just want to talk and gripe. You put a call for action in front of them, and you'll scare every single one of them away. I'm not hopeful. I don't know what everyone else tells you, but these groups aren't the answer to our problems.*

I tapped my temple with the quill, getting the feather caught in my hair netting. I wanted to keep it away from the page so I didn't blurt out my thoughts to Ralrek. Vulnerability with him was something I was still working on, overcoming eras of emotional stunting at his past bullying. Opening up was not easy, but it was necessary.

ZEKE: *Ralrek, I need help. I'm in trouble.*

After a few minutes of updating him on the latest with Chax, Seraph, Leo, and the Abandoned, I felt comfortable that I had conveyed the seriousness.

RALREK: *That's fucked up, Zeke. I wish there was something I could do.*

ZEKE: *You could try not letting these groups die.*

RALREK: *The Council isn't playing around anymore. You're not here to see it. It's dangerous to act against them.*

ZEKE: *It's dangerous to be living in the Overworld as an Abandoned demon and watching your friend die while you live every day paranoid that an attack waits around every corner. Ralrek, the Council wants me dead. They're not going to come at me directly because they don't have to. They have enough demons working for them. I need somebody on that side. Somebody besides Dialphio.*

RALREK: *What about Bilba?*

ZEKE: *What about him?*

RALREK: *Did you talk to him about this?*

ZEKE: *Of course! He's busy preparing for the Passage and he's struggling. Plus, he's helping me find information about Hex magic and curses.*

RALREK: *Hex magic? Oh, for Cancer's situation? This sucks.*

I pulled my notebook further away from my face, refusing to believe Ralrek's detachment. Was he going through such an existential crisis about his former rule–following ways that he was too conflicted to see the reality that the Council was an enemy? This wasn't the overbearingly confident demon I used to know. Did I even know this incubus anymore? Maybe I was taking a risk even talking to him?

Before I said something I regretted, I told him I had to get going.

RALREK: *Okay, Zeke. Write again when you get time. Send me those movies too, don't forget.*

I didn't bother responding, slamming my notebook closed and stomping back into the kitchen to finish preparing and serving the evening's meal for Olympia's neediest citizens.

My punch seemed to fill the Lion's Den.

"Careful, I don't want you busting that bag wide open at closing time," a voice said behind me.

Leo.

At a metallic jingling, I turned to see the gym owner, swinging a lanyard attached to a ring of keys in a circle. He wore a jacket and stretch pants that were part nylon, part spandex. His scrunched face told me he was curious.

I stepped back from the heavy bag I had been working my incubi–inspired frustrations out on. The bag took the brunt of my emotional turmoil because I couldn't treat the two incubi who deserved the actual punches to them. I was so frustrated with Bilba and Ralrek I had chanced a run-in with the Abandoned, where I would have been at the disadvantage, by going to the Lion's Den during operating hours. Now, after an hour of hitting the bag, my wrists were sore and stiff. I hadn't noticed until Leo interrupted me. "Don't tell me you're shutting up shop for the night?"

Leo nodded, his eyes prying into me. "What's up with you, man? We're fifteen minutes past closing time. The last member left a half hour ago. We made that deal so you could come after I closed. Tonight, you come by when I had members in here, man. You didn't realize we closed. How safe does that make you if you're so oblivious to your surroundings? And I've definitely never seen you abuse a bag like that. What's going on?"

There was no way I could tell him about my friends back in Hell, one with his personal pursuits, and the other suffering from a bout of untimely apathy. Leo didn't need to know anything about my connections when his remained a mystery.

"Sorry, just have a lot on my mind," I said, unstrapping the gloves and tossing them into my new gym bag, which was half-full with gear. A month ago, I didn't even have a gym bag.

He cocked his head to the side. "Need to talk? I've got time. We could go grab a drink or something."

I shook my head as I bent to retrieve my bag. "Just a lot of bullshit, Leo. I think I could hit that bag all night."

He smirked. "I don't think so. Another half hour and you'd have bleeding knuckles and two broken wrists. You'll be sore tomorrow."

No sense in revealing my unique healing properties. I nodded with a snort of agreement.

"So, what's going on? I've never seen you like this, even after everything we've been through. Well," he said with a chuckle, "the first time doesn't count since I knocked you out cold."

"You sucker punched me," I clarified.

He lifted his shoulders, the keys dangling from his hand. "It's a matter of interpretation. Listen, man, if you don't want to talk, that's fine. You just look like you could use it. If it's a problem I can help you with, let me know. My life has been a lot easier since the angel disappeared." He tipped his head and thrust his chin forward. "Did you have something to do with that? Did you handle it on your own? If so, you're more of a badass than I thought."

Leo's life was peaceful now? What a novelty. Frustration churned inside me. Though it wasn't his fault, he was a contributor to what I was feeling. Unlike Bilba and Ralrek, Leo was standing in front of me.

"Glad you're not having any troubles anymore," I said caustically. "I can't imagine what that must be like. It's been," I paused, putting a finger to my chin as if I was in deep thought, "years since I could say the same."

"Whoa, man, calm down. I was just offering to listen, if you had something on your mind. Don't attack me. I didn't do anything."

I stabbed a finger in his direction. "That's the problem,

Leo. You didn't do anything. I took care of your problem with the angel, but you haven't told me a blessed thing."

"About what?" His tone was decidedly less friendly than seconds before.

"It's a little convenient that you've got a group of thugs as members," I said, stepping forward. "You're also working a deal with some mysterious demon to get back to the Underworld, but you haven't told me who. You haven't told me how it actually works, which doesn't help me or Cancer. I've given you plenty of chances, and I took care of your problem in good faith. I wanted you to see whose side I was on. Yet, it's been weeks and I've waited. I'm still waiting. And nothing. All the time, Cancer has... suffered. You could have helped change that. What are you hiding?"

He pulled back. "That's not cool, man. I'm not hiding anything."

"Then who is working to get you to Hell?"

Leo broke eye contact, blinking as his eyes scrunched. "Man, I can't talk about that stuff. If I do... he'll break the deal. I can't risk that. I've got to take care of my family. You know that. You met them, and you know how we got screwed because of their problem with my uncle."

The mention of Aries dampened my internal fire. I rubbed a hand over my forehead.

"What's going on, man?" Leo asked again, this time more benignly.

"I know your family doesn't deserve what happened to them," I said as patiently as I could manage. "And I'm not asking you to put them at risk, but I need to know who you're working this deal with. I've got problems of my own. Giving me that name might help me solve them."

Leo swirled the keys once more in a big arc, catching them in his thick palm. His eyebrows raised in a pleading look. "If I give you the name, I ruin my family's chances. I won't be able to save them, man. Please, I'm asking you, I'm *begging* you to drop this. I can't do that to them. I'm sorry if that causes trouble for you, and I'll help how I can. But I can't do that."

"You won't do that, you mean," I retorted.

"Come on, man," Leo said, dropping and shaking his head. "Sometimes you have to let shit go. I'm not saying I would understand if the shoe was on the other foot, but I'm being totally straight with you. And I'm asking you, man to man, to figure out another way to do what you need to do. Stop asking me who's working the deal. Please."

I had heard enough. Giving my bag a jerk around my shoulder, I stormed past Leo. "Fuck you," I snarled, slamming the gym door open, and stepping out into the cold Olympia night.

My anger accompanied me home, filling my head to the point where I didn't care if the Abandoned were lurking in the darkness.

"Let them come," I growled to myself.

All I wanted was a name. I didn't ask for more than that, and I definitely didn't ask Leo to get involved. He didn't need to be a middleman. A name given, and I would work the rest to stop the Abandoned and Chax. A name was all I needed to take care of my business.

I threw open the apartment door so hard it slammed into the bumper, startling Cancer in the other room.

"Zeke?" she said with fright.

I caught the door before it banged into me. "Sorry. Didn't mean to do that." I did. I tossed my shoes toward the mat. They bounced off the wall and rolled on their sides, neither landing on the mat. Then I saw Cancer's face, and I understood.

I understood everything Leo had just said.

'Sometimes you have to let shit go,' he had said.

Admittedly, I was probably the worst incubus in the Underworld when it came to letting things go. I saw that clearly, looking into Cancer's startled eyes. Frail and fragile, she sat on our couch with a blanket up around her chest as she slowly breathed a sigh of relief. Cancer was in the Overworld because of me. She didn't know me from Beelzebub when she had asked for the favor of helping remove her curse. Desperation and empathy drove her. She faced her family's greatest enemy in the form of Seraph to testify on my behalf and try to save me from Abandonment. Her consequence? Abandonment. Now, her decay, coupled with a possible curse set by Seraph's family, was rushing death in her direction.

My fire was extinguished, tendrils of its smoke blown away in a wind of compassion.

Without a word, I went to her. Sitting, I hugged Cancer, burying my head in her shoulder.

She wrapped around me. "Wha—what's this about? Is everything okay?"

"Tell me something, Cancer," I said, pulling back slightly, but keeping the physical connection with my hand on her leg.

Uncorrupted apprehension scoured her expression. She cocked her head slightly to the side. "Of course. Ask me anything you want. What's going on? I've never seen you like this."

"Why do you put up with me?"

Cancer gave an awkward chuckle, as if she wasn't sure I was serious. When I didn't respond, her fragile smile fell. "Because we're friends." It was a statement but sounded more inquisitive than confident. "We've been through heaven and back, and we did it together. Why?"

"We have been through a lot, but that's not what I mean," I said, leaning back against the couch and rubbing my head.

"You've got to tell me what's going on," she said. "I'm worried."

Behind the protection of my hands covering my face, I admitted, "I failed Aries, and I can't help but feel like I'm failing you."

"Failing me? You're not failing me," she said with an unconfident chuckle. "How do you think you are?"

"You're working your ass off so we have a place to live in a decent neighborhood," I said, pulling my hand away and gesturing at the room. "You're killing yourself with the hours you work, but you still do it without complaint, all while decay and the curse wears you down. You work three times as hard as I do, and you're still so focused on others. I haven't done anything to help... I haven't been honest."

She blinked, looking stunned, but didn't shift away. "Honest about what?"

I stared up at the ceiling. "You know, for the longest time I thought I was the considerate one. Always thinking of others and what they needed. The truth is, all those thoughts were tainted by my own needs. Infected by the things I desired. I wanted. I needed... or thought I did. What I wanted for others is what I prescribed they needed. And the kicker is," I said, slapping my leg. Cancer watched, not saying a word. "It's always been about me. For years, I've said I was done letting the Council affect me. That I was done letting that asinine nickname they gave me when I was a child oppress me. That my family's humiliation would no longer hurt me. But the Lucifer-honest truth is, it has. And it affects how I treat others."

"Zeke, you're a good incubus," Cancer said tenderly. "Where is this coming from? What haven't you been honest about? Maybe you just need to get it off your chest? Maybe I can help?"

"See? That's what I'm saying," I grunted. "Look at how late it is. I come barging into the house with you asleep from a long day, drop this in your lap, and you still want to give more. How much have I given you? Nothing, that's what. I've been hiding something because I thought it was the best thing to do for you. Now I see it was only best for me."

I sat up, faced my roommate and friend, and told her

318 | PAUL SATING

about Seraph's visit. On the other side of the veil, I no longer cared if anyone was listening. If they were, I would welcome them to the Overworld in style. Telling her didn't go down well. I couldn't be upset that she was upset. After her fiery reaction, Cancer simmered enough for us to talk it through.

"And it's not just you," I admitted.

"You've lied to others?"

I shook my head. "No, not lied. I berated and pouted like an impling. I chastised my best friend because he's preparing for the biggest event in his life, and he couldn't drop everything to help me research a counter spell to your curse."

The corner of Cancer's lip turned up. "Well, no one ever said you were a scholar. Needing help with research makes sense with your book smarts. That might have been wasted effort."

Though I appreciated her attempt at humor—Cancer was rarely funny—this moment was too serious. I promised myself to laugh later. "The thing is, I didn't need to wait for him once I found out about the Abandoned. With Cassie here and agreeing to wait to act on Leo, I have the power to change things. I don't have to wait for Bilba. I can't force it. But I wanted it both ways. I've been walking around this Lucifer-blessed town on eggshells for weeks, instead of solving the problem myself and helping you, which is what I truly wanted to do, Cancer. I hope you believe that?"

Cancer placed her hand on top of mine. "I do. Do you think I'd go through this if I didn't think you were a good incubus? I wouldn't, in case you needed help with the correct answer. You have a kind heart, even if your actions are sometimes misguided. Please try not to beat yourself up over this."

Finished, Cancer laid back, pulling up the blanket. Soon, her eyes drifted closed.

I needed to say my piece before she fell asleep and we started a new day as if none of this happened. "I've been selfish, and I'm sorry, Cancer. If you're not happy here, please don't feel you need to stay for me. This is my fight, and I can do it alone. If you don't feel safe, I will understand."

Cancer's eyes weren't focused, snapping back in my direction as if she suddenly heard me, and then drifted away. "Thank you, Zeke. You're a good guy."

And with that, she was snoring within a minute. I sat at the opposite end of the couch, her feet kicked out over me, watching her rest and swearing to Lucifer I was done making everything about me and how I was getting screwed. From now on, the Overworld would not be a Zeke–centric one.

22

OLYMPIA

DIALPHIO: *Write back as soon as you see this.*

Fact is, I had lost track of time and had no idea how many hours passed since her message. After last night's admission to Cancer, I had all intentions of waking up early to catch her before she left. Sleep had come in fits and spells after a long struggle. After helping Cancer to bed, I lay in mine, staring at the ceiling and wondering how in the heaven I was going to do better. By the time the blanket of sleep fell, the rest of the world was halfway through their slumber. I wasn't surprised I woke well after Cancer left for another ten-hour shift.

Trouble was my only breakfast partner. Well, I had its unwanted company and a pot and a half of coffee, to be fair. The gray Olympia sky hung low, muting sounds of daily life from the street below as morning rush hour cars passed. The dreary day chased the few pedestrians into buildings and homes. Even Olympia's homeless, sheltered against the gray. On my balcony, deep in thought, only the far-too-many cups of roasted coffee beans in liquid form staved off the chill.

I only saw the message notification in the demonic notebook because I had gone to my bedroom to grab a hoodie. The notebook was on my nightstand, and I almost missed the glowing blue seal of Lucifer. The series of v-shapes and swirled lines beckoned. I snagged the notebook and read it on my way back to the balcony.

I sat in the chair and slipped the quill from the leather loop.

ZEKE: *Hey boss, what's going on?*

By the time I refilled my coffee, Dialphio's new message had arrived.

DIALPHIO: *We're safe to talk?*

Code. She wanted to talk about something serious without worrying about someone seeing or finding our missives.

ZEKE: *Yes. What's going on?*

DIALPHIO: *Serious events, Ezekial.*

ZEKE: *Like?*

DIALPHIO: *I've told you a number of cells are working in your favor, right?*

ZEKE: *Sure. What about them?*

DIALPHIO: *Some members of these groups are well-placed demons with connections. Advantageous connections. They've been hearing troubling things about your situation.*

ZEKE: *Troubling? Like what? I know all about Chax, but I haven't been able to find him.*

DIALPHIO: *Well, that came from a source I have. They confirmed Chax got to the Overworld via one of the Council members. The source wanted to clarify that it wasn't the Council itself that sent him, just one member in particular.*

ZEKE: *Let me guess. Seraph?*

DIALPHIO: *The one and only.*

ZEKE: *How good is the source? Who was it? Do I know them?*

DIALPHIO: *I can't reveal that. Not yet. The time will come when they can be revealed. No matter how safe these messages are, I can't take the risk of naming them. You understand?*

ZEKE: *Of course.*

I didn't have to like it, but I definitely understood. The

322 | PAUL SATING

name wasn't important, just the information they had and were willing to share.

DIALPHIO: *That doesn't absolve the Council, though.*

ZEKE: *Absolving them of what, Dialphio?*

DIALPHIO: *Don't let this upset you. I'm telling you because I care. Information is your friend, now more than ever. We need it to figure out what to do next. If there was anything I could do, I would. I'm still working with a few trusted demons, but this is a very sensitive situation. Please know you're not alone. I'm doing everything I can.*

ZEKE: *Okay. Please let me know what you're talking about. I'm in the dark here.*

DIALPHIO: *Yes, I'm sorry. The entire reason you were Abandoned was to get you into the Overworld where you're vulnerable. I think you know that.*

ZEKE: *I do.*

DIALPHIO: *They want you gone. They want Creed removed from the equation, figuring that if you were to meet your demise, the halberd would become nothing more than a very exquisite piece of wood and metal. The halberd chose you, so they believe it is eternally tied to you. Aries was its protector. Even if we will never know how or why he came by it, we know that much. You and it are linked because of your shared purpose.*

ZEKE: *And without me, Creed's magic is inert?*

DIALPHIO: *I can't be sure. But that seems to be the consensus. The Council is willing to hedge their bets of that not being in your favor. Get rid of you and they get rid of Creed, the one thing they fear more than anything. The most powerful weapon ever created, one which they have no influence over. Powerful demons don't react well to things they can't manipulate and control.*

ZEKE: *So killing me is their answer?*

DIALPHIO: *Except they haven't been able to. They've tried. Each one has failed.*

ZEKE: *Well, I wouldn't say that. I'm just harder to kill than they thought, and I recover quickly.*

Dialphio couldn't see my snarky smile of false bravado, directly leading to the joke's inability to land.

DIALPHIO: *Be that as it may, they're growing desperate. The Overworld war is still restricted to the other side of the world, correct?*

ZEKE: *Things are heated here, but only in terms of debate. The only people who really think about it are those young enough to be drafted by the mortal Army, or those who have family who might be. Beyond that, people don't appear concerned. The war is too far away to be important, I guess.*

DIALPHIO: *Far enough away to not impact you. Don't be surprised if you get a draft notification from the mortal Army.*

ZEKE: *Are you saying the Council is trying to set that up?*

DIALPHIO: *That's one of their options.*

ZEKE: *I'm not going back into the military, Dialphio.*

DIALPHIO: *The Council is going to do whatever they can to get you out of the picture. If their assassination attempts don't work, they'll figure out a way to get you into the Army and have you sent into the war zone. Of course, that's not their only option, just one they've been throwing around. Word is, something else might happen.*

ZEKE: *Something else?*

DIALPHIO: *There are rumors that if they can't kill you in the Overworld, they'll get Lucifer's approval to have you executed.*

ZEKE: *Executed? Lucifer can't come here to do that.*

DIALPHIO: *Exactly.*

ZEKE: *Wait, Dialphio, are you saying what I think you're saying? Is the Council going to bring me back to Hell to kill me?*

DIALPHIO: *Exactly.*

So, the Council might bring me back to Hell to rid themselves of me? Perfect.

23

OLYMPIA

"WE NEED TO TALK," the text message read.

I stared at my cell phone, loving the magic of human Technology Abilities. The text had come in while Dialphio was telling me the Council might bring me back to Hell with the express purpose of getting the Big Man involved in my life in a one-and-done interaction. Now, my friend and roommate was telling me we needed to talk. Far be it for me to think I'm the smartest incubus in the world, but I know enough to know when a roommate of any flavor tells you they need to talk, it rarely means anything positive, or enjoyable, or positively enjoyable.

"About what?" I texted back.

"On my way home now, see you in a few minutes."

I paced the kitchen while I waited. The chicken cacciatore in the oven filled the apartment with a wonderful smell. My stomach growled, but that was the only positive reaction to dinner I had—and I usually had strong reactions to dinner. I still feared I had upset Cancer. I ran over our conversation, trying to unweave the tangled mess between my ears. Soon enough, footsteps approached the front door, followed seconds later by the metallic clinking of a key in the lock.

"Hey Zeke," Cancer said as she stepped into the apartment.

I rounded the corner of the kitchen too quickly, startling her.

A hand pressed to her chest, she laughed. "What did you do that for? You nearly gave me a heart attack."

Even after a long shift at the hospital, Cancer looked brighter than I had seen her in months.

"Good day on the job?"

"An excellent one," she smiled, her brown cheeks radiating. "That's what I wanted to talk to you about."

"Okay, good," I said, confused. "You had me worried that something was wrong… or that you were going to tell me how much of an idiot I was last night."

Cancer put a hand against the wall as she bent, pulling one foot up to rest on her knee so she could unlace her shoes. "An idiot? Not at all. You were amazing. If it wasn't for you, I wouldn't have had such a good day. I have you to thank for it."

"Well, that's great, I'm glad I could help," I said, having no idea why, and I didn't care. I was happy that Cancer was happier and was thrilled she looked so reinvigorated.

She bounced to the other foot, repeated the shoe untying, and kicked them toward the wall. Both flopped on their sides and Cancer didn't notice. Her nostrils flared. "What is that? It smells wonderful."

I half–turned to the kitchen, waving with both arms. "As soon as you're ready, I would like to invite you to join me for chicken cacciatore."

Her eyes widened. "You made chicken cacciatore? Boy, am I being spoiled or what? You're up to something, Ezekial Sunstone, being so good to me."

"Not nearly as good as you've been to me," I said with all seriousness.

Cancer followed me into the kitchen, plopping down in a chair after grabbing a glass of water.

I looked at her askance. "Aren't you going to shower first?"

"Are you saying I stink?" she said playfully.

"I'm saying you usually shower before dinner," I laughed. "You must be starving."

She grabbed the fork next to her plate, holding it upright in her fist, looking every part of a medieval queen on a food bender. "Blessed right, I am. But I also wanted to talk to you."

I pulled open the oven door, clutched the dish, and set it on the hot plates. "About what?" I asked, peeling back the aluminum foil, and receiving a face full of heated aroma as a reward.

I was still inhaling the earthy tomato sauce fumes when Cancer answered. "About me leaving."

Whether because of the contents of her message, or her seriousness, I lost my focus on the wonderful dish. I stared at the red sauce covering the ingredients as if it would tell me I didn't hear her right. It didn't.

"Zeke?" Cancer said.

I let go of the foil and slowly turned, worried that I had truly pushed her away last night, the last thing I wanted to do. Forming the single word response was difficult. "Leave?"

"This is why I wanted to talk to you face-to-face," Cancer said. She set the fork down as if it were the most fragile item in the world. Her chest rising with a deep breath, she said, "I didn't want to do this through text or the little notes we leave around the apartment for each other. Can we," she said, pointing the fork at the dish, "keep that covered? I'd like to take a quick walk with you because..." she tugged on her ear before swiveling her finger in the air.

I understood. "Sure, let me just grab my jacket."

The walk to my bedroom was like walking through the gateway terminal in the Seventh Circle I had marched through on my way to boot camp. Frightening, long, and seemingly over too soon.

Once we were outside, Cancer started walking around the apartment building.

I cast occasional glances in her direction before her silence forced me to ask, "What did you mean about saying you are leaving? Where are you going?"

Cancer pulled her jacket tightly around herself, tucking her hands under her arms and smiling. I hadn't seen her look this happy since our Abandonment. "Remember that wonderful nursing program I told you about?"

I did. She had mentioned it in passing more than a few times. "The one overseas? 'Nurses Overseas', or something?"

"Nurses Abroad. The administrators have been expanding it as the war expands. My mentor at the hospital has been keeping an eye on it as well. She heard me talking about my time in the war in the break room one day. I was telling a peer how I'd go back again if I could. My mentor thought it might be a good fit for me. With everything going on, with you doing better, with being Abandoned in Olympia... I would be able to serve victims of the war again, just like I was doing in Baghdad! Except, this time, I would have the full support of other staff and supplies and equipment. And a budget! I would be able to serve those poor people and make a difference. Make a real difference."

My mouth dropped open but I clamped it shut again. The urge to tell Cancer she was making a difference at the hospital and local schools, and at the Lion's Den, wanted to burst forward. I wanted to highlight how she made a difference in the lives of all those people she served in Olympia. I burned to tell her how much of a difference she made in my life. But I stopped myself. Learning to be a non-whiny version of myself was the most difficult challenge I would face until the next time I saw a Council member. Almost as hard as keeping my stupid mouth shut right now.

Her smile threatened to disappear underneath worry. I smiled and rubbed her shoulder. "That... that sounds amazing."

Cancer burst out with a laugh so hard that a few drops of spittle flew from her mouth. "Oh, Zeke, you're a terrible liar."

"I'm not lying," I lied.

She slapped my shoulder. "Stop it, you're killing me. Seriously, I know this isn't exciting news for you. And I know I've been talking about it forever, but it probably still feels like I'm dropping it on you. I'm not asking you to be thrilled. Not at all. I understand this is a shock."

"You could say that again." The response came out too abruptly, too much like the Zeke I was trying to bury. I softened my voice. "It is a shock, Cancer. But I know you're not happy here. You deserve to be fulfilled. If going over there is what you want, then I'm all for it."

I wasn't, but that was because I was dealing with six thousand years of baggage, six thousand years of seeing life in a certain light, and now trying to shift that perspective. Just as Cancer needed time to do what she needed for herself, so did I. Here was to hoping it wasn't going to take thousands of years to set a new course.

We rounded the next corner of the apartment building, heading back up the parallel street.

"I want to be serious for a minute, Zeke," Cancer said hesitantly. "Please, be patient and hear what I'm saying."

"Okay."

She drew a deep breath. "I'm tired. Very tired. I don't know if it's the decay, or the curse, or whatever. And honestly, I don't care. If there is a cure for the curse, then I hope someone finds it. My family could use the break. But I can't wait. I can't let more time pass without doing something meaningful. Day after day, I'm more exhausted. The weakness," she said, pulling a hand free and placing it against her stomach, her fingers extended as if she were trying to reach into her stomach, "is seething inside me. I feel it spreading. Remember when I told you I don't know how much longer I can do this?"

"Yeah." I forced the word through my rusty throat.

Cancer slipped her hand around mine. I didn't let go. "It was the truth. I'm getting weaker. I can fight things, you know that. I can be stubborn if I want to. I've kept the toll it's taking on me from you because... because I wasn't sure you could deal with it. Ever since we were Abandoned in Seattle, you've focused on the unfairness of everything, but I don't think you were ready to deal with it."

"And that's changed?"

"*You've* changed, Zeke," Cancer said, squeezing my arm. "You're not a brat anymore, for starters. Now, you... I don't know. You carry yourself differently. It's like you've realized that life is going to serve you dishes you don't want to eat, but they're still good for you."

"So you're leaving because I decided to eat my veggies?" I teased.

She tugged my arm again. "Because you're ready."

Her comment hung between us, not pushing us apart, but as one that wrapped its arms around us and pulled us closer.

After a moment, I grunted, seeing the humor in her reflection of her own personality, but struggling to find joy in the observation. Thankfully, Cancer snickered.

Waiting until a couple in their fifties passed, their gloved hands wrapped around each other's, Cancer continued, "But I'm not so stubborn as to not see the truth. I faced the fact long ago that I'm decaying. Dying. I can't stop that, and I can't change it. I'm not going to beg and plead with the Council to change their minds, and I'm not going to wait for them to either. And... and I love you for what you're trying to do for me. Bilba, too. It is so humbling to know how much you care." She gave my arm a tight squeeze. I squeezed back. "But my days grow shorter, and my desire to help those in need grows larger. Please forgive me for deciding this."

"There's nothing to forgive, Cancer," I said, turning to face her. A man behind us nearly stumbled into my abrupt stop, navigated around us, and continued on his way. I watched him for a few seconds. When he was out of earshot, I said, "This is your life. I'm happy you're doing what you want with it. I envy you, honestly. Not," I said, holding up a finger and smirking, "that I'm looking to go back to that part of the world, by the way."

Eliciting a laugh from Cancer was my greatest achievement of the day, even better than the chicken cacciatore.

"Come on," she said with an appreciative smile, tugging my hand. "It's cold and getting colder. Just like our dinner."

"When are you leaving?" I asked with great hesitation.

She shrugged. "As bad as the war is, they sped up the application process. They're in desperate need of nurses. My supervisor helped. She called in a favor to get my application reviewed today. I had a telephone interview at the end of my shift and they accepted me. They said they were going to send me an email with the specifics, and I haven't had a chance to look yet. It will be fast, though. I know that. But don't worry, you're stuck with me for a bit still."

We rode the elevator to our floor in silence. Cancer stepped in front of me at the apartment, digging through her pocket. She freed her keys, immediately fumbling with them and dropping them. She stifled a groan that still slipped as she bent to pick them up. I couldn't stop my small frown. The click of the lock echoed in my head like an eerie sound in a horror movie. This version lacked women running through strangely lit woods. This version was much more frightening.

I watched her, knowing I was going to miss these times. She stepped inside, leaving the door open, and kicked off her shoes. She was halfway to the kitchen before she stopped to look over her shoulder. "You coming? Because I'm not waiting. I'm starving. If you don't hurry, I'll eat the entire thing myself."

With a laugh, she rounded the corner, out of eyesight, leaving me in the hallway. Alone.

With Cancer leaving for the war, I was going to have to finish this business with Chax. Leo, the Abandoned, and the stupid Council on my own. But I *was* going to finish this business. For her.

24

OLYMPIA

"THAT'S IT, ISN'T IT?" Cancer asked, squatting on the ground and taping the last box closed.

I wiped the sweat from my forehead, taking a moment to look around the living room, inhabited with boxed stacks of her life. "Yep. Who knew you had so much stuff? Where did you hide it? Heavens, working as much as you did, when did you have the time to buy so much?"

"Lunch breaks, mostly, when I could get away from the hospital," Cancer answered nonchalantly. "Plus, I had to have something to do after I got off shift and before I headed over to the Lion's Den."

"Have they replaced you yet?"

"Yeah, I recommended one of my coworkers to Leo. They seem like a good fit," Cancer said.

I watched her add tape to the boxes like she needed to waterproof each container. We were almost done, which was a good thing, because we had to get downstairs. I watched her, because it was easier than seeing the three suitcases standing sentry by the door, reminders of what was coming.

"We have to get going," I said, my voice shaking in my own ears. My moment of vulnerability distracted Cancer from the boxes. "I can finish that. You don't need to miss the airport transport."

"But I don't want to leave you with all this work." She pointed at the boxes.

"Don't worry about it." I waved away the small inconvenience that would actually be a hell–sent curse. I needed something to distract me after I walked her downstairs to the transport. This task would do nicely. "You still want them taken to the donation center on Fourth?"

Cancer stood, brushing off her hands. "If you wouldn't mind, I'd really appreciate it."

"Of course. I don't mind at all."

We both knew only moments separated us from saying goodbye. I didn't want it to happen. By the way she bravely fought off tears, I don't think she wanted to either.

"Thank you for everything, Zeke," she said, her bottom lip trembling.

I needed to get her out of the apartment before we both became babbling implings. "Come on, grab your jacket. Let's get downstairs. Once it arrives, they won't wait forever."

I threw mine on and zipped it. The weather had taken a turn for the colder in the week since Cancer volunteered to travel around the world to return to work in a war zone. "Do you think it's going to be this cold in... over there?" I covered my slip at almost mentioning Baghdad, Cancer's home away from home-away from home. Standing in a sanctuary meant speaking in code to ward off Hell's eavesdroppers.

"Maybe not this cold, but the winters get cold, especially to us," she said with a smile. "I was hoping becoming mortal would mean I would adjust to these Overworld temperatures more quickly. Even after years here, I still haven't gotten used to it. The winter is so blessed cold."

Her laugh was light, the joyous type. She was heading off to do what she wanted, and I could only imagine the weight this turn lifted from her shoulders. Her smile in the past week reminded me of that of an impling's without a concern in the Underworld.

Cancer drew a deep breath as I held two of the suitcases, waiting in the hallway. She paused in the doorway and took one last look at the apartment, releasing her shaking breath. "I'm going to miss this place," she said as she locked the door.

"And it will miss you," I said. "And so will I."

Her hand found my back as we entered the elevator and punched the button to the bottom floor. The elevator doors slid closed, marking a turning point in our lives. "I know, Zeke. I'm going to miss you too. Look at it this way, we can stay in contact without using a demonic notebook. Well, unless the cell towers are knocked out. But if they're not, we can get online and see each other and catch up on what's going on, and the Council won't be any the wiser. How cool is that?"

"Very cool. I would like that," I said with a smile I was completely faking. This was for her, I reminded myself every three seconds, because it was the only way to stop myself from becoming a pouting lunatic.

A future without Cancer was scary. Very scary. Not only would I be alone in the Overworld, without much in the way of friends, but I wouldn't be around to protect her. I hid my worry that Seraph would somehow find out and send Chax following her to Baghdad. That incubus was the very definition of cowardice. He would stay as far away from that the war zone as possible, until he was told to go by his auntie. Still, the thought unnerved me, as did understanding I couldn't help if Cancer needed someone.

A brisk wind struck us as we stepped out onto the sidewalk. Good or bad, I wasn't sure, but the airport transport was idling at curbside as we stepped into the day I no longer wanted to face. Cancer waved to the driver, and he disembarked to load her suitcases.

"Blustery day," the heavy man with fading brown hair that poked out from underneath his watch cap said. "Hope you're flying somewhere south."

Cancer beamed like an excited tourist. "I am."

He nodded as if he had a personal investment in the situation. "Good on you then. Wish I could join you."

He finished sliding the suitcases into the storage bin.

"Can you give me a minute?" Cancer asked. "I need to say goodbye."

"Sure thing," he answered, his eyes offering me an apology, as if he understood. He had probably seen it dozens of times in the past month, but this was mine, and this was hard.

Cancer faced me, cinching her jacket around herself as the wind blew sideways, pushing her loose curls into her face. Every time she tried to pull them behind her ear, they were pushed back. I grabbed her by her shoulders, smiling, and turned so she was facing the wind while I did my best to block it. With her hair blowing back, keeping her face clear, we restarted this difficult farewell.

"Better?" I asked.

"Much," she answered, turning serious. "I'm going to miss you. I'm going to worry about you. We need to stay in touch as much as possible."

"I wish you wouldn't worry about me," I said, recalling Leo's unintentional message that woke me to a new reality. "You're going to have so much on your hands. You'll be busy doing important stuff and I'll be playing video games when I'm not at the store or the soup kitchen. Plus, I volunteered at the shelter too. Tons of demands on my time now. It will be lonely for a bit, but I'm sure I'll make new friends."

She squinted, her mouth curling in a smile. "Like Cassie?"

"Huh... uh... no," I said, a little too forcefully, eliciting a laugh from my ex–roommate.

"Sure, Zeke, keep telling yourself that," Cancer laughed. "But if you do find yourself hanging out with her, don't do anything dumb, okay? You seem to have trouble thinking whenever she's around."

"I have no idea what you're talking about," I said, knowing exactly what Cancer was talking about. That didn't mean I'd admit it, so I changed the focus of the goodbye. "Are you nervous?"

"Without a doubt," she said, confidently. "Scared out of my mind."

"You still could change your mind," I said, only half–joking.

Cancer's eyes fell to the middle of my chest. "No, I can't. This is what I need to do. This is who I am," she said, her eyes drifting back to find mine, holding them. "It's beautiful. To be able to choose how I live my last days. That's all I can ask for. Even if this is the last thing I do in the Overworld, I get to choose it. I'm at peace with that." She grabbed my hands, squeezing. "I want that for you, Zeke. You deserve that. Do me that favor, if nothing else. Don't wallow in your loneliness, and for the love of Lucifer, stop being angry about everything. If you truly see me as a friend and you are serious about this whole change of personality phase, even though I still think you're a pretty great guy, do that. Promise me you'll live the life you choose to live."

My stupid throat constricted again. "I will, Cancer… I promise."

She inhaled and smiled broadly. "Come here, give me a hug. I've got to go."

Right there, under Olympia's perpetually gray sky, on a sidewalk in a blustery wind, I hugged Cancer, and she hugged me. Two ex–demons who had been to the Overworld and back, and back again, coming together one last time before separating, probably forever.

I don't know how long we held each other, both of us not caring to hide our tears from the two passengers on the transport bus.

At some point, the driver called out through the doors he had cracked open. "Sorry, folks, but I've got to get going. Got another pickup before we head to SeaTac."

"Okay," Cancer answered, her voice quivering. She pulled away, her full cheeks wet with tears. Mine were too. "Goodbye, Zeke."

The one word, a single word, so hard to form. "Goodbye."

I stood on the sidewalk and watched her take a seat on the bus, waving when she waved, watching the doors close. The bus slowly rolled out onto the street. I stood my ground as the taillights blinked out when the traffic light turned green and the bus pulled through the intersection, rounding the corner to head toward the highway. I stood my ground, facing the blustery late autumn wind, underneath the blanket of ominous gray above that promised to piss rain if I stayed much longer.

Even when the bus disappeared from sight, I kept my ground until I was ready to head back into the apartment alone, ready to face my life's reset.

25

OLYMPIA

"No, slide your hand down a little further. I'm talking half an inch. Nothing more," Leo said, pointing at the spot on the bar I held.

"Here?" I asked.

"A little more," he replied. When I slid my finger to where he wanted, he shouted, "Yes, right there!"

We were standing in the middle of the large bay of the Lion's Den, where Leo was teaching me how to balance a bar on a single finger. The bar was much heavier than Creed, but the principle of the training was my aim. The burning in my shoulder from holding the bar for so long was just the bonus. He felt so sorry about Cancer leaving and claimed he didn't mind taking time to teach me. Without a class going on, coupled with a healthy dose of guilt from unresolved business with my ex-roommate, Leo seemed more than happy to help.

I thought I knew how to use a long weapon after having Creed for years, but I had never thought about using the balance of a weapon to create momentum for more powerful strikes. Now I would, and I had Leo to thank. Well, thanks to

Leo feeling sorry for me. Hey, I'm not above leveraging sympathies where needed.

After Cancer loaded on the transport, I busied myself in the apartment. Cleaning her room occupied an hour or two of my day. Rearranging her boxes so I could load them into the Mustang she sold to me—charging me a dollar, because she couldn't stop taking care of others right up until the end—took much less time. It didn't hurt the sales price that she never had the car repaired after the altercation with the van. Keeping myself busy didn't distract me from the over-whelming solitude, which wasn't peaceful. The place just wasn't the same without her. So I headed to the Lion's Den and informed Leo she was gone and that I needed company. He was kind enough to put aside any hard feelings over the way we left our last conversation. Plus, I think weapons training was something he didn't do often enough, because he jumped in with both feet. That only amplified as days passed.

As he watched me practice balancing the bar while rotating it in mock striking movements, he led the conversation while I tried to focus. I don't know if he felt obligated to fill in the silence or if he was truly commiserating over the loss of Cancer. Maybe it was part of the training. The distraction was effective, even when talking about my recently departed friend.

"I'm sorry about Cancer, man," he said. "I'm definitely missing her presence here, and it's only been a week. I'm sure you will too."

"I already do," I said, trying to focus on balancing the bar in my palm as I rotated it over my head.

"Any idea what you're going to do with the apartment? Need a roommate?" he asked.

"Not sure yet," I answered honestly, because I didn't. I could afford the apartment for a few more months, between my departing gift from an unnamed demonic friend and the little I had put aside. Cancer had transferred most of her savings to my bank account, saying she wouldn't need it in the war, which was probably true. She forced me to take it and told me not to complain. I capitulated, not uttering a single complaint, at least not to her face. "I'll figure something out."

"Well, let me know, man," Leo said. "A few members are looking for a place. Speaking of." He stopped and jerked his head toward a small group working out in the corner. "I need to kick them out. It's closing time again. Sorry, man."

"Don't worry," I said, pulling the bar back down and tucking it under my armpit in a smooth move.

"Impressive," he said. "You're picking it up fast."

"I've had some experience," I said. "I'll put this back and get out of your hair."

"Give me a second," he said with a wave of his hand. "I'll kick them out, lock up, and we can go have a beer. No sense going back to my place already. I wouldn't mind grabbing a drink. You down for that?"

"Sure," I said, finding it desperate to be so ready to stay out of the quiet apartment.

By the time I put away the gear and packed up my bag, Leo had emptied the gym. Creed nearly burned my hand as I shoved my gloves underneath it inside my bag. I straightened, snapping my head around. Something was wrong.

Leo was at the front of the building, closing down the reception area as I crossed the open bay.

"All locked up," he called out.

Trying to sense what Creed was acting all petulant about, I was about to tell him I was ready when exploding glass behind me made me spin. I dropped my bag as another window was shattered. And then another.

"What the fuck?" Leo shouted from the front room.

Another window exploded inward. Thrusting my hand into the gym bag, I snagged Creed. It burned in my hand.

Even as Leo ran into the bay behind me, multiple figures in black jumped through the four shattered windows.

"Shit!" I said, instantly recognizing the attire. The Abandoned had arrived.

All in black, none of the figures wore masks, allowing me to identify the few I recognized. Fifteen imposing people, obviously not looking to get free lessons on how to roll around on a mat from Leo.

I stepped backward, closing my eyes for a brief second to extend my senses. The invisible wave rippled out, sensing Leo's emitting immortality just behind me. As it rolled over the black-clad group, I received emission signatures from multiple people. The signature of immortality was too strong, almost as if the ex-demons emitting were—

My eyes snapped open. In the back corner of the group, the strongest emissions were coming from Virgo. He was not who had my attention.

Standing next to the intense fighter, much shorter, thinner and physically less intimidating, was a demon I knew all too well. Not an ex-demon, but an actual living, breathing one. Chax Vicu had finally shown his cowardly face. Not alone, of course. Protected by fifteen ex-demons—and probably some ex-angels I couldn't sense—Chax also had something I didn't anticipate. A familiar.

The lizard was the size of a household devildog, similar size to a Labrador. Black scales covered its body, dotted by ovals of orange. White teardrop colorations lined the bottom of its jaw, and the creature's orange eyes darted back and forth. Constantly flicking its tongue, the familiar raised his spiked tail over its barbed back. The tail featured a protruding stinger that was at least six inches long.

"Sunstone," Chax said with the confidence of someone with an immortal nature and superior numbers.

"Nice to see you brought a few friends to the party," I said more confidently than I felt, pointing at the familiar.

"But we don't allow pets, even stuffed animals. Gym policy."

Chax glanced at the giant lizard which kept its unblinking orange eyes on me. "Who? Rimmion? I figured you wouldn't expect a familiar in the Overworld. Bringing him will help finish this business without much trouble from you."

"Took you long enough then," I snarled. "How long have you been stalking me?"

Chax, his skin as pasty as ever, pulled his lips back in a snarl. "Long enough to know everything I need. I mean, it helped that Leo gave us so much information about you. Really sped things along. Though, I would have got it on my own after a little time."

I took a larger step backward to put Leo in my periphery while keeping my eyes on the group. Leo faced them, his legs spread in a stance that kept his balance. Though he eyed me, he was aimed at the group. This wasn't the stance of someone ready to betray me, at least I hoped. But if Chax was telling the truth, Leo already had.

"Is he the one you made the deal with?" I said, Creed pulsing in my grip.

Still facing the group, Leo nodded. "He is. But this," he said, thrusting his hand at his broken windows and those who busted them, "wasn't part of the deal. I swear, man."

"What was?"

"He wanted to take his mommy and grand-mammie home," Chax laughed from the back of the room. Most of his group laughed. There was one notable exception. Virgo stood to the side of Chax, his arms crossed, watching me with his intense eyes.

"You know what I wanted, man," Leo answered in a low tone.

"And what did you have to give him?" I asked.

"Information, man, I swear that's all it was," Leo answered. "He came to me, I don't know, a couple of months ago, maybe, and told me to hire Cancer. That's when he told me who he was. If I hired her, he would do favors for me in return."

Chax's group spread out around the gym, keeping a few feet of space between each other

"Then came the promises how he'd help take care of your family?" I concluded.

Leo's cheeks flushed. "Yeah. When you started coming around, he changed. Started freaking me out, man. Started dropping these hints about what he wanted me to do. I avoided him, man, I swear. It was only ever supposed to be information."

The black-clad Abandoned began pressing in, their ominous intent etched on their faces and the way they rolled their shoulders, smacked weapons against their open palms, rolled their heads, and snarled. A smorgasbord of violent intent.

Leo looked startled and confused. But he also looked pissed off. If he was on my side, Chax's sidekick Virgo would have someone who could match him on the grappling side. All I had to do was handle a demon and fourteen associates, plus one ugly lizard.

"Well, you're going to get a chance to prove whose side you're on," I told Leo, giving Creed a shake.

As the halberd expanded, Chax screamed, "Get him!"

His fighters moved forward, but not before Creed was at its full length, displaying its half-moon and a spiked asymmetrical double-axes, partnered with the wavy dagger jutting from the bottom. The metal was cold steel, containing none of the Hellfire.

"Come on, you stubborn stick," I complained, willing it to display its magical properties. Dormant in my hand, the halberd denied me. "I'm burning you after this is over."

I lowered Creed into middle guard, keeping one eye on Leo as Chax's fighters moved to flank us. Behind them, Chax crossed his arms over his thin chest, a smug smirk making his jaw jut out. He had kept his lizard and Virgo near him.

The blue matting on the floor creaked under my shifting weight. "I swear Leo, I've got your back if you've got mine. But I also swear, if you are in this with them, when I'm done beating them back to their grandmas, I'm coming for you."

"Remember the deal, Neto," Chax called out, taunted. "Would sure be a shame if you broke it now. Well, unless your mommy is enjoying her life in Olympia. Because, if you make the wrong decision, this is where she'll die. You will too."

"He'll do it anyway. He'll break his promise," I warned even as Chax's thugs moved in. "Right now. When we're done cleaning the gym floor with them. Tomorrow. Next week. It doesn't matter, Leo. He will not hold up his end of the deal."

The noose was tightening. A decision needed to be made in the next second or I would make it for everyone.

"I've got your back, man," Leo said, raising his fist and turning to face the gang on his side.

A rattling chain drew my attention to my left. Chain Queen was here and was more than an annoyance. She snapped her gum. "Let's do this, boys," she said, swinging the chain.

At her order, the crew lunged.

I was not waiting for close combat. One of the advantages of being armed with the halberd was the separation I could create if I didn't feel like getting intimate.

"Get him!" Chax screeched.

The order didn't seem to move the Abandoned. They closed in on the same creeping direct line. Great 'leadership' by Chax. No wonder he never made a good sergeant in the Army.

A man came straight at me, wielding a katana. I raised Creed and brought it down in a diagonal strike, cracking the haft across his skull before he could slash. He collapsed in a heap. I spun to my left, facing a man who couldn't be a week into his twenties, carrying a metal bat. He raised it and took a healthy swing, which I ducked under easily. Spinning behind him, I swung Creed to wipe his legs out. He fell on his back, the bat thumping against the mat and rolling away. Before he scrambled for it, I held Creed crosswise in both hands above my head and brought the haft down on the top of his head. He was out.

Jumping to my feet, I spun to analyze everyone's position. The rest of the gang slowed their approach after seeing their side go oh-for-two. To my side, Leo wrestled with one man, who had pulled a stun gun from his belt, while also thrusting kicks to ward off another two who were attempting to grapple him to the ground. This was going to be an arduous struggle, unless I did something soon.

"No, seriously, any time now you want to help," I told the stubborn halberd.

"Get the bastard!" Chax shouted. The familiar at his side made a clicking sound, like thin sticks rapidly struck against each other.

Behind me, someone yelled as a bone snapped. Leo had been on the ground with one of the gang members on top of him. But the gang member had his arm behind his back, and Leo used his leverage and fighting skills to make sure the man wouldn't be able to use it anymore. He rolled off Leo, holding his arm against his body, sobbing while Leo scrambled to his feet. Eight more to go.

The group approached swiftly now, probably thanks to Creed deciding now would be a wonderful time to not be a badass. Most brought their own weapons. Bats. Knives. One guy had a T-baton. Some of them had picked up loose items from around the gym to use as weapons. One I sensed as an ex-demon grabbed a pair of cables and started swinging them like they were nunchucks. A large man—or possibly an ex-angel—pulled a small punching bag from the wall, holding the circular wood platform like a shield. Another held a black steel chair like we were going to take the professional wrestling route. Weapons to maim, not kill.

That didn't mean I felt the same way.

Leo fought a pair who didn't look ready to quit. I had taken down two easily enough, but I knew the bulbous-nosed female's skill with her chain. If she snared me like she did in the gravel yard, I was going to be in a world of trouble since Creed had still not drawn on the Hellfire. Without its power, the halberd was just a stupid halberd. They wouldn't be dumb enough to try to take it this time. They didn't need to. All they needed was me out of the picture and Creed would become a nice wall decoration for Chax.

The problem was, the cantankerous halberd seemed to be in a mood, cold gray steel confirming it had no interest in showing its true power.

Four Abandoned closed in. The woman with the bulbous nose and chain accessory led the charge.

One swallowed my backhand. Two other men danced side-to-side. The Chain Queen whipped the steel like it was a lasso at my feet. I leaped over the uncoiling metal snare as she spun away before I could target her and carry out weeks' worth of building revenge.

Behind me, Leo puffed with exertion. I knew his decay was much slower than what Cancer was experiencing, but he had admitted his fighting career was over because of how weak it made him. This fight would drain him soon. I didn't need to add his two fighters to my equation. I also didn't need to add his injury or maybe even death to my history of failing others. Facing his Nana after I allowed her grandson to be killed was not high on the list of 'fun things to do while in Olympia'.

As the group tightened their circle around us, I raised Creed above my head in an open palm and began spinning it. Round and round. Most eyed the halberd warily. The air moved as Creed whirred faster. I soon had it spinning with blinding speed. The halberd was far more dangerous now, and even for me, nearly uncontrollable. Two of the gang stepped to the side in opposite directions to flank me. Time was up. Leo sounded exhausted, and I could only balance Creed's spin for so long. At some point it was likely to shoot out of my hand and topple harmlessly to the gym wall.

Spinning my body in a full circle, I lowered Creed and allowed the momentum to carry me around and around, transforming me into a whirling dervish of destruction. This was going to be gruesome, but what choice did I have? What was about to happen should never have to occur. But, then again, neither was my death on a stinking blue mat in the middle of a stinking gym in the suburbs of this stinking city.

With Creed leveled, rotating faster than a top, I tore through the gang, Creed's metal blades slicing into flesh and breaking bone. No momentum lost as Creed ripped and severed. The screams were horrific, making me grimace even as I carried out the group's execution. At this speed, I barely registered the bulbous–nosed woman's widened eyes right before Creed cut through her stomach, tearing it open. I did not stop until I had spun twenty feet away. When I did, I held my semi-faithful weapon at middle guard against any attack coming my way, and nearly vomited at the carnage on the blue mats.

Eight gang members who pressed to take my life now lay across a wide expanse of gym mat. A hand here, an arm there. Someone lost their entire lower half. The thick, upper torso lay fifteen feet away, intestines splayed across the mat. Chain Queen's mouth was open in an eternal O-shape.

The scuffle between the two gang members Leo fought was the only sound. One slapped the other on the arm, gesturing at the gruesome scene. His partner swallowed noticeably.

"Let's go!" Chax snarled at Virgo and nodded toward the

window. Chax ran back to where he'd come from. Virgo followed, grimacing. The lizard familiar continued clicking away, its jittery eyes fixed on me. The two gang members fighting Leo raced to escape.

Chax paused at the window. "Rimmion, kill!"

At the command, Virgo snatched at the lizard, but missed. The familiar scurried on its four legs directly at Leo.

"Don't!" Virgo shouted.

But the lizard closed in on Leo, ignoring the intense fighter who had yet to get involved. Thank Lucifer for small miracles, am I right?

It crossed the mat toward the gym owner, dodging bodies and body parts even as Chax climbed through one of the broken windows. The two surviving thugs who had been fighting Leo followed. Only Virgo hung back, his jaw grinding. His intense brown eyes watched the giant lizard. As much is I wanted to follow Chax and make him pay, I couldn't let Leo fend off the familiar by himself.

Rimmion stopped short of Leo, out of range for the ex–demon to use whatever fighting skills he had against a giant reptile. A row of spikes, like wet fur on a devildog after a walk in the rain, raised like hackles. Just really, really big hackles. They rattled. The curled tail with a half–foot long barb twitched, but it was the spikes that were positioned to do damage. The lizard spun, one second facing Leo, and the next its back to him without a single shuffle of the feet. It simply jumped and spun a full one hundred and eighty degrees. The spikes on its back clanked. The lizard's clicking became rapid.

I sprinted across the mat toward Leo.

A spike loosed itself from the lizard's back, propelled at the gym owner.

"No!" The shout hadn't come from me but from Virgo, still standing at the back of the gym. He inched toward the lizard and back to the window, grimacing.

The spike shot the twenty feet to Leo, faster than my sprint, striking him in the shoulder and spinning him with such force he was thrown backward, flying through the air as if an invisible game show pulley had yanked him. His scream filled the bay.

The clicking lizard raised its spikes again. Leo rolled on the mat, blood soaking the back of his shirt as he screamed in agony, holding his shoulder. Another spike tearing into him, especially in the prone position, could do irreparable damage. I still had a wide swath of mat to cross when the lizard loosed a second spike.

Like the previous one, it shot across the open bay toward Leo. Because of his injury, he writhed and rolled on the mat. That probably saved his life. The spike dug into the mat where he had been seconds before, tearing the blue matting open to expose its black foam guts.

The clicking lizard raised the third spike—this thing was persistent—and loosed it. With another five spikes on its back, it wouldn't stop. The freaking beast didn't have to. Leo's luck would not last, even if he rolled behind the octagon.

As the spike flew through the air, I tossed Creed like a javelin. The halberd intercepted, the wavy dagger tearing into the spike. It exploded in a cloud of fine dust, sending the halberd thumping across the mat.

The lizard sensed a new threat in me. With a half-turn jump, the familiar faced me before raising its tail over its head and lowering its barb in my direction.

"Shit," I said. This was going to hurt.

On a good note, the barb on the lizard's tail gave no sign of being detachable like its spikes. The clicking lizard scurried in my direction, its long body swiveling side to side as it covered the distance between us. Too quickly.

"Creed!" I called out to the halberd.

It stood on its wavy dagger blade, shuddered for a very

long second, and then flew across the gym. With arms wide open, Creed slapped into my open palm without me taking my eyes off the ugly orange-eyed lizard. As it closed, I lifted my halberd-turned-javelin with the double-ax head toward the rear, the dagger pointing forward. "Let's see how you like shit being thrown at you."

I propelled Creed, the halberd spinning in tight rotations. Just as I predicted, the tiny reptilian brain couldn't calculate the risk. Chax's familiar was bent on one thing and one thing only. Programmed to kill or be killed, the poor creature didn't stand a chance. Creed's dagger buried itself into the lizard's neck. The black scaled creature screeched as the blade bit deeply. Apparently, that was the way you communicated in the fraction of a second between registering pain and exploding into a powder puff of black and orange dust. Creed dug into the gym mat at an angle that made it convenient for me to run forward and dislodge it without breaking my stride.

Virgo bolted from the gym by leaping through the window that framed the black night.

I raced to Leo, sliding to my knees next to him. "Are you okay?"

Leo rolled onto his back, clutching the shoulder underneath his bloodstained T-shirt. The lizard's spike was gone, apparently disintegrating with its death. But Leo's injury was still very real.

"Burns like heaven," he grimaced.

I looked around and found gym towels on a rack along the near wall. I gathered as many as I could carry without letting go of Creed and brought them to Leo, sliding a small stack under his shoulder and pressing two on top of the wound.

I glanced over my shoulder.

"Go get him, man," Leo groaned. "If you don't, he'll come back."

"I've got to help you," I protested, feeling the tug of rage.

"I'm fine." He winced. "Get that sonofabitch now."

I didn't need any more encouragement. Jumping to my feet, I raced across the gym and dove, headfirst, through the window. Since the gang had blown it inward, no glass lay on the ground outside. I hit the blacktop in a roll and jumped to my feet.

The night was almost still. Almost. Above me, I heard mumbled arguing on the roof.

"Drop it, Virgo," Chax said with snobbish conviction.

"Dead," Virgo said in that deep rich voice that, even painted with anger, resonated beautifully. "They're all dead, Chax. You said it wouldn't go this far. You told me he was an outlaw and was supposed to be brought back to the Council. The Council! Where were they? They didn't show up. What was that bullshit down there? You weren't trying to apprehend him. You tried to *murder* him."

"Let go of me!" Chax screeched, no longer hiding his presence atop the building.

More scuffling. More voices. Chax and Virgo weren't alone. I imagined the other two surviving gang members were there too. The four were going to get a rude surprise.

Hefting Creed like it was a javelin again, I flung it at the zenith of the wall. The wavy dagger sunk into the corrugated metal siding. Pausing until I was sure no one above me heard the slice of blade through metal, I raced up the ladder. It wasn't until I was halfway up that I remembered; I don't like heights. At all. Twenty feet off the ground was fifteen feet higher than I wanted to be. But this was my chance to snare Chax and make him pay for everything he had done. For everything the curse, if it were real, would be doing to Cancer even now, somewhere in the Middle East.

"Shut up," Chax said harshly. "What was that? I heard something."

"I don't know," one voice said.

"I think I heard a noise too."

"Be ready," Chax whispered.

I grinned wickedly. I was ready, thanks to my superior senses; they were guessing. Maybe even jumping at shadows. At the top of the ladder, I swallowed my fear, released my death grip on the rung, and pulled Creed free from the wall. Hopping over the upturned beam forming a shin-high wall, I landed on the roof with Creed at the ready.

"Lucifer, Sunstone," Chax said with a smarmy grin, "you insist on dying, don't you?"

I groaned. Surprise was no longer my advantage. In fact, it had been Chax's all along.

Chax was most definitely not alone. Not only did he have Virgo and the two gang members, but there were another twenty black–clad men and women, probably with a smattering of ex-immortals along for the ride. I snapped my eyes shut, sending out my senses. Besides Chax and ex-demon, Virgo, others were definitely emitting. How many ex-immortals occupied this space was impossible to tell with so many bodies so close together and having used all my time-outs. Trouble. Again.

"Where's your aunt, Chax?" I asked, trying to nudge him toward making a stupid decision while I bought time to figure out how I was going to take on so many enemies without Leo's help. "Why don't you call out to her? This is a perfect opportunity for her to get what she wants. Me dead."

"I can handle my own business, Sunstone," he spat.

"You haven't yet," I teased and got the reaction I was hoping for.

"Fuck you, Sunstone!" Chax screeched, jabbing a finger at me. "Wish I could say it's been nice knowing you, but that would be a lie. I'll make sure I let Nijal know what happened. I hate the thought of searching for her, so why don't you tell me where she's hiding? We won't drag out your demise if you do. I can't say the same if you choose to play stupid. But I want you to know, either way, I will find her. I want you to know right before you die that I'm going to drag her death out. That bitch has a lot coming and I'm going to enjoy it. See you." He turned to the armed Abandoned. "Earn your pay. He'll kill you if you don't kill him first. Take him out!"

The black–clad gang hunkered in defensive positions even as Virgo grabbed Chax by the collar and pulled him close. "Stop this, Chax!" Virgo growled.

Chax must have spent good money to upgrade his equipment. Everyone was armed. And when I say armed, I don't mean with chains and baseball bats. I mean, armed, like with guns.

"Stop them!" Virgo shouted.

Chax threw his arm up, trying to swat away the larger ex–demon's arm, which didn't budge. "Get him away from me," Chax ordered the men nearest him.

Three of them moved toward Virgo, who shoved Chax away. The coward stumbled and fell, yelping when the roof's pea gravel dug into his arm. The fighter didn't wait to be subdued. He went on the attack. Spinning, he thrust a kick into the midsection of the nearest man, bending him in half and sending him backward. The second one received a spinning punch to the cheekbone that knocked him out. Virgo was on the third and had him in a headlock before the man even recognized what was happening.

Then all heaven broke loose.

The remaining gang of thugs looked around, blinking at each other. Confused or not, they did what unsettled armed people always did. They reacted with false courage inspired by handheld firepower.

I dove for cover just as the first bullets tore into the roof at my feet. The air-conditioning unit was easily three bodies wide. Hiding gave me a second to collect my thoughts, but it wouldn't give me more than that. The gym was a wide, long building, but it was mostly an open rooftop with no escape except for a fall to the ground far, far below—yes, twenty feet is far. Within seconds, they would round the unit and open fire and I would end my life by becoming yet another gun violence statistic.

Rapid pinging against the metal told me they weren't even going to wait that long. My brain was scrambled. How did I fend off so many armed enemies?

A hiss escaped the air-conditioning unit when a bullet punctured one of its lines. I cowered and army crawled—see, there was something good to come out of my military time— behind an electrical box. This was smaller than the air-conditioning unit, but in the cover of the night, it gave me a chance to hide as long as the group thought I was still hiding in my original spot.

In the corner, Virgo fought two men, even as they screamed for him to calm down. Whether he was doing this to save my life or save his own now that he had committed against Chax, the fact was, he was still drawing attention away from me. Without help or forcing me to submit a request in writing.

Creed's double-ax head and dagger blades burned blue with Hellfire, casting a haze around me and illuminating most of the electrical box. In the darkness, it was like a beacon in the middle of a wasteland. The pinging of bullets striking metal and flying chunks of rooftop material verified Creed had given away my new hiding spot.

"Are you freaking serious? Now?" I chastised. Creed vibrated in my hand, the blue light glowing brighter. "Oh, you're begging to become bonfire fodder now. What do you want me to do?"

The halberd vibrated again. And then my arm seared with pain as a bullet tore through the box and into my left triceps, flinging my arm forward. Creed tumbled to the roof, still illuminated.

"Shit!" I grabbed my triceps, warm blood oozing between

my fingers. I pinned my arm to my side. Bullets sprayed around my location, sending gravel, blacktop, and chunks of concrete flying everywhere.

"Creed," I croaked.

The halberd stood on the dagger once more and flew into my open palm. Holding my arm against my side, I used the full length of the halberd to pull myself to my knees. I scanned for another hiding spot that would give me time to catch my breath and isolate a few of the gunmen. No way I could take all of them at once. They were too spread out. Piecemeal picking was the way to go. Then I had a chance to survive long enough to bleed to death twenty feet above the surface of the Overworld.

I rolled to check on Virgo. Another gunman joined the smaller squad in trying to subdue him. They wrestled. One dropped his pistol while trying to free an arm. But Virgo was too strong. He spread his legs to gain a wider base as they tried to pull him to the rough roof surface. An uppercut rocked one man's head, sending him reeling backward. Two held Virgo around the waist when a larger man charged. Far away and busy bleeding to death, I could only watch as the big oaf tackled Virgo. Often, demons will say that it's a stereotype that big oafs lack intelligence, but they would not be stereotypes if they weren't constructed from a good chunk of truth. This guy proved my point when he tackled Virgo at chest height, sending them both reeling backward. The back of Virgo's calf caught the rooftop edge, and they tumbled over, out of sight.

The one hope I had was gone.

"Find him!" Chax's voice pitched into the night. "Light up this entire blessed rooftop if you have to, but find him!"

Focused white circles appeared on the rooftop as the group of armed thugs pulled out flashlights to search. Though I held my arm, I no longer felt it. Numb. Glancing down, I pulled my hand away. The front of my bicep was still intact. The bullet had not gone all the way through. Good? Bad? What did I know? The only medical professional who could help me was halfway across the world—or further, I couldn't remember. Overworld geography was hardly a strong suit of mine.

The sweeping beams of light grew denser as the armed thugs closed. Seconds were all I had left. A few seconds to realize I had just changed my outlook on life to follow Cancer's wonderful example. A few seconds to realize not only had I failed Aries, but I wouldn't get the chance to tell Cancer I had failed her a second time. A few seconds to think about Chax torturing the life from that beautiful soul. A few seconds to grow viciously angry.

Growling, I gripped Creed tighter. "This isn't how it ends. Are you with me or is it time for your nap?"

The blue glow surrounding Creed's blades brightened and pulsed.

"Fire!" someone shouted. The flashlight beams swiveled in my direction.

The rooftop exploded around me with shards as bullets tore apart the roof. Shoving Creed's dagger into the blacktop, I left the halberd standing upright, and raced around the side of the roof, staying low. Bullets ripped the rooftop around Creed, my decoy, as I closed in on the first gunmen, taking him out with a clothesline and elbow to the face.

The next one didn't see me coming either. I was behind him, flying through the air and snagging his neck before he could turn at the crunch my feet made. Cinching his neck as I flew over him, I drove his face into the jagged rooftop. The crack of bone on roof told me he wasn't going to rejoin the fight.

Still, I scrambled to my feet, looking for my next target.

"Back here!" a woman screamed. My sneak attack was done, advantage vanquished with a shrill cry. I'd only taken out two more gunmen, far short of what I needed.

"Creed!" I called across the rooftop. It wiggled free and shot in my direction. As I caught it, a bullet took my leg out from under me. I screamed into the Olympia night.

"Kill him! Kill him!" Chax shouted frantically.

The new pain in my leg made the world spin. I squeezed my eyes closed tight against the agony. So tight that my vision filled with white. And then I waited for death.

The poor Council; they would not bear witness to my demise.

I waited.

And waited.

Death never came.

Instead, screams filled the night as pain tore through my head. At the base of my skull, one of the gunmen must have jabbed a knife into my thin skin, trying to pry open my brain's bone container. Boy, would he be disappointed.

More screams.

More jabbing pain as the thug pushed the knife deeper.

Wait.

No!

Not a thug.

Not a knife digging into my skull. This was a headache, a migraine. White light.

Angelfire.

Prying my eyes open, I watched as heavenly white light tore open the gunmen on the rooftop. I pushed myself up and backward, away from the fight, using Creed to accelerate my retreat. Blood seeped from just above the edge of my shorts where the bullet had torn a chunk of my leg. At least it hadn't hit my tibia or an artery. I was still able to use both legs, even if the injured one sent me clear signals it was not happy about being made to move. It didn't get a say in the matter. My arm was still useless, so I needed both legs to get to safety.

I wasn't in this fight alone anymore.

At the far edge of the roof near the ladder stood a form,

shining against the black backdrop, shrouded in the brilliance of her Angelfire. Through blurry eyes, I reveled in the beauty of Cassie exacting retribution. Short bursts of white light, like lasers, shot from her extended hands. Not random, but deliberate. Terror and vengeance with purpose, taking out solitary gunmen, one with each burst.

Bodies drifted into the night like smoldering paper from a cooling campfire as her Angelfire ripped into them. Screams faded to nothing as the mortals and ex–immortals died.

"No! No! No, stop it!" Chax screamed.

She shot one beam after another each time a thug raced for escape or to take aim on her. They didn't stand a chance against her beams, which tore into flesh, bone, metal and concrete with equal aplomb.

And then Chax's hands were moving. The tickling in my brain was immediate, just subdued by the searing migraine–like headache of Cassie's Angelfire. Chax was using his Discernment Ability on Cassie. The slight distraction of his mental manipulation could delay her long enough for his crew to take her out.

Growling against the protesting of my limbs, I used Creed to stand. Every inch of my body shrieked as I hobbled in Chax's direction. The tickling in my brain intensified. His spell was growing, maturing in his recitation. I was running out of time before he loosed it on the angel who'd intervened to save my life.

Lowering Creed to mid-guard position, I yelled, pushing my will into the petrified dark cherry of the halberd's haft. Creed responded, the blue glow around the axes radiating, pulsing, vibrating… bursting. A blue ray of Hellfire shot from the spiked end of the halberd. Toward Chax.

I had the satisfaction of watching him turn, seeing me and the blue ray of death that bore down. His eyes widened and thick lips spread in horror as the beam consumed. Chax didn't even have time to scream as the Hellfire sought justice.

Creed's fury tore into Chax's chest, the blue Hellfire burned golden upon impact before exploding outward in a burst.

A smoldering pile of white ash lay on the rooftop where Chax had stood seconds before.

I collapsed to my hands and knees as Creed cooled, the blue glow of its axes and dagger fading. Somewhere in the distance, mortal and immortal cried their final cries as Angelfire rained down.

As the blackness of the night smothered me, the sounds of death settled to silence.

Technically, I was still conscious when hurrying footsteps crunched across the rooftop. Conscious enough to feel the warm, soft hand on my arm.

"It's okay, Z-Zeke," Cassie said, "I'm here."

26

OLYMPIA & BEYOND

"It's MIRACULOUS," Cassie said, her crystal eyes sparkling with delight. "I've never seen anything like that."

I smiled through my grimace. "I'm full of surprises if you give me a chance."

There was a grunt to my side. "Do you think now is the time to flirt, man?" Leo replied with a stunted laugh, then a wince. "Ow, that hurt."

"Then don't laugh," Virgo said, holding his ribs.

Cassie was kneeling in front of the three of us, lined up along the interior wall of the large bay inside the Lion's Den. Three ex–incubi and one angel. "Good to know us angels don't have much to fear from the Underworld."

I gave her a raised eyebrow.

Her finger swayed across us. "Look at you three, and I'm feeling just fine."

"You came into the fight after Leo and I did the hard work," I said.

Cassie snorted. "We need someone to look at those injuries. I'm not good with medicine."

"We can't call an ambulance," Virgo winced, holding his side.

"And you shouldn't talk," Cassie chided. "Every time you do, you aggravate your injuries. Just rest. I'll figure something out."

Leo raised his hand, waving it back and forth as if he was saying hello to someone on the other side of the room. "Don't worry. I called Leanne." He glanced at me. "She's Cancer's replacement."

I asked. "Is she safe?"

Leo knew what I meant. None of us could deny the drastic scene sprayed out before and above us. The Lion's Den was a display of destruction. The remnants of Chax's gang here and on the roof, a testimony to absolution by rage and Angelfire.

"She is. She has to be," Leo nodded. "Cancer said she would trust her with any secret."

"Okay. Let's hope so. We don't have any other options," I said, sucking in my breath as I moved too swiftly for my arm.

"I'm not gonna let her walk into a shock, man," Leo said, dipping his head at what remained of his blue-matted kingdom. "I told her to be ready for a gruesome scene, and I explained what happened as she got ready. She had me on the phone a while, but she was in the car before we hung up."

As if on cue, a tentative "Hello?" came from the reception area. A blond stepped into the bay, halted, swallowed noticeably, and then raced in our direction. "Oh my God, this is... let me see your wounds," the woman, who was presumably Leanne, said as she kneeled next to Cassie kneeling before us.

I would like to tell you I didn't scream like an impling as Leanne dug the bullets from my arm and leg. But I did. I screamed and screamed and screamed. On a good note, Leanne seemed pleased with how the impromptu and unofficial procedure went. She had me bandaged and wrapped not long after.

Tending to Leo was much quicker. He and I sat close as she checked on Virgo, who seemed least damaged of all. The large man who had attacked Virgo, sending both of them over the rooftop, was the one who landed on the dumpster, cushioning Virgo's fall. Leanne checked him for internal injuries. Virgo said he had none, though he still held his side.

"I'm sorry about this," I said to Leo.

"And I'm sorry I didn't tell you earlier about that dickhead, man," Leo responded. "If I knew it was going to come to this, I swear, I would have cut off contact with him right away."

I shook my head. "Chax was on a mission for a powerful family member. He wouldn't have stopped, trust me."

"Still feel bad."

I lifted my arm and placed it lightly on his good shoulder. "Don't. You were thinking about your family, trying to take care of them. I don't fault you. I would have done the same thing. Probably."

Leo laughed. It was a weak, exhausted laugh. "No, you wouldn't have. You're the Segregate, man. A hero to some demons. Now, I see why. You would have done the right thing. I know that, man."

"I thought you gave up that nickname for your new one?" Cassie teased.

"Don't you start," I said with a wink before turning back to Leo with more seriousness. "Don't feel bad about any of this. If nothing else, at least we're even now."

Leo gave me a confused look at my bad joke.

"I was talking about your uncle. You know, that whole touchy subject that I'm flippantly trying to make light of?" The weak smile slipped from my face. "I'll never be okay with what happened to him, and when I told you how much he meant to me, I was being genuine."

Leo's head dropped. "He was a great incubus. You would have liked him if you'd been given a chance to get to know him. They took that away from you, man. They took that away from both of you. As bad as you feel about that situation, I feel equally shitty about this. Except I'm more at fault. I could have stopped this. You couldn't. Not with the Council, man. Stop thinking you could."

"You just wanted to get your family home," I replied. "There's no crime in that."

"Yeah," Leo said, gazing into the distance.

I imagined losing his family's opportunity to get back to the Underworld was gone forever. He was going to deal with the consequences of tonight for the rest of his mortal life. I had a feeling we all would. Then his eyes cleared and turned back to me. "I don't know what's going to happen now."

"Don't worry about the bodies," Virgo grunted from a few feet away. "I'll take care of this. Our crew can make it disappear."

The three of us looked at him, waiting for an explanation, one he didn't provide. No questions were the best questions in a situation like this.

"But the Neto family will move on, man," Leo said, refocusing. "I promise you that. We won't let this go, and we won't rest. We're going to keep seeking justice as we can, and if it never comes, at least we have each other. We're all together, and we're going to enjoy the time we have. I hope you can too. You're one miserable bastard sometimes. So serious."

"I'm working on that," I admitted.

"Let it go, man," Leo said, now resting his hand on my shoulder. "My uncle would be proud to know the type of incubus you are. What you stand for is right in line with what he talked about all the time. Whatever you need to tell yourself to make peace with your role in his death, know that no one in my family holds you responsible. Let it go. Stop blaming yourself. Just." He stopped while I tried to draw breath. "Just promise me you'll carry on being the good incubus you are. If you truly want to honor my uncle's memory, make peace with yourself. Okay, man?"

After six thousand years of brain training that preached

incubi are not supposed to cry, especially in front of other incubi, I felt no shame in letting the tears flow freely.

———⯈

"WANT MORE WATER?" CASSIE ASKED, HOVERING OVER ME AS I sprawled out on my couch. The court scene from *A Christmas Carol* played softly in the background. Cassie turned to watch before her eyes danced over me.

"What," I said with a goofy grin.

"Oh, nothing. Well. I'm enjoying the irony of a demon watching a Christmas movie," she laughed, light and pleasant. Water trickling over rocks. "Definitely on my list of things I never thought I'd see."

"One day, we're going to talk about your bigotry toward demons," I said with a wink before closing my eyes and putting my forearm on my forehead, feeling the surge of raw, returning energy swelling inside me. "But right now, I'm too mad at you for making me rest."

Hours into the new day, I had the energy to walk from my bed to the couch. I didn't want to lie down. I wanted to head to the Lion's Den and help clean. But Cassie had called and told me Virgo followed through on his promise. The gym was nearly spotless, and the damage to the roof was unnoticeable from the parking lot and street. Leo had even contacted a contractor to replace the windows.

Cassie giggled. "Stop being so glum."

My eyes still closed, I responded, "That's hard after everything that happened last night."

"Why? Ch—Chax is no longer a threat, and the Abandoned won't be bothering you again. What could be wrong?"

"Cancer," my answer came through a constricted throat.

"What about her? With Cha—Chax out of the picture, she's as safe as she can be, Z-Zeke."

I ground my teeth. "I wasn't thinking last night. I saw Chax ready to... to hurt you. I didn't think. I just wanted to stop him."

Cassie squatted next to the couch, her hand on my chest. "What is it? What's wrong?"

"The curse," I said as I tried to control my voice. "I don't trust Seraph. She told me only the demon who set the curse could remove it. I planned on making him recite the cure. It was all Cancer had left. Who knows if it would have worked or not, but it was worth a shot. And now it's gone. Killing him means I've condemned Cancer. There is no way to stop the curse now, if it's real. And it's my fault."

My chest heaved as I blew out a deep breath. Cassie rubbed it.

"You don't know that for sure, do you? For absolute truth?"

I shook my head, unable to speak. It was true, there was still Bilba and Melchiot and their research side-project. Dialphio was conducting independent studies on the topic. The curse might be all in Cancer's head too, something she believed without evidence. As soon as I felt better, I was going to figure out how I could help.

"Plus, you said she wanted to go back to the war to help the mortals in need. That was the only thing she wanted to do with the time she had left, right?"

I nodded. It was the only thing I could do.

Cassie's hand rubbed lightly. "While you're making peace with yourself over A-Aries, be sure to do it for Ca-Cancer too."

"What do you mean?"

Cassie sighed. "You are pretty thickheaded. Did you not listen to L—Leo last night?"

"I did."

"Well then, you would have heard what he said about

absolving yourself for what happened to A-Aries. It's the same thing for C-Cancer. Just like with him, you didn't have any responsibility to her. You did what a friend does, and she wouldn't expect anything more." She paused, watching me. "And she's your friend. She knows what you did, but she also knows you did it out of kindness. You did the most selfless thing you could by supporting her decision to go back to a dangerous war zone to do meaningful work. If she was here and saw you acting like this, I bet she would kick your ass."

I loosed a shaky snort. Mucus flew from my nose onto the back of Cassie's hand. She grimaced and wiped it on my shirt.

"That was gross." She watched my face before smiling. "But not as gross as what you look like when you're upset."

I smiled. "Thank you, Cassie. Thank you for everything. When I feel better, I'll take you out to dinner and repay you for what you did."

"I didn't do anything you wouldn't have done for me," she said nonchalantly, pressing her hands to her knees and pushing herself up. "Now—"

Her eyes widened.

"What's wrong, Cassie?"

"I've… I've got to go. Sorry. I'll check back soon."

She scrambled for the front door, throwing it open.

"Cassie, what's going on?"

Before she answered, the front door slammed shut.

I laid my head back and groaned. Angels, I just don't get them.

But what I did get is another visitor, approximately twenty seconds after my angelic friend bailed.

My living room sizzled with a tear in the fabric of space.

"Lucifer, bless it," I swore, hearing clinking coming from within the rift. "Creed."

The halberd flew around the corner of the hallway and was in my hands as the first pair of armored legs stepped through, followed by three more.

Four Council guard spread out, armored in their honorary black armor, holding staffs tipped with the blue light of the Hellfire.

"What the heaven do you guys want?" I said with a growl, trying to push myself up off my couch. My bullet-free triceps flinched at being forced to support me. By the way, it did a piss-poor job.

A fight was the last thing I needed. Though I have supernatural—even for immortals—recovery powers, being shot twice sort of balances the equation. I could walk stiffly, but fighting was a day or two away. That was why the Council was showing up now.

Legs adorned in a black robe trimmed with red, denoting the appearance of one of the five most powerful demons in Hell, appeared in the rift, leading the rest of the body in. My fuzzy brain didn't even care to guess which Founder was making a guest appearance. When I saw it was Azazel, relief washed over me before the feel of his listening ward followed.

"Young Mr. Sunstone," he said apologetically. "I hope you're feeling better after last night's events." He stopped, alert as he looked around the apartment, bending to see around the rift. "Is she gone?"

I played dumb, something I do very well. "Who?"

"The angel," he answered matter-of-factly. "I delayed as long as I could to avoid the others knowing about her. But I couldn't wait much longer. Please tell me I've missed her?"

I nodded, looking at the four guards.

"Don't worry," Azazel said. "They're loyal to me. This is pretense and formality. There are things I can manipulate, and things I cannot. Who I choose to have at my side, I control. Why we are here, I cannot, I'm afraid. But rest assured, they won't betray the fact she was here."

"Why *are* you here?" I asked.

"To bring you home, young Ezekial," Azazel said, a haunting dominance in his voice.

Dialphio's frantic warning flashed in my mind, knocking thoughts of Cassie, Cancer, Leo and the like, out of the way as it barged forward.

They want you executed, she had told me.

Now I had a Founder and his guards in my Overworld living room to bring me back to Hell.

"Don't I get a few days to recover?" I asked, knowing the answer.

Azazel shook his head. "Unfortunately, I was outvoted in the matter. I thought to do just that, reasoning you wouldn't be well enough to travel through the rift. The others... didn't seem too concerned that traveling might be traumatic in your current state."

"So I could conveniently die in the rift?"

Azazel clasped his hands in front of him and lowered his head. It was the only answer I needed.

I gave Creed a shake. When the truncheon expanded into halberd form, the guards jumped. Two of them shifted their hold on their staffs. Fighting position.

But Azazel's arm shot up. "No!" he ordered and then looked at me, his face sagging in a begging expression. "We don't need violence. Please. There are... reasons I have for asking you to come peacefully."

Grimacing, I pulled myself to a standing position, the ache in my leg shooting up through my back, making me go stiff. It hurt less than my arm, so there was that. "I'm not looking for a fight, I'm looking for help standing, because a whole bunch of someones tried to have me killed last night. This," I said, dipping my head toward Creed, "will help me accomplish that. For the bonus, I'll even be able to walk with its assistance. You're going to have to be okay with that... unless you want to try to take it from me?"

Azazel's lips moved for a few seconds before he mumbled, "Of... of course not. You can use it to assist you. I'm sorry for the misunderstanding."

I narrowed my eyes and smiled at the first test of wills of many that were to follow if my instincts were correct. Cancer would have been proud, which made my chest swell in vengeful pride. Before leaving, she had asked me to live the life I chose, and that started right here, right now, with the first interaction with a Founder. If I was going back to Hell, I was going on my terms. The line in the sand had been drawn, and I drew it with Creed's dagger. The Council might think this maneuver was giving them the upper hand. Sadly for them, they had no idea what was going to walk through the rift. Had they ever faced an Abandoned demon with an inferno raging in their gut? They were going to get an Ezekial Sunstone, a Segregate, like they never knew. Maybe the Great Prince would make an appearance.

"Thank you," I said, my voice full of fortitude.

He studied me. "Shall we?" Azazel said, half–turning and gesturing toward the rift.

"After your monkeys," I said with a nod. None of the guards responded. "I need a moment to gather my things."

Azazel nodded. I hobbled to the bedroom to pack a bag with my clothes and essentials. Not that I had much to bring with me. I had acquired so little of true value during my Abandonment. I doubted the Council was going to let me come back, something that tore at my insides while I packed the few things I refused to leave behind.

A demonic notebook was one such item. Before packing it in the bag, I ripped a page and scribbled a quick note to Cassie, for when she came back looking for me, which she surely would. Briefly, I described what happened and told her where to find the remaining notebooks I had scattered around the apartment, explaining they would be our way of staying in touch. Then I scribbled a separate note to Dialphio, informing her of what was happening and asking to pass along the situation to my best friends and mother.

The party waited for me in the living room.

"I'm ready," I said.

"Thank you for making this easy," Azazel said. He flicked his hand and the four guards took their leave through the rift.

I gave Azazel an appreciative nod.

Exhaling, I took in my apartment. I had no special attachment to it. I'd only lived here for a few months and never truly felt at home in the Overworld. If I made it back to this realm, I would correct that. I would reach out to Leo, and maybe even Virgo. I would catch up with Steve and ensure he was doing well, and if he wasn't, I would help however I could. I would spend more time at Stacy's soup kitchen, giving more of myself. I would do these things with the lust for life that Cancer exhibited. I would live Aries's legacy. I would live the life I wanted to live.

I still would, even if that life was a short one in Hell.

Azazel stood by quietly. After too short of a minute, he said, "We only have seconds. The rest of the Council is waiting. They expect us back. I will tell you this once and then we need to move. Be very careful and deliberate in how you act. You have the fire of a young incubus. That serves you, but it is also something you must manage or it will mislead you. I think you know you have friends throughout the Underworld. I know you have them here as well, to a greater extent than many realize. And you will have enemies the moment your feet touch brimstone. Don't let that distract you from those who are allied to you. When we walk through this rift, I will lead you. Keep a cool head. Whether this is the end of your journey or just beginning. Your destiny is of your choosing. Let no others choose it for you."

Oh, I was all about choosing my destiny. No more regret. No apprehension. Cancer taught me that when she grabbed her future by the throat and directed it where she wanted it. I was simply modeling her extraordinary example.

"I imagine this hasn't been easy for you, Azazel," I said to the Founder, "but I appreciate it. I recognize what you've done for me. So, let's go. I'm ready."

Azazel nodded, his bottom lip pushing his upper lip toward his nose, making his long goatee jut out. As I neared, he held up a finger. The listening ward was still up. "Keep this safe."

I looked at his extended hand and noticed a folded piece of paper.

"What is it?"

A mischievous grin spread across the ancient incubus's face. "Do you remember the Horn we sent you on a mission to retrieve?"

I nodded. "Yes, of course I do."

"Conveniently, that powerful item, the one that was so important we had to regain possession of it from the Hammerwulf family, hasn't been seen in quite some time. A powerful, powerful item. For its whereabouts to be unknown is disturbing on many levels. The odd thing is," he said, pausing to tap the paper in his open palm, "these are the coordinates to where I believe the Horn was taken. Were that item to fall into the possession of someone like..."

I filled in his pause. "Me?"

Azazel's eyes looked a half million years younger in that instant. He smiled. "That would be terrible. Such a terrible thing for some of the Underworld's most influential demons. That should never happen. Ever."

Azazel was still smiling as he slid the paper into my palm and wrapped my fingers around it, encasing it in my hand.

He pulled his hand away and looked over his shoulder at the rift, releasing the listening ward. His eyes held a devious glint. "Shall we head back to the Underworld?"

"Yes," I said with a firm nod. "I'm dying to see everyone again."

THE END

WHAT'S NEXT?

Hell's reject is called back home? What plans do the Council have for Zeke? Why did Azazel provide him with possible coordinates to the Horn and what are his plans for it?

Find out in the next part in Zeke's story. Grab book 6, "Virgo's Vigilantes" now.

REVIEWS HELP

If you enjoyed this book, I would really appreciate getting a review from you.

Reviews not only help other readers find something they might like, but they help me as an author. Your reviews are important to me because they allow me to see what readers like you enjoyed about the book and what I could have done better.

Thank you to each and every one of you who takes the time to leave a review!

DON'T GET LEFT OUT!

Get the latest news, special deals, exclusive stories, first looks at book covers, and more by signing up for Paul Sating's newsletter!

Sign up for Paul's newsletter to follow all the news and special deals for upcoming novels, and to catch up on the latest regarding his podcast at http://www.paulsating.com.

BE PART OF THE EXCLUSIVE CLUB

More stories! More exclusive Paul Sating fiction, including free audio books, in podcast form!

Become a Patron & enjoy more content. Go to paulsating.com and click the Support tab to find out how, or simply go to patreon.com/paulsating.

ACKNOWLEDGMENTS

This book was one of growth and change, not just for Zeke, but for me. For those of you who aren't part of my newsletter (please join me if you've read through the fifth book in this series—those folks get so many deals and insights) or my Facebook group, you might not know that this book is not only the biggest of the series to-date, but it is also the fastest I've written a novel.

The first draft came in at around 125,000 words, nearly twice the size of *Bitter Aries*, and was done in eighteen days (though the editing, as it does, took far longer). Eighteen days! Who knew that was even possible?

How can we know what is real, what is possible, if we don't push ourselves?

It all started as a public commitment to document the writing of the book for other writers and authors. Inspired by Chris Fox, a SciFi author, who did a similar challenge years ago, I knew doing daily YouTube videos of the project would force me to push through the slow days. The challenge kept my butt in the writing chair on weekends, when I typically don't put in full days of writing unless I'm working toward the end of a novel. 125,000 words in eighteen days (I still can't believe it). Crazy! But I owed it to the fans of Zeke, and to those writers I was hoping to inspire, to dedicate myself to the project, even at the risk of publicly humiliating myself. And it worked. Since writing *Leo* in October of 2020, and writing these Acknowledgments in March of 2021, I've already written another *four* more books! Three of them are the first books in a new fantasy series I'm starting that falls in line with what you might expect from a Conan/Witcher mashup, and the fourth being *Virgo's Vigilantes*, the sixth book of the Zodiac (more to come about that when the time comes). Join the newsletter and/or Facebook Group to get those scoops along with chances to read the books before anyone, for free, by the way, and other book deals.

As we move deeper in to 2021, I'm thrilled to have grown as an author, now capable of getting more books into the world. Sharing the stories in my head with people around the world is one of the most humbling and transcendent events in my life. The future holds more of those opportunities now that I'm leveling up my writing game, and I couldn't be more thrilled.

The Pride of Leo also brought growth and change for Zeke. Even since we closed the doors on *The Gemini Paradox*, I've been dying to bring Cassie back. As a storyteller, it's important to me to tell stories from different perspectives. Writing in third-person is a wonderful way to do that, but the first-person perspective of the *Zodiac* doesn't allow me that chance. Cassie being an angel is a vehicle to bringing a different perspective to this story world. Who wants to see this story just from the demon's perspective? Not me, I say! Having an angel involved, and *not* be the enemy, is a lot of fun to explore. As the movie in my head plays out, I love watching this dynamic between Zeke and Cassie as his world becomes more complex. Don't be surprised if you see her again.

As for Zeke, I've been itching to mess with on an entirely new level, more severely than he has been messed with up until this point. Not that I didn't have fun putting troubles in front of him in the first four books, I did. I love messing with Zeke. But I've been itching to take his journey to the next level, and this book was the beginning of that for our favorite demon.

Over a twelve book series, you have to be deliberate in where you take your characters. If an author isn't careful, they tend to kill their series. The character never develops, remaining the same person/demon/fae they were in book one as they are in the series conclusion—something few readers reach because they've become bored out of their minds by the character. That happens if the character "peaks" too early and the author hasn't thought through where they want the character to be at the end of the series. Sure, throughout the first four books, I wanted to have Zeke do and say things that I ultimately stopped him from doing and saying. The struggle is real—especially when you receive "those" reviews of your book where someone slaughters the character, not understanding that what they're seeing is only a snapshot of that character's life, not giving the character room to grow—as we should all be afforded. So, yes, it feels good to begin taking the shackles off my man Zeke. Long may he be messed with! Thank you for being the type of reader who understands that and for sticky with Zeke through five adventures.

As with all my books, *The Pride of Leo* wouldn't be possible without special people in my life.

First and foremost, my lovely wife, partner, best friend, and cruel (that's a joke) alpha—first—reader, Maddie. Who knows what Zeke would have been, or if he even would have existed outside of my mind, if it wasn't for her. From the moment she read the first words of *Bitter Aries*, I had the confidence to fully explore Zeke's world because of her. She often tells me that this series is the first time she cannot "hear" me in the stories, and I'm dull-witted enough to still think she means that as a compliment. My life is enriched by this amazing force each and every day. Wherever I would be if she hadn't come into my life, it wouldn't be this. That, I know for sure!

My daughters, Nikki and Alex, inspire me to be the best I can be each and every day. Growing up, entering the workforce and college in this day in age has to be frightening. I'm one of the lucky "old" people, someone who grew up in a time where going to college opened many doors for you. The younger generations face so many challenges, small and big, people my age never had to face. I don't envy them. Which is why I love seeing how hard these two young women are working to chase their dreams. It reminds me that I'm not ready to quit on life, that I want to be fully engaged in this ride until I check out. I want them to be as proud of me as I am of them.

Jon Grilz of Creepy Pod is such a quiet, unassuming, and under-appreciated human. I'm grateful that he came into my life when I was heavily involved in fiction podcasting. When my daughter was looking at universities in Washington, he was there to offer a contact who helped her make one of her first major life decisions. When I lost my job and decided to go at this writing thing full-time, he was there with kind words, compassionate actions, and even advice from his own experience. Jon is one of those people who doesn't act with kindness because of what he might get out of it in the future, he acts out of kindness because he *is* kind. Without him, Zeke, Leo, Virgo and the ladies in the octagon wouldn't have been so fleshed out, because I enjoy watching MMA, but I've never been in the octagon—and never plan to be. Without his help, I would have never known what I do about the inner-workings of martial arts gyms, their politics, and their intrigue. There's an entire book that could be written about what he shared. I hope the Lion's Den does you honor, Jon.

As always, the most wonderful readers I could ever ask

for were a big part of this book. These brave souls read *The Pride of Leo* long before it was ready for the world. They are such a critical piece of how books are received by the greater world, giving authors such as myself a fresh perspective on the story. We get lost in the details—okay, I can't speak for all authors, but I can speak for myself, and that is absolutely true. The forest is crowded by trees that are hard to see past. Without these people, I'd be swimming alone in the vast sea of story—a truly frightening place. I'm so honored to have them as part of the "Paul's Peeps" team! Thank you to Lori Peterson, Adina Dumitrache, Kevin Rowlands, Erica Stensrud, TC Grassman, Alli R., and Stephanie Mikkelsen for seeing Zeke's blemishes before the rest of the world did.

SciFi author Blaze Ward, for telling me to trust my author voice. This bit of advice was critical to speeding up my entire writing and editing process. Who knows where it'll lead, but I'm excited to explore.

Eric Thomas and Nancy Nelson, thank you for your "inspirational" Creed comments

To each and every single Patron who donated on a monthly basis throughout 2020. Yes, they receive exclusives and bonus content, but I would be remiss if I didn't mention how amazing and humbling their support throughout the unforgiving year of 2020. We'll always remember the year for the difficulties it brought into most of our lives. In that spirit, it amazes me that so many of you stuck by my side through that tumultuous year. You are absolutely epic.

Lastly, to you, dear reader. Thank you for walking with Zeke. He's a handful, I know, but his heart is good and he appreciates you always being there with him as Lucifer's minions insist on serving up headache after headache. Without you, there is no Zeke. Thank you for ensuring that he never truly walks alone.

ALSO BY PAUL SATING

Fiction

Fantasy

The Zodiac Series

The Fall of Aries (Free for newsletter subscribers)

Bitter Aries

The Horn of Taurus

The Gemini Paradox

Cancer's Curse

The Pride of Leo

Virgo's Vigilantes

Libra's Liberation (2022)

Battleborn Series

Bloodborn (Free for newsletter subscribers)

Battleborn Trilogy

Fireborn (Coming 2022)

Rageborn (Coming 2022)

Battleborn (Coming 2022)

BoneBreaker Trilogy

King of Bones (Coming 2022)

War of Bones (Coming 2022)

Breaker of Bones (Coming 2022)

Crown of Thieves

Birth of a Thief (Free for newsletter subscribers)

Horror

The Scales

12 Deaths of Christmas

The Plant (Free for newsletter subscribers)

Suspense

RIP

Chasing the Demon

Nonfiction

Novel Idea to Podcast: How to Sell More Books Through Podcasting

Podcasts

Audio Fiction with Paul Sating Podcast

(Exclusive to Patrons)

Urban Fantasy Author Podcast

(Available on all major podcast apps)

ABOUT THE AUTHOR

Paul Sating is an author, podcaster, and self-professed coolest dad on the planet, hailing from the Pacific Northwest of the United States. At the end of his military career, he decided to reconnect with his first love (that wouldn't get him in trouble with his wife) and once again picked up the pen. Years on, he has published eight novels and he hasn't even screwed up his podcasts, which have garnered over a million downloads.

When he's not working on stories, you can find him talking to himself in his backyard working on failed landscaping projects or hiking around the gorgeous Olympic Peninsula. He is married to the patient and wonderful, Madeline, and has two daughters—thus the reason for his follicle challenges.

Find out more about his other books and free podcasts from his website: paulsating.com.

CONTACT PAUL

How to Contact Paul Sating

Published by Paul Sating Productions
  P.O. Box 15166
  Tumwater, WA 98511
  paul@paulsating.com

Follow Paul:
  Facebook: www.facebock.com/authorpaulsating
  Bookbub: bookbub.com/paul-sating
  Instagram: @paulsating
  Pinterest: pinterest.com/paulsating
  Twitter: @paulsating

EXCERPT FROM BOOK 6 "VIRGO'S VIGILANTES"

Pick Up "Virgo's Vigilantes" to Continue Your Adventure With Zeke and the Gang!

Seconds After Leo

NOTHING SAYS "WELCOME HOME" like having two spear points pressed at your neck the second you walk out of a rift. The self-contained flames of crackling Hellfire dancing over steel tips will get your attention. It definitely got mine.

I'm not saying Azazel had this planned all along—he didn't and wouldn't—I believe that, because I was in no position to distrust him after what he had done in Olympia just moments ago when he handed me the supposed coordinates to the missing Horn. Well, coordinates to an ancient, powerful artifact and a message of warning and empowerment. Enemies and friends awaited my return to Hell. With the spear points, I'd already met some of the enemies and was really looking forward to seeing the friends.

The problem was, I was in no position to request or

demand much of anything. He knew that. Distrust of the elderly Founder wasn't something I needed to waste energy on. Now standing in the Council chamber, I had enough to go around with the other demons I was about to confront.

The rulers of Hell, Lucifer's Third Council, had called me home to answer for something I did to upset them. It would be outlandish. Trumped up. Laughable. Gross. Spurious. In other words, everything you'd expect of politicians.

This farce wasn't about crimes or not-crimes. This was about getting me back into the Underworld so they could force me in the direction they wanted me to march. A death march. Beyond any other evident truth there was this; Lucifer's Council wanted me dead.

One way or another, I was here to fill that destiny.

Dropping my bag at my feet, I raised my arms, showing the pair of unintelligent chamber guards I was no threat. They took synchronous steps back, spears raised back to vertical positions without a word. A statement of power, as if I needed to be reminded the Council ruled here.

The guards were not the only demons awaiting my return from Olympia. I wasn't surprised because Azazel had prepared me before leaving the apartment, but there was still an ounce of turmoil rocketing around inside my brain at seeing who the Council had gathered for this latest farce. My parents stood across the room, about as far away from me as possible. The other pair of demons were two I'd include on the invite list if the Council had asked.

"Wow, it's so good to see you," Bilba said as he approached, his arms outstretched long before he was close enough to embrace me. We hugged, only long enough to not lose any cool points, before separating. I turned to the tall, handsome demon with perfect jet black hair who stood next to him.

"Zeke, great to see you," Ralrek said with a sad smile.

"Ezekial," I corrected, pausing to ensure he flinched. I only allow my friends to call me by my nickname. For six thousand years, Ralrek hadn't been counted among those few. That changed only in the past few years, but toying with him was still a favorite pastime.

We clasped hands, bounced chests off each other, and separated as quickly as we joined.

"What are you guys doing here?" I asked.

Ralrek tipped his head toward the front of the chamber where a long jade table so dark it might as well have been black sat upon a riser, dominating it and the room. The table had to weigh more than ten chimera. "They told us we had to be here."

A group of ancient demons sat behind the extravagant table, leaning toward each other and speaking in low, conspiratorial voices throughout the seconds of my return to Hell.

Lucifer's Third Council. The five most powerful demons except for the big guy himself. Azazel was one of them, but not one of them. Not anymore. I was still trying to wrap my head around the fact that he was actively, if not subversively, working against them. What that meant for me was unclear. Too much to ponder at the moment. Upon leaving my Olympia apartment, Azazel had warned me not to forget I had friends here, that over-reacting might be to my detriment. As we returned through the rift between the Overworld and Hell, I was not a lamb being led to slaughter. What I was, though, was unclear. I guess I might define that in the next few moments.

The presence of the five most powerful individuals in the demonic realm, only one on my side, was enough to temporarily unsettled my nerves. My angst remained untouched. Heavens, I was still sore from a fight to the death the night before, and missing the friends I left behind, including an angel who saved my ass.

Basically, I was trying to keep my shit together.

I faced Hell's rulers. Yahweh could torture them for eternity as far as I was concerned. Michael, Beelzebub, Seraph, and Apopis, dressed in their formal attire. The fact they had donned those robes meant this little get-together was not going to be fun for someone, and that someone was me.

"Before we begin," Azazel shambled over to stand between me and the table, "I must prepare."

Michael nodded. Beelzebub grunted.

"Hurry up," Apopis hissed, his tongue flicking at the corner of his mouth.

Seraph leaned forward over bent elbows planted to her side. "We would like to move these proceedings, Azazel. Be quick about it, please."

Azazel ambled toward his personal chambers. Never one of the quickest demons at his advanced age, his stride was shorter and wobblier than seconds ago in the Overworld. I couldn't help but smile. So nice of him to provide more time to commune with my friends to calm my nerves.

"Are you okay?" I whispered to the pair. Inside the Council chambers, the Founders could read thoughts of demons. Well, except for me. Not that I could claim any credit for it. My ability to block their mind reading came down to the fact that I possessed the most kick-ass halberd in creation. Creed blocked them from dabbing their claws inside my head. But Bilba and Ralrek didn't enjoy the same luxury.

"I've been better, to be honest," Bilba said, the tips of his protruding ears turning a darker pink. "They didn't tell us what this was about. We didn't even know you were coming back."

"Not until that rift opened. Once it did, it was pretty much a no-brainer. Especially since they are here," Ralrek said, casually tossing his hand in the direction of the older demons who stood nearby.

Next to one of the large pillars supporting the expansive ceiling painted with an image of the Hellfire stood my parents. Underneath the flame of annihilation the cruelty of the Council was proven once more. Bringing my parents in to witness my final demise was no surprise. I expected nothing less juvenile from Hell's rules. But still, a part of me twitched with anger and humiliation. Only a twitch this time, I swear. Old Zeke was still somewhere back in that Olympia apartment. The me who stood in the Council chamber now was a different demon altogether. My parents' presence felt more like a pathetic power play. Too bad the Council hadn't yet realized their extra player advantage wasn't going to sway me.

Mother clamped her hands at her waist, squeezing them tightly enough to meld into a single lump of flesh. Lilith Sunstone usually had deceptively hard eyes, but now they quivered when she looked at me. Her square chin, easily the most intimidating one in Hell, trembled. The incubus at her side was much taller, his gray hair slicked back. His cold eyes stared ahead, toward Hell's leaders.

Oh, joy.

Some things in life repel one another. Oil and water. Magnets. Succubi and incubi who aren't tall, dark, and handsome. Add to those examples this farce with the combination of the Council, my presence, and that of my parents and two best friends, and you've got yourself a party.

My parents' presence only reinforced my belief that Azazel was going to have to call on a miracle of Lucifer to get me out of what was going to be a bad day.

"Did they say why they were called?" I asked my friends.

Bilba shook his head.

Ralrek harrumphed. "Your father wouldn't even look at us."

"Your mom was friendly. She gave us hugs. But your father ignored us. I'm sorry, Zeke," Bilba said.

"There's nothing for you to be sorry for. You didn't do anything."

A door clunked closed from the back of the room, as loud

as a hardback textbook dropped on cold tile in the middle of a library. With Azazel in his chambers, I was alone with my best friends, my parents, and the four powerful demons who were going to ruin my day.

My mother shifted on her feet, her hands still gripping each other. My father was stoic, lifting his chin as if aware I was examining him. I couldn't say I was surprised. During my entire Abandonment, I hadn't heard from him once. I wasn't bitter. It was what it was.

"I guess I should go say hi," I said begrudgingly.

"Good luck with that." Ralrek sniffed.

"She loves you, Zeke." Bilba shot Ralrek a sneer. "This is just a lot to deal with. Most demons never go through this once in their life. Your parents have been dragged through it over and over. Be patient. She misses you, and this is how she is reunited with you? So cruel. So unjust."

"Be careful," I said with a nod toward the four demons behind the jade table before tapping the side of my temple.

"I don't care what they think about me," Bilba said, his tone firm.

My friend's determination was encouraging, but his timing still sucked. Any other day, any other time, any other situation, I would have praised him for his display of fortitude. But not with the Council on a mission. They didn't need to be handed anymore victims.

"Do it for me then." He shot me a confused look, so I clarified. "They're on the warpath. They have something planned; I don't doubt that. Let's just keep their attention on me and away from the two of you. Whatever they're planning, I'm pretty sure I'm going to need you to get me out of trouble."

"Again?" Ralrek said, a faint smile playing on his lips.

"Just think how boring life would be if it wasn't for me constantly getting in trouble," I said before going to my parents. Four heads from behind the jade table moved to watch each of my steps. Their conversation continued while I crossed the room, but they made no secret they were more interested in watching me than they were in each other's words.

My father stiffened as soon as I stepped their way. My mother looked like she could have crumbled. But neither moved toward me.

I hugged my mother first. "Hi."

She pulled me against her, cupping the back of my head as if I was still an impling. "Oh, Ezekial. I never thought I would see you again. My boy. My precious boy." She pulled back, keeping contact but making enough room to look me up and down. "You've lost too much weight. I need to put food in you. No worries. The first chance I get, I'll cook something special. I promise."

I didn't want to bring up that I might not have the freedom for her to cook for me. Also, the last way I wanted to be welcomed home was with my mother's cooking. Culinary arts aren't much of an art for Lilith Sunstone. But I love my mother far more than my desire to be honest with her. If I made it out of this, I'd eat a thousand of her dinners.

I turned to Kanthor Sunstone. "Father." A single word. Nothing more. Yet so difficult to form.

His gaze remained forward. "Ezekial."

I waited, but he offered nothing else.

My mother wrapped her arm underneath mine. "I'm so glad you're home. After this is over, we need to catch up. I'll make tea. I've got a few boxes at the house from a new product line I'm testing. We can have that. I plan on hearing your stories long into the night. No early bed for me."

The click of a door handle brought my attention back to the corner where Azazel had disappeared, pulling me away from teasing my mother about her ever-deepening involvement in pyramid schemes. The ancient Founder stepped out, now wearing the official black robe. He ambled toward the jade table at a pace that would make a sloth look like a sprinter. Never once did he cast a glance my way.

Time crawled as he climbed onto the riser, shuffling to his position at the end of the jade table. Behind his chair, he paused, putting a finger to his lip and tapping it as if he'd forgotten something.

"Will you hurry up?" Beelzebub growled from the second chair. The demon, as big as a chimera and hard as brimstone, crossed his arms, flexing his biceps underneath his robe. His dark eyes fell on me, a satisfied grin on his face framed by the pork chop sideburns he bleached blond to contrast his dark skin. The jig was up.

The bad news train was barreling down, and I was tied to the railroad tracks.

Azazel patted his chest as if he had left his note-taking material inside his robe. "I seem to have forgotten where I set my quill and paper. Allow me a moment to return to my chambers."

"Just send the guard. We don't have an eternity," Apopis snarled, his eyes scanning the chamber guards. He pointed at the nearest one. "You, there. Go retrieve his quill and paper."

The guard snapped to attention and almost ran to Azazel's chamber.

"Quickly," Apopis shouted after the guard, who sped into an actual run.

Azazel frowned.

"Mr. Sunstone, step forward," Michael, the leader of Lucifer's Third Council, said from the left side of the table. The first chair. He still wore the neatly trimmed beard and mustache he always did. His light brown eyes fell on me unflinchingly.

I moved in front of the table. Creed hung in collapsed form from the loop at my side, warming at Michael's attention. I ignored it for now.

"Unfair, but necessary," a voice whispered. From where, I

couldn't tell. I snapped my head to the side, not expecting someone to sneak up on me in such a serious situation.

No one was there. Bilba and Ralrek were a few feet away. After a moment, Bilba squinted as if confused. I scrunched my eyes. The smartest demon I knew, he could be thick-headed, especially when it came to defending me. The confused glance he and Ralrek shared at my examination hinted it might not have either of them who'd made the comment.

Deciding to ignore the voice and move on to the Council's latest screw job, I faced the jade table.

"We won't spend long on this hearing, Mr. Sunstone. Understand, it is of utmost importance that we dispense with this as soon as possible," Michael said.

"Which shouldn't be difficult considering the gnat's actions in the Overworld," Beelzebub said. A deep chuckle rumbled somewhere in his chest.

Creed thumped against my hip. "What actions are you talking about?" I asked, my eyes sliding across the members behind the table.

"Your actions that upset the Balance," Apopis spat, his close-set eyes narrowed to slits.

Unlike the past, his half–tattooed faced no longer bothered me, though I was still curious to discover what the stupid inscriptions said. I imagined it was a dare from his college days.

Creed warmed a few more degrees. He didn't like Apopis either.

I answered the thin Founder, but my eyes were firmly on the only succubus on Lucifer's Third Council. "And what actions were those?"

"Would you like us to read the entire list of infractions, Mr. Sunstone?" Seraph asked, her voice raised in a haughtiness undeserved for someone so despicable. Until recently, I found the slim Founder stunning. Now her cheekbones were too bony. Her long, blond locks, too stringy. The slivers of wrinkles that hinted of the possibility of mature seduction looked more like cracked porcelain.

My mouth moved before my brain engaged. "I would be honored. In fact, I would be happy if, for once, just once, this blessed Council was forthcoming about something."

So much for playing it cool.

Behind me, my mother gasped. Ralrek groaned, and Bilba made a noise like a trilling ember cat. And those were the funny reactions. Not so funny were the Council member's reactions.

Azazel, whether fabricated or not, blubbered something to his chest. His long goatee, gray but tipped with orange, poked his stomach. Beelzebub actually had the audacity to make a fist and pound it into the open palm of his other hand. Apopis pulled his lips back and hissed. Seraph's icy blue eyes flashed. Only Michael remained composed, which I would expect.

He leaned forward, tapping the jade table with his finger. "Mr. Sunstone, you have worked for the Council for years. You understand the duties and responsibilities we hold, and, despite your recent actions, I had hoped you would be civil enough in these proceedings that we could address the challenges before us without antagonizing one another. This is not pleasurable for any of us. But it is something we must do."

"It is necessary," Apopis said.

"Again, I'm at a loss over what I've done that is so bad to be called back from Abandonment. I didn't even think that was a thing."

"It has happened before, though not for many ages. Not common, definitely a unique situation," Azazel said.

"A situation that, nonetheless, must be addressed," Michael said, sitting straighter. He held the air of authority with his posture and his position, and he knew it. "Azazel is correct. Calling someone back is rare, indeed. But there are times when it must be done to preserve the Balance."

"Still not sure how I affected the Balance," I said, eyeing each of them before tapping the halberd on my hip. I swear they flinched. Even Beelzebub. "Unless you're talking about me using this, which of course, I wouldn't have had to use if you hadn't sent your assassins and your nephew, Seraph, to kill me."

Lucifer, it felt good to name her. Petty? Maybe, but I was past caring about pettiness, especially toward the pettiest demons in creation.

"You think too highly of yourself, boy," Beelzebub laughed, crossing his arms. "You were Abandoned. We would have no reason to bother with you, never mind sending someone to kill you."

"Yet, you did," I pressed.

"We did no such thing," Michael interrupted as Beelzebub's arms flexed.

"True enough. We didn't. Yet we cannot explain why Chax Vicu, Seraph's nephew, was in the Overworld," Azazel said, bringing his goblet to his lips, looking straight ahead as he sipped and waited for a response.

"I have my reasons." Seraph's head snapped in his direction. "None of which is any of your business."

"They may not be, but it provides cause for young Ezekial's actions," Azazel replied.

"You dare justify the murder of a demon by an Abandoned?" Seraph shot to her feet, her knuckled hands clenched. "That demon was my nephew. My family. And he was killed in cold blood by that criminal."

Azazel slowly set his goblet on the table. Even from thirty feet away, his hand shook noticeably.

Heat rose up my neck. My pulse galloped. "Chax Vicu has been after me since I wanted him to halt a curse on an innocent demon. The demon you knew about and did nothing to help. Because you supported your family's vendetta."

"This is highly unconventional," Azazel blurted in a wobbly voice.

"Insolence," Apopis spat.

"Michael, do something about the boy, or I will," Beelzebub boomed, tipping forward.

Behind me, my mother whimpered, infuriating me. How dare they put her through this?

Creed pulsed.

"What will you do?" I challenged.

Bilba gasped.

We were in Hell; the Founder could do nothing to me here any worse than what the Council already had done. Without permission from Lucifer, they were powerless to kill me. Besides the big guy Himself, no demon could kill another in Hell. Well, except one.

Me.

If Beelzebub wanted to dance, I was ready to tango. I had Creed and two left feet. My day might not be enjoyable, but I would walk, or crawl, off the dance floor. Beelzebub lacked that same guarantee.

"Enough!" The command from Michael boomed across the chamber. "Enough," he repeated, softer this time. "I will not allow this to be reduced to a juvenile squabble. Seraph, sit down."

All attention in the chamber moved to the succubus standing at the fourth spot. She was still half-facing Azazel, about to protest.

"Sit," Michael repeated.

Her eyes flashed once again before she whirled to her chair, yanking it back. The chair legs cracked against the riser. Sitting in a huff and scooting forward, she waved her hand in a few rolls. "Well, then, let's get on with this business before we completely capitulate to this imp."

"I don't believe that's what we're—" Azazel started.

"There will be no capitulation," Apopis said. "Regardless of his desires, thoughts, or opinions on the matter, we should be done with this discussion and move on to the punishment."

"So I'm to be punished for defending myself."

"You murdered a demon in the Overworld," Michael said as if it settled the argument. "And that is not the worst of the matter."

"The heaven it isn't," Seraph said.

"Seraph," Michael tilted to see around Beelzebub, rotating his head in her direction and basically cutting off everyone in the room who wasn't in his line of sight. "You will get your say in the matter. I'm going to ask you... again... to stay true to our purpose."

"What purpose is that?" I asked.

"To determine the punishment for your crimes," Beelzebub snarled from behind his crossed arms.

"It's not a crime to defend yourself against someone trying to kill you," I argued. "You'll need to do better than that."

"And consorting with an angel?" Apopis retorted. "What would you say to that, Sunstone?"

Well. Shit.

Beelzebub barked a laugh. "The boy thought we didn't know."

Honestly, I didn't care if they knew as long as that knowledge didn't put Cassie in danger. She proved she could handle herself against someone like Chax and his crew. She could deliver pain and death in a sneak attack when the rest of the Underworld didn't suspect her presence. The same way she did as part of the angel crew that attacked the First Circle at Gemini's attempted execution. But I doubted she had the same chances when it came to facing down a Founder or two. Even if she could stand up against them, that didn't mean I wanted to poke that blazebull. Cassie would have enough troubles back in the Overworld. Best to keep her out of the matter.

"I'd say your spies need to get better at their jobs," I said, hoping to plant doubt. "Either that or you are imagining things. Angels? That's ridiculous.'

"Our reports say that Angelfire was used in your attack on Chax," Seraph said.

"Again. Defending myself, not attacking him. Though, I guess you're not going to listen. He didn't listen to me either, and look where that got him."

She shot to her feet.

Creed burned against my side.

I concentrated and projected my senses outward. If someone was tapping into their Ability, I'd know it the instance they touched it. In the past, I only felt when a spell was being prepared. As my Creed-gifted senses improved, I was even more sensitive to magic, and honestly, I'd take any advantage I had. Pricking at the fabric of the room, I reached, my Sensing coming back empty.

But one wrong movement from her, or any of the Founders not named Azazel, and I'd have Creed in my hands, ready to do to the Founder what I did to Taurus. And the assassin. And Chax. This list was getting long.

Before returning to Hell, Azazel asked me to not rush into any situation, to trust I was not alone in what was to follow. Maybe he should have begged.

The last thing I felt was the comfort of company. Even if Azazel suddenly reversed the aging process and became a more youthful, powerful version of himself, even if Bilba and Ralrek made the bad decision to fight on my side, I doubted it would end well for the good guys. Someone I cared about, someone who was on my side, would pay a heavy price. No one needed that.

"Trust," someone whispered, the voice wispy and ambiguous.

I risked a glance away from Seraph, half-worried I had just made a mistake. The succubus was conniving enough to use the diversion, but she didn't. Whoever spoke gave away no sign. Disguised in ambiguity, the voice gave no hints to the speaker.

Trust what? Trust who? Was I just hearing things? Had something happened inside the rift on my way back through to the Underworld? Rifts could be dangerous, even to experienced travelers. Though I had crossed between realms numerous times since working for the Council and never experienced any severe reactions, there was always the chance I would. A matter of when rather than if, I guessed. Maybe I was hearing remnants of traveling through the magical device.

Great. A convenient bout of delusion to go along with whatever the Council was readying to serve up.

"Murder. Consorting with angels. The death of Cancer Nijal," Michael said, his voice steady. "That is why you are here, Ezekial. To face the charges and, if found guilty, be sentenced. Stop with this other folly if you want to preserve what few rights you have left."

"Wait. What? Cancer?" I said, shocked and stumbling through broken thoughts.

"She's dead, boy," Beelzebub taunted.

"Abolished, Sunstone," Apopis said.

Cancer? Abolished?

"How?" The word creaked out of my throat.

Apopis's laugh sounded like a rattle. "As if you don't already know."

Cancer.

I hadn't heard from her since she flew to the other side of the Overworld to return to the war zone to serve humankind. Abandoned along with me, she was decaying—dying, as mortals said. Everything dies. Humans. Demons. Planets, suns, and their solar systems. Nothing is free of death's touch.

A natural process for immortals and mortals, it happened much more quickly for us when we were cast to the Overworld. Her desire was to leave a positive mark on the world with the time she had left. I had figured I would hear from her when the time was right. Now...

"I... I..." Forming a response was impossible. Somewhere behind me I heard Bilba say he was sorry. A disembodied comfort.

I felt detached. Cancer, gone.

"There's nothing to hide, boy." Beelzebub's deep voice shook me out of my thought-tornado.

Seraph said nothing, just bore holes into me with her gaze.

"But... I haven't seen Cancer since—" I cut myself off out of instinct to protect her. Whatever this was, I knew I was innocent. If something had happened to her, it wasn't at my hand. The guilty party was likely sitting in front of me.

"So unfortunate," Apopis said, shaking his head.

I swore he was smiling, but my eyes were blurring with tears.

Something ruffled to the side of the room, but I was too busy mourning the loss of my friend. I drew a breath and lifted my head, readying myself to ask the Council's favor for a moment. I needed to collect my swirling thoughts tucked behind the image of Cancer's face. But Michael wasn't paying attention to me. Instead, he gave a slow blink and head nod to a guard at the side of the room. It was only then I realized that the ruffling was from a guard going through my personal items.

Dizzy, I couldn't think straight. Any momentum I had gained by coming out swinging at the Council was lost.

A thick incubus with brown skin that never met a razor, he straddled my bag, which gaped open. In one hand, he held my copy of *The Histories of the Balance*, the most important book in Hell, gifted to me by my ex-boss, Dialphio Tywald. The Council feared the book so greatly they had my original copy burned, by Apopis's own admission. Now, they had their filthy hands on the last copy. The guard also pulled out the only demonic notebook I brought home, leaving a bundle in my apartment in hopes Cassie would find them.

"A demonic notebook?" Seraph asked. "How does an Abandoned book stocker afford one of those?"

I shrugged, hoping I looked more nonchalant than I felt. "You paid me well to do your dirty work."

"Hmmmm," was all she said in response.

"Doesn't matter. Bring the book here. Leave the notebook," Michael ordered the guard, who complied.

Numb, I watched as the incubus delivered my book to the leader of the Third Council. His black armor rattled as he stretched to set the tome in front of Michael, who didn't touch it until the guard departed. Beelzebub looked at it as if it were a coiled snake. One corner of Apopis's lips pulled back, spreading his smile half across his face.

"Is that what I think it is? The heretical writing?" Azazel asked.

Michael nodded. "It is." He tipped the book so that it stood on its end.

"Where did you come by this, Sunstone?" Apopis said, his head rolling to the side, jutting in my direction.

I wanted to smile. They thought they had the upper hand, but the book was something I didn't need any more. I understood enough about the nature of Hell's history, the magical halberd I held, and how astray Lucifer's Third Council had gone from its original intent. Let them keep the blessed thing. Plus, knowing Dialphio, she'd probably made another hundred copies by now.

"I found it in a bookstore in the Overworld. It's the most popular book up there. All the mortals are reading it," I teased.

Apopis's brows drew together. "You treacherous, little bastard."

Bringing my height into the discussion was a low blow.

"Possession of heretical items, murder of my nephew and of another Abandoned, and consorting with an angel." Seraph tipped her fingers down to the table, pressing them so hard against the dark jade that the tips turned white. "Is there anything more to discuss, Michael? Or can we finally dispense justice? It's obvious Mr. Sunstone has committed a number of egregious crimes. We have too many things to accomplish to spend any more time debating his future."

Michael watched me, stoic. Not a hair in his well–groomed beard twitched.

Beelzebub slapped the table. My mother yelped. "I agree with Seraph. Let's be done with this."

"It would be appropriate to take a vote," Azazel said.

Michael slowly set *The Histories* down, his hand lingering on it. When he spoke, it was as if he were addressing the book. "Agreed. It is time for us to deal with this permanently." He looked me in the eye. "Mr. Sunstone, you've been given many opportunities to change your course, yet you continue to take the wrong path. It is unfortunate, but our attempts to help you see the light have failed. We have done all we could. Now, we determine your fate."

"I say we Abandon him. This time we choose where he spends the last of his days, rotting away. Some particularly grim locations come to mind," Beelzebub said, sitting back, extending his arms. The balls of his biceps twitched.

Was he seriously flexing?

Seraph snorted. "How many times do we send him to the Overworld where he can cause problems? Plus, if we Abandon him again, he will just reach out to the angel. Do we want to give him that chance?"

Apopis's tongue flicked to the corner of his mouth. "We can't take chances with this one. I vote that we keep him closer, here in the Underworld."

"But if he remains in the Underworld, he remains immortal," Michael countered.

"We have to do something. Something permanent, and something now, Michael," Seraph said, swatting one hand at him. "His consequences must be as grim as his actions. We need to make a statement."

There was silence behind me, both from my parents and my friends. I was grateful for that. I didn't want any of them to make a comment. This chimera wagon was rolling, gathering speed, and anyone who cared about me would get run over.

"Then are we ready for a vote? Because it doesn't sound as if we are," Michael pointed out. "We can discuss the terms and conditions later. First, we need to determine if he will be Abandoned or imprisoned. Once we set that, then we can decide how he will spend his remaining days."

"There's always another option," Apopis sneered.

"Would we be willing to discuss that?" Michael asked.

Seraph turned to take in the slender, half–tattooed Council member. "Get approval for an execution? Do you really want to go through the process? Public trials, where he'd have witnesses and could appeal. The time it takes. Time I would rather spend on other things than seeing Mr. Sunstone for one more day."

"Seraph is right," Beelzebub chimed in. "I'd rather not spend another day on this issue. Heavens, I don't want to spend another hour dealing with this gnat. Let's choose. Abandonment or imprisonment? Let's be done with it. If we go with Abandonment, I will take care of the logistics."

Azazel slowly raised his hand, a finger extended.

Michael acknowledged him. "What do you have?"

The oldest Council member chimed in, his voice weak and wavering. "There is yet another option besides imprisonment, Abandonment, or wading through an execution trial."

"Such as?" Apopis sneered.

Azazel spread his hands. "We know nothing we've tried has worked. We have already imprisoned Mr. Sunstone. We have already Abandoned him. Yet he continues. We want swift action, which is why we are here. Past Abandoned were always adjudicated at lower levels. So there is a way that we can swiftly address this."

"What way is that?" Beelzebub grumbled. "Out with it."

"A trial by combat," Azazel said.

My mother gasped. My eyes shot open. Ralrek scoffed. But the wheels were turning in the minds of the Founders. They were entertaining Azazel's proposal.

"Interesting. Definitely interesting," Michael said, tapping his finger absentmindedly on *The Histories of the Balance*.

Beelzebub rolled his bottom lip out of his mouth, sitting back and crossing his arms. "I would be okay with that. We could take him to the fighting pit in the Seventh. I haven't been back in ages and would love to visit my old stomping grounds to watch Sunstone being torn apart, limb by limb."

Seraph watched me as if I had already found the unlocked door and was waiting to dash to freedom.

"Interesting proposition," Apopis said. "Do you have an opponent in mind? Someone carrying the criminal guilt equal to Sunstone?"

"I have a few candidates. There's a demon in San Jose who offered to spy for the Upperworld," Beelzebub offered.

Michael tilted his head, his eyebrows raising. "We do have the Jordanian politician. It would be difficult, of course. But he needs to be brought to justice as well."

"Hardly an opponent worthy of young Ezekial," Azazel said.

With that, Apopis agreed. "That is true. Sunstone would walk free a minute after combat started. No, he needs a more dangerous opponent."

"There is the former Third Circle Administrator—" Seraph said.

"I don't want him back in the Underworld," Beelzebub barked.

"We have to choose someone, or go with another option," Michael said before another verbal battle kicked off.

"Do I get a say in the matter?" I risked asking.

Beelzebub lunged forward, his finger shooting out in my direction. "No! And say another word and we will cast a Silencing spell on you. I promise, it will be a permanent one. You won't even be able to say goodbye to your loved ones. Keep your mouth shut."

Michael pushed his hand to the floor as if he were trying to subdue a faerie. "Let's keep this moving." The leader of the Council looked down the table at the opposite end where the oldest among them sat. "Azazel, this was your idea. Do you have anyone in mind?"

Just above his long, pointed goatee, Azazel's lips rolled in and out. "Actually, I do. Another demon who has gone... wayward. Someone I believe can be more than a match for young Ezekial."

"Good then," Michael said. "Who is this demon?"

"I'd... rather discuss that in private. Young Ezekial should not be privy to this information out of... security concerns." Azazel wagged a finger at me.

Heads turned to Michael. Including mine. Had I not been completely thrown off my game learning about Cancer's death, I might have confronted Azazel's apparent setup with a dose of Creed for the Founders. Right now, I could barely remember to allow my automatic biological processes to do their thing.

The leader of the Council nodded. "We'll talk about the specifics later. I think—"

"We're going to take the word of this senile bastard?" The shout cut Michael off. Seraph was on her feet again. "Enough of this. I'm not just going to roll with whatever is thrown out, without thought. We need to be deliberate and we need to do this right. I'm not willing to take a chance on Sunstone escaping justice again. Beelzebub?"

"I am of no mind to give Sunstone any breaks. Whoever we choose, it needs to be done quickly, and with the right opponent. Like Seraph, I am no longer willing to take chances."

"Are we all comfortable with a trial by combat? Can we take a vote on that, at least?" Michael asked his peers.

The Founders voted in favor of a trial by combat in less time than it took my mother to burn dinner. Apparently, my fighting days were no longer behind me. Though I had done nothing wrong, I was now going to have to fight for my life. And by the speed at which everything was moving, it was going to happen soon.

"Now, the matter of Sunstone's opponent," Seraph said, finally re-taking her seat.

"If you will just give me time, in private, I'll explain my—" Azazel tried to speak but Michael cut him off.

"This is a matter we will continually circle around," Apopis said.

Beelzebub grunted. "I'll fight the gnat myself if I have to."

I welcomed that proposition.

Seraph closed her eyes, breathing in slowly through her nose. Her agitation was palpable. "Let's call on Him. A quick conversation and all will be settled. Let's not waste any more time."

Beelzebub leaned forward without unlocking his arms. "Are you sure? You know how He can be. The vote needs to be unanimous."

"Highly unconventional. Highly unconventional," Azazel complained.

Her top lip peeling back, baring her teeth, Seraph said, "Again. We need to move forward. Invoking Him will be faster than making the allowance for an execution trial. We agree a trial by combat is the way. Let's make this next decision even simpler. I invoke Lucifer."

What in the heaven did that mean?

"I second the motion," Beelzebub said, slapping the table.

Michael's hand slid to his side to where he kept the gavel. He picked it up, raising it at a slight angle. "All in favor?"

"Aye," Apopis said.

"Well, I have already stated that I believe this is highly unconventional. I believe that we can make the decision ourselves without invoking Him," Azazel argued, his cheeks wobbling in frustration. "If you but listen to my justification for—"

Beelzebub leaned back in his chair, tipped on its hind legs. His massive hand gripped the jade table so he didn't tip over. I imagined those thick fingers around my neck. "Yes or no? It's that simple."

Azazel blinked a few times before answering, looking at the others for help. None came. "Then... yes."

"Aye," Michael said. "We will invoke Lucifer and return to this matter. We're done here." He tapped the jade table with the gavel.

Accused of murder and consorting with demonkind's eternal enemies, facing a trial by combat against an unknown opponent selected by the Lord of the Underworld Himself. Talk about an epic homecoming.